THE RISE OF ADSCENDO

THE RISE OF ADSCENDO

TOMORROWLAND
& JESSICA THORNE

English edition first published in Belgium in 2023
by TL International BV/Tomorrowland

ISBNs
Numbered Limited Edition: 9789464752007
Limited Edition: 9789464752014

D/2023/TL International BV, uitgever

Typeset in 11.5pt Adobe Caslon Pro and Caslon Antique by seagulls.net

Printed and bound in the Netherlands.

TL International BV
Korte Vlierstraat 6,
2000 Antwerpen,
BE

www.tomorrowland.com

FOREWORD

Every year Tomorrowland presents a new festival theme, which comes to life via a beautiful trailer, on the legendary Mainstage and throughout the festival grounds at Boom in Belgium. As the stories and characters of each theme cannot be expressed fully during the festival, we have dreamt for years of taking more time to develop them, all the while writing down our ideas, creating the new worlds and stories that inspire our festival themes.

Now, after years of worldbuilding and story development, Tomorrowland Fiction will bring to life the magical worlds and storylines of our themes. A new fantasy universe to inspire readers around the world with stories about all the good things in life: friendship, love, freedom, unity and the beauty and importance of nature. Stories about passion, courage, and possibilities. Stories with characters we hope you will fall in love with as much as we have, who live and work in magical and wonderful new realms, in cities and towns, on land and sea and in the air. Worlds that are just waiting to be explored.

We look forward to sharing our stories with the world in the years to come and are thrilled to share with you here that our first novel to appear in bookstores will be book one of Tomorrowland's first trilogy, coming in fall 2024.

And for now, we are very proud to present to you here our first origin story, the Adscendo festival theme novel: *The Rise of Adscendo.*

TOMORROWLAND

CHAPTER 1

The alarm bell hit Ro like a punch to the guts. She was on her feet running out of the mess hall before she even realised what was happening. As she raced to the muster point before the stone docking jetties on the heights of Mount Nest, the jolt of adrenaline made her heart pound in her throat.

"What is it?" Derren Loft shouted, his voice still bleary from sleep. How he'd been able to sleep was beyond her. Whenever she was on duty she couldn't even close her eyes.

Emergency calls like this were common. No one slept for long. Seasoned hands didn't even try.

"Calm yourself." She dragged Derren along behind her in the right direction. He pulled himself free and glared at her in that way all the new Windriders learned to do pretty soon after they'd got to active duty. She was used to it by now. No one wanted too close an association with any member of the Swift family. "We'll be there soon enough."

"Yeah, but … what's the shout? It's barely dawn."

Barely dawn or barely dusk, it didn't matter. They were on call and that was that. She grabbed her flight jacket from the hook beside the gleaming brass pole and slipped into it. The flaps hung beneath her arms, pulling them down with the weight of the material. Plain, functional, lifesavers. The flight jacket felt like a second skin to her.

"All hands to stations," the aeronaut called from their designated balloon and Ro jumped for the pole, wrapping her legs around its sleek surface as she slid into the gondola of the balloon.

Derren landed beside her with less grace. Trying not to be too obvious about it, she kept him upright to check he'd put the jacket on correctly. Another scowl told her he didn't want her help. Great. Just great.

The balloon lurched upwards, loosening its tethers on the cliffs of Mount Nest, home of the Windriders' Guild, and the highest point of the city of Arcadiana and its surrounding islands. As they rose, she gazed at her home, the walled city occupying the whole of the central island. Beyond it the ocean speckled with its attendant islands. The gondola was higher than the Aviary in moments. The Aviary, the home of the Birdsingers, was the only Guildhouse which reached almost as high as her own. Beneath them the city spread out with its spiderweb of irrigation channels, its slate roofs gleaming in the dawn. Gold decorations on the blue and red walls flickered into life with the sun.

The shadow of one of the soaring isles passed across the harbour beneath them and on out to ocean. One of the higher ones, she figured, far above them, floating in the air. She squinted up but saw nothing except a shadow in the distance.

Dark and ominous, the huge floating mountains ranged across the sky, far above her island home, but they were beautiful as well, some bare rock, some covered in vegetation.

All around them balloons were rising, patterned and brightly decorated, lifting broad gondolas beneath them. It would look festive if she didn't know that they were all Emergency Response teams.

A flock of gulls flew around the balloons and she glanced at the Birdsinger standing with the aeronaut on the raised dais in the centre of the gondola. Young, probably a friend of Saran's, but not someone she knew. Her brother didn't exactly socialise with her. He never had the time.

The Birdsinger said something to Windrider Gayle and pointed east.

"Stand by," Gayle shouted. Ro watched the osprey who aided him in his work rising high above them on an updraft and then dropping again to guide them. Gayle might have smiled—no more than a tightening of his grim mouth really—and then the balloon followed the bird and caught the breeze it had detected.

It didn't take long to reach Ilana, an outer island in the archipelago.

Two balloons were already there, hovering over the crash site, and the crew looked like ants on the ground beneath them. Individual Windriders descended through the air, arms outstretched as they glided in formation with each other towards the scene. A third balloon was down, the great red and white punctured envelope billowing out across the field in which it had crashed like a blood-soaked flag. The gondola looked like kindling spread across the ground. There were boulders strewn across the scene.

"Rockfall," one of her companions whispered and glanced up as if expecting another strike from above any second.

"Medics to position one," the aeronaut's voice rang out again. "Rescue on the count of two. Clean up, take the rear. Windriders ready."

They all shouted the affirmative. This was why they were here. This was what they lived for. All that training, all those drills, all leading to moments like this.

Breathe in, Ro told herself firmly. *Breathe out. Do it again. Keep going.*

Ro pulled her visor down as the hatch in the side of the gondola opened. The four medics went first, followed by two rescue. The air sucked the remaining four Windriders out towards the empty sky.

Ro closed her eyes, leaned back and let the wind take her.

She fell, spiralling down and then, once safely clear of the balloon, she spread her arms wide. The jacket did the rest. The flaps on either side of her body lifted her into the sky, and transformed her into a glider. For a moment all was peace, perfect peace. She rolled in the air, graceful and at home.

Derren plummeted past her like a stone, screaming. Bloody idiot. He'd had training and drills. Never under stressful circumstances like this, clearly, but he should know what to do. They would never have cleared him for active duty otherwise.

Cursing, Ro dragged her arms to her side, and fell towards him, her makeshift wings no longer holding her up. She grabbed him and they fell together.

"Open your arms," she yelled at him. "Now."

Training kicked in, as it always did once her voice cut through the panic. She couldn't fault the Windrider Academy in that. They drilled obedience into every last cadet as if their lives depended on it. Because usually it did.

She had been the only one where it hadn't quite taken the way it should have.

Derren's arms snapped out and she released him so he could glide away.

Her own descent wasn't as graceful because she didn't have the time to readjust. Not anymore. She came in hard and too fast. Rather than alighting like a bird, she slammed into the ground, rolling to prevent the worst, and finally came to a stop sprawled on the ground, breathing hard.

"Elegant as ever, Ro."

She recognised the voice. How could she fail to? From anyone else it might have been a compliment, or even a light joke about her landing, but Ro and Grayden had history. He was there every single time she messed up. Grayden Mistral had taken to command like he was born to it, which was exactly what had happened, really. He had been born for it, as the son of Flight Commander Mistral. His rise through the ranks was meteoric. The fact that he actually earned all those promotions rather than had them handed to him by his mother as Guild head just grated all the more. As leader of the Windguards, the elite security force of their shared Guild, of course he would be here first, in case any Guildless were tempted to loot the wreck, or had caused the crash. Ro glared up at him from beneath the visor, unable to find enough breath to form even the simplest words, let alone a witty retort.

"We have survivors over here!" came the distant shout and Grayden broke into a sprint without another glance at her. Always heading to the thick of the action, always in pursuit of glory. That was Grayden.

It had never been very hard for him to leave her behind.

Ro struggled to her feet, her body aching from the impact, and lurched after him.

Duty was duty.

The balloon had been struck from above, a shower of rocks falling from one of the soaring isles. Crumbling. Treacherous. Some of them too high for conventional balloons to reach.

The rocks that came from their crumbling edifices, great and small, were deadly. They picked up speed as they plummeted towards the land beneath, punching through anything in their way. Most hit the ocean, or the less inhabited outer islands of the archipelago. But they were a constant threat.

The debris had torn through the material of the envelope, destroying the air valve so the whole thing had just dropped out of the sky. Then they'd pulverised the gondola underneath. The balloon had come down in a tangle of material and wood, spewing its cargo and passengers across the plain beneath.

The medics triaged survivors and arranged airlift to the nearest infirmary, where the Birdsingers specialised in healing would help with the more serious injuries. Then there wasn't much left to do.

With every crash, every earthquake, every flood event, every catastrophe on the islands, the Windriders were called to the scene to pick up the pieces as best they could.

It was a thankless task.

They catalogued the dead, removed the bodies in much the same way as the living, although with less urgency.

The members of Ro's crew were soon the only ones who remained. They searched through the wreckage, matching items found to inventory so that it wasn't just spirited away by any Guildless who might happen upon the scene. They were notorious for picking through crash sites, often despatching survivors to cover their tracks. Another reason why it was so critical to reach them in time. And why the Windguards went in first.

Sometimes, the rumours went, the Guildless would cause accidents in the first place, just for looting opportunities.

But now all that was left was inventory.

Ro kept her head down and helped haul the remains of cargo and belongings from the broken balloon, prepping it for transport and ignoring the fact that the others barely included her in conversation beyond the necessary. If she wasn't used to it by now, when would she be?

One broken box spilled out a selection of tapestries, the colours so bright and beautiful that she couldn't help but pause to look at them. They were master works of the Weavers' art. She reached out to stroke the soft threads and unrolled one on the ground to get a better look.

The bird portrayed there was like nothing she had ever seen in real life. It was the blue of a cloudless sky, its wings splayed wide as it came in to land on top of a waterwheel. Its long tail split in two, a huge V with trailing feathers on either side, just like the symbol of the Birdsingers' Guild. It glimmered with golden threads and the eyes glittered in the sunlight. They were little pieces of amber, she realised, stitched into the embroidery. It looked as if, at any moment, it would rouse itself from its world of thread and stitches, and take off, soaring high above them all.

A Golden Auric, one of the most beautiful depictions of one she had ever seen. The myth of the great birds who lived on the furthest of the soaring isles, the High Eyrie, was one every Windrider grew up hearing. So did everyone in her world, she supposed.

Ro had dreamed of them all her life, but never seen them. No one had except fools and liars. The stories said they were the children of Amare, birds of legend, creatures formed of magic and joy.

Even when she was little, before her brothers left, before her parents died, especially back then, when she still had hopes and a future, when she still believed in stories, she had dreamed of them, dreamed of flying alongside such beautiful creatures. Silly fantasies perhaps, but they had shaped everything. All her life, those dreams had been so real.

Her life had changed after her brother Matias was arrested and Ro turned down the offer of marriage from Grayden Mistral which most people would have killed for. Half the Windriders wouldn't even look her in the eye anymore. Far more than half. When her parents died, she knew she would never receive another offer of marriage. She lingered at the bottom of the Windriders' hierarchy and there she would stay. True, she could seek out her brother Saran and beg for his help, but the thought of that made her flush with shame. He'd asked her to join him in the Birdsingers' Guild but she'd said no. She couldn't go running after him now. Not when he was fast becoming the universally adored protector of their people, the one everyone looked to. She would look pathetic.

Her hand trembled and she dropped the tapestry.

"What are you doing there? Put that down."

The harsh barking voice made her spin around. A Flight Officer bore down on her, a thin, little, weasel-faced man puffed up on his position. Eno Hale. He'd been friends with Grayden in the Academy. She cursed under her breath.

"Ro Swift, I might have guessed. Leave that alone. The owners are here to collect."

That wasn't right. She faced Hale before he could walk away.

"Procedure says they have to be documented and the ownership papers matched to the manifest back at base so someone doesn't just—"

He leaned in over her, pressing uncomfortably into her personal space. He smelled of too much aftershave and stale breath. "I said the owners are here to collect them. Step away, before I write you up for looting." He growled out the words and Ro felt the skin at the back of her neck tighten in disgust and outrage.

For a moment she just stood there, and felt her hand slowly ball into a fist. It would only take a fraction of a second to draw it back and bury it in his stupid face. He turned away from her, not even concerned that she might react with anything other than deference.

Another hand closed around her clenched fingers, not tightly but firm enough to stop her.

"Not worth it," said Tomas on a breath. She released her fist and turned, startled to see him here. He didn't even look at her but stared past her like the perfect servant, his hand still curling gently around hers, behind her back. "Forgive us the interruption, Flight Officer Hale. The Weavers are most eager to collect their cargo."

Hale scowled at Ro, and didn't even deign to acknowledge Tomas Harper, a mere Labourer. "We'll talk about this later, Swift," he said and stalked away towards two brightly dressed men who had pulled up with a horse and cart.

"Tomas? What are you doing here?" she whispered.

Tomas just grinned, that same old dazzling smile which made her breath catch in her throat. His coal black eyes sparkled beneath the fall of his dark hair. "Keeping you out of trouble, it seems."

"I don't think you succeeded, but thank you for trying." She shook her head, then glanced at her superior officer. "He'll report me anyway, even though he's the one breaking the rules. Malicious little—"

"Ro, stop. It's okay. The Weavers are the owners, I promise. I came with them. Let's leave them to it."

"Aren't you meant to be working? I presume you're here as their muscle."

He flexed one of those spectacular muscles at her. "What else is the Labourers' Guild for if not lifting and carrying? But they'll understand."

All that was left to do here was the mundane gathering of debris and scavenging anything that might still be of use. And making sure that any surviving goods made their way to their proper owners. The grunt work. The jobs the Windriders gave to those who ranked lowest in the hierarchy of their own guild.

People like her.

She was sick of it.

And trapped by it.

Tomas had a way of making her forget about this, almost. He threaded his fingers through hers and she smiled up at his face. Tomas was the one bright thing in her life.

"I'll be paying for it later anyway," she told him. "I might as well deserve it."

CHAPTER 2

Tomas only breathed easily once he managed to whisk Ro away from the site. He wasn't sure what might have happened if he hadn't seen her and intervened. He'd never met anyone quite so capable of getting themselves into trouble. Just like Matias really. Ro's eldest brother had been his closest friend but the things Matias had dragged him into … it didn't bear thinking about. But Matias had that golden touch, that ability to wriggle out of trouble without any problem at all.

Until the end. Until it hadn't been an option anymore.

Tomas had only managed to avoid the same fate because Matias had taken the blame. All of it. To save him. To save all of them. To save the movement. And Tomas had let him.

But Tomas had promised, eight turnings ago, when he said goodbye, that he would look out for Ro. Because that was what friends did, wasn't it? They thought her parents would be there for her. And their other brother, Saran. But it hadn't worked out that way. Now there was just Tomas.

A sennight ago, Tomas had found ruins halfway up the hill in the middle of the little agricultural island. Abandoned, but still beautiful, the remains of the old world, the place their ancestors had lived and worked. He had known right away that Ro would love them. The stones carried carvings, beautiful, intricate things which captivated the eye. Abstract swirls and spirals, like someone was trying to draw the wind. And birds, of course. Birds of all shapes and sizes. The creatures their ancestors had revered, that their culture still venerated.

The Birdsingers' Guild had the ability to interpret birds' flight patterns and their songs, but many people had birds who worked alongside them, helped them and guided them. Images of the birds decorated every building, from the grandest to the poorest, carved into eaves and etched in lintels. They were vital for the Windriders when it came to navigation and carried messages between the islands. Ro had always shown an obvious affinity for them, so much so that her family had once thought she would be a Birdsinger herself, like Saran.

Tomas shuddered at the thought. Imagine if she had.

Don't let that happen, Tomas, Matias had said grimly. *Whatever happens. My parents think it would be wonderful, but I dread to think what the Birdsingers would make of her. Saran's already changed.*

But Ro had made the decision for herself. She hadn't wanted to change Guild. She remained a Windrider.

"So what did you want to show me?" she asked, drawing his attention back to the here and now.

"This." He gestured to the stones, with their beautiful carvings. The sunlight was slanting just the right way, picking out the lines, shadowing the hollows so that the image was clearer than it would be at any other point of the arc between sunrise and sunset. He couldn't have chosen a better time. Like it was meant to be.

Ro traced her finger along the lines and smiled, instantly captivated. Tomas knew he would do anything to see that smile.

There was nothing so beautiful to him in the whole world, not this land, not the carvings, not the birds circling overhead. Nothing.

"It's Amare," Ro said. "Oh look, you can see the feathers. It must have sheltered here. The details are incredible."

The Great Bird of the High Eyrie was the guardian spirit of their islands. Ro loved the stories about her. She always had. He knew so much about her hopes and dreams, about the girl she had been.

But the woman she had grown into could still be a mystery to him. Why did she care so much what the Windriders thought of her? Why did she bother when they treated her so badly? Why didn't she just leave?

But where would she go? To Saran and the Birdsingers? That would be unbearable, lifting her out of his reach. And he would never ask her to leave everything behind to be just a Labourer with him. That wouldn't be fair. Especially since his life was far more complicated than he let on.

"I really need to draw this," she murmured, still staring at the carvings as if she didn't even know he was still there. "The image is one of the clearest I've seen. How did you find it?"

He shrugged as nonchalantly as he could. He wasn't about to tell her that. That he had been sneaking around here in the dark meeting people he really should not be meeting. Because while he would trust Ro with his life, he couldn't risk dragging her into it.

"I just heard a few things. Came up to find it a few days ago. I thought, since we were close—"

"It's almost like that tapestry, back at the crash site. The one your Weaver friends were picking up. But this is old. This must be from the old world itself." She carried on examining the images, captivated, and then as if she had just realised what she had said, she dug in her flight suit pocket to pull out a notebook and the stub of a pencil.

He watched her fondly as she settled on the grass and sketched, completely focused on her task. Tomas settled down beside her to wait, content to watch her work. He hummed an old tune, one from their childhood. Pretty soon she was singing along with him, not even aware she was doing so, he suspected. Her clear high voice entwined perfectly with his baritone. As if they had been created to sing in harmony.

The valley spread out beneath them, the early sunlight like honey. There was nowhere else like this in the whole world. The light on the islands was unique. He sat looking towards the ocean and the other islands of the archipelago, in the opposite direction to the crash site. The surface glittered as if studded with diamonds. In the distance, the walled island city of Arcadiana rose from the waters of the bay, pointing towards the sky, its many towers and turrets glinting in the light. In the distance, docked balloons on Mount Nest looked like bright decorations.

A wren began to sing along with them, looking for attention, a long trill of music intercut with chirps and scolding cries. Tomas looked up to see it on the top of the stones, a tiny brown bird with a surprisingly loud voice. It began its song again, delighting in the morning and the melody.

They didn't see the cat until it was too late. Black and sleek, beautiful but deadly, it slid through the shadows at the foot of the stones, then pounced.

The noise was a single, terrible squeak of pain and terror.

Ro yelled and surged forward. Tomas was already moving, his arms wide, his body low, his gaze fixed on the animal with the bird caught firmly in its jaws. All birds were sacred on the islands, revered and beloved. And while the cat was needed to control vermin, that should never include birds.

The cat backed up, growling at him, but didn't run. As he reached the cat, his touch calmed it. He had that ability with animals, always had that soothing presence and charm which made them trust him. That extended to people too. It had always been that way, even when he was young. Very useful for a Labourer, dealing with livestock on a regular basis. Or even irate customers. People trusted him. He relied on that daily. The cat was no different. Where anyone else could be scratched and clawed, Tomas just scooped up the creature and removed the tiny bird from its mouth.

The cat struggled under his arm, but he held firm as Ro took the bird from him. The wren's body didn't even fill the palm of her hand. For a moment he feared the worst. It lay so still, its eyes unmoving, its soft round body hardly any weight at all.

As Ro breathed out, a disappointed sigh, they watched as the bird's feathers ruffled, but other than that, it did not respond. Perhaps shock had killed it outright.

Tomas could see tears, unexpected and sudden, glittering on the edge of Ro's lashes. It sent a pang through him. It was only a bird. Just a tiny bird, not even important in the grand scheme of things. He knew its kind aided farmers planting seeds, or disposing of insects, but though it sang beautifully with them, wrens were so humble that most people barely noticed them. Except for Ro. Tomas knew he would have done anything to help. But all he could do was offer the most basic comfort.

"We'll bury it," he said, stroking the cat which had now stopped growling and settled into his arms. It was still watching the bird with hungry eyes though, so he wasn't about to release it. Ro was glaring at the animal and Tomas smiled with regret. "It's just a cat. It's just doing what comes naturally. It's probably from the farm down there."

A flash of anger shot through her eyes. "It should stick to the farm then, deal with vermin. If a Birdsinger caught it—"

She never finished the sentence because suddenly in her palm the little bird shuddered and shifted. It righted itself, perching on her finger, and watched them intently for a moment before it began to move, hopping up to her shoulder where it settled again.

It began to sing, a scolding refrain directed, he was sure, right at the cat.

Tomas released the animal and it slunk away, slowly at first and then faster, racing back down the hill towards its home, a black shadow on the grass.

Ro was right. If a Birdsinger caught it hunting birds … well, it wouldn't be pretty. At best the owners would be fined. They were just Labourers like him, simple farmers. They couldn't afford that. Birds were revered on the archipelago. They helped people, worked alongside them, sewing, harvesting, controlling pests, even the smallest birds. To kill a bird, or be responsible for its death, was a terrible thing.

If the Birdsingers were feeling particularly vindictive …

"I'll talk to them," Tomas said. "I'll warn them. But Birdsingers never come out here."

"They'd kill it, Tomas, and it's not the cat's fault." She sighed, staring fondly at the wren. "I thought it was dead."

So had he, but clearly they were both wrong. That bird was very much alive.

The wren sang again. For a tiny bird it had a big voice, and even bigger opinions.

Then it took off, its wings moving so fast they were a blur. They watched its looping flight with relief until it was out of sight. A moment later, it was back, perched on Ro's shoulder again. She reeled around, torn between delight and surprise.

It took off once more and then came back, singing intently. As if it was trying to tell them something. As if it wanted them to follow it. Ro glanced at Tomas, seeking guidance, but he felt just as bemused as she looked. Birds often acted as guides; he knew that. Sometimes individuals and birds bonded so closely they could understand each other, like Ro's friend Ameris and her crow Zen. Like Saran and his magpies. No one got anywhere among the Birdsingers if they didn't have that kind of bond with at least one bird. Any number of Windriders had birds who helped them with navigation, especially the aeronauts who were in charge of the great balloons.

But not Ro.

This was different. This wren was trying to take her somewhere, to show her something. Definitely her. Not him. It was ignoring him.

"Follow it," he said.

"Follow the bird?"

"Yes. Go on. It's a sign."

For a moment she hesitated. Her voice sounded distant and dreamlike. "When I joined the Windriders, my parents warned me there would be no more time for playing with the birds. But before that … Sometimes I wondered if I had dreamed my closeness to them." Now? Now, suddenly, she was not so sure. He could see it written all over her face. "Matias said I was imagining it. That it was wishful thinking."

The wren had stopped on another arrangement of boulders, and hopped back and forth impatiently. As they approached, it tapped the stone with its beak, the noise surprisingly loud. Ro frowned and leaned down to examine the moss covered stone.

At the base of the stones something else glinted in the sunlight. A feather. A single golden feather.

Ro reached out one shaking hand and the wren sang again so suddenly that she snatched it back. The bird stopped singing, though still hopped up and down insistently on the stone.

"All right," she murmured. The feather was as long as her arm. It was soft and pliable, but there was no doubt in Tomas' mind that it was also made of gold. Or something like gold. Some kind of living metal.

Impossible, unbelievable. Except that she was holding it in her hands.

"It can't be ..." he whispered.

He thought of the tapestries Parsa had sent him to collect, particularly the one Ro had been looking at when he got there—the blue and gold bird, the bird that had not been seen in living memory.

"We need to show this to Ameris," she said.

They wrapped the feather up in Ro's flight jacket and bundled it back into the pack, hiding it from view. If any of the Birdsingers saw it, they'd seize it immediately. They always did. Anything magical, anything from the soaring isles was theirs by the agreement of all the Guilds. Especially something like this.

But the wren had brought Ro to it and neither of them wanted to hand it over. Ameris on the other hand ... well, there was no one they trusted more.

CHAPTER 3

The Ateliers' Guildhouse was busy as always, housing all the workshops and accommodation within its walls, which meant Ameris was always working one way or another, whether she was in the forge, drawing up designs in her chamber, or toiling away in the general workshop assembling parts for one of the masters. She could spend her whole waking span somewhere in that network of buildings on the hill overlooking the eastern wall. Lines of smoke rose from the furnaces and forges. The waterwheel that powered it all creaked and groaned. The sound of metal on metal rang out like music. It was constant noise and rigorously organised chaos.

The other Ateliers might not entirely respect her, she knew that. She was young, and never spoke up for herself. That was why she ended up getting the variety of jobs she did. She didn't know how to say no. And she had to admit, the intricate miniature water turbines she was helping assemble were a beautiful piece of work. The new adaptations to the irrigation system were being prepared to power great signal towers on the walls of Arcadiana, to act as beacons for shipping, but she could see all sorts of applications for them elsewhere.

Ro told her constantly that she needed to stand up for herself more, especially to her mother. Because even when you were the brightest flame in a fire, the hearth itself contained you. And Ameris' mother, Devera Flint, Master Atelier of the Guild, contained everything.

The supervisor cleared his throat pointedly. She looked up from the reverie of her work, forcing her eyes to focus on the distant door to the workshop where two figures were silhouetted.

"Ameris!" Ro waved brightly, either oblivious to her supervisor's displeasure, or just exaggerating because she knew it would annoy him.

Tomas at least managed to look contrite. He knew and understood in a way Ro never would. Ro simply didn't seem to care if her superiors were unhappy with her. Sometimes it almost seemed she relished getting into trouble.

Ameris had just finished the piece she had been working on. She placed the intricate contraption of overlapping blades set around a rotor in the box set aside for it, and tidied away her tools.

"May I leave?" she asked with all due deference.

The supervisor rolled his eyes. "It's your break time, Ameris. You can waste it as you wish."

Ameris nodded, because what else could she do? Time with her friends was never wasted. Protest and it would be all she'd be known for: the Master Atelier's daughter making a fuss. Everyone would be looking at her. And they were always just waiting for her to make a mistake.

"You're more talented than anyone else your age, Ameris," her mother had once told her, rubbing the back of her neck with strong and supple hands. "But they won't thank you for that. If anything, they'll see you as a threat. People can be so jealous when you're gifted. I can't be seen to give you preference."

She slipped out of the workshop, pulling the two friends along with her, turned down the long corridor and out into a sunlight cloister. The garden in the centre was a sea of herbs and flowers, waving and dancing in the light breeze. It was an oasis in the dark halls of her Guildhouse. The low wall to the south overlooked the harbour district, where the fishing boats set out with gulls reeling all around them. Birds flitted across the garden, tiny finches and larks darting around.

A harsh croak greeted her as she stepped out into the sunshine, and, in a flurry of black feathers, her crow flew to her shoulder.

"Hello, Zen," she murmured and reached up with her hand. Zen rubbed his head against her fingers and gave a series of rumbling, throaty sounds indicating his pleasure at seeing her again. "Miss me?"

Ro shook her head. "You and that crow," she muttered. She was holding her bundled up flight jacket to her chest and there was an air of excitement about her. Tomas too. Something was up. It had to be important for them to show up here during her working hours.

"What is it?" she asked. "What's wrong?"

Tomas grinned. Nothing wrong then. But something was definitely happening. They were up to something.

"Ro has a surprise for you."

Ro unrolled the jacket to reveal, first just a glint of gold, and then, impossibly, a gleaming feather.

Her breath caught in her throat. Before she knew what she was doing she held out her hands and to her even greater surprise Ro gave it to her. Just like that.

"Where did you get it?" she asked in wonder, running her fingertips over the feather, testing its strength, its flexibility. It was metal, but such a metal as she had never seen.

The feathers left behind by the Golden Aurics were legendary relics. The blue ones could sometimes be found. A beautiful colour perhaps and one the Weavers prized. But the golden feathers, the ones actually made of that precious metal and riddled with a peculiar and vital magical energy, were rare beyond belief. Legend had it that the only one had been found many turnings ago and the Birdsingers had claimed it at once. People argued that, like the birds, the golden feathers didn't really exist. Ameris barely heard as Ro described the location on one of the outer islands, and said something about a wren. She was captivated by this bounty.

The things she could do with it. The possibilities were already unfolding in her mind. It was exactly what she needed.

"Ameris, it was Amare. I have sketches of the carvings. The clearest yet." She pulled out her notebook and opened it so that her drawings were visible. Ameris studied them. Ro was right. It was definitely the Great Bird herself.

"Amare." She smiled as if greeting an old friend. "She's always guided us, Ro."

"Can you use it?" Tomas asked.

The feather seemed to vibrate in her hand, full of promise, glittering with magic.

"Oh, yes. Just you wait. It's perfect."

¤

Zen was always at Ameris' side when she worked on her own projects. The crow had been little more than a scrappy fledgling when she had found him as a young Atelier. He'd looked half dead, tossed out of a nest or, more likely she later realised, having fallen out due to a misadventure. She rescued him, hand fed him, nursed him, even while others told her he would never make it.

But he did. She had been determined that he would live and so he did. In doing so he rescued her as well.

Zen brought her gifts, little trinkets he found, glass beads, scraps of metal, and tiny stones. She had threaded them all on her bracelet, the one her mother had made for her when she was a child. Each turning that passed she added another link to it.

But it was Zen who provided the decorations.

"You'll never find a partner with that crow courting you," her grandmother liked to say.

But Ameris didn't care. She had her work. She had her crow.

It seemed almost a sacrilege to melt the feather down. She knew that any of the Ateliers would tell her to do it. Or offer to take it off her hands. The Birdsingers would use it for their magic, pulling out the energy without so much as a thought to the other possibilities. Even the Windriders would find some way to use it, even if only as a lucky charm. But it wasn't a store of energy or a talisman. It was a gift from the great birds, the children of Amare, left behind to be of use.

Still, it was so beautiful that she hesitated. Just for a moment.

The forge was dark and hot and the feather caught the light.

Ameris had been named for Amare, the Great Bird, the guardian of her world. She wore the name with pride, even if others liked to tease her about it.

Ro was one of the few who never had. Since they had been girls, Ro had looked out for her and even though Ameris was of a different Guild, a step down in the hierarchy, Ro had always been her friend. Ameris knew she would do anything for her.

Like this. There was no greater gift.

Carefully, Ameris shaved slivers of gold off the feather which she would melt down, and began the first of her many experiments.

¤

"Ameris?" The voice woke her from her sleep, her face pressed to the table with the designs under her cheek. She started, bewildered, and then flushed. She'd nodded off working on the drawings. Had she been drooling?

Zen cawed softly from the rafters where he had been roosting and flew down to her shoulder.

And standing in front of her, looking down on her, was Guild Master Flint, her grey eyes missing nothing.

"You didn't attend dinner. Again."

A thousand apologies leaped up into Ameris' mouth, but she didn't say anything. What could she say? She couldn't deny it. But she had no idea what time it was or how long she'd been here. She couldn't even tell if it was dark outside because her workshop was in the depths of the warren of rooms and next to no natural light got in at the best of times.

"Whatever are you working on?" Her mother picked up the sketches Ro had left, studying them, and then her gaze strayed to Ameris' designs. "Interesting. How are you compensating for the weight?"

"Mother, please …" she began but her mother's glare fixed on her then and she couldn't protest. "I have an alloy I've been working on."

"Show me."

"It's not ready yet."

"You're being very circumspect. What are you up to? Is this one of Ro's crazy ideas?"

It was the way she said Ro's name. Ameris bristled. "Yes, one of her ideas. And it's brilliant. If I can get it working, it will change everything."

"*If you can get it working,*" her mother echoed. "Oh, Ameris, why do you let her lead you so? There are so many things you could be working on, so many other Atelier projects that would be happy to have you."

Ameris pushed down the surge of outrage inside her and schooled her expression to the careful blandness that got her through times like this.

"Mother, please. You have a reputation to uphold. I have always understood that. You always taught me I can't rely on your reputation to get by. And I wouldn't. So let me do my own work. I'm so close."

To her surprise, her mother sighed. "But close to what, my love?"

Ameris frowned. She didn't want to show her, not yet. Not if it wasn't ready. But she was indeed so close.

And where was the harm? Guild Master Flint was a fellow of the Guild, its leader, and not to mention her own mother.

Reluctantly, she showed her the alloy, and the pieces that were already in place, light as a feather, a metal which glimmered in the candlelight as if gold dust had been trapped inside its surface, frozen in silvery ice. She showed her how vibrations affected it, the way the same flecks moved like living things. And finally she showed the design for its intended use. Her mother listened in silence, her keen eyes missing nothing at all.

"I call it a Wing," Ameris said.

CHAPTER 4

The wind was right, and the air was right. Ro knew it, right down deep inside her, that feeling of the moment being here, being now. It had to be today. There wasn't going to be a better opportunity. The weather was perfect.

The cart was not cooperating. Every time she leaned left it went right and the wheels rattled and bumped along the path. The donkey was being true to its nature: stubborn, a pain. And Ameris wasn't helping either, her arms folded across her chest as they jolted around on the hard seat. Once again Ro wished they could have got a balloon to bring them up but that was not about to happen. Not if she was the one asking. The first aeronautical division were running endless drills today. So the Ateliers' Guild cart and recalcitrant donkey it was instead.

Not to mention the recalcitrant creator. Ameris was sulking.

"What?" Ro asked again.

"Nothing."

"It's clearly more than nothing."

"We're not ready for this. I'm not happy with the tension yet. And the blades aren't light enough. I need more time to refine it. And—"

Ro pursed her lips and chose her words carefully. Ameris was a genius, but she was so wedded to the world of the Atelier Guild which had so many rules about testing everything to within an inch of its life. There was no risk involved. Not in Ameris' world.

Her mother wouldn't allow it.

Even getting her to take part in this scheme was a miracle.

There was a secret rebellious streak in Ameris that she took great care to keep hidden from her Guild. Not from Ro though. She couldn't hide that from her. Ro was the one who had found it and nurtured it, and had seen the joy it brought to her friend's life, even if Ameris sometimes didn't.

"It will be fine. It's a flying machine. They're meant to fly."

"Spoken like a true Airhead," Ameris muttered.

At least she was talking now. And insulting her. Which was a good sign really.

Ro grinned in response to the attempted insult. "I'm not an aeronaut. An aeronaut is in charge of a balloon. If anything, flying this, I'd be a pilot. A real Windrider."

Ameris shook her head in despair. She had been like this for a sennight already, ever since she'd finished the Wing and Ro had said they had to test it. And while Ro knew they had to wait for the right conditions, Ameris was taking it all too far.

"Ro, this isn't safe. You know it isn't safe. And yet here you are about to strap yourself into an untried flying machine and throw yourself off a mountain. It's foolhardy in the extreme."

Ro lifted her head to drink in the sunshine, the breeze ruffling her copper hair, loosening the tendrils that had escaped the tie. She closed her eyes and listened. The birds were singing. So many of them. Away from the crowded city, she could hear them at last. A chorus, a symphony. From the time she could first walk, she would follow the birdsong outside. Saran couldn't join the Birdsingers quickly enough, rocketing up the hierarchy, and he didn't have half the affinity Ro had.

But Ro was, first and foremost, a Windrider, like the rest of her family. The Birdsingers and her brother might think they were further up in the steps of the hierarchy, but she was proud of who she was and where she came from.

And she longed to fly.

Not to drill. Not to glide down to pick up debris. Not to march and guard things.

Today was the day. It had to be. Everything was right. The Wing. The weather. The wind.

Looking up she saw the distant shapes of the floating mountains above her small world, the soaring isles. Some of them were quite close—the Maiden, with all its brightly coloured flowers spilling from cliffs and catching the sunlight, and the Fountain, water cascading down its slopes, making rainbows in the sky, before dispersing into the lightest dusting of mist or rain.

Some of the isles were distant shapes, too high to reach, even for the aeronauts in their great balloons. Others were close enough to reach by conventional means, the smaller ones mined or used for other natural resources. Labourers fired up grappling hooks, attached to lines which they then scaled, dangling precariously over the world before abseiling back down once they'd finished their work. Sometimes they made attempts to tether the isles to the ground, to better make use of them, but the isles always tore free, the magic which drove them far stronger than any manmade ropes or cables. She remembered that a full moon ago three Guildless had been stranded on one as it sailed off. They'd been up there for eight sunsets before it circled back close enough for the Windriders to mount a rescue.

Part of the role of the aeronauts was to bring Birdsingers as high as they could to reap magic from the clouds. But it was hardly worth the effort anymore. At least that was what people would mutter whenever another name was added to the Wall of Heroes, the place where those Windriders who had died in the sky were honoured. The magic was fading, or at least it was drifting higher, out of reach. Perhaps that was why everything seemed to be falling apart. The magic that kept the soaring isles aloft, and the archipelago afloat, was leaving them. Many people tried different ways to alleviate the problem. They'd been working on solutions for many turnings, all without success. The Birdsingers tried magic, and the Ateliers worked on their various inventions, but nothing worked. The soaring isles would soon all be out of reach.

Farthest of all, the High Eyrie, where the Golden Aurics lived, was no more than a shadow against the sun, far too high to be reached by the balloons and flying machines available to them today. That's where that miraculous feather came from. The one that had made this invention possible.

"The wind is right," she told Ameris for perhaps the hundredth time and urged the donkey on up the slopes of the mountain.

"Everything is right. Weather conditions, the wind direction and strength, everything. Once I'm airborne, you'll see. The Wing will do all the work. I'm sure of it."

"Well, I built it and I'm not sure at all. And the Master Atelier will have my hide if she catches me up here with you. We shouldn't be doing this."

She couldn't just say her mother. And it wasn't Master Atelier Flint they needed to worry about. If Commander Mistral got a hint of what they were up to …

Ro shook her head, feeling that surge of reckless wonder that always filled her jittering heart preflight. "It's our day off. We can do what we want with our day off. Besides, it's the perfect day."

Ameris didn't know the sky like she did. She didn't know the air and the currents, the way it would work with you if you just read it right. If she had learned nothing else from the other Windriders, Ro knew that. She might not have a bird to guide her, but she knew she could do this. She'd checked with the Elder Windriders who read the weather patterns. She'd watched and she had waited. And waited. It simply had to be today. Every single instinct in her said that.

"I should be working on my design for Ateliers' Prize at the Carnival of the Birds. The alloy will revolutionise all kinds of things, but I need to do the work. That isn't just going to—"

"Oh, hang the Carnival. This should be your entry, the Wing. It would surely win. Can you imagine? We could unveil it there. I could fly it for you there, right over the crowd."

"You're a complete Airhead." Ameris sighed. But she didn't argue. The Wing did indeed have a shot at winning the prestigious prize. Ro knew that as well. But first they had to prove it worked.

The donkey came to a halt at the top of the path where the ground flattened out to a ledge. There was no one else around. It was an older embarkation point, hardly ever used now.

"Are you really ready?" Ameris asked.

"Always," she replied.

It didn't take them long to prepare. Ro was already wearing her flying jacket as a safety precaution. Ameris pulled the tarpaulin off the cart and began to prep the Wing.

It didn't look like much. Not compared to the great balloons which rose like leviathans into the air, or the flying machines the Windriders were trialling which skittered along the ground like fledglings. This was small and slight, but where most flying machines were made of canvas and wood, Ameris had used metal. Not just any metal either. She had created the alloy from the Auric feather. It shimmered like oil on water, silver with ethereal bands of colour in the sunlight, with a faint dusting of gold threaded through it. Ro didn't ask how she'd made it, mainly because she knew Ameris would go into a long and complex explanation, with diagrams, which Ro wasn't certain she would understand. She just knew it was thin and light, flexible but strong. When the wind struck it just right, it created a vibration which made it lighter than air, lifting an array of primary, secondary and tertiary feathers made of metal which rested against the next, avian anatomy made anew by human hands.

By Ameris' hands.

Instead of a machine to carry someone aloft, the Wing became part of the human body, and the human body part of the Wing.

Once again Ro found herself catching her breath in wonder. Her friend had done that. Well, the two of them had. But Ro's part had mainly been to *'stand there,'* '*hold that'* and *'No, Ro, leave it alone!'*

"Are you sure?" Ameris asked again, scrunching up her nose. Her dark brown eyes were full of doubt.

Ro held out her arms. "Of course I'm sure. Who wouldn't be?"

"Someone sane," Ameris muttered under her breath. Ro pretended not to hear.

Ro pulled down her visor to shield her eyes as Ameris lifted the Wing up for her to slide herself in. When she did, the wings became extensions of her arms, her fingers controlling the feathers. Strapping herself in was simple enough.

Ameris carried on checking everything yet again and they went through the preflight checks. Everything worked perfectly. Of course, she expected it to, but she still relished that sense of relief.

"You have your flying jacket, right?"

Ro lifted one arm to show her. The left side of the Wing shot out to the right, startling the donkey. Ameris cursed and moved to calm the creature.

Right, the controls were sensitive. She'd have to remember that.

"Of course I have the jacket. I'm not an amateur."

"You checked it, didn't you? It's in working order?"

"Of course I—"

Well, she was pretty sure she had. She always did. Her jacket was her jacket.

"We're about to launch you off the mountain. You'd better be certain you did."

"I did, Ameris. Let's go."

"You'd better stay safe. Bring this back in one piece if you can, but most of all bring yourself back in one piece. Ready?"

"Ready."

The wind was right, the weather was right. Everything was—

She didn't count down. You were always meant to count down. Everyone knew that. But Ameris just shoved. The Wing, complete with Ro, leaped into the air, arching up gracefully like a bird taking flight, before plunging off the ledge towards the city walls and the ocean.

The wind sang around Ro, and the metal of the Wing sang with it, in perfect harmony. So did every sense she possessed. Ro adjusted the feathers with her fingertips and then spread the wings wide. It was as if she had been hooked from behind and dragged upwards. She caught the updraught, spun around for a moment and then … then she was flying.

It was perfect. More than perfect. It was everything!

Just a little flex of her fingers and the wings kicked in again, a single mighty beat sending her higher and adjusting effortlessly for the airflow.

Beneath her the ground fell away, the cliff, the mountain, Arcadiana itself. The ocean spread out in the distance, a hazy blue which went on and on until it merged with the sky on the far horizon. She turned, swooping around to face the mountain. Ameris, standing there with her hand shielding her eyes, and her donkey munching on the grass, were mere specks. Ro had to keep going higher. She twisted her head to look up. Only clouds overhead. She beat the wings again and felt the machine respond like a finely tuned musical instrument.

Letting out a whoop of delight, she flew, she turned, she rolled. She rose to the crest of a wave of air and dropped again before pushing the machine higher and higher. It was perfect. It was more than perfect.

It worked. It actually worked. When she'd first shown the sketches to Ameris she'd been so unsure. But then her friend had told her about the experiments she'd done on lighter alloys. And they'd worked on a design, using the drawings of the Aurics and Amare as a basis. With the feather it had all fallen into place.

And here was the proof. She was flying higher than any of the Windriders, higher than any of the balloons, and had travelled further than the other experimental flying machines.

A flurry of movement to her left caught her attention and suddenly she was right in the middle of a flock of birds, a vast murmuration of starlings, moving like a cloud, but one made of living things. They adjusted to make space around her. No, to *accommodate* her, making her part of their pattern. She could follow them, let them guide her. She gave a gasp of wonder as it all fitted together, as she flew with them, watching them roll and dart around her. It was a thing of wonder.

Ro was one of the birds, at one with them. She never wanted it to end.

She thought back to the little wren she had scooped up in her hand, the way it had weighed almost nothing at all. It had watched her with such knowing eyes before taking flight. And oh, how she had envied it.

Now she knew the feeling. This was what it had known, the relief, the freedom, the wonder.

A loud twang sounded behind her head, somewhere out of sight. Discordant and far too loud. Panic speared through her, but for a moment nothing else happened. She tried to breathe again, but the moment she did, she felt the Wing dip and collapse around her.

Cursing under her breath, she scrambled for control again, but was met with only the grating whine of metal on metal. She had to stay calm. She had to keep control.

This was bad. Really, really bad.

She wasn't giving up the Wing. She just wouldn't. It was hers to fly. It was meant to be.

Something fell by her face, something like … a metal feather. And then the whole Wing lurched against her back, shoving her forwards, as if she had been knocked from the sky. She dropped like a stone.

The wind buffeted her as she fell. She was tumbling past the birds, through the clouds and towards the ocean. She closed her eyes, fumbling for the release. Her hands slipped against it, sweaty and shaking, and just when she thought it was too late, the Wing detached. She spread her arms wide and was jerked upwards by her jacket. Her head jolted back as it struck a piece of falling metal and a blinding pain turned her vision white and then red. The copper tang of blood filled her mouth. The visor spun away, but instinct kicked in, and she spread her arms again, the flying jacket deploying at last.

Just for a moment, she hung there, watching the remains of the flying machine tumbling away beneath her towards the base of Mount Nest.

Something hot and wet covered her face, blinding her. She blinked furiously and everything turned red again. Blood. She was bleeding, her world spinning, the back of her head pounding. But she was safe.

And then she heard the rip.

It was an awful, jarring noise, one which tore at her chest. She jerked her head to the side, in spite of the wave of nausea which swept through her with the movement, looking at the jacket flap. Her eyesight was blurred, the wind blinding her, but even then she couldn't miss the problem. One of the metal featherlike pieces from the Wing had stuck in the material and she heard it slowly, inexorably tearing through her only hope of safety.

This couldn't be happening. She looked down. The cliffs were coming up fast. Maybe if she pulled hard one way she could swing close enough to attempt a landing. Or make the jacket come apart faster. It was that or the ocean.

Something struck her chest hard, snatching her up. Air rushed from her lungs as bands like iron gripped her body and bore her upwards. She blinked furiously, trying to focus, to see what had plucked her from her fall. What had saved her.

Claws. They were claws, the colour of gold. Four long taloned digits wrapping around her waist as if she was prey, but they didn't hurt her.

Great wings of blue, turquoise and gold spread out over her, the wingspan beyond estimation.

It couldn't be. It *couldn't* be.

They were a myth, a legend. No one *believed* in them anymore. Not really. Oh, the Birdsingers might go on about them but no matter how high the Guild members flew, no one had ever seen one. Ro had even found a feather, but that didn't mean she believed …

The Golden Auric carried her higher. Up, away from land, away from the mountain, and the Aviary, and the city and the islands below. Up beyond the reach even of the balloons, its great wings beating like her heart, and all she could do was hang there, watching in wonder and dread.

They passed the Maiden, and the Fountain, and three other floating mountains Ro didn't even remember the names for. Beneath the motion of the great wings, she saw them fall away, and her body wilted in the bird's grip.

Golden Aurics were guardians and guides, heralds of good fortune and most notably, not meant to be real anymore. But here she was, being carried off by one.

It let out a trilling call, a sound like trumpets, and looked down at her. Could a bird look smug? She had no idea, but that was the impression she had of it. It was proud of itself, triumphant. Or possibly making fun of her for trying to fly too high, for having the temerity to imitate it and enter its domain.

Was it going to eat her? She didn't know if they were meant to be carnivorous, but given the size of the thing, it had to be. She tried to remember the old stories her grandmother used to tell. There was nothing on their diet. It was more about how they appeared when disaster struck, whenever they were most needed.

Which, given her circumstances, was logical.

They flew higher than all the other soaring isles save one now, the High Eyrie.

Up here, the air was thin and heady, almost scented. Or maybe she was hallucinating. That happened when you went too high, or so the Windrider Elders taught. You could lose all sense of yourself, throw yourself from the balloon, think you could walk on the clouds or …

Or imagine an enormous blue bird with feathers made of gold …

Her head hurt. Her back ached. She was losing feeling in her hands and feet. Ro's vision swam and a sick sweetness began to fill her mouth as if, at any moment, she might throw up.

The bird landed and set her down gently on a sandy ledge. Ro lay there, breathing hard, struggling to tell if these would be her final moments, but the Golden Auric just stood over her, wings spread to shield her from the sun. Mantling her like an eagle ready to feast.

No, it was protecting her.

How did she even know that?

Birdsong surrounded her. Not the song of the Golden Auric but other birds, countless birds. Tiny jewel coloured hummingbirds and finches, ominous birds of prey, graceful and elegant songbirds … she ought to know their various voices, and at one time, when she was little, she would have known. Ro had forgotten too much. She and Saran used to call out to them and follow them and …

There were flashes of light, birds that vanished as she tried to look at them, birds so fast they appeared as no more than a blur of colour shooting by. Birds she had never seen before. Perhaps no one had.

Slowly, her racing heart calmed, lulled by the music in the air, or by the air itself, and the pain in her head seemed to ebb. The atmosphere here was sweeter than anything she had ever experienced, with a spiced scent. The sun seemed brighter. Beams filtered through the quills of the Golden Auric's wings, as if through stained glass, and fell on her face. Slowly, she tried to sit up.

At least the bleeding appeared to have stopped. She opened her mouth, licked her lips and worked her tongue around her teeth. She could still taste the blood but there was nothing fresh and the pain was gone. That throbbing faded as if she was waking from a dream. Or a nightmare.

Tentatively she reached a hand back to her scalp. Dry blood still matted her hair. She could feel that. But there was nothing fresh and it didn't hurt to touch. She ran the hand over her whole head, but there was nothing. No sign of injury at all.

Another thing to ponder later.

She stared up at the Golden Auric again. It was watching her closely, as if curious to see what it had snatched out of the sky.

Ro raised her hand awkwardly. "Hello," she said and instantly felt foolish.

The Golden Auric cocked its head at her and leaned down as if to smell her.

Its eyes were the colour of amber, she realised, deep and endless, aglow from within. Just like the stories. Just like the tapestry she had seen at the crash site.

She shuffled back and the bird took a step away from her. Opening its golden beak it let out another trilling cry. Further off, something answered. Oh ancestors, there was another one.

Tears welled up in her eyes. She couldn't help it. She thought of Ameris, back down there on the island, trying to explain what had happened when she wouldn't even know. And Tomas …

What would Tomas say?

But the birds were not attacking her. Far from it. The one that had saved her still stood over her and the others had not come any closer. She could only see her rescuer, which bent its head towards her. It watched her with its bright orange eyes, blinking as it continued to examine her and then, finally, nudged her ever so gently with the curve of its beak.

Get up, it seemed to be saying.

Pulling herself together, Ro scrambled to her feet, at which point she heard the bird give some kind of satisfied rumble. Or a purr. Did birds purr?

She choked on a laugh and the Golden Auric turned its head again, tilting it to the side as if asking a question.

All birds were intelligent. She knew that, but she had never seen the fierce intelligence she saw now in the Golden Auric's eyes.

It had brought her here for a reason.

She looked around. The cliff face rose in front of her. It was like a terraced garden, rising up in a series of ledges. High above them, at the summit of the Eyrie, she could make out a tree, or at least it looked like a tree. It shimmered with light, impossibly tall and slender like an enormous silver birch, with white and grey bark. Yet its leaves were gold, and all of it iridescent and aglow with light. Was it reflecting sunlight in the refined air up here, or was there actually light coming from it? Its roots winnowed their way down the front of the cliff, framing the area right in front of her like a great arch, a pale grey colour threaded with silver light.

The bird peered closer at her, cocking its head to one side.

"What do you want?" she asked. Not the politest question maybe but she was still shaking. "I owe you. I understand that. You saved my life." Then she added, belatedly, "Thank you."

The funny purring noise rumbled from the Great Bird's chest again, a soft vibration of the air. The feathers fluffed out, so soft and bright, blue and gold, glittering with magic. It lived and breathed magic, of course. She could see that. The air felt alive around it. The golden feathers were the same living metal as the one she had found and brought to Ameris.

Was that why it had come to her aid?

The Golden Auric turned away and strutted towards the cliff face, its great plumed tail sweeping behind it. Even folded, the tail was several yards long, and the two feathers which trailed out on either side reminded her of a peacock, more decorative than functional. They were the twin feathers which formed the symbol of the Birdsingers' Guild.

She tried to imagine what the Weavers would make of those colours. All those shades of blue. She'd never seen anything like it. Even the beautiful tapestry she had seen didn't capture it.

As Ro admired the Golden Auric, it leaned forward impatiently and tapped on the rock face with its beak. A sharp cracking sound echoed around them, and Ro looked on, fascinated. The bird tapped again and then turned its amber eyes on her pointedly.

The wren had done that when it had showed her the feather.

"Okay," she replied, having no idea what it wanted.

It drew its head back, glared at her and then tapped at the rock-face again, where the roots of the Tree formed an archway.

"You want me to look at the rocks?"

She walked forward, under the shelter of its chest, and stared at the stones. Flat and smooth. Unnaturally smooth, she realised. She reached out and pressed her hand to its surface. It was polished. Or at least it had been at one point. It had weathered, up here on the highest of the soaring isles. But she couldn't deny that this was a worked stone surface.

All around the edge of the space she could see the remains of carvings, intricate and beautiful, just ghosts of them visible now. She traced the lines with one finger, its tip fitting perfectly into the indentation.

"It's beautiful," she murmured. The Golden Auric purred again. Then it took another step forward, its body colliding with her back, and urging her forward again. "All right, all right, hang on."

She searched the surface of the stone and then, just when she was about to give up, turn around and start trying to apologise to the profoundly pushy bird, she saw another indent, different from the rest. Not merely decorative. When she pressed her hand against it, she felt it give, and it sank into the stone in two parts to reveal … a handle?

A human sized handle.

There was no way something the size of the Golden Auric could open this. Which meant it hadn't been made by them, or for them.

But no humans had come up here in at least a lifetime. Maybe more.

No one except her.

She sucked in a breath of excitement, or fear—she wasn't really sure which—and with her heart hammering away behind her ribcage, she grabbed the handle and turned it.

There was a clunk, and a grinding sound of stone on stone. It took a long, agonising moment, and then, a door opened.

Dust fell from the edges, and she shook her head to keep it out of her eyes and mouth. The Golden Auric gave a squawk of triumph, a most undignified sound, and took to the air. The wind of its wings beat against her, sending her staggering forward and the dust swirling around her.

Half blind now, she reached out for the walls to steady herself, and when she touched them, for just a moment, they glowed. Long lines wove their way along the smooth interior of the passage, swirls and spirals intricately interlaced, a blue-green luminescence which lit the way forward. The Tree's roots? They had to be, winnowing their way through the heart of the Eyrie. They gave off the same glow, brighter in the dark, and somehow clearer. A tunnel stretched back into the mountain. A distinctly human sized tunnel with smooth floor and walls.

She took a step forward and hesitated. What if she stepped inside and the door closed? What if she was trapped there in the dark? What if she never got out?

But the Golden Auric had brought her here for a reason. It had saved her life. She'd been hurt and she suspected that it, or this place, had healed her.

It had chosen her.

And where else did she have to go?

She'd wanted to make discoveries. She'd wanted to explore the unknown. And what could be more unknown than this?

"Right," she told herself, winding her courage around the core of her being and forcing herself to stand upright, to take that next step. "Here goes nothing."

CHAPTER 5

Tomas realised he was being followed the moment he stepped out into the plaza that opened onto the harbour. It was just a feeling at first, but one he knew not to ignore. He'd learned his lessons well. An unexpected chill crept up his spine and he glanced behind him. There was no one there. No Windguards, no Guildless, no one at all. But he couldn't shake the feeling that someone was watching. Not a sensation he would ever be comfortable with. If someone was watching that meant he'd been noticed, and he didn't like to be noticed. He slowed his step, waiting, watching, and then made his decision.

He walked calmly on his way, letting the city life swirl around him. At the corner by the fishmongers' hall, he turned sharply down towards the harbour itself. He paused at the quay. His meeting wasn't time sensitive or even particularly secret. It would be easy to explain if he was questioned. All he was doing was passing on information by word of mouth. He could afford the time.

The ground rumbled ominously and the water swelled against the stones of the harbour wall, suddenly angry, as if intent on tearing them away. Tomas watched with a shiver of alarm, waiting, but the tremor subsided just as quickly. The busy harbour seemed to breathe again, as everyone went back to work. The business here didn't wait for anyone. Labourer boats were coming in with the catch, gulls wheeling in the air above them, cormorants perched triumphantly on the bows, their black wings spread wide to dry, their work aiding the fishermen done for the day.

When a patrol of Windguards stamped by him, he folded back against the wall of the harbourmaster's office to get out of the way, just like everyone else. But they were gone in seconds without offering a glance in his direction. And yet the feeling of being watched didn't fade.

He entered the bustling taproom of Harbour House, the inn much busier than he had expected. The smell of working men and women, of the ocean and ale, was heavy in the air.

There was no one out of place in there. Yet the unsettling feeling persisted.

The barman nodded to the left, where a door led to a smaller private room.

Tomas made a face as he realised what that meant and the man grinned at him, before shaking his head regretfully, and turning his attention to someone at the far end of the bar yelling for ale.

Tomas pushed through a rather rowdy group of dockers on their break, then slipped through the door and down the narrow corridor.

The noise fell away.

He waited, leaning nonchalantly against the wall, listening to the hum from the taproom. If they followed him in here, if they tried to take him, he'd have an advantage. He could hold the space long enough for the people in that room to get away. He could do at least that much. He had to.

But it wasn't the Windguards watching him.

A second before Tomas gave up waiting and knocked on the door to the private room, the boy appeared. His head darted around the corner, but when he saw Tomas, his eyes grew wide and there could be no doubt who had been following him.

Tomas' hand shot out too fast for him to evade it, grabbing him by the scruff of the neck.

"And what are you looking for?" he asked, not unkindly. To be honest he didn't have the heart to be threatening and there really was no need. The boy looked as if he was going to wet himself.

A skinny little thing in plain homespun clothes, he had dark eyes so big they seemed to take up half of his lean face. The boy shrank in his grip, making him look even smaller. The tug he made to escape was pathetic, and not at all likely to succeed. But at least the threat Tomas had felt was now diminished.

Tomas knocked on the door to the private room with his free hand and heard it open behind him. He didn't take his eyes off the boy though. He'd been bitten by that before. Sometimes literally.

"Hello, Tomas," said a familiar jovial voice. "What have you found?"

The boy looked even more terrified now. Tomas didn't blame him.

"I don't know," he replied. Finally he turned to look at the man. Shorter than him and almost twice his age, dressed in a flamboyant robe of many colours, his long hair was swept back from his face, marked by streaks of grey at the temples. He smiled, that same, familiar smile. "Is this yours, Parsa?"

Parsa Craft the Weaver shook his head and glanced over his shoulder. "Not mine. Looks like one of Nazir's though."

Someone else gave a gruff rumble from inside the room and the boy wilted in Tomas' grip. All semblance of innocence melted away. "Not good enough, Erik. What did I tell you?"

The boy, Erik, looked close to tears. "Don't let him see you," he mumbled, reluctant to admit that this was exactly what had happened.

"And what else?"

Tomas slowly relaxed his hand, letting the boy go.

They were all looking at the boy now. "It's only a game if you're not caught."

Nazir levered himself out of the chair in the corner and moved slowly across the room. He walked with a limp and carried a stick to help him, but Tomas knew never to count that as a weakness. There was nothing weak about Nazir. Broader than Parsa, he stood a head taller than his partner. And where Parsa wore all the colours of the rainbow, Nazir would dress entirely in black and grey, all the better to slip into the shadows or move through the night.

He took some copper coins from his pockets and held them out. Erik hesitated—no fool he—but when the hand didn't move, he darted forward to take the coins.

"You said five," he gasped, having counted only three.

Nazir grinned, unrepentant. "I said five if he didn't catch you. Go on. Two for your mam, remember?"

And just like that the boy nodded solemnly and was gone.

"Come in, Tomas," Parsa said, going back to the table. The surface was spread with papers and drawings, scraps of materials and threads of many colours. Tomas dreaded to think what he was working on. It looked like a design for a spider's web. There were flames and something that looked like grappling hooks.

"Are you spying on me now?" Tomas asked.

The older man huffed out a laugh. "What would that gain me? I know all your secrets, Tomas. I just wanted to test him."

Tomas shook his head, pitying the poor kid. "What did he do to annoy you?"

"He's an uppity little one, that boy. Thinks he knows everything already."

"A bit like someone else we know," Parsa chimed in as he began to tidy away his papers. His precious designs, which he hardly shared with anyone. That's why their meetings tended to be secret. Because Parsa had a million secrets and he never shared them all.

Tomas gave him a marked glare which he completely and pointedly ignored. Nazir had taken his place back in the corner, his stick beside him.

"Test him or test me?"

"A bit of both perhaps? Don't want you to get rusty."

"Shut the door," Parsa said, the paraphernalia on the table now safely back in various bags and pockets. "Have you eaten? You should eat. The stew here is very good. They use fresh star-root and a wine imported from the south. Yalla brings it up by sail all the way from Fristena, on the mainland, at great personal risk."

"Yalla is a pirate and a smuggler and if the Windguards find out—"

Parsa just laughed, cutting Tomas off. "Well, we'd better hope they don't. She's paying them enough and I don't want to have to rely on that pissy cider from the outer islands."

Tomas thought back to the reports that came in this morning and winced. "There won't be many orchards left the way the outer islands are flooding. Then you'll be sorry you weren't more appreciative of the cider."

"If you think I will ever be appreciative of third rate—"

"What he's trying to say is that it's good to see you and we've been worried about you," Nazir cut in before Parsa went completely off on a tangent. "Are you well? Are you eating? Have I covered everything?"

It was like having two overly protective fathers who knew everything about his life but tried to politely pretend that they didn't. Tomas knew that there was no hiding anything. He didn't even bother to try. Their pretence wasn't even very good.

They had saved him long ago. He'd been even younger than Erik. He wasn't the first and he would not be the last. He owed them everything.

Because in every society children fell through the cracks from time to time. The Guilds were meant to be there for them, but invariably they weren't. Luckily people like Parsa and Nazir were.

Even if a boy or a girl picked up a somewhat unique skillset from them along the way.

"What did you hear?" he asked when Parsa came back from ordering some bread and stew that Tomas hadn't asked for. Fussing over him again. He took a seat across the bare fireplace and watched Nazir warily.

"A Golden Auric feather?" the old man prompted.

Tomas had to suppress the wince. "Yes?" There was no point in lying.

If Nazir was disappointed, he didn't show it. He didn't show much of anything. "Didn't you think we could have used that?"

Oh, he was sure they could have. He didn't want to imagine what use it might provide though. If nothing else the thing was probably worth a fortune. If they got it off the islands he was sure there were people who would pay a king's ransom for it. He was only surprised it had taken them this long to find out about it. Or perhaps it had only taken them this long to issue the invitation to him to join them here.

They might be like family, but that didn't mean family couldn't be annoyed with him.

Nor he with them. "Ameris needed it."

Someone knocked on the door, a definite prearranged pattern of knocks, and Parsa went to answer while the other two stared at each other in silence. Parsa took the tray and set it on the table. "Now, here we are. Come and eat. I swear, you're wasting away."

He really wasn't, but if he didn't sit down and eat he was never going to hear the end of it. He kept his eye on Nazir as he levered himself back out of the chair and sat at the table.

The food really did smell good. His mouth was already watering. He ate in silence as Parsa fluttered back and forth around the room, while Nazir stared at him in stony silence.

"There's a new flying machine," Parsa said at last, pausing to preen a little at his reflection in one of the polished copper vases on the shelf. "Weren't you going to tell us that either?"

He shrugged and tore off a hunk of bread. "Clearly you found out anyway. Ameris is working on one."

"More than *working* on one," Parsa replied, without turning back to him. In the reflection, his smile was a bit more fixed. "They went off to test it this morning."

They had? Tomas stifled a groan of annoyance. Of course they had. Because telling him and letting him help them would be far too much to ask. Ro would be more than eager to throw herself off a mountain to test her theories.

He hadn't expected Ameris to be quite that fast building the thing but then again, he should have known. When she focused on something and got stuck into her work, there was nothing she couldn't do.

But he had truly thought they would tell him first. Parsa and Nazir knew more than he did. As usual. It annoyed him.

"Did you find out how it went, as well?" he asked, tartly.

Nazir gave a single cynical laugh.

But Parsa seemed to have frozen, still staring into the copper vase's shining surface. His hands shook against the bright colours of his robes, making the material quiver. Food forgotten, Tomas pushed himself to his feet.

"Parsa?"

Nazir reached Parsa first, his arms encircling him, holding him gently so he didn't fall. After Tomas grabbed a chair, Nazir lowered him into it.

"There," the older man whispered gently. "It's okay. Tell us what you see, Parsa. We're here. We're listening."

It didn't matter how many times Tomas had seen Parsa in the throes of one of his visions. His innate magic incapacitated him and rammed images directly into his brain in a chaotic jumble that frequently made no sense. If only he had been given some useful gift, he would moan when recovering, like healing, or the ability to predict the winner in a sporting competition. The flippancy didn't help, even though it was his way. When you cared about someone it was upsetting to see the pain etched on their face. How Nazir stood it, Tomas didn't know, but they had been married for so long they seemed to know exactly what to do for each other at any given moment.

Parsa's voice was a whisper at first, a stream of words falling over each other to leave his mouth. "The blue bird in flight, the flash of gold, the darkness. She steps inside and it closes. Follow the lights, little bird. Follow the … The shimmer is closing in, drawn to her. It will take her, swallow her down and drain her. She should fly. She must fly. The glass will guide her, the glass of time, the sands fall only one way. But she can change it. Only her. She can …"

Suddenly the words stopped and Parsa's glassy eyes fixed on the door as if he could see something or someone there.

Something terrible.

"The Collapse is coming. The skies will fall and the ocean will rise. I see a lake where the Aviary was, the great Auric sculpture spanning it like a bridge. Water running, channels of it everywhere, turning wheels, lighting sparks, fires blazing. It's all falling apart. All of it. Light the candle. Listen, Nazir, can you hear it? The wind? The air? It's coming. We must ascend. We must fly. All of us together. Light the candle. Or all will be lost."

Nazir's voice, so gentle that many people would never believe it was his, normally so gruff and caustic, whispered, "I'm listening, love. I promise, I'm listening. Come back to us now. Come back." He stroked Parsa's black hair back from his brow, his bronzed skin a stark contrast to his husband's waxy pallor.

Parsa drew in a single, shuddering breath and then relaxed against him, his eyes closing at last. Slowly his breathing fell to an even rhythm.

Hastily Tomas poured some water from the jug into a goblet and passed it to Nazir who lifted it to Parsa's lips. He drank cautiously and then made a face.

"You couldn't find the wine? The good wine?"

A smile flickered over Nazir's dour face. "Drink the water."

Parsa obeyed, just a little, and then seemed to shake himself awake. He gave Tomas a weak grin of embarrassment. "I didn't make a fool of myself, did I?"

"You never do," Tomas assured him. "You were talking about a bird. The one in the tapestry, I think. And about the Collapse. Do we need to step up the preparations? I can get word out across the movement and—"

Before Parsa could reply, someone hammered on the door with their fists. Both their fists from the sound of it, a rapid explosion of noise. Tomas jumped up, his heart racing in panic. Perhaps the boy hadn't been the only one following him. Perhaps—

Nazir had already slipped between Parsa and the door, his stick held out like a weapon, ready to take on whoever was trying to get in.

"Tomas, take Parsa out the back." Nazir nodded to the far corner, the place he had been sitting. Behind his chair there was another door, smaller, a servants' entrance to the room. Nazir and Parsa would never let themselves get stuck in a room with only one way in or out.

But then Tomas heard a voice he knew too well. Not a Windguard. Far from it.

"Tomas? Please! You have to help me!"

It was Ameris. A different kind of concern turned his stomach. He waved Nazir back and opened the door. Ameris fell into the room, her eyes red with tears and wild with panic. He caught her before she could hit the ground and lifted her up. He'd never seen her like this.

"What is it? What's happened? What are you doing here of all places?"

He stared past her, out into the hallway, looking for Ro. Because Ro had to be there. She was always with Ameris, especially when there was an emergency.

There was no sign of her. Something inside him froze, poised to shatter into a million pieces.

"She's gone." Ameris gulped out the words, frantic with grief. "It all went wrong. The Wing crashed."

CHAPTER 6

Ro had only taken a few steps down the passageway when she heard a terrible scraping noise behind her. She spun around, but she was already too late. The great stone door closed, shutting off the light and sealing her inside. She ran back, trying to push it open again, scrabbling around to find the handle, but there was no handle on this side, just smooth, polished rock. Like a tomb.

How could she have been so stupid? She should have blocked it open. But looking at the size of the thing and its obvious weight, she knew it would have crushed anything she could have moved.

For a moment she didn't know what to do. She stood there, frozen.

There was air and she was alive. There was a passageway. If something wanted her in here, there had to be a way out as well. The Auric had brought her here for a reason and she didn't think sealing her up alive in a cave was the type of thing the children of Amare would be known for.

Panic later, she told herself, closing her eyes and trying to calm herself. *Plenty of time for panic later.*

Putting her trust in the giant magical bird no one believed in, which had just saved her life, seemed to be her only option. She pressed her hand to the smooth walls of the passage and forced herself to breathe. To draw air in and out of her lungs and to calm herself, to slow her racing heart.

Deep in the rock she felt a deep rumble, like the sound the Golden Auric had made.

When she opened her eyes, there was light again. A hazy watery blue-green light, but light nonetheless: the light that had drawn her inside. Light flowed through the rocks, like seams of precious stones or the veins in her arm, like roots in the ground, glowing with a blue-green colour that shifted and moved, reflecting up on to the ceiling as if she was underwater.

But she wasn't.

Far from it. She was in the air, inside a floating mountain, so many miles above the ocean she didn't even have the ability to guess how far it was.

The light led her down, into the heart of the Eyrie. She followed, her feet finding the path smooth and even, the steps easy to follow. They curved around in a spiral, leading down and down, so deep that she began to believe she might just fall out of the bottom of the Eyrie entirely.

In the watery light she could make out carvings on the walls and ceiling, like those she had known all her life. Birds and clouds, buildings and people living in the air, the soaring isles, balloons, flying machines … But these weren't worn and damaged. They were crisp and beautiful as if they had been carved only recently.

But no one had been here in an age.

Something had preserved them. Something in the air, a frisson of energy, magic all around her, prickling against her skin. She could feel it, taste it, like a sweet juice with the scent of spring flowers and spices. Her senses were sharpened with it. She could hear only her footsteps ringing against the stone floor, and her breath.

Keep breathing, she reminded herself.

At the bottom of the steps, she stepped into a circular room. On its wall, illuminated by the glow, the old world surrounded her, picked out in a mosaic of polished precious stones, gold and silver. It glittered as she walked around, studying every detail. Amare soared overhead, the image dominating the ceiling, the Great Bird captured in a moment of elegance and grace Ro wouldn't have believed anyone could master, so lifelike that at any moment she might leap from the stones and take off. All around her she found images of cities in the air, surrounded by clouds and blue skies, and in each one, the birds in a million different colours and shades, mundane and magical.

Ro stopped, unable to move. She was overwhelmed by the beauty of it, of what had been, of its portrayal, the artwork and the skill that had captured this glimpse of a lost world. Tears stung her eyes and slipped down her cheeks, blurring her vision until it seemed that it all came to life before her, swirling and living and breathing. She could hear the birdsong, the wind, the voices and laughter of the people who had lived here, all resurrected as a million ghosts of a long lost world.

She didn't know how long she stood there, trying to take it all in but eventually she turned her attention to the rest of the chamber.

In the middle of the room stood a raised block of stone, as intricately decorated as everything else there. On it the stub of an unlit candle stood, trails of old wax attaching it to the stone like a parasite, and an hourglass, the frame of which looked like it had been carved from the same shimmering wood as the tree above, the tree whose roots surrounded and illuminated the chamber with blue-green light. But the hourglass was solid, a pale white, without the light of the living version. The sand was still flowing within the glass, glittering as it fell from the top bulb to the bottom in ceaseless movement. Even as she watched, convinced that the movement of the sand would stop at any moment, it kept going as if it had no end. There was hardly any left in the top. It had to stop.

But it didn't.

Ro moved closer, leaning in to peer at it, but as she did, her foot caught against something on the otherwise smooth floor.

A circle of pale stone large enough for someone to stand on jutted from the ground. It depicted an axe, the symbol of the Labourers' Guild. It was identical to the seal and the shield over the door of the Guildhouse. Further on, she saw another circle in the floor, of the same pale, unadorned rock carved this time with the needle and thread of the Weavers' Guild.

A brief exploration of the other side of the room led her to carvings representing the sextant of the Windriders, and the hammer of the Ateliers. It was only when she walked to the far side that she found the last one, the only image it could possibly be given the others. It depicted a bird flying towards the table, the carved feathers captured in exquisite detail. The wings were spread wide, and the tail split in two, and trailing out behind it, the distinctive lines of a Golden Auric. It had to represent the Birdsingers.

Each of the circles were no more than an arm's length apart. Five people standing on them could reach out and hold hands, encircling the whole stone table.

What was this place? It was clearly imbued with magic, and such magic as she had never seen. The people who made it must have poured all their skills and abilities into it, to create the most beautiful and enchanting room she could ever have dreamed of. And then they had just left it. Why?

She touched the hourglass gently. It wasn't large. One hand could envelop it almost entirely. She hadn't even been aware of moving towards it or reaching for it, but suddenly she was holding it. The surface was warm to the touch, as if someone had just been holding it a moment before her. The glittering sand inside kept flowing with a soft whisper.

She turned it over.

Impossibly, the sand kept flowing in the same direction, now from the bottom glass bulb to the top.

She stared at the hourglass, turning it again and again. Nothing changed. The sand flowed steadily in one single direction no matter which way she turned the thing.

The magic in it had to be powerful, but to what end? Why was it here and what on earth could it possibly be doing?

She lifted it up again, shaking it to see whether that made a difference. She peered inside its contents, squinting at the sand which glittered and shifted and whispered. It didn't change no matter what she did. Impossible. And yet she couldn't deny it.

Movement in the far corner of the room caught her eye. It hadn't been there a moment before. She almost didn't see it now but the room itself was so still. Nothing in it moved apart from her, and the sand in the hourglass, and the strange shimmer of misty light, whatever it was. A chill crept over her, and a curious sort of numbness tingled in her fingertips.

Ro frowned at the mist, trying to bring it into focus, but she couldn't. It seemed to slide around the edges of her vision, like a mirage or a heat haze. There was a light to it, yet no source of light that she could identify. And it was definitely moving, slipping around the edge of the circular chamber, closing in on her. A shimmering wisp of light.

A shimmerwisp. She'd heard of them. Everyone had heard of them.

Be good or a shimmerwisp will get you. Don't go out in the dark or a shimmerwisp will be waiting.

But they weren't real. They were just a story to frighten children.

And right now it was frightening her.

Still holding on to the hourglass, she stepped back from the raised stone, and carefully retreated, keeping her eyes locked, as much as she could, on the strange anomaly. Something about it made her skin crawl. She couldn't say why. It didn't look dangerous, just wrong.

So very wrong.

As Ro backed towards the entrance, she glanced over her shoulder for just a moment, some instinct warning her. There was another shimmerwisp. Two of them now, closing in on her. On the far side of the stone table, a third flickered to life, and then a fourth, at the foot of the stairs. She froze, trying to watch them all at once, and realised she still had the hourglass clenched in her hand.

"Okay, okay, I'll put it back," she murmured gently in case this was some kind of magical defence against theft. She stepped back up to the table and carefully replaced the artifact.

The moment she did, they surged towards her. In a blind panic, she grabbed the hourglass again and they stopped in their tracks as if they had run into a wall.

"This isn't good, is it?" she said to herself. "Right, think."

The shimmerwisps resumed their slow approach. They were coming for her regardless, but if she let that hourglass go, they were going to be too fast to evade.

The only way out was over the table. She made her decision and moved, leaping up, sliding over the surface and throwing herself towards the stairs which had brought her here.

She slipped as she hit the bottom step and fell forwards, the hourglass rolling out of her hand, landing a couple of steps up from her, out of reach.

She lay there, winded, helpless.

The shimmerwisp nearest to her spun back and rushed towards her just as she came to her senses and scrambled up the steps. She reached for the hourglass once more. Not fast enough though.

The light wrapped itself around her leg, holding on to her, and pins and needles engulfed her calf. It was burning and freezing at the same time, draining her lower leg of all strength and feeling. A terrible numbness, followed by stabbing pain, as if her skin was burning away. The breath left her body. She didn't even have enough left to scream. Instead, she threw herself forwards and snatched the hourglass up again. She found the wherewithal to gasp for breath as the thing released her leg.

It seemed more solid now, more like a glowing mist, as if it had drawn some kind of sustenance from her. Fed on her. A cold wave of nausea passed through her body.

A shimmerwisp will get you …

They needed to feed, that was clear, whatever it was they fed on … and she was the only source of food.

The shimmerwisps stopped where they were and then began their approach once more, still slow and undulating. Ro didn't know which was worse, the gradual advance, or the shocking speed. They were relentless.

The hourglass might be slowing them down, but it didn't stop them. She didn't know what might manage that, but one thing was for certain: she wasn't going to let one of them touch her again if she could help it.

Stories were no use at all. They had nothing to say about how to deal with these beings. The end of such tales was as inevitable as the tides. The shimmerwisps got you.

Ro knew she couldn't stay in the chamber. She limped back up the steps, praying that the hourglass would keep the shimmerwisps at bay, holding it in front of her like a weapon. She was only halfway up when she realised her mistake. The door was still closed and she'd just retreated into a dead end.

This couldn't be happening.

"Come on!" she yelled in frustration, the echo of her voice bouncing off the narrow stone walls and the low ceiling, reverberating back on her like mockery.

The shimmerwisps were getting closer, only a few feet away now, clustered together on the narrow steps, a wall of mist and swirling light. The hourglass was barely holding them back. Any moment they'd be on her and once she reached the door, she'd have nowhere else to go. She shouted her frustration to the Auric which had brought her here. It had to still be outside. It couldn't have just flown off, could it? "If you brought me here only to let me die in a hole in the ground—"

But it wasn't the Auric that answered.

The ground shook under her feet, and the mountain groaned. The whole soaring isle gave a lurch to the side and she was thrown against the wall so hard she almost dropped the hourglass again. But she clung to it with a death grip. She heard a sound like a strangled growl, the scream of rock on rock …

The wall opened up.

It was a gaping hole out into the air, not onto the surface of the soaring isle above but into empty space below. She could see the clouds and the birds, but no land. Just a narrow ledge.

And then, emptiness.

Swearing to herself, Ro looked back down the passage. The shimmerwisps were still coming, still closing in on her.

So her choice was to give in, let them come and drain her of all life, or throw herself into oblivion.

She swallowed hard. She still had the flight jacket on, but it was damaged and she wasn't sure how long it would hold. More than that, flight jackets weren't meant to be used at this altitude, not to mention for the length of time it would take her to get safely to solid ground.

Then, below her, she saw something. One of the other isles passing slowly across the skyline. The shadow of the Eyrie fell across it. Maybe, if she aimed for that, and then for another one, maybe … maybe …

The wind rushed by her, tugging at her as if daring her to jump, promising to help her. Its roar deafened her and stole her breath.

Better than staying here to face the tender mercies of those mindless things.

She was running out of time and she didn't have any other options. Securing the jacket as best she could, she muttered a silent prayer to her ancestors and threw herself into the air, arms spread wide, the hourglass still clutched in her hand.

CHAPTER 7

Ameris didn't want to believe it, but all the evidence was insurmountable. Ro was gone because of her, because she'd let Ro persuade her to test the Wing even though she'd had her doubts. Even though she'd known it wasn't ready. Because Ro always persuaded her to do things.

She should have known better. She was the reliable one. The one who kept them safe. The one who would never do anything quite as stupid as this.

Telling Tomas had been the worst moment of her life. She knew how he felt about Ro, everyone did. Except maybe Ro herself.

Letting all her fears out in front of the two strangers was a terrible mistake, but she couldn't keep it in any longer. She didn't know who they were and didn't really care, but they were clearly known to Tomas.

She'd just needed help. She'd wanted someone to tell her not to be silly, that Ro would be fine, that everything was going to be all right.

But he didn't. Instead, he just stood there, holding her, with a look of devastation on his face.

The next thing she knew the men with him were organising searches and before long, people were heading out in parties to look for Ro. Birds were dispatched with messages. It seemed to shake Tomas to life again. He was at the centre of it all, directing people with an authority she'd never seen him wield before.

But for Ameris, hope was dying, especially as the sun continued to cross the sky and more people were becoming involved in the search. Something nagged at the back of her mind, something she didn't dare name, a suspicion that was dangerous. She knew as well as Ro did that Tomas had some kind of connection with the Unity movement. But it couldn't be more than that, could it? She'd said it once to Ro, who had laughed out loud.

"Tomas? Part of a criminal movement? Don't be silly. Could you imagine it?"

But he definitely had contacts. He was often down here at the harbour. That was how she had found him, and everyone knew him. He was trusted, loved. It could be as simple as that, she reminded herself. The Unity movement was dangerous and while she felt sympathy for their stated aim of improving the lives of every person regardless of guild, in practice everything they did caused trouble. People got hurt. People got arrested. Tomas would never be involved in something like that. He just had a way with people.

Later he insisted on taking her home. She wished he hadn't, but how could she argue with him? The harbour area wasn't as bad as somewhere like the Mire, but it wasn't exactly safe either.

A group of Windriders brought back the shattered remains of the Wing just after Ameris arrived home. They'd found it at the foot of Mount Nest. Standing in the yard, within the walls of her Guildhouse, Ameris didn't want to examine it. Tomas pulled back the tarp and stared, unmoving for so long she knew she would have to join him.

The broken Wing was sprawled out on the bed of a wagon similar to the one she'd borrowed to take it up the mountain in the first place. The one she'd … Where had she left it? Somewhere by the gates maybe. She'd have to explain that to the Guild too. She was going to have to give so many explanations. They'd probably order an investigation. She might even get herself thrown out of the Guild altogether. What would her mother say then?

"Ameris," Tomas said gently, his hand warm and firm around hers. "You're hyperventilating. Just focus on your breath. Slow it down. Can you do that for me?"

She tried, just because he asked, not because she thought it would help. But it did. Somehow it did.

"What did I do?" she whispered.

"It isn't your fault."

"I built the stupid thing."

"And Ro wanted to fly it."

That wasn't the point, she wanted to say. Instead, she peered at the heap of metal. It wasn't actually that bad when she looked at it now. The analytical part of her mind told her she could probably repair it. Everything looked intact except for the cables connecting the pinions of the left hand side. They had snapped.

"Perhaps it needed more flexibility to account for torque?" said a too familiar voice. "Or was the diameter too small on the connections? It must have been under tremendous pressure to shear off like that."

Ameris froze, the shame and regret twisting her stomach until she felt like vomiting. Tomas bowed his head and took a step back, releasing her. Because he had to. She needed to face this on her own.

"I should have—"

The Master Atelier raised a hand for silence. "It's an untried alloy. Besides …" Her mother sighed heavily. "I know Ro too, Ameris. I doubt you could have stopped her leaping off that mountain even if you tied her up and locked her in your workshop. Experimentation is never without risk."

Not this kind of risk, Ameris wanted to shout. Not at this cost. But she couldn't find the words.

"The next time you will know better," her mother finished. "Now, I have news. Good news. She's in the infirmary at the Windriders' Guild. No more than a few cuts and bruises and a suspected sprained ankle."

Ameris felt her heart leap up into her throat. "She's alive! Why didn't you start with that?"

Her mother continued as if Ameris hadn't just spoken. "Very much alive. And being the type of patient you would expect her to be."

Spinning around, Ameris seized Tomas in her arms and hugged him. He trembled against her for a moment, looking as if he might burst into tears of relief.

"There's a carriage ready to take you there as quickly as possible," her mother said. "You too, Tomas. And thank you for looking after my daughter. I know this cannot have been easy on you either."

"Master Atelier, thank you." He swallowed his relief in a layer of deference that made Ameris profoundly uncomfortable. But Tomas was a Labourer and he was keenly aware of it.

No, he couldn't be part of the secret movement. Not with the way he was bowing his head like that.

Her mother nodded, dismissing them, but as they made ready to leave, Ameris saw her stop by the Wing and examine it.

"It's quite remarkable, Ameris. I look forward to seeing the improved prototype. Be sure to show me before trials. Well done."

Well done? She'd almost got her best friend killed and she got a well done?

She would never understand her mother. Never.

¤

The gates guards at the Windriders' Guild took one look at the pair of them and promptly refused them entry, looking down their pompous noses at them, evidently disgusted that an Atelier and a Labourer might think they could enter. And then, point blank, the foremost guard told them to go away.

"But we're here to see someone in the infirmary," Tomas protested. "Ro Swift. She was brought in earlier."

"That fool?" one of them laughed. "Well, you'll have to wait until she's released. She's got a lot of answers to give yet. Trying to fly ill-made prototypes is probably the least of her worries."

"What did you say?" Ameris snarled, her temper lashing out in a way it never did normally. How dare they talk about Ro like that? Not to mention her Wing.

"What? That she's as much a fool as she's always been? Or that whoever designed the contraption she was trying to control should be locked up?" He sniggered with his companion and Ameris felt tears burn like acid in the corners of her eyes.

"Enough," a voice snapped and the two guards shot to attention, their eyes fixed on the far distance, their faces masks. "You two need to learn some manners. What kind of reception is this? I'm putting you both on report. I won't have that kind of talk here, understand? This Guild has its honour to maintain. To behave like this, standing under our very symbol …"

Grayden Mistral stood in the doorway behind them with a face like a thunderstorm. The banners of the Windriders' Guild billowed behind him, the sextant symbol picked out in gold against navy blue. He was as ridiculously handsome as always. It was a pity about everything on the inside. But for once, Ameris was almost relieved to see him. Almost.

He looked past her at Tomas and his face hardened in that superior way she had grown all too familiar with.

"Ameris, you can visit her, but only you. The medics don't want her to over-exert herself so they're restricting visitors at the moment. I'm sure you understand."

He stood there, waiting, forcing her to choose Ro over Tomas. Knowing she would.

"It's okay," Tomas said, avoiding eye contact with either of them. "Tell her I was here. Tell her I'm glad she's okay. I have work to do anyway." He nodded curtly to Grayden and then turned away, his shoulders slumped.

Ameris glared at Grayden. "That was unkind."

He didn't look in the least bit apologetic. "Perhaps I'm doing Ro a favour. I still care what people think about her, even if she doesn't. He's trouble, that one. Ro needs better friends."

Tomas was so far away from being trouble that this didn't even warrant a response. The urge to slap Grayden in his all-too-handsome face was never far from the surface. He probably wouldn't even notice if she did, yet she wanted to all the same. How dare he imply this was for Ro's own good? He was just jealous and refused to admit it.

"Does that include me?"

A brief smile flickered over the sour line of his mouth. "Why would it ever include you, Atelier?"

Just like that he stuck the knife in and twisted. She was just an Atelier. Both being the children of Guild leaders they should have been something approaching equals, but the hierarchy said differently. As a Windrider, Grayden would always be higher than her.

As she valiantly tried to dismiss him from her thoughts, Ameris pushed past and strode down the corridor, passing the Wall of Heroes. Pennants fluttered overhead, strung across the ceiling, some of them ages old. They depicted family symbols, each one entwined with the sextant, and beneath them the white marble walls displayed name after name. The lost Windriders. Everyone entered the Windriders' Guild this way, forced to see the countless lives given up to protect the islands, to serve their people. Windriders died all the time. Every call out could be their last. They threw themselves into danger for the sake of others. She supposed they were lucky Ro wasn't joining them up there, her name etched in stone and painted with gold. If they'd even bother to do this for her.

Of course they would. Tradition and all that. Grayden would have seen to it. The traditions of the Guild were everything to him.

Ro had flown an unauthorised machine without her commander's permission. Not just flown it, crashed it. The Windriders didn't take that kind of thing lightly. Ro was in trouble and they would want to punish her. She was forever breaking rules. This could be one rule too many. They might throw her out of the guild.

People were expelled for far less. They ended up in the nastier parts of the city at the mercy of criminals, dragged into illegality through no fault of their own. Or they went to one of the outer islands where they tried to scratch out a living. Or they left altogether like Ro's brother Matias had. Gone with the sunset.

More people were leaving Arcadiana every day, driven out by the dangers of rockfall or the rising ocean. Or by the increasingly strict laws governing them. The Birdsingers said it was to control resources and to ensure public order, but even Ameris wasn't sure of that. It seemed to get worse every day.

Ameris ground her teeth together as she turned the corner towards the infirmary. She could hear the footsteps from Grayden's ever so shiny boots on the marble floor behind her. He was still following her. Accompanying her.

Ancestors forbid that a lowly Atelier should walk through the hallowed halls of the Windriders' Guild on her own. The sky might fall.

She didn't have to acknowledge him though.

The path led upwards, through a wide-open gallery overlooking the terraced gardens that covered the lower mountains. They were nourished by streams from the mountain which fed into the city's irrigation system, running little channels of water everywhere. In turn, the water powered waterwheels and turbines, generating the city's industry. Her mother was working on several improvements, and it took almost all of her time. She was obsessed with it.

The gallery hugged the side of the mountain that led up to the higher levels of the Guild, away from the work yards and the Windguards' barracks. Arches lined the other side, each framing views over the city, while the solid wall was lined with tapestries and panels painted in an array of jewel colours, highlighted with gold. The curved roof had been painted like the summer sky, dotted with clouds. Below it lay the officers' quarters and the docking ledges for the balloons, while up above the infirmary occupied a wide building constructed into the face of the mountain, like most of the Guild.

When she reached the airy white halls, all thought of Grayden vanished, even if he himself did not. The medics were clustered around the door of a single chamber, desperately trying to not look as if they were following the altercation going on inside. Ameris recognised Ro's raised voice right away and started forward.

"And *I* keep telling *you* I'm absolutely fine."

"No one could be *fine* after what you just did. No one normal. Just let me examine you, for the love of the ancestors!"

Grayden's hand on Ameris' shoulder stopped her. "Birdsinger Finch is with her. Hold on a moment."

Ameris wanted to push him away and stride in there, wanted to tell him she didn't care who was in there with her friend. Ro didn't have anyone else in the world. And from the sound of it the argument with the Birdsinger attached to the Windriders' infirmary was going badly in the extreme.

Ro had never been a good patient and now it sounded as if she'd graduated into a total nightmare. There was no reason for her to refuse the Birdsinger's examination of her. No one was more skilled in the art of healing magic. Which meant Ro didn't want to be examined for a reason. Which meant she was hiding something.

It did not bode well.

Then another noise reached her ears. A harsh croak, one that was all too familiar.

"What is that crow doing here?" Birdsinger Finch blurted out in exasperation.

"Zen!" Ro cried out. "Ameris, are you here? Where are you?"

Grayden let out a single long-suffering groan and released her. “Go on,” he said, but it was hardly necessary, for Ameris was already running, the charms on her bracelet jangling against her wrist. She pushed her way through the stunned medics to get to the room where Ro was sitting on the edge of a bed, which she pointedly refused to get into as well as be examined or be in any way apologetic about either fact.

Zen perched on the headboard. *Look,* he seemed to say with a triumphant look. *I found her for you.*

“Thank all the ancestors you’re all right!” Ameris gasped. “What happened to you?”

“The question we have all been asking,” Grayden said pointedly from behind her. “And the one she’s been refusing to answer. Maybe she’ll talk to you. Birdsinger Finch, a word, if you please. The rest of you, don’t you have work to be doing?”

And just like that he cleared the room, closing the door firmly behind him.

“Don’t be fooled,” Ro said, pulling a sour face. “He’ll be back. He’s been hovering around me ever since I got here.”

“How?” Ameris asked again, exhausted and exasperated. “How did you get here? I saw the Wing come apart in the air. I saw you fall, Ro! What happened?”

Ro grinned, that same maddening reckless grin Ameris knew all too well. “You mean you didn’t see the Golden Auric?”

CHAPTER 8

Ro watched Ameris turn the hourglass over in her hands, studying it. Under the bright lights of the hospital, the brass still looked as if it had been polished recently, although that was unlikely. The wood was pale and almost like bone, and the glass bulbs sparkled. The sand flowing from the uppermost glass bulb to the lower never ceased. It sparkled as it fell. When Ameris turned it upside down, the direction of the flow never changed.

"Impossible," she muttered, yet again.

"I told you," Ro replied. "How does it do that?"

"It shouldn't."

Ro had insisted that they pull the curtains around the infirmary bed. She didn't want to chance someone peering in on them and seeing what they were staring at.

"And yet …" Ro gestured at it and Ameris shook her head, clearly at a loss at how to explain it. Which was deeply annoying because that so rarely happened. Ateliers were always able to figure out how things worked, especially Ameris who figured out everything. Ro had been relying on it.

"And you just found it?"

"Yes."

"And took it?"

It wasn't as if she'd stolen it. Well, not really. She had no idea who it belonged to or when anyone had last found their way into the cave. It had seemed like the best thing to do at the time. And when had she ever thought things through anyway?

Besides, it had been the only thing that seemed to slow down the shimmerwisps and she didn't want to think about what they would have done to her if they'd overwhelmed her. Just the touch of one on her leg had been agony.

She had been meaning to take it straight to Ameris, but when she'd reached one of the lower soaring isles—the mining isle known as the Rock, as it turned out—and seen a transport balloon in the distance it had made more sense to signal to it that she was in distress. To be honest, she was. The flying jacket was just about ready to give out and she wasn't sure she would survive another jump. Her arms ached. Everything ached. And she was exhausted.

When they picked her up, they were shocked to find her alive. That was how she found out about the search for her.

It was just a little bit gratifying. Clearly enough people cared that she didn't die.

They insisted on taking her to the infirmary, refusing to even entertain the idea of going anywhere else. The aeronaut in charge of the balloon had been adamant. So that had been that. Once she was here, there were medics, Birdsinger Finch, and worst of all, Grayden throwing his weight around. She had been about to try hurling herself out of the window when he turned up. She couldn't tell them about the hourglass.

"It was just sitting there. Besides, I think the Golden Auric wanted me to find it. I think that was why it took me there."

Ameris was the one person Ro went to when she needed answers. They had been friends since childhood. Not even the rules and strictures of their paths in life could get in the way of that. Ameris always felt the need to look at things from every angle, to examine every permutation. Sometimes Ro felt like it took her an entire season or more to make a decision, but her diligence was mostly a positive.

"The giant bird that only exists in legends," Ameris said dubiously. "The child of Amare, that no one, not even the Birdsingers, have seen for fifty turnings or more."

"We know they exist. The feather proved that. The one I gave you."

Ameris inclined her head to one side, still unconvinced. "The bird that plucked you out of the sky and saved your life."

"Something saved my life," Ro said, irritated now. They'd been going back and forth over this ever since Ameris had turned up at the door of the infirmary. "And I needed this to get away from those … whatever they were."

"Shimmerwisps." She sounded like she wanted to believe Ro's story. But at the same time, it was difficult. "Have you told anyone else about them?"

"Who's going to believe me?"

"I believe you," she said at last, her voice very gentle. "Tomas would."

Ro smiled at the thought. "They wouldn't let him in, would they?" She knew he would have been here if he could. She'd never doubted that for a moment.

"They barely let me in," Ameris replied. "You should thank Grayden for that much."

Thanking Grayden Mistral. Not high on her agenda. She was already sick of his too-handsome supercilious face. He was probably still outside the door listening in on everything she said. But she couldn't do anything about that right now.

Ameris turned the hourglass over again and almost growled at it. "And what is it for?" Ro wasn't even sure her friend was talking to her.

"That was something else I was hoping you'd tell me. It's magic, isn't it?"

"It's something," Ameris replied thoughtfully.

The shimmer of the sands when the light hit it made Ro shiver inside. The hourglass defied all logic. Things fell down, not up. Every Windrider knew that.

Ameris was taking it as a personal affront. "I don't know what. This is far beyond anything I know. We need to ask someone. My mother, perhaps?"

Ro didn't like the idea of it though. It felt … wrong. Something like this, which defied reason, would hardly find understanding with the Ateliers. They didn't like things that didn't obey logic. Even Ameris was clearly having a tough time dealing with it. Besides which, they'd inevitably hand it over to the Birdsingers. That was what you were meant to do with anything magical.

Mind you, the same thing went for Golden Auric feathers. And that hadn't happened either.

Ameris shook the hourglass hard and glared at it again. Nothing had changed. Next she'd want to take it apart to see how it worked. If she didn't break it in frustration first.

Ro took the hourglass back and cradled it in her arms. "I don't … I don't think we should give it to her. I mean … don't get me wrong, but your mother doesn't like me very much."

Ameris smiled in a knowing way. She understood her mother better than Ro did. "I don't think she likes anyone very much. But fair point. What about Commander Mistral? She's head of the Windriders. She may have seen something similar. She's flown higher than—"

"Grayden's mother *definitely* doesn't like me."

"The Birdsingers?" Ameris asked. "They'd know. Or they could ask the birds."

Ro pulled a face. "Birdsingers. They'd just confiscate it."

"Only if we let them. But we won't let that happen. Finders keepers. That's a law, isn't it?"

Ro groaned, suddenly certain where this was going. "That's not a real law, Ameris."

But her friend just smiled, delighted to have wound her up just a little. "Send a messenger bird to Saran. He'll help us. He's your brother, after all. He has to help."

¤

The sun was already dipping towards the horizon before Ro was finally allowed to leave the infirmary. Grayden had tried to interrogate both of them, but they didn't answer any of his questions.

It was market day in Arcadiana. All across the plaza in front of the Aviary, stalls spilled everywhere in a noisy colourful display. But the noise seemed more forced than usual, and the stalls not as many as in previous sennights. People gossiped in groups, but it seemed like they fell silent when someone they didn't know drew closer. Suspicion rippled in the air like an undercurrent. People were worried, scared. They just didn't want to show it.

In front of the central fountain decorated with carvings of a thousand birds, glasslarks circled a musician who played a lute, darting about in time to the music, relishing it. The sunlight refracted through their gossamer thin wings, sending tiny rays of light glimmering around them. It was almost as if they were dancing to his tune, little sparks of iridescent colour reflecting in the fall of the water. Ro threw some coppers into the basket at his feet and he turned his head towards them, nodding his thanks.

Weavers and their associated artisans had commandeered the whole section of the market to the east, bright fabrics and tapestries tumbling across counters in a riot of colour, artwork and items of such beauty that no one could fail to admire them. A variety of birds flitted from stall to stall singing as they went, harmonising with the chatter, laughter and arguments, making a symphony of sounds. The Labourers had turned their section into a food market, filled with the finest produce. Birds flew in with orders, fluttering down with little scrolls of paper tied to their legs. The Ateliers were here too. Ingenious inventions and tiny marvels which would help in the home or the workplace abounded. At the far end, a flock of harperbirds sang in elaborate harmony which sounded like the stringed instrument they were named for, and a group of people had gathered beneath the shade of the wide spreading charnut tree to listen.

And everywhere they heard murmurs, whispers, rumours. Trouble on the outer islands. People fleeing across the ocean. The Unity movement organising ships. And the Windguards closing in on their leadership.

As they passed the Ateliers' stalls, Ro almost lost Ameris altogether to a display of fine tools for metalwork. The looks she got as she drew her friend gently away were not overly friendly, but what did she expect? None of the Guilds particularly liked each other on principle. They were too different: Birdsingers full of magic and mysteries, Windriders with their heads in the clouds, Ateliers bent over some new invention, Weavers marrying colour and fabric in ever more beautiful creations and Labourers tending the earth or fishing the oceans. They might work together, but they rarely socialised. Her clothes marked her out as a Windrider, the neat tailored flight suit, even her hair tied back from her face so as not to get in her eyes. Whereas Ameris, with her blacksmith's apron, neat bodice and heavy boots, was clearly an Atelier.

Ro had long ago decided not to care what others thought of her. Ameris cared too much, but tried not to show it.

A raucous caw sounded as they reached the far side of the market and Zen circled down to land on Ameris' shoulder. He dropped something into her hand, a tiny brightly coloured stone.

Ameris smiled. "Thank you, Zen. A beautiful gift."

"Who did he steal that from?" Ro asked.

"He doesn't steal." She ruffled the feathers at the back of his head. The bird leaned against her, preening. "He liberates."

A thin roll of paper had been tied to his leg. He pecked at her hair impatiently while she pulled some nuts out of her pocket and held out her hand. He hopped along her arm and helped himself with a triumphant cackle.

"Saran's in the Aviary," she said, after untying the scroll. "He's teaching this afternoon so he can't come here. But he said to go there and tell the sentries he sent for us."

She supposed they were lucky he could find the time to see them at all. He was so busy. People sought him out for one thing or another, and she knew he prized his teaching time most of all. He was shaping the future of the Birdsingers' Guild.

Perhaps Ro should have been the one to send the message, but it was easier to let Ameris do it. Zen was faster and smarter than any hired messenger bird the Aviary could provide, and Zen knew Saran well. Having no bird of her own to help her, Ro often relied on Ameris and her crow.

In the distance the Aviary rose out of the sprawl of the city, the centre of the Birdsingers' domain, their Guildhouse, notable for the willowy tower which saw birds come and go at all times of the day, and the great glass domed enclosure filled with plants and avian life of all kind.

As they drew nearer, the architecture around them changed, subtly at first. There was more greenery, trees, and parks. Houses stretched upwards, three and four storeys high, some even higher than that. The many balconies which clung to them were festooned with flowers. Birds of all kinds perched there and flew between them.

A shadow passed over them and Ro looked up. Far off, among the clouds, one of the soaring isles sailed by. A common enough sight, but now, with the increased rockfalls, a sense of foreboding came with it. People looked up as its shadow passed, pausing, waiting, ready to run for cover. She could see a number of birds around it, circling idly, hovering on the updrafts, which was probably a sign it was stable enough. She thought of the Golden Auric and squinted, shielding her eyes against the sun. That floating mountain couldn't be the High Eyrie. The birds were too small, and too many, and the isle too close.

Everything seemed to freeze for a moment as the shadow passed over the street, but there was no ominous rumble, no rain of rocks from above. Every eye turned up, watching, waiting. Just in case. But the isle was a stable one. As she watched she picked out the unmistakable shapes of Windriders leaping off it in formation and circling down. They must have been scouting up there. Or seeking out any Guildless who might be pilfering resources found there. She watched them until they were out of sight, gliding back towards Mount Nest.

She wondered whether the Birdsingers would believe her if she spilled out everything that had happened, if she told them about the Eyrie. Would Saran believe her?

Nobody could fly that high to begin with. And no one would believe that a Golden Auric had revealed itself to someone who wasn't a Birdsinger. She imagined what their faces would look like if she told them, the disbelief, the outrage.

Saran would be mortified if she announced something like that. He would think she was trying to make herself special, to make herself as important as him, or even to outshine him. For a moment she hesitated. She didn't want to embarrass her brother. He was so well loved and respected, and she was proud of his accomplishments. He was still the only family she had. But she didn't know what else to do.

The shadows were already lengthening as they arrived at the gates. Above them an enormous sculpture of a Golden Auric spread its wings wide. The stonemasons who had made it long ago were masters of their art. It almost looked as if it would tear itself free at any moment and glide over them. The details around the head were uncannily accurate. Ro had to smile. She might be the only person alive who knew that. The guards seemed less than impressed with their presence regardless of how presentable they looked. They were left standing outside for a long time, during which Zen got bored and flew off overhead, cawing too loudly. Probably to harass some unsuspecting pigeons. Eventually they were admitted and directed down a long colonnade of white marble through lush gardens, and across an arched bridge over a reflecting pool, into the central courtyard. In the middle of it rose the vast dome, of coloured glass panes amid a filigree of metal, the heart of the Aviary. The tower beside it rose like a slender tree, beautiful and delicate, home to the Birdsingers' elite.

As they entered the dome, warm air rushed over them, the heavy floral scent almost overpowering at first. Ro didn't know where to look, the press of the vegetation all around them rich and lush with life, a kaleidoscope of colours. Water flowed in little channels, the complex irrigation system mirroring that of the city itself, adding its own melody to the music of birdsong and the rustle of life. Most of Arcadiana was fed by the spring deep beneath the Aviary.

Ameris and Ro followed a slender winding path which led them through the gardens. Amid the shrubs on either side, she saw ground dwelling birds, small striped quail which rushed towards them as they approached, looking for food, or just curious. They knew no fear, she realised. Nothing would threaten them here. Overhead she heard the songbirds, and brightly coloured finches took flight in a flurry of brilliant feathers. Sparks of light denoted the places where the glimmerlarks darted in and out of the fabric of their world. No one knew where they went the rest of the time.

In the centre of the dome the plants fell away to reveal a shining pool of water, the surface as smooth as a mirror. Above it hung a covered structure like a tiny version of the tower itself, elaborately decorated, suspended weightless in the air by cunning magic. Inside, spilling over the lips of the carved openings, water flowed in a never-ending stream. The outer pillars were blue with flourishes of gold, and birds in flight were carved at various intervals around it, wings spread wide, each feather intricately crafted. The inner ceiling had been painted like the sky on a spring day, a pale blue with white clouds billowing across it. On top, a slender gold spire pointed skywards.

Although Ro and Ameris had seen it before, it never failed to impress. There was something ethereal about it, the last piece of the old world suspended in the middle of the dome, the Heart of Arcadiana.

Something about the place just made you want to stay forever. Ro looked around for more of the magical birds which were known to frequent the dome. A sparkling wandered along the path, its long tail trailing lightning flickers behind it. Overhead she heard the sweet song of a mimic, like bells ringing, lifting the heart of anyone who heard it. Noble birds, the Birdsingers called them, those who lived and breathed magic. But there was none so noble or magical as the Golden Auric.

A fluttering by Ro's ear made her start and when she looked, she saw a tiny brown bird with a pale breast, perched on her shoulder. A wren. Nothing magical about it. Just a wren. Just like the one she had saved.

Exactly like it.

Enchanted, Ro brought her hand up, slowly, carefully. The bird didn't move away. If anything she thought it leaned in towards her.

"I see you have a friend, Ro," said Saran as he approached. At the sound of his voice, the bird took flight and vanished into the trees above them. His gaze followed its departure and he smiled fondly. "A shame. They aren't normally so fickle. How are you?" He leaned in to embrace her. "What was it you wanted me to examine?"

Saran was still as Ro remembered, with more of a look of their father about his eyes now. He wore flowing robes which fell like wings from his broad shoulders, fine silk hand-painted with coloured feathers. Only the best for a Birdsinger. Especially one like him. They said her brother was one of the most powerful Birdsingers ever born, with a natural affinity for magic, which made the fact of him being the child of Windriders something of an embarrassment all around. But Saran rose above it. He applied himself, dedicated himself to his Guild, and had gained respect and admiration through his good works, his wisdom and his skills.

The wry expectant smile he turned on her left her with little room for manoeuvre. She opened the satchel she had slung over her shoulder and took out the hourglass. She didn't want to hand it over to him. She didn't want to hand it over to anyone. It felt wrong, but what could she do?

Besides, she told herself firmly, Saran was her brother. She could trust him.

Saran took it gently from her, examining it, and to her surprise a frown deepened the line between his eyebrows. His nose twitched.

"Where did you get this?" he asked, and every last trace of tranquillity drained out of his voice.

CHAPTER 9

"Give it back, Saran." Ro held out her hand firmly, surprised that it didn't shake.

All around them the Birdsingers working in the Aviary frowned at them, staring while pretending not to. Saran's students, all in their white robes, hung like ghosts nearby, watching everything, their eyes full of adoration for him, and suspicion of her.

"Of course," he said as he gave it back reluctantly, his gaze still clinging to it as she took it and slipped it into the pouch at her belt. He breathed out a long rush of air and fixed her with his soft gaze. "But where did you find it?"

That was the one question she really didn't want to answer, but it was also a fair one. She could lie. Or tell him the truth. She wasn't sure which would be better.

"Ro saw a Golden Auric," Ameris blurted out.

For a moment the whole Aviary went quiet. Even the birds were silent. Ro squirmed, aware that every eye was on her. The birds began to edge closer. They looked plaintive, as if they were worried about her.

She shook her head. The birds weren't worried about her. That was ridiculous. They were just birds.

His whole demeanour changed in an instant. "Come with me, both of you." Saran led them through the plants and the arches of flowers, until they reached an ornate white door.

"Where are we going?" Ro asked, beginning to worry now.

He released them as he opened the door and ushered them inside.

"Out of earshot of all the people who might lock you up for just having touched something with that much magic in it. Quickly, Ro. Someone is probably already reporting it." When she didn't move, he let out a heavy sigh. "*Please.* I'm not going to hurt you, neither of you. Or get you into trouble. You're my sister, for the love of our ancestors. Just … please, go inside. This is just the way to my chambers where we can discuss this in private."

The three of them filed into the round hall at the base of the tower, its cool darkness such a contrast to the bright warmth of the dome that it took more than a moment for Ro's eyes to adjust. The slender windows were stained glass, blue and green in elaborate patterns which, combined with the thick walls, made the space feel cool and dark. The stone stairs wound up in a spiral. In the centre, a long tapestry hung down, depicting the city on both sides, with thousands of intricately detailed birds, all circling the island of Arcadiana. It must have taken turnings to create, and yet they hid it away in here for themselves alone. Ro frowned at it the whole time they climbed the stairs.

Saran led the way up. It was so quiet she could hear her own breath along with their steps on the stone stairs. Only Saran moved soundlessly. They wound around the inside of the tower, circling that wondrous tapestry. They were almost at the top when he finally stopped. He unlocked a plain wooden door and opened it.

His quarters were neat and orderly. The window looked out over the dome of the Aviary, all those sparkling panes of multicoloured glass stretching out on either side of the central beam. It also had a view of Mount Nest and she wondered with a pang if he sat here sometimes, thinking of home.

Beyond the city, she could see a small group of Windriders performing drills in the air, whirling around in formation, gliding downwards. Just drills. Ro had heard that they were considering raising the threat level just this morning. There were going to be a lot more drills happening from now on.

Saran wasn't looking at the view, or the Windriders.

"Close the door," he said, and Ameris, who was last in, quickly obeyed.

Saran reached up to one of the shelves and brought down a heavy book. Ro watched, wary as a hare, as he put it down on the desk where she could see his notebooks in neat piles, the pens lined up beside the ink bottle. He opened the book to reveal an illuminated page. Colours stretched across the vellum, intricately decorated with ground lapis, oxblood ink and gold. But she recognised the image framed in the centre instantly.

A Golden Auric.

"Tell me," he said at last. His voice sounded more like her brother again.

This image was a lot more accurate than the tapestry had been. Beside her, Ameris drew in a wondering breath but when

Ro looked up, Saran was watching her with all too knowing an expression.

"Is that what you saw?" he prompted.

Ro nodded and his shoulders sagged. Saran sighed. "I feel the magic clinging to the hourglass even now. There's a scent … a taste … I don't know how to describe it if you haven't— Look, it doesn't matter."

Ro remembered the scents of the air up on the Eyrie and she understood. There was no other way to describe it. Floral and spiced. It was distinctive. And Saran knew that.

"It *does* matter," she said. "How do you know that?"

He clenched his jaw. "I know it because it's the way magic smells and tastes. Because it acts on our senses and there is nothing else like it in the world. This is an artifact of the old world and I need to know where you got it." His expression softened again with concern. "It could be dangerous."

"It's an hourglass. What's it going to do to me? Get sand in my eye?"

But Saran didn't laugh. He didn't have a sense of humour anymore. Maybe the Birdsingers had drained it out of him. "Did you break it?"

"No I didn't break it. Ameris, help me here. My darling brother is a bit slow on the uptake."

"Ro," Ameris replied, her face grim. "Ro, just show him."

Ro pulled out the hourglass again and held it in her hand. This time he didn't take it and she was grateful for that because she wasn't sure what she would do if he tried.

A squawk drew her eyes to the open window. Two magpies were perched there, just inside, glaring at them with tiny black pebble like eyes. Saran's magpies. She'd never liked them.

Now they were gazing at her with far too much interest. It made her skin crawl. What had he called them? Silk and Steel … something like that.

"Should they be in here? There are rare documents and priceless treasures," she asked, giving the book a pointed look.

Saran just shrugged and put the book back on the shelf. "They'll behave. This is their room too."

Ro wasn't so sure. She didn't like the look they were giving her. The magpies fluttered over to the top of the shelves and hopped up and down tormenting each other.

Meanwhile Saran fetched a box and set it down on his desk. Inside she saw a pile of dusty old scrolls. He opened them, carefully enough, one after the other until he found the one he was looking for.

It was covered with drawings, pictures of birds, great and small.

In the centre was a drawing of Amare and in her talons she held an hourglass.

"That's not possible," Ro said, moving forward, straining to see. But it was. She knew full well where she had found it. She just didn't want to tell Saran. Or any Birdsinger for that matter.

She'd thought it was because they'd never believe her, but perhaps she was really worried that they would.

And then what?

The sketch was so tiny. You couldn't even see it clearly. That was what she kept trying to tell herself. But there was no doubt.

"It's exactly the same," Ameris said.

There was a word written underneath it. Something in an ancient language, and an ancient script. She squinted at it and before she knew what was happening, her mouth tried to form the word.

"*Adscendo.*"

The air trembled and in front of her, for just a moment, a tiny ball of flames coalesced in the air. Just for a second, but then it was gone, leaving only a patch of warmth, as if she had simply imagined it, the air scented like at the High Eyrie.

Saran jerked her back from the scroll. "Don't say it. It's not something to simply *say* like that. It's old magic. Ancestors, Ro, you're so reckless sometimes." She closed her hand about the hourglass, but Saran grabbed her wrist, stopping her putting it away again. For a moment he wasn't her brother at all. He was a stranger. "I don't know what you're playing at or what you've got yourself involved in this time, but you need to give the hourglass back to me. Before anyone else sees it. Just tell me where it came from, which box in the archives, and I'll put it back. No one will know. I promise."

"Which *box?*" She was really confused now. And not a little frightened. What was he talking about? She tugged her arm, trying to free herself, but he didn't let go.

"Saran, stop it," Ameris protested.

"It's dangerous. And if the hierarchy finds out you have it, whether you saw an Auric or not, whether you've worked out how to use magic or not, if they think that you *stole* that from us—"

It was like a bucket of cold water had been dumped over her head. Even the way he said *'whether you saw an Auric or not.'* He didn't believe her. Not for a moment. "I didn't steal it."

"Then how did you get it? *Where* did you get it? Is this something to do with Matias and—"

"And what?"

He didn't answer, but she knew. Matias and the Unity movement. Enough. She'd had enough. How dare he? And how dare he suggest she'd stolen it?

Which … well, maybe it could be seen that way … but there had been no one there. It was clearly abandoned. And besides, the Golden Auric had brought her there. It had wanted her to take it. She knew that. She was sure of that.

But he didn't believe her. Her own brother. He didn't believe anything she told him.

Her heart thundered in her chest and she finally ripped her arm away from Saran. She made for the door. He might be her brother and he might be a Birdsinger, he might be their best and brightest, but that didn't mean he could treat her like this.

The magpies gave a single joint cry, a squawk of anger, and took off from their perch, swooping down, directly at her, beaks and claws ready to attack.

Ro threw her hands up over her face.

But something else got there first. A shape made of coal black feathers and outrage came through the open window, twice the size of the magpies. Zen's cry was a harsh croak, but it sent the other birds scattering for the ceiling. Saran fell back against the table which skidded across the marble floor, the legs making a scraping noise like a scream.

A chill passed over Ro's body, a numbness that was so like what she had felt in the cave that for a moment she thought she was back there.

And then, between her and Saran, a shimmerwisp appeared, a drifting cloud full of glimmering lights.

"What's that?" Ameris asked, fascination filling her voice. She even took a step towards it. Show Ameris a mystery, any mystery, and she would want to solve it. No matter what the risk.

"No!" Ro exclaimed in horror.

At the same moment Saran shouted, “Don’t touch it!”

The shimmerwisp lurched towards Ameris hungrily.

Ro threw herself to one side, pulling Ameris after her. She held on to the hourglass like grim death.

“Ro, don’t make any sudden moves.” Saran didn’t sound angry now. He sounded terrified. Terrified for her.

What did he want her to do? Stand there and let it have her? She tore open the door and careened down the stairs, Ameris close behind. She glanced back. The shimmerwisp was still following them, but its attention was fixed entirely on Ro and the hourglass. She had to get the bloody thing out of the Aviary. There were too many people here.

Beyond the tower, in the dome, sudden noise erupted, human shouts and the shrieks of birds, all rising to a deafening roar.

“Take cover!” a voice screamed. “They’re everywhere!”

Someone slammed against the door, threw it open and flung themselves inside the room at the foot of the tower. Two terrified Birdsingers sprawled there, their unadorned white robes pooling around them as they tried to escape. Another shimmerwisp surged through the door after them. Saran gave a roar of dismay as it bore down on his students. Ro and Ameris reached the foot of the stairs and folded back against the wall, but the original shimmerwisp shot by them and joined its fellow. The glowing mist-like shapes descended on the students as they scrambled back against the far wall. The boy raised his hands, performing a complicated dance with his fingers, and the air around them tingled with the magic in use, making Ro’s skin crawl in recognition. The second joined in and she realised too late what was happening. They were trying to shield themselves, but the presence of magic was just drawing the shimmerwisps to them.

"Don't move," Saran yelled, this time at the acolytes. Tears streamed down their young faces. They looked to him with desperate hope, with absolute trust. Ro held her breath as he raised his hands and unleashed his magic, driving the shimmerwisps away, slamming them against the wall to the right and trapping them there. More came as if called, or as if attracted by his power. Like sharks scenting blood in the water.

Magic. It came to him as naturally as breathing and she could sense the power he wielded.

She'd done that when she accidentally conjured the light up in his room. On a much smaller scale, but it was the same feeling, the same vibration beneath the skin. It was nothing compared to the power her brother unleashed now. He rushed to the defence of the acolytes, magic pouring out of him, forcing the other shimmerwisps back. She'd never seen anything like it. He threw himself into the fray to protect them. He glowed from within, magnificent with it.

Ro seized her moment, grabbed Ameris and pulled her back to the now open door to the dome, with Zen ghosting after them on his broad wings.

The dome was a scene of chaos. Birds flew everywhere, dive-bombing the misty shapes that had sprung up amongst the terrified Birdsingers, shrieking at them, from the smallest to the largest. Magic flared and died. Shimmerwisps came from the undergrowth, from the canopy, they came from everywhere. And the Birdsingers were panicking instead of fighting back like Saran had.

"What's going on?" Ameris cried out in fear. "What are those things?"

People screamed as if acid were eating through their skin. From somewhere Ro could hear Saran shouting instructions, loud and firm. His voice galvanised the other Birdsingers into trying to mount a more effective defence. Magic bristled in the air again. The Birdsingers were following her brother. He was a natural leader, someone they trusted. Somewhere underneath the terror, she felt a surge of pride.

Ro and Ameris ran pell-mell through the madness, the fear in her chest bubbling up the back of her throat where it burned, but she had to keep going. She had to get them both out of there.

The two women burst through the doors, out into the open, skidding across the cobbles of the Aviary's main courtyard. The birds roosting there took off in a great cacophony of cries and flapping wings and began to swirl overhead, but Ro didn't stop.

It was her, she realised. The shimmerwisps were following *her*. It was something about the hourglass. Or the Golden Auric. Or the fact she'd been to the High Eyrie, gone into that chamber, and survived.

They were after her, the one who got away.

Only in following her, they'd found the Birdsingers, people who lived and interacted with magic on a daily basis. And shimmerwisps fed on magic. That was what all the old stories said. They would gorge themselves in there. She only hoped Saran could protect the others from what she had unleashed.

Get a hold of yourself, she repeated in her head. *Get a hold of yourself and calm down. Otherwise—otherwise—*

There was another burst of commotion behind them. She glanced back to see the Windguards pouring out of the barracks and heading for the dome with shouts that they were under attack, and calls to defend the Birdsingers. Saran would tell them what had happened. It was only a matter of time before they'd be coming after her as well.

After both of them. She'd got poor Ameris into this.

They rounded the corner, forcing themselves to slow to a brisk walk so as not to attract even more attention. The gates stood wide open, and the sentries there were staring back towards the dome in utter confusion. They weren't even looking at the Windrider and Atelier hurriedly leaving the scene of disarray and turmoil. No one would ever put it together, except perhaps her brother.

He would. He already had.

She'd said that word, worked that spell up in her brother's room, standing over that ancient book. The little flame had been conjured into life. And they had come as if called.

Birds were still circling overhead, angry and confused. Everyone was looking up at them.

Ancestors, what had she been thinking? She should have just let Saran have the bloody hourglass. He would know what to do with it. She should have just—

But why did every instinct tell her not to let it go?

The market was packing up for the night, but it was mostly deserted now. She and Ameris skirted the edge of the marketplace and then plunged into the warren of alleyways at the far side, Ro running again and Ameris stumbling after her. The streets closed in around them, the lanes narrowing, the buildings less beautiful. Ro had thought they were heading for the harbour, but she must have taken a wrong turn in the tangle of alleyways. It was growing dark. The lamps flickered on as they found themselves in an area of disrepair and dilapidation.

Finally, Ro slowed to a halt. She had no idea where they were. The path ahead smelled of fish guts and old litter. There was hardly any light down here and all she could see at the far end was a boarded up door. No way out.

She turned around, covering her mouth to fight against the stench, and saw their way back blocked. Three figures stood there, one leaning nonchalantly against the wall picking at his teeth with his fingernails. The other two formed menacing towers next to him.

"What have we got here?" the one leaning on the wall drawled.

This was bad. She knew where they were now. Where they had to be. The Mire. The section of Arcadiana where no one wandered unwary. Every city had somewhere like this. Beyond the archipelago people said it was the same, or even worse. Although Ro knew next to nothing of the countries of the mainland, there were always stories. And everywhere had somewhere like the Mire. Because every light had to have a shadow. Even Arcadiana.

"We ... we're just leaving," Ro said, shoving Ameris firmly behind her and making her way determinedly towards the tiny gap between the larger men.

The gap closed. Ro's heart sank. This couldn't be happening. They'd escaped shimmerwisps, for the love of the ancestors. A group of Guildless thugs weren't going to be the end of her.

"I don't think so, love," he said. "I don't think so at all."

They didn't so much seize Ro and Ameris as herd them back down the laneway, towards the boarded up door. Heart thundering, Ro tried to think of a way out, a way to protect Ameris and somehow make this not turn into the nightmare it was rapidly revealing itself to be.

When they could retreat no further, Ro stood her ground, hands balled into fists in front of her. She'd had the same basic combat training all Windriders were required to take. She hadn't been very good at it, but she might be able to hold her own long enough for Ameris to make a run for it.

"Don't you touch us," she snarled, hoping she sounded fierce rather than desperate.

"No one's going to touch you, love," said the man with a weasel grin. "It's not worth our skins to cross him. You're under his protection." They all laughed at her confusion. It wasn't a pleasant kind of laughter. "You come in the Mire, you've got to pay the Piper. And we've been watching out for you."

CHAPTER 10

Tomas had left Ameris at the door of the Windriders' Guildhouse as she went to the infirmary. There was no point in arguing. The guards had already made up their minds and Grayden Mistral was not about to help him get inside. Especially not to see Ro.

He'd made his way around to the kitchens and talked his way in there. It wasn't difficult. All the gossip in any Guild ended up in the kitchens. He just had to ask the right questions.

"I heard she was picked up by one of the high altitude balloons," the pastry chef said. "The one Birdsinger Finch was on, doing his—" He waved his flour dusted hands in the air in a suitably mysterious way. "You know, gathering magic from the clouds."

"Not sure it works like that," the pot boy said with a mocking grin.

The chef rolled his eyes. "Like you'd know. They found her way up on the isles. Almost killed herself getting down that far, I heard."

Lots of speculation and very little information other than that Ro was safe and seemingly unhurt. At least he had that small comfort.

As he left, the wagon delivering supplies to the kitchen arrived so he stopped to help the driver Spira Wheeler unload, and then he took a lift back towards the harbour with her. She was an older woman, with greying hair in a long plait and a round, pleasant face. "You heard about Ilana then?" she asked, as her donkey lurched forwards.

"No, what happened?"

The outer island of Ilana, the very one where he and Ro had found the feather, was home to a small farming community and not much else.

"Their seawall went. Couldn't build it up fast enough. The whole place is sinking."

Ilana didn't have many resources. The Birdsingers had denied them aid, saying they had to fend for themselves. Clearly that had not gone well.

"What about our Guild?" he asked.

Spira shrugged, a look of guilt married with helplessness on her face. "We only have so much to go around, Tomas. You know that. Everything's going into the projects here. There's talk of an evacuation, ships off the islands. I reckon Ilana will be deserted before the Carnival. If it isn't entirely underwater."

She was right. There was only so much that anyone could do. People were leaving. Some quietly, some loudly proclaiming their exile, because no one could help everyone. Not even the Unity movement. Not anymore.

"What do you reckon?" Spira asked, as she pulled up outside the next stop on her round. Tomas hopped down and the old woman gave him a speculative look. "Time to evacuate, is it?"

"While we live we have hope. Isn't that what they say?"

Spira snorted out a laugh. "Do they? I don't know. I reckon we all need to head for higher ground, like the Windriders on their mountain or the Birdsingers with their tower. Could do with a nice house on a hill somewhere at the very least. If they weren't already taken up by the rich. Failing that? Time to find passage on a ship, I reckon. Take care, Tomas."

For a few hours he carried out the inspections of work he had scheduled. The irrigation upgrades were proceeding apace. As he walked the city walls, the breeze whispering against his skin calmed him. New tethering rings were being sunk into the ground beyond the walls and he had the perfect view of the latest works. The Windriders had contested the locations at first, arguing that all the necessary docking areas for their balloons were already available on Mount Nest. It had taken seasons of careful diplomacy on the part of Parsa, Nazir and the head of the Ateliers' Guild Devera Flint, and many others, to get the go ahead to sink the huge anchoring rings in the ground and to reinforce the foundations around the walls. Debate still raged. Why did they need to be so big? Why did they have to drill down so far to anchor them? Mount Nest only offered a certain vantage point, the Master Atelier had reasoned, and this way they would cover far more space. They would also allow people to maintain the signal towers being installed all along the walls, guiding lights for ships and air traffic, like the balloons, permitting night flights.

The Windriders still weren't happy about it, but some of them at least saw sense. Commander Mistral, Tomas suspected, saw it as a way to expand her Guild's influence over other parts of the city. She was already planning garrisons to be stationed on the walls at every anchoring point. That was the payoff, he supposed. The Windriders would manage the signal towers, but at least they would still be built. It was a safety and security matter.

If that was what it took, then so be it, Parsa had said, shrugging his shoulders. Nazir said nothing, which was his usual approach. He had his own opinions about Mistral and her ambitions.

The torches located at fixed points on the battlements were another new addition. When lit, they would illuminate the walls of Arcadiana, with flames rising through glass tubes into the night. Whether they would actually work to guide ships in the dark, or were purely decorative conceits, remained to be seen. Other than the fishing fleet and the rare traders allowed to dock in the harbour, there weren't a lot of ships that needed such guidance. Certainly not those putting the archipelago firmly behind them. But for the increasingly complex night flights the Windriders wanted to undertake, they would be invaluable.

Parsa had used his charm, wit and when all else failed abject flattery to get his way. The torches would be beautiful, he said, and that was as good a reason for him as anything. The sconces were indeed ornate and when they caught the setting sun, they gleamed like the flames they would one day contain.

But as to their usefulness? Tomas wasn't so sure.

After checking the intricate machinery which would power the torches—cogs and gears, tiny flints and complex machinery that would set the flames—under the watchful eye of an extremely suspicious Atelier who didn't want an intrusive Labourer anywhere near his precious equipment, Tomas stepped away. He knew better than to ask too many questions. He wanted to know every last detail, but that would only draw attention to him and he couldn't afford that. One day, he promised himself, he would ask Ameris to explain it all and she would have the time of her life. Only one glance and his friend would have it all figured out. He only hoped he would understand her explanation and not have to see her make that face, the one that made it seem like he had just proved himself to be a total idiot.

The afternoon was speeding onwards. Knowing he couldn't put it off any longer, he made his way towards the Mire.

If the Aviary was the heart of the city, the Mire was its bowels, a rank warren of narrow streets, where things went to decompose. Everything, from food, to garbage, to people.

But the Mire was home. While he may not like it or live there anymore, he couldn't deny that it was where he had come from. He couldn't help but go back. He supposed he should be grateful that Parsa had plucked him out when he did. Guildless children didn't fare well in places like this. No one knew that like he did.

However, the people here were proud, and determined. They didn't want charity, or the Guilds interfering with their lives. Within the walls of Arcadiana, the Mire was the last bastion of the Guildless. The numbers allowed to live there were severely limited, and the actual headcount a secret closely guarded by the inhabitants. If anyone was asking questions, they clammed up. If the Windguard came around, the doors closed and the windows were immediately shuttered. Ateliers tended to ignore its existence entirely, unless they wanted some commodity that was more difficult to obtain. Or entirely illegal. If the Weavers showed up with aid, they were mocked and jeered. Even Labourers were barely tolerated, although many of the Guildless who left the Mire joined the Labourers, often the only guild that would take them. At least it meant honest work.

And Birdsingers? No Birdsinger would willingly set foot in the Mire.

Even Harbour House was a world away from this place, with its ocean breezes and sunshine, its laughter and welcoming air. Harbour House was the one place that Tomas felt most comfortable, most at home. But the heart of the Mire was a place he knew, and a place where he was known, inside and out.

He opened the door to the Piper's domain and stepped inside.

"Just here to light the candle," he said.

The elderly man behind the grubby bar eyed him suspiciously at first and then, as his rheumy eyes adjusted to the outside light, nodded in recognition. There was no one else here. Tomas didn't need to say another word and in truth he was just too tired to get into any kind of conversation. The code word greeting was enough.

Strange how something so awful as the thought of anything happening to Ro could tear all the energy from him and leave him hollow inside. Now, knowing she was fine and that the Windriders had closed ranks around their own, all that rush of adrenaline had drained him. At least here, there would be no lies, no questions, no performance. Just him.

"Some ale?" Creed asked. No one knew exactly how old Creed was, but he was easily the oldest person in the Mire. Like the young, the old didn't last long here either. It was the place of last resort. It was here, or exile. Or the grave.

"Thank you," Tomas replied. "And the reports?"

"Awaiting your attention." Creed had already shuffled away towards the grubby little kitchen he kept at the back of the house. Whatever agreement Creed and Nazir had come up with so many turnings ago, it served everyone well enough so long as the rest of Arcadiana knew nothing of it.

The Unity movement wouldn't survive without the Mire or this sorting house of information, a place where debts were bought and sold, where promises were kept no matter what, where dark deeds could be done.

No one hated the thought of that more than Tomas, but sometimes such things were necessary.

He sat down at the desk in the corner, his back to the wall, and started to read through the various papers waiting for him. Some of it would not be of any import, or at least nothing that was obvious now. But later, in the future it might be helpful to know for example, who was having an affair with whom, whose family was experiencing hard times, who had made comments which might be more obviously sympathetic to the movement.

Some things needed more immediate action. He mentally made notes of things to report back to Nazir. He didn't write anything down. Later on Creed would burn all these reports. They kept nothing. It was too dangerous. If the Windguards ever found this place, it would all go up in flames before the word could be spread. Preferably with their enemies still inside it. Creed would see to it.

Tomas studied the papers in the dim light until his head began to ache. The ale didn't help as much as he had hoped it would.

The not terribly hushed exchange outside brought his attention back to the here and now. It was rapidly turning into an argument and Creed was getting more irate.

Damn it. He shoved the papers back into the pouch and pushed himself to his feet.

Price's voice reached him. "Well, I reckon he's going to want to know."

The thief could be useful, but Avon Price had a mean streak that set every nerve Tomas had on edge.

"You shouldn't have brought them here," Creed snarled with unexpected vehemence. "Even an idiot knows that much. Take them away, lock them up and we'll deal with them later. They shouldn't even be seeing this place."

"Well, you can always put those pretty eyes out yourself. You'd probably enjoy it, you sick, old—"

"Enough," Tomas barked.

Creed turned towards him, guilt all over his ancient face. Price let his face split into a broad grin.

"Piper, you're here. The man himself." Price sneered. "Thought you were too good to slum it with the likes of us. You made it out of the Mire, didn't you? But you still come slinking back."

Tomas narrowed his eyes. "What do you want, Price?"

Price snarled at him, but Tomas didn't flinch. He kept his face completely impassive. Show any fear and he was done for.

"Brought you a gift, didn't I? A pair of little ones that got lost in the woods."

Price's goons shoved Ro and Ameris in through the door. The shock on Ro's face when she saw him quickly contorted to appalled horror. Ameris was white as a sheet. It took every ounce of control Tomas possessed to keep his face unmoving.

This was bad. Really bad. He couldn't think of any words to explain his way out of this.

"Well, Piper? Nothing to say?" Price asked. "I thought you were friends. Or didn't you share all this? You might want to ask these two what they got up to in the Aviary. Word is someone attacked the Birdsingers in their heart of hearts. You wait, Tomas. They'll be blaming it on us regardless."

Of course they would. Anything like that was blamed on the movement. Sometimes with good reason, but the Guilds knew how to pick a scapegoat. If it wasn't the Guildless, it was the movement that tried to help them, and everyone else, to achieve what the Guilds denied them—parity, equality, unity.

He didn't want to know how Price knew about his friendship with Ro or why he'd brought her here. Sheer devilment, perhaps. Tomas had tried to keep their association secret but everyone had known Matias Swift. Or at least they had after he'd been arrested. Even in the Mire they'd recognise his face.

Tomas had just assumed that no one here would know about Ro. She never came to these parts. As a Windrider who wasn't connected to the Windguards, she'd have no reason to.

And likewise, he'd never mentioned any of it to her. Matias had been scrupulous about keeping his family out of all Unity activity. Which meant Price had to have been watching them. Or this was more widely known than he cared to think about. It felt as if the earth was dropping out from under his feet. He'd thought he'd been so careful.

Clearly not.

"Get out. All of you." Tomas made his voice like iron, the only type of tone these men would respond to.

Price just smiled again, a lewd and awful expression. He even gave Ro a suggestive wave as he retreated.

Ro started to say something which would have made matters even worse, but Tomas moved like a blur, wrapping his arms around her and pressing his hand over her mouth. She gave a muffled cry of outrage, though this was also laced with unexpected fear, and he heard Price's laugh echo back down the narrow lanes in response like a nasty barb.

A cold feeling of disgust crawled over Tomas' skin, but he didn't dare release her. Not yet. He gazed into her furious frightened eyes and tried to pretend he couldn't feel the way she was trembling. Ameris said nothing, but stood behind them, her arms wrapped around her body, frozen in fear.

When he was finally sure Price was gone, he loosened his hold on her.

Ro shoved her way free. "What do you think you're … How do you even know him? He called you the Piper, Tomas. Like the man who Matias …"

The words trailed away as she realised what that might mean.

Tomas decided to ignore all of this. He couldn't even begin to explain. Not in a way she'd understand right now.

"Come on," he said curtly, without deigning to indulge her questions. "We need to get you away from here."

They stared at him like he was a stranger, like another person was somehow inhabiting his body. They didn't know him. Not like this.

"We didn't do anything," Ameris began to say. "It wasn't our fault, the Aviary. We—"

Tomas shook his head. He didn't want Creed to hear anything they had to say. The less anyone in the Mire knew about the two of them, the better for everyone concerned. "Explain later. Creed, shut up after me. Say nothing of this to anyone."

The old man nodded, still eyeing the two women with hostility. "As you wish, Piper."

Ro flinched at the sound of the name. He saw it. He couldn't pretend otherwise.

He took Ro's hand, threaded his fingers with hers and for a moment he thought she'd pull away. But she didn't. Her grip tightened, trying to hide the way her hand was trembling against his, but he felt it. He reached out for Ameris as well. He couldn't risk losing either of them. Not here.

Without further argument he led the two of them out of the Mire.

Ro avoided looking at him, concentrating on the path ahead. Tomas felt a pang of loss spear its way through him. She was trying to work out if she could still trust him. He'd never thought she would have to question that. Except ... except he did, he had. All the time, if he was honest. He had been waiting to see that look in her eyes for far too long. She'd just seen a glimpse of the other side of his life, the side he never wanted to reveal to her. Because she wouldn't understand.

But right now he needed to get her away and somewhere safe. It was Ro. He would do anything to keep her safe.

The Harbour House wasn't far. But despite the fact it was his preferred bolthole, the place would be busy tonight and there would be too many eyes on them so he made for the bakery around the corner instead.

The baker let them in and didn't ask any questions, but then, he never did. He even handed Tomas some warm rolls to take with them as they made their way upstairs to the safe room. Tomas closed the door behind them.

"What happened?" he asked at last. "In the Aviary."

Ro pulled a little hourglass from the pouch at her belt. Delicate, beautiful workmanship, with a carved frame of pale wood, with brass details and a fall of glittering sand that never ceased. When she was certain he was looking at it, she turned it around and the sand didn't change direction. "This happened."

His mind gave a twitch of disbelief. But he couldn't deny what his eyes saw. It was beautiful but at the same time ... it sent a shudder of alarm through him. "Where did you get that?"

Ro told him everything. How she'd tested the machine and almost died, how the Golden Auric had saved her and brought her to the High Eyrie. How she found the chamber, and in the chamber she found the hourglass. How the shimmerwisps had attacked her. And how she had escaped.

He sat there, breathless, listening to her, pushing down the fear of what might have been. He could have lost her.

The idea of Ro no longer being in his life was almost too much.

"Saran wanted it," Ameris said. "And then the shimmerwisps appeared in the Aviary."

Ro gave another growl of frustration and Ameris shrank back a little, clutching the roll in her hands. He'd never seen the two of them like this.

"Explain," he said carefully.

"Why don't *you* explain, Tomas?" Ro snapped. "Who were those men? How do you know them? What were you even doing in the Mire of all places? Are you the Piper?"

His throat closed up and he stared at her, helpless. "It's … it's a long story. We don't have time."

"We're just sitting here. You want answers and so do I."

"I didn't … I wasn't always a Labourer, Ro."

Something in her glare faltered. "You were Guildless?"

"I was an orphan. I grew up there. Which has nothing to do with what happened in the Aviary."

She glared at him, vibrating belligerence which was much more like her. But she answered him at last, ignoring his revelation, which was a relief.

"I think the shimmerwisps followed me there, or the hourglass …" She trailed off, but he knew there was more. She didn't want to elaborate on it. He frowned. Ro normally told him everything.

"Can I see it?" he asked.

Ro swallowed hard. He watched her throat move, and for a moment wondered if she would refuse and what that could mean. But slowly, she pulled the artifact back out of the pouch and held it out to him. He waited, studying her face before reaching for it. She gave away nothing further.

The glass and metal were very cold against his skin, but the wood felt warm. It wasn't large. It wasn't heavy either. The wood was extraordinarily light and the brass fittings quite slim. The glass was too. It barely felt real and so very fragile.

An awful lot of fuss over so tiny a thing.

"What do you know about magic, Tomas?" Ameris asked, her voice very quiet. At least she was speaking.

"Magic?" He frowned at the hourglass. Was it some kind of trick question? "Nothing much. No more than anyone else. Why?"

"Because I think that is what this is all about. I was hoping Saran would explain it, but he … he didn't believe us … and then the shimmerwisps came …"

He didn't like to say what he thought of Ro's brother Saran, who had never been his favourite person in the world. Too full of himself and filled with a sense of undeserved self-importance. Though only four turnings younger, he and Matias had never seen eye to eye either. Matias had feared Saran was too concerned with being a Birdsinger to look after Ro properly so he asked Tomas to watch over her instead.

And what a fantastic job he was doing of that.

He thought of her standing there, trying to protect Ameris, with a bastard like Price bearing down on her. He felt sick. Bringing her to him was a message. Price knew his weakness now and when the time came he wouldn't hesitate to use it. And that risked the Unity movement itself.

"Maybe they came to take back the hourglass?" Ro said.

"Perhaps," Ameris said. "It's powerful, full of magic. I wonder if it's affecting you as well. In Saran's room you—"

"Then what do we do with it?" Ro cut in sharply, clearly trying to stop Ameris from saying something important. "The only people who know about magic are the Birdsingers and after what happened in the Aviary today … Saran's going to be furious with me."

"It's magic," Ameris replied carefully. "And we don't know how that works. I don't think you called the creatures. They just appeared when you—" Again, Ro glared at her and Ameris winced and her tone became almost apologetic. "But we're going to have to find out how they appeared somehow and what is drawing them to you."

The room was very quiet. Tomas could hear their breath and all those other unspoken questions. About him, about the Mire, about the Piper, about Unity itself. Neither Ameris—who could normally work out any problem in moments—or Ro—who usually had a smart answer for everything—knew what to do.

But he did.

"There's someone who can help. But you're going to have to trust me. And I need to take the hourglass."

"I'll come with you," Ro said instantly.

He shook his head. He couldn't let her see any more of what his life could be. He couldn't pull her any further into his world. No more than he could safely reveal any secrets relating to the Unity movement. Not even to her. It was bad enough she knew he was the Piper.

"No. I'll see you two back home, after dark."

But Ro wasn't to be put off. "You have to be careful with the hourglass. I think it's dangerous."

Dangerous? It didn't look dangerous. It looked beautiful but harmless.

But then, Tomas knew he had all the affinity for magic of a large rock.

Ro, on the other hand …

She should have been a Birdsinger like Saran. She'd chosen differently, but that didn't change what was inside her. Matias had told him everything. Saran's affinity with birds as a child had been a pale shadow beside Ro's.

Was that what had happened? Something to do with magic? Was that what she was stopping Ameris from saying?

"I'll be careful," he promised and gave her the most reassuring smile he had in his arsenal.

She may have been embarrassed enough not to ask any more about the Mire and his past, but that didn't mean she had forgotten. And she was smart enough to know that, at best, he was lying by omission.

¤

The niggling feeling in the back of his mind was not unfamiliar. Tomas struggled to ignore it. Once fully dark, he and Ro walked Ameris back to the Ateliers' Guild, and then turned north, towards Mount Nest. The mood in Arcadiana was wary, and the rumours flying around about what happened today at the Aviary were making him twitchy. Ro noticed it too. She had fallen quiet as she walked at his side.

He listened carefully, and the various sources he knew were reliable had nothing specific, nothing which would identify either of them. The Birdsingers had shut everything down immediately. But people still talked. And Tomas had always made a point of paying attention. It was his talent.

There had been an attack on the Aviary, specifically on a number of the more powerful Birdsingers. Two dead, many more injured. It hadn't taken long before they started to blame the Unity movement. They were always a useful excuse.

He'd promised Matias that he would look after Ro and he had, as best as he could. He kept so much of his life to himself that it was second nature now. But that didn't mean he didn't want to tell her. He wanted to tell her everything. He just didn't know how and it was not safe to do so.

Now she'd caught a glimpse of it. And she wasn't stupid.

"What's that?" he asked, pointing to the starlit sky, where a balloon loomed high above them and flickers of movement cut through the dark.

"A night-flight," she murmured, and a frown creased her brow. "I didn't know one was scheduled. Commander Mistral is working everyone twice as hard these days."

A night-flight was one of the more dangerous exercises of the Windriders. Figures high in the sky above them wheeled and rolled through the darkness. They were just shapes against the night, like bats moving through the air, the flying jackets spread wide. Only a single balloon watched over them, still tethered to the mountain, its burner a bright flame in the night. Disasters didn't just happen during the day and an incident at night could be devastating. They were drilling more frequently every passing day, as if they knew something was coming, as if they too felt the inevitable approach of the Collapse.

If only they would do more than drill. Like help people.

He sometimes wondered what else the Windriders flying through the darkness saw from up there, who they watched, how much they saw of the city beneath them. The Windriders in flight made almost no sound. He watched two alight on the roof of a building below the gates, silent and stealthy before dropping down to the ground and walking away together. They could spy on the darkest places of the city. They could arrive in silence and melt into the night. No one would ever know.

At the gate of the Windriders' Guildhouse Ro stopped and turned to him. It happened so quickly he was standing too close to her and her hands came up against his chest. She stood there, in the circle of his arms and stared into his face.

"Just don't do anything stupid."

He forced a grin onto his face. "Don't I usually have to say that to you?"

She didn't return the smile. Her gaze was intense. Like she knew what he thought. Like she knew he was lying to her. Like she finally understood the perilous path he walked. He'd thought she would be disgusted, but this was something else.

"I mean it, Tomas. If something happened to you …"

He tried to laugh in that easy, carefree way. Even he was aware that it wasn't convincing. "Nothing is going to happen to me, Ro."

"I don't know why you're involved with the … those men … with any of it … but I know, after Matias … just be careful." She shook her head, as if unwilling to leave him yet, which made a small flame of hope leap up inside him. Then she rose up on her toes to kiss his cheek, before leaving him standing there, astounded.

The door closed before he could find the words to reply, before he could make his brain lurch back into gear. It was just a kiss. The simplest of things.

He made his way back towards the city with the skin of his cheek still tingling.

The Weavers' Guild doors were firmly closed by the time he reached them, of course. The great water wheel had slowed to a crawl, but never entirely stopped. When he was young, when he had first arrived here, he'd been convinced that if the wheel ever did cease to turn the world would end. Probably some tall tale of Parsa's. Here he was, with the world crumbling around him, and the wheel still turned, creaking and groaning as the soft whisper of water drove it on.

He knocked on the door. No one answered so he made his way around the side to the place where the dye vats were kept, and where the swathes of recently coloured fabrics hung on lines to dry under canvas canopies. Everything rippled in the ocean breeze.

Like the Labourers' Guild, there were no walls and gates here, no guards. It wasn't in the nature of the Weavers. The light from the windows beyond was warm and he could hear music. Flutes and a harp by the sound of it, harmonising with the water wheel and the rush of the stream. The Weavers, entertaining themselves, practicing their art.

He slipped around the side of the shed and leaned against the wall, studying the sky and the roofs nearby for anything untoward, before reaching up to tap gently against the window. Three times, a pause, three times again, another pause, then two.

It took a moment. Something shuffled around in there.

Two taps came back from inside. *Wait.*

It didn't take that long. Tomas stood against the wall, gazing up at the sky. It was a clear night and the moon was bright. A scattering of stars spread out overhead. There were no signs of the Windriders' night-flight now.

Just a drill, an exercise, he reassured himself. Nothing to worry about. They weren't watching him. They couldn't know where he was or what he carried.

The hourglass, wrapped up in the pouch on his belt, felt unbearably heavy. A secret. A treasure.

Tomas didn't know if the hourglass was dangerous in itself, but if it acted like a magnet for monsters made of mist and light, he knew it needed to be investigated. And there was only one person he would trust with that.

Nazir finally came out. "What is it? What's wrong?"

"I need to see Parsa."

"At this hour? He's already in bed. You know what he's like. If he doesn't get enough sleep he'll be a bag of cats in the morning."

"All the same. It's important, Nazir. I wouldn't ask otherwise."

Nazir sighed, and didn't argue anymore because he knew that at least was true. "Don't make too much noise. The children are asleep."

Tomas followed Nazir inside through the empty boot room. Beyond it, the stores and the workshops were still and quiet. They passed the dormitories, and Tomas saw the sleeping forms of those who had found shelter here, much as he had once upon a time. The Weavers had taken him in, a Guildless boy from the Mire, who could easily have turned out just like Price and his gang. Parsa and Nazir had found him trying to pick pockets and failing. They'd brought him home, fed him and taught him better. They would have sponsored him in any Guild, but Parsa always said *follow your heart.* And he had.

It should have led him straight to Ro, but he couldn't live a lie.

The network extended to every Guild, because of the children they helped, the friends they made. Tomas was almost as good at making friends as the older Weaver. But Parsa had a plan. He made connections. He encouraged cooperation. And relationships. *With everyone we help,* Parsa often said, *we light a candle. And candles stand for hope.*

They called it Unity, a movement of cooperation which reached out between the Guilds in every way. It wasn't all kindness and collaboration. It couldn't be. Not with the way Arcadiana worked. The Mire alone was a tangle of rats turning on each other and any who stretched out a hand to help them. The Unity movement had teeth and sometimes they had to be used.

It was dangerous work; he had always known that. The upper hierarchy of Guilds had outlawed the movement long before Tomas had become involved. Windriders regularly raided the poorer areas of the city, and took in anyone suspected of involvement for brutal questioning. Even one of their own like Matias. People had died, their secrets still held close. Few people knew as much as Tomas, and only the council of Unity, those secret leaders hidden in Arcadiana, knew everything. Information was kept in closely guarded cells, like the one in the Mire, with a keeper like Creed, willing to die to protect it.

Matias had sought out Nazir when Tomas was just a boy and had quickly become a vital part of the movement. Few Windriders were tempted by Unity, their loyalty to their Guild beyond question. But Matias had seen something greater, something more important. He'd seen a way to protect his sister and the future that seemed to be bearing down on them all as their islands slowly disintegrated. By twenty-four turnings he was running the network Tomas now maintained, all the while mentoring Tomas himself.

Matias would have sponsored Tomas to become a Windrider, when the time came at his eighteenth turning day, which as far as everyone else was concerned would be a great honour, but Tomas refused. He'd hated everything the Windriders stood for, the boots kicking in the doors, the enforcers dragging away his people for questioning. Perhaps he'd been naïve. Matias said nothing would change unless they changed it from within. Tomas had called Matias gullible.

If, in the intervening turnings, Ro had become a Birdsinger, Tomas would not have had a single doubt that Parsa would have pushed him harder into her sphere, into marriage and children and a life together. A life Tomas had so desperately wanted. It might have even worked. Although how he would have fitted into that life, a Labourer living among the Birdsingers, only accepted by marriage ... no, he would have ruined her chances among them. Or she would have rejected him outright. It was bad enough as it was. He was a weight about her, he knew that. But she didn't seem to care.

And still, a treacherous voice whispered that it could have been. That they would have found a way to make it work. That he and Ro could be together somehow.

But he could never shake the fear that it would all be a lie. That he would be with her because Parsa and the other members of Unity wanted it. That they had somehow tricked her into marrying a worthless boy from the Mire.

He couldn't betray her.

Like he was about to betray her now.

Parsa appeared at the door of his chambers, hair dishevelled, eyes bleary. He wore loose pyjama trousers and a multicoloured dressing gown. "What is it, Tomas? Whatever is wrong?"

"This," he said, holding out the hourglass. "Parsa, I need you to tell me what it is. And if it's dangerous."

CHAPTER 11

They arrived at Ro's sparse quarters far too early in the morning. Instead of birdsong, she woke to the sound of boots in the corridor outside. The door burst open before she could even open her eyes. Hauled to her feet, she stood there, swaying as someone shouted at her to stand to attention, to answer their questions.

Hale. It had to be Hale. She'd know his nasty bullying voice anywhere.

"You've really done it this time, Swift," he said on a breath, delighting in his power over her. "They're going to have your guts. If you're lucky."

When had she ever been lucky? she wanted to reply but this was not the time. Every surviving instinct told her that, even in her sleep deprived state.

"Where is it? Where did you hide it?"

She blinked. The hourglass, he was after the hourglass. But who had sent him? Ro chewed on her lower lip and fixed her eyes on the wall of the corridor outside.

There were far too many Windguards in her room, bustling around, filling the narrow space with threat.

"Search everywhere," Hale ordered. "You, outside." That was directed at her. When Ro didn't instantly move, he grabbed her arm and pulled her after him. Behind her, she could hear her room being upended, her belongings pulled out and everything turned upside down.

"Enough, Hale," came a cool voice from the corridor outside. There were people everywhere, peering out of their own doorways, gathering together at the end of the corridor by the washrooms. Hale stood to attention so quickly Ro could have sworn he vibrated. "Swift, come with me please."

Please ... That must have been a joke. She had absolutely no choice in the matter, and no way out of this. Not when the head of your entire Guild told you to do something. She may have said please, but it was not a request. Ro knew that.

Commander Mistral did not make requests.

Ro followed her out of the dormitories, through the refectory and down to her office, knowing from long and bitter experience that this particular walk of shame never ended well.

Mistral's office was as stark and neat as the woman herself. Ro had never seen her out of uniform, with her hair scraped back from her face, her collar perfectly starched. No wonder Grayden was always first in his class. He wouldn't want to disappoint her.

Perhaps it explained more about him than Ro cared to understand.

Still in her nightclothes, her hair loose and unbrushed, Ro stood in the middle of the room while Mistral took her seat, and then leaned forwards, elbows on her desk, chin on her hands. The commander clearly didn't like what she saw.

But when she spoke, her words were unexpected. "What am I going to do with you, Swift?"

Ro found her voice somewhere. "Do with me, ma'am?"

"The Birdsingers have informed me that you have a valuable artifact in your possession, one which you did not declare and did not relinquish when you were instructed to do so. Something which is not yours."

So, Saran had spilled everything. She should have expected it, of course. He needed to explain what had happened to his superiors as much as she did. And he had got his side of things in there first. At least she didn't have to lie.

"I don't have it," she said.

The commander raked her hand through her short steel grey hair and sighed. "Where is it?"

Ro kept her eyes focused on the wall behind her head. "I don't know." That wasn't a lie either. Not exactly. She knew who she had given it to, but she didn't know where Tomas was right now. How could she?

"This isn't good enough, Windrider Swift. You know that. There will be consequences."

"With respect, ma'am, they're already tearing my belongings apart back there."

The commander didn't exactly roll her eyes. She'd never do anything as petty as that. But Ro was certain that she wanted to.

"*Worse* consequences. Do you have any idea of the trouble you're in right now?"

Same as she was usually in, she supposed. There was no politic answer to that question so she fell back on ages of tradition. "Yes, ma'am."

"I don't believe you do. The Birdsingers are not happy. There was an attack in the heart of the Aviary when you were there. Two of them are dead. They can demand I expel you from the Guild. What do you think would happen to you then?"

Another Guild might take her in. Unlikely though, if the Birdsingers had demanded her expulsion. There wasn't really a way to live in the city without a Guild. She thought of those men in the Mire. And Tomas, who clearly knew them. Was he really the Piper? Matias had mentioned the name once or twice. More as a joke than anything else. But everyone knew that the Piper was high up in the Unity movement and had been for many turnings. He'd been the one Matias had been protecting. How could that be Tomas? He'd only been eighteen turnings when her brother was arrested.

Had the Piper been Matias? Before him? Was that what her brother had been hiding and was that why he had been forced into exile? There had always been rumours in the Guild, whispers as she passed. Was that why Mistral and her people hated her so?

She shied away from that thought as quickly as she could. She didn't want it to be true. She didn't want to inadvertently say anything that might convict her brother or incriminate her friend. And anyway, it had nothing to do with this. This was personal. It had to be.

She couldn't live the life of the Guildless. Which left exile. Trying to buy passage on a ship which would take her the ancestors alone knew where. If whatever ship she found didn't throw her over the side once they were out of sight of land. There were rumours of more preparing to leave every day. Maybe she could find Matias.

What was he now? Thirty-three turnings? He'd have made a life for himself somewhere, surely.

She didn't have enough coins anyway. Which left trying to stay on the islands and eke out some kind of miserable existence in the shadows between the Guilds. There were people who did that.

They just didn't survive very long. Or they fell in with the lawless of the Mire. Or the Unity movement …

It all came back to that. Every thought. And with that, Tomas. She couldn't afford to say it out loud.

"Not so amusing now, is it?" Commander Mistral said in weighted tones.

If only she knew. But then again, better not. "No, ma'am."

"I don't know what your parents would have said. They struggled enough to get over Matias' defection but even that shame doesn't come close to this. People are dead. The Heart of Arcadiana defiled by shimmerwisps. Where is the hourglass?"

Ro tightened her lips and felt the tears she could not shed sting her eyes. Shame and rage burned through her and choked any possible words in her tight throat. She didn't want this to be her fault. She hadn't meant to summon shimmerwisps into the Aviary or put the Heart of Arcadiana at risk. But the hourglass had to be protected. She didn't know why. It just did. She drew in a breath that sounded more like a sob and struggled to keep her voice as even as she could. "I haven't got it."

And she was not going to hand it over, even if she did get it back. Perhaps she was being unreasonable, but every instinct told her that she herself had to do something with all this. Not Saran, not the other Birdsingers. Her. The bird had chosen her.

"Swift, this is your last warning."

"I can't," she blurted out. "I was brought there for a reason. The Golden Auric saved me and brought me there to find it."

"Brought where?"

It all came out in a mad tangle of words. She couldn't help it.

"To the High Eyrie. To the cave at the foot of the tree. You have to believe me. There were things in there, things attracted by magic, shimmerwisps, and I barely got away. But the Auric wanted me to have that hourglass. I don't know why or how or what it wants me to do, but I can't give it up."

Commander Mistral's eyes had taken on that flat, disbelieving gaze which Ro dreaded seeing. "A Golden Auric? Children's stories."

"Well, how else do you think I got it?"

The commander leaned on the table and pushed herself up to standing. "The Birdsingers tell me you stole it. Your own brother told us." She paused, pointedly. "Saran, I mean. He might have left us for another Guild, but he isn't a traitor. He is worried about you. He says you have fallen in with the same dangerous crowd as Matias did. You took the hourglass from the Aviary for them. I find that eminently more believable than fairy tales." She stood up, her chair scraping across the floor. "Let me make myself clear, Swift. Get that thing back from wherever you hid it. Bring it to me, by tomorrow morning. Or you will leave this Guild forever."

¤

Hale and his team had really done a number on Ro's room. Her belongings were strewn everywhere, the drawers and wardrobe emptied, her sketches crumpled on the floor with her clothes and any trinkets and memories of her parents tossed carelessly. She stood in the doorway, shaking from head to foot, though whether from anger or grief, she couldn't tell.

This was all she had left. The Guild. This mess. Everything in her world. And now they were threatening to take that away. They thought she was part of the Unity movement. What she saw in front of her was a message and it was loud and clear. If she didn't do what they wanted, this was the end of her life here. The Birdsingers would see to that and so would Commander Mistral. She would relish the chance to get rid of her.

She couldn't believe Saran had turned her in. Her own brother. How could he?

Worried about her, Mistral had said. Maybe. But still …

Slowly, carefully, she knelt down and tried to gather the pieces of her shattered life together.

The soft fluttering of tiny wings made her look up. The wren had perched on her windowsill, watching her with a curious gaze, its little head tilted to one side.

"I don't know what you're looking at," she told it. "This is all your fault."

"How is this my fault?" Grayden said from behind her, his voice wounded. "I wasn't even here." She spun around on her knees to find him in the doorway, his falcon, Pel, perched on his shoulder, talons digging into the heavy material of his uniform jacket. Its sharp eyes were fixed on the wren, but it didn't move.

Ro swallowed hard on the lump in her throat. No matter what she didn't want to let Grayden see how upset she was. Her pride wouldn't stand it.

"Go away."

"What happened?"

"Your mother and your mate Hale happened. They wanted something I don't have. And now I'm being told I'm going to be kicked out if I don't deliver. Happy now?"

He didn't look happy. If anything he looked embarrassed.

"He's no mate of mine."

That was news to her. It probably would be to Hale too. She noticed Grayden didn't attempt to deny his mother, but that would have just made her laugh in his perfect face so it made sense. Grayden knew her as well as she knew him.

She turned back to her devastated room and began to grab armfuls of her clothes and bundle them back into the drawers in no particular order, just to get them out of the way. Out of sight. The wren was still on the window ledge, eyes locked on Pel.

"Go on," Ro said. "Shoo."

"Is that to me or the birds?" Grayden asked.

"All three of you."

Grayden gave a long suffering sigh and Pel took off from his shoulder, flying so low over Ro's bent head she could feel the air move. He landed on the windowsill, but the wren didn't budge. It didn't even seem worried. Now both birds were watching her and she didn't like it one bit. It also meant Grayden hadn't gone anywhere. He started to pick up her sketches and flatten them out again, carefully smoothing the creases.

"These are beautiful."

It was all she could do not to snatch them out of his hands. She just grunted in reply and picked up the necklace and bracelets her mother had left her.

"Is this Amare?" he asked.

"Yes, of course it is. What do you want, Grayden?"

"Just to help."

"I don't need your help."

He cleared his throat, looking around the room. In spite of the amount she had already cleared, it still looked like a whirlwind had swept through it. "I beg to differ."

“Did your mother send you?” That would be just like her. Send Grayden in when Ro was at her lowest and get him to find out where the hourglass was.

What was she going to do? She couldn’t just hand it over. But she wasn’t sure what else she *could* do. She didn’t want to lose what little she had left.

“No. In fact, she told me to keep a wide berth.”

“Such a shame you don’t listen. But you never did.”

That was the moment she found the little clay bird she’d made when she was five and painted as a gift for her father. The exposed clay was a deep orange, crumbling in places. The exterior had been blue once, but now it looked more grey. The paint had been chipped and the colours faded. But that hadn’t mattered, neither to her father nor to her. Her voice died in her throat. He’d loved it, made sure it had pride of place in their house. He’d pointed it out to everyone who visited. That was so long ago. Before Saran left. Before Matias fled. When their family was whole. Now, just like her life, it was broken into pieces.

The sob ripped its way out of her throat, completely unexpected, raw and violent.

Grayden didn’t react. He didn’t try to hug her or hold her close for comfort. She wasn’t sure what she would do if he did, but it wouldn’t be pretty. He just carried on, clearing up her belongings, as if he wasn’t the son of the commander at all, as if he was just a friend.

Ro sank onto the edge of her upturned mattress, cradling the broken bird in her cupped palms. Only the slightest sound alerted her to the wren flying to her. She watched as it alighted on her fingers beside the lumps of clay.

“I didn’t know you had a bird,” he said at last, sitting down beside her.

"I don't." Didn't she? The wren seemed to think otherwise. "Or at least I didn't until the other day. It just turned up. And it doesn't seem to want to go away."

Grayden smiled gently. "Yes, it can feel like that. I'm sorry, Ro."

"About the wren?"

He shrugged. "About all of this. Do you want to tell me what actually happened?"

What actually happened? She gave a deep sigh. "Hale took the opportunity to deal out a bit of his usual bullying. It doesn't matter."

"But it does. I'll talk to him. It won't happen again."

"Grayden, that won't help. It's only going to make it worse. I don't know why he hates me."

"He's jealous."

"Yeah, right. Of all this. He has your mother's ear anyway and—"

"She would never condone this."

Ro laughed, a brief and bitter sound. "I love that you believe that. And you should. She's your mother. But she's my commander. And she really doesn't like me."

He looked almost distraught. "I'll talk to her too."

"You can try. I doubt it will make much of a difference though."

"She's stepping down, you know. Any day now."

That surprised her. Ro's heart gave a little wriggle of hope. She looked up at his face, but he wasn't paying any attention to her. He stood with his back turned, staring fixedly out of the window.

"When?"

He shrugged. "At the start of the Carnival of the Birds."

Not long then, but not soon enough either. Besides—

"So you'll be Commander at last. Good for you."

Except it wasn't. Not really. He lived in his mother's shadow. He always would. He might have wanted to be his own man, but he'd need to defy her if that was ever going to happen. There was no point in saying it again. It had caused the fight so long ago and nothing had changed.

"You know it shouldn't be hereditary, don't you?" he muttered. "The commander should be the best of us. Not—"

She didn't know where the words came from. Just that they were true. "It would still be you, Grayden. We all know that. Even me."

He shook his head ruefully, unwilling to pursue it further. "What is this hourglass everyone is so interested in?"

Here it comes, she thought. He'd get the information his mother wanted with kindness instead of threats, that was what he thought. Suddenly she regretted what she'd just said about him.

She retold the events again, even though he wouldn't believe her anyway. They thought she had stolen it from the Aviary. The commander hadn't believed a word of her story. Why would her son and heir be any different?

Grayden just turned and stared at her, perplexed, his perfect brow wrinkling as he frowned. Eventually he came to sit at the other end of her bed.

"A Golden Auric?" he asked eventually.

"Yes. And there were stones in the cave, each one marked with the symbol of a different Guild. And these things … shimmerwisps, like the old stories. They were made of mist and light and they were coming after the hourglass. Or me. I don't know which. Both maybe. One of them touched me and … It hurt, Grayden. I mean, it really hurt. So I had to get out of there. The balloon with the Birdsinger was gathering magic from the clouds and I barely made it down to them." She stopped speaking and tried to wipe her face, hoping he wouldn't see. He studiously ignored the motion and waited for her to continue. "When we went to show the hourglass to Saran, the shimmerwisps turned up again. That's what happened. Everyone says it was an attack by the Unity movement, but it wasn't. They lied about that too. Saran lied about the hourglass. I didn't steal it."

Grayden rolled his eyes. "If Saran thought this hourglass of yours was important enough to lie about, it must be special."

Ro frowned at him. "What do I do? Give it to him?"

"Ancestors, no." He got to his feet and Pel gave a low cry of agreement. "That's the last thing to do. Our illustrious Birdsingers are altogether too demanding. Half of Arcadiana might think your brother a wonder, but he leads a faction within that Guild that thinks itself far above the rest of us. They believe they can take whatever they want."

Ro stared at him in shock. She'd never heard him criticise the Birdsingers. No one did. It was a short step from that to being accused of treason, of being part of Unity, to being cast out. Grayden met her gaze. "Where is it? Did you give it to Tomas?"

His mouth twisted as he said Tomas' name. Her stomach sank. She'd been wrong. He was there for information and he'd already guessed. But then to her surprise, Grayden just shook his head again before she could tell him to go to hell.

"No, don't tell me that. If he has it … well, we can only hope for the best. Do you honestly think it's safe?"

She nodded. That at least she was certain of. Tomas would keep it safe for her. He'd keep it hidden and so far no one else had mentioned his name. She could trust Tomas.

At least, she thought she could. Her memory threw up the image of his face in that room in the Mire, shadows slanting across his familiar features making him a stranger. And a flicker of doubt made her stomach turn. *If he has it …* Grayden had just said. He hadn't sounded like that was a good thing. What did he know about Tomas?

Come to that, what did he know of the Unity movement? He was privy to all the intelligence the Windriders gathered. He was in charge of the search for members of the movement. With their capture and punishment. And he was good at everything he did.

Windguards were constantly trying to track down the leaders of Unity. Grayden was in charge of all the Windguards. Soon he'd be in charge of all the Windriders, and with that all aspects of security in Arcadiana and the surrounding islands.

If he knew that Tomas was the Piper … If she let that slip …

She may not be sure if her suspicions were actually correct—she had to ignore the nagging voice which knew, just *knew*—but she could always trust Tomas. Every fibre of her being told her that. She had to protect him in return. This new side of Grayden might be trustworthy when it came to her, but otherwise? No. She had to be careful.

"So what do I do?"

Why she was asking Grayden, she didn't know. Maybe it was just a way to change the subject and she needed someone to talk to. She may not have liked him enough to marry him, but she knew his honour was everything. And she couldn't think of anyone else.

Grayden shook his head. "I'll see what I can find out, if you want. But the easiest thing would be to get the hourglass back and hand it over, wouldn't it?" He wasn't wrong. It would be so much easier. Grayden smiled at her, that same charming smile that won everyone over. It said he knew her better than anyone else, which was not true. All the same, her thoughts had to be written all over her face. For a moment she thought he could just look inside her head and see everything. He had that way about him. He always had. "You've never picked the easy way, have you?"

He turned to go.

"Grayden?" she asked suddenly. "Why are you helping me?"

He gave a brief, dismissive laugh. "You were always so suspicious, Ro. Besides, someone has to."

"But you hate me."

A flicker of something she couldn't quite read travelled over his face. Regret, perhaps. Or betrayal. "No, I don't. I never did. But you were right. We would have been a disaster together. And I appreciate your candour. Maybe I didn't back then. But I do now." He shrugged and gestured to the room, which was almost back to normal, but still ragged around the edges, her belongings still skewed and stuffed back into the wrong places. "That was the past. And even if I did regret it, it doesn't mean I want this for you. I'll talk to Hale. It won't happen again."

He nodded to himself, a decision of some kind made. But at the doorway he stopped again, hand on the frame. He hesitated as if trying to will himself to leave. Or to stay and say something else. The latter instinct won.

"Be careful of Tomas Harper, Ro. His *friendship* ruined Matias' life. I wouldn't want that to happen to you too."

CHAPTER 12

"Just hold it still," Ameris grumbled as Ro's hand moved the wrong way *again,* and the piece of iridescent metal she was trying to secure slipped.

"I'm sorry. I'm trying."

"We're never going to get this new version built if you can't focus."

Ancestors, Ameris was tetchy when she was working. To be fair, the new prototype of the Wing was mostly finished. Somehow it seemed lighter than ever. Ro wasn't sure what changes Ameris had made to the design—it was bigger, sleeker—but she could sense the improvements, and she itched to slide herself into the flying machine again. It might even carry two people if you could secure them correctly. Would Ameris take that leap with her? Would Tomas? No, someone smaller, slighter, especially for a test flight.

Strange, she thought, *I ought to be afraid, given what had happened the last time.* There ought to be lingering doubts and uncertainty. But all she could think of was the way it had felt to fly like one of the birds, the sheer freedom and exhilaration she had experienced. She wanted that again. She wanted it more than ever.

She needed it.

Flying would mean not thinking about what had happened this morning, about the search of her room and the threats the commander had thrown at her. Or about Grayden's bizarre behaviour. She still couldn't figure that out.

A hand of friendship? But why? What would he gain from that, especially now?

And as for her gnawing doubts about Tomas ... Why did Grayden, of all people, feel the need to warn her about him? Apart from the obvious.

"Ro! Focus!" Ameris snapped at her.

Tetchy.

She wound a slender length of wire around something Ro couldn't quite see and the featherlike panel slid into place. It vibrated for a moment, the metal gleaming. The light in it rippled and the Wing seemed to rise, just a little, just for a moment.

"There," Ameris said, happy at last. "Right. Take a break. I'll need to get more wire and then we can do the other side. I thought I had made more of it. Someone has been making off with my alloy, I swear."

Ameris never swore. She had the vocabulary of a saint.

Ro, on the other hand, did not. She muttered a curse under her breath as Ameris left the workshop. She'd thought they were finished. And now there was a whole other side.

She hadn't been able to find Tomas. There didn't seem to be a trace of him anywhere. That wouldn't normally have worried her.

When she added the hourglass and the Piper and everything else to the equation, a chill passed through her. She had gone to Ameris in case she had seen him and was quickly roped in to repairing the Wing. It wasn't as if she had much else to do and it meant she wasn't at the Windriders' Guildhouse.

She wasn't hiding. Not exactly.

But if she was hiding this would be the one place he would know to find her.

He just hadn't turned up yet and she was getting nervous. What if something had happened to him? What if the Birdsingers had figured out he had the hourglass and had arrested him? Or Tomas had gone back into the Mire? What if he was lying in an alley with a knife in his guts?

That happened to people there all the time. Even to people who knew their way around. Even to people who came from there, who thought they belonged.

But Tomas didn't belong there. Not the Tomas she knew.

It was his friendship that ruined Matias' life …

Ameris was halfway to the door when the ground beneath their feet rumbled, the tremor shaking through them both. Their eyes locked and they froze, waiting for something worse, for the walls to fall or the ceiling to crack. It was only a moment and then it subsided. Everything went still and quiet again.

Heart racing, Ro steadied the Wing and then let out her breath. "That was strong."

Ameris nodded, her face pale. "I'll be back in a moment. I need to check there's no damage elsewhere and no one was hurt. Stay here. Mind my Wing."

There wasn't much Ro could say to argue with her. Ameris was gone before she'd even thought of saying something.

Alone in the workshop, Ro went to the window and pulled back the blind, allowing the evening light to pour in from the courtyard outside. It bounced off the metal of the Wing, making it gleam, become alive with light. It really was beautiful, a work of art as well as engineering. Ameris should be so proud of it.

It had an ethereal quality, as if it might take off and fly all by itself. Once again, she itched to put it on.

"There you are," said a voice behind her. "Ancestors, you're so difficult to track down."

Ro turned on one foot, surprise making her movements sharp and unstable. "Saran!"

He filled the doorway, his robe fluttering around him. "I wondered where you were hiding."

She backed away, looking for an escape but there wasn't one. Unless she could dive through the window and run. Had he come to turn her in? To demand the hourglass again?

Saran stopped and held up his hands. "Ro, I come in peace. Please, just listen to me. I'm sorry. Things got … out of hand yesterday. Let's talk. Just you and me."

"I don't have it," she warned him.

If it was disappointment in his eyes he masked it well. "Fine. But we still need to talk. About the hourglass, yes, but more importantly about what happened yesterday. About the shimmerwisps. And what happened to you. *Please.* You're my sister and I'm worried." He spread his hands wide in a gesture of peace. "Just talk. Come with me to the gardens. It's quieter there."

It wasn't as if Ro had much of a choice. Saran had cornered her. She followed him cautiously outside, waiting for guards to seize her. But he was alone.

Maybe he did mean to help her. Maybe ... She wanted to trust him. He was her brother, her blood, her family. All she had left.

The gardens of the Ateliers' Guild were not as ornate as those of the Birdsingers, nor as large as those of the Windriders which wound their way up the side of the mountain between the docking jetties. In between the workshops and the forges, there were pockets of green, dense with vegetables and herbs, planted for practicality rather than aesthetics. And yet, there was beauty here as well. Lush and green, cared for and nurtured so astutely by the Ateliers. While their forte was engineering and invention, they appreciated beauty as well.

With the sun setting in the distance, the knot garden beneath the northern wall of the Guildhouse was stunning, brushed with the soft red-gold light, creating long shadows that striped the gravel paths. Above the wall, the trees of a public park on the upper level draped long willow branches down like hair.

Their feet crunched as they walked, the only sound of human life out here. There was no one else outside and the Ateliers had long ago perfected a way of soundproofing their workrooms. But there were birds, of course, singing as they settled for the evening, great and small, those who had made their homes in the gardens as well as interlopers too.

Saran's magpies hopped around the central lawn, flashes of black and white, cackling away to themselves, and setting off the alarm calls of a dozen smaller birds in the bushes around the edges. Saran sat himself down on the low wall overlooking the harbour to the southwest. He had their father's nose and jawline, she realised with a jolt. She'd never noticed that before. Like her, he had their mother's eyes and colouring.

"First of all," he said, his rich voice flowing through the evening air, "I want to apologise." He didn't look at her when he said this. Perhaps he couldn't bring himself to make eye contact.

"You do?" She lingered at the edge of the lawn, nervous.

"Yes, of course. I should have been more patient. I didn't think. But a discovery of that importance, Ro …" He sighed, reining himself in again and this time he did look at her. His familiar gaze captured hers and held it, until she couldn't doubt his sincerity.

"You told them I stole it."

"I apologise. I thought … I was wrong, clearly, and I'll make that known. But I need to talk to you about what happened. With the shimmerwisps."

This was what she was afraid of. The hourglass was one thing. The shimmerwisps were something else entirely. She said nothing. She didn't know what to say even if she could force words out through her tight throat.

"Ro," Saran said in his smoothest voice. And for a moment it was almost as if they were children again. "It's just me. Don't be afraid. Just tell me what happened."

Easier said than done. But something in her relented, relieved to have his ear at last.

"They followed me, I think, from the High Eyrie."

"And the magic? Have you done that before?" When she shook her head, he pursed his lips in thought. "What about the bird? Did it follow you from the Eyrie too?"

"The wren just showed up. And then the Auric …" She hesitated and he saw it.

"You always called birds to you," he whispered.

"When I was little, Mother used to say we talked to the birds. Danced with them. She thought we would both be Birdsingers."

"I remember. Why didn't you? You clearly had the same calling as I did. With a strong ability for magic apparently. Why didn't you come?"

"Matias left. I couldn't …"

"Ah," he said slowly.

Holding out his hand to her, he waited and Ro had little choice but to move closer and take a seat beside him. She didn't take his hand though. She gripped the edge of the stonework, where there was a carving of a repeating pattern of birds in flight. She dug her nails into the indentations. Saran let his hand fall.

"I never apologised, did I? For leaving. When our parents died, I thought … I thought you'd surely come to me at the Aviary and join me. Has no one ever explained the nature of the Birdsingers' calling?"

She stared at him as if he'd asked her to explain a mathematical problem so far beyond her she'd look like an idiot if she even tried to solve it. He thought she'd just leave everything and go to join him? That she'd abandon everything that mattered to their parents like he did? Of course no one had explained the Birdsingers to her. Who was there to explain any of it? He had left.

"We all form emotional attachments with birds," he said and one of the magpies flew to his shoulder. It perched there, preening itself and casting her the occasional smug glance. She ignored it. "We share empathy with them and they act as our guardians and our guides. You've seen that with Ameris and her crow. But for Birdsingers it is something more. We share their souls, if only for a little time; we share their magic. When a bird flies high into the clouds they bathe in the magic of the High Eyre and bring it back to us."

Ro thought of the wren and almost laughed. "And if my bird is a wren? They don't fly high at all. They barely get off the ground."

Saran smiled, his face transforming back to that of the boy she had known, and shook his head. "No. It is the humblest of them all, that's true. But the wren is special in its own way. Some people call the wren the king of the birds, as unbelievable as that might sound. I can tell you the story if you want?" Bemused, Ro nodded, so he went on. "Once upon a time all the birds held a competition to see who would be king of the birds. Amare herself was to be the judge. She flew far overhead and hovered, watching, her glorious wings of many colours wide-spread. Up and up they flew—the eagle, the hawk, the albatross, all those great winged birds—striving higher and higher but one by one their wings failed them. Only the Golden Aurics were left, Amare's own children. And the strongest of them flew higher and higher until all others were gone. 'I am the king,' the victor cried out, but then the wren which had been perched on his golden crest leaped into the air, even higher, singing out her triumph. And Amare declared her the king of the birds. The Golden Auric was angry, said the wren cheated, but Amare just laughed and said that being clever wasn't cheating. She told her child to learn that lesson and never dismiss the wren."

When Ro was little Saran used to tell her stories. She would sit there, spellbound, as his beautiful voice wove fantasies and wonders. A warmth inside her bloomed, something she had almost forgotten existed.

"It's just a story though," Ro said. "The wren isn't at the top of the hierarchy of birds. She certainly isn't a king. She's just … she's just a bird."

"Of course. But the wren can be wise. And stories teach us things, don't they? What do you think it's trying to teach you?"

Ro didn't know. It was just a story like she said. But Saran was looking at her so expectantly that she had to try to find an answer.

"Sometimes the wren needs help?" she asked.

"Yes. And she's smart enough to find it. If she looks."

His meaning was clear enough. "Fine. So help me, big brother." She faltered then, the bravado slipping away. "I … I don't understand what is happening to me."

"I've read all there is to read on the old world. It is a special project of mine. And what I don't know I can find in the archives. Please, trust me. You used to."

He'd always been the cleverest of them. And he knew it. But for once she decided she wouldn't hold this fact against him. He was trying to help.

A special project, he said. "What kind of project?"

At that, his face fell. "Ah, well, you've noticed the rising waters, and the soaring isles beginning to crumble?" It was a rhetorical question, the kind he always had liked to ask. There was no way she could have missed any of those things. She nodded. "Long ago our ancestors lived up on the soaring isles before the Collapse. The magic in the air was rich and plentiful, but our enemies came across the ocean to steal it. They took too much and destroyed the delicate balance. There was a war and we drove the others out, cut off our lands from them and laid out the laws of access and exile, but by then it was too late. The islands were beginning to fall."

Ro had heard some of this before, but not all of it. She knew about the ancestors and the war with the other nations. Everyone knew that was why they lived in isolation, because it was just too dangerous, because what little magic was left was too precious. Saran went on, his eloquent voice enchanting her.

"From my research, I believe our ancestors tried to stop the process and created a spell to hold their world together. It only worked in part and they all died in the effort. Some islands sank altogether. Some came to rest in the ocean, and those are the ones we live on now, while others continued to rise, pulling away from the rest, like the Eyrie, the most powerful and magical of them all, perhaps the source of magic itself. And sadly out of our reach now. The Guilds were formed to represent each of those heroes who tried to save us, who at least slowed the Collapse long enough to give us a chance." She knew that. Everyone knew that. But Saran wasn't finished. "Our islands are sinking, the others breaking up as they pull away into the air. The spell was incomplete and while it bought us time, the Collapse continued to happen, our islands and the soaring isles pulling away from each other. It began with a spell and I believe that spell could save us. With enough magic, it could be reversed. But the air from which we gain that magic, like the Eyrie, is far beyond our reach now. Or at least it was. Until you went up there, took the hourglass and awoke something inside yourself."

She remembered the chamber, and the shimmerwisps. The little wisp of flame—the magic she'd conjured in Saran's chamber when she said the word *Adscendo.* But she had never been able to do anything like that before she went to the chamber in the Eyrie … Before the hourglass …

"One of the shimmerwisps up there touched me."

Saran recoiled in sudden alarm. "Truly? And you lived? Ro!" He sighed out her name in relief and horror. "You were so lucky. They killed and injured a number of my people yesterday before they could be driven off. But they don't gift magic. They drain it, steal it, for what purpose I do not know. But magical objects attract them as well. And of course, someone like you."

Is that what it had tried to do to her in the cave? It had hurt so badly, that awful tingling numbness. And once it had a taste of her …

"They followed me. I brought them to the Aviary, didn't I?"

Which meant the dead and the injured … she was responsible for that. The thought made her stomach twist into knots.

He shook his head and hugged her. Unexpectedly, after so long on her own, such a simple gesture from him meant so much. She buried her face in his shoulder and his voice rumbled through her as he patted her back. "You weren't to know. When you said the word to activate the spell, holding the hourglass … well … They appear from time to time when magic is worked. We have ways of dealing with them. It's not something we like to admit. People would panic. You know how they are in Arcadiana. Even my people panicked. They know of them, and are supposed to know how to shield themselves from them but when faced with one in real life … well … We're all fallible. There were more shimmerwisps than anyone had ever seen before and it all happened so fast."

So fast. She sighed. Yes, it had been fast. It had been horrifying. And it was all her fault. No matter what he said, they'd come after her because she took the hourglass. And they found the Birdsingers instead. People who used magic, who gathered it and stored it. It had been like releasing starving dogs at a feast.

"You talk of magic like it's a food or drink. Like it's life's blood."

"Perhaps it is. Magic is everything to us. To all living things really. We would not exist without it. And it is in everything around us, from the greatest to the least of us. Without it, there would be no life. We would be like ghosts, echoes of what we once were. Not to mention that our world as we know it, these islands, would tear themselves apart. Sometimes I think magic is all that holds everything together. With it, anything is possible. It can turn back time, rejuvenate the ill, repair injuries. That's how we heal others. But the effort is enormous, the cost very great."

"What does it have to do with me?" she asked.

At this he finally smiled again. Right now, it felt as if he was the only person who could possibly understand what she was going through. He was her brother again. Tears stung at the corners of her eyes and she looked away, blinking furiously to fight them back.

"It has everything to do with you, Ro. I believe the Golden Auric chose you to find the hourglass, to bring it to us. You were born to be a Birdsinger, one of the greatest of us all. I don't just say this as your brother. Even our family name—Swift—is a Birdsinger's name as well as a Windrider's. I don't think the wren is your guide, but rather it is drawn to you because you are *our* guide. Your affinity is with the Golden Auric itself, the most magical of the noble birds. It took you to the Eyrie, showed you where to find the hourglass. It must want you to help us. You've been chosen and we need to find out why."

The Golden Auric had saved her, that was true. But the wren had been the one to stay with her, to help her, to comfort her. How could the Auric be the bird she had bonded with? And yet, if Saran said it, it had to be true. He would know.

"It wants me to help you stop this Collapse?"

He laughed as if she had said something vaguely amusing, or terribly naïve. "I wish that was still possible. But we have a chance to avoid it, to lift our island into the sky, or at least part of it, to join the soaring isles. It's a spell. A ritual. I've been working for turnings to bring it about. But it has never worked. We have tried, but the situation just gets worse. And now, with you and your power, your affinity with the Auric, with that hourglass, I believe we can do it. If you'll join me. If you'll take your rightful place among the Birdsingers as my sister." He held his hand out to her again. "We can save many lives, Ro. We have to try."

This time, as if in a dream, Ro let his fingers close over hers. Something inside her shivered. But she couldn't pull away. He only wanted to help, she knew that.

"I have a way to save our people, Ro. I know it will work, especially if you're by my side. Not everyone, maybe, but I have to try. I have to save as many as I can. That's my purpose, my calling, do you see? I've studied the archives, and here you are with the final part of the puzzle. I need you, not just the hourglass. You. The Birdsingers need you. All of Arcadiana needs you ..."

The evening sun was now gone, sunken beneath the horizon, leaving a line of light along the edge of their world. The ocean caught its last glimmering, and she stared at the far horizon. Gulls reeled around the mouth of the harbour, and overhead, she could see the bright flashes of fire-crested herons, their wide wings leaving trails of light in the darkening skies, which sparked for a moment in the night and then faded like fireworks.

She was on the verge of losing everything. He had to know that. He had told everyone she stole the hourglass. She couldn't forget that. Though Saran had always thought he knew what was best and he had apologised for that. He was offering a new life. A better life. And he was the only family she had left. He only wanted what was best for everyone. He was offering her a purpose, a way to help everyone, to save the islands.

"I want to know about this spell myself." She remembered the strange word, the way the air had shivered around her when she'd uttered it, the flame bursting into life from nothing. It had been magic. She'd worked magic. Just like that. As easy as breathing.

"Of course. I'll show you everything. But the details, such as they are, are documented in the old language. I'm not sure you'd understand. I'd be happy to translate, of course. The Elders said that the right person could just place their hand on the book and see everything, see what needed to be done." He laughed softly, a self-deprecating laugh that made that familiar smile tug at her lips. He sounded more like her brother again. "I suppose we've never found the right person. But luckily they wrote it down as well. Let me help you. And you can help me. Together we can help everyone."

She'd never been a student of languages and the old language was difficult to comprehend for most people. But still … *Adscendo* … the word hung in her mind, calling to her. Taunting her. Begging her to say it again.

"So, only one question remains," he went on when she didn't speak. "Where is the hourglass? Is it here?"

Slowly, carefully, she slid her hand from his. He barely seemed to notice, his eyes fixed on some far distant, glorious future she couldn't see. She felt suddenly cold and unsure. The breeze coming off the ocean was chilly, and the shadows seemed darker than ever. Something was wrong. Very wrong.

"Saran?" she whispered, and then her voice died in her dry mouth. "I … I should go. Ameris will be wondering …"

"Ro, think carefully about this. This is the offer of a lifetime. Few others will ever get the same chance. The world and the hierarchy of Guilds is changing. It has to change before it is lost. We will lead them."

Lead them? Since when were either of them leaders?

"I didn't say I don't accept. I just … I need to think."

In the corner of her vision a flicker of light spiralled up out of the ground, a little whirlwind of shimmering mist. It moved too fast for her to keep track of, swirling to their left. But that didn't matter because there was another one on the right. And another. And yet another.

Shimmerwisps.

They came from all directions, glittering and insubstantial.

“Saran!” she shouted, panic infecting the sound of his name, twisting it to a cry of dismay. But it was too late. They surged towards her all at once.

CHAPTER 13

Parsa had refused to do more than glance at the hourglass.

"It's too late now. Come in, get some rest. There was a lot of trouble today. You shouldn't be out and about. The Windguards are everywhere."

As if Tomas didn't know that. He was just grateful he'd got Ro and Ameris to safety.

He had slept at the Weavers' Guild, rather than go back to his small neat room in the Labourers' Guildhouse, lulled by the soft creaks of the waterwheel, the music of his childhood here. In the morning he'd discovered Parsa had already gone out. And then the children had wanted his attention. By lunchtime, he still hadn't broached the subject of the hourglass. Nazir had a whole consignment of tapestries to pack and ship out to various locations around the islands. Tomas was soon roped into that. Each one contained coded instructions, woven in with the images of birds, of the city, of the clouds. And apparently it was imperative they went out as soon as possible.

It was becoming entirely too clear that the two Weavers were putting off talking to him about the object Ro had entrusted to him and he didn't like it. There was so much work he suspected that, as they had when he was a child, they were throwing jobs at him to tire him out, distract him. Or to keep him busy and off the streets. It might have worked back then, but not now.

"Nazir," he said, as evening approached.

"Just another two boxes," Nazir said cheerfully, tapping them with his stick. Tomas gritted his teeth and loaded them into the cart.

"I need to talk to him. Now. I can't leave it any longer. I need to take it back to her." Otherwise she'd think he'd made off with it like Saran had tried to do. They still hadn't talked about what happened in the Mire, what she'd seen. And he knew she had a million suspicions. She wouldn't be Ro if she didn't.

"He's busy." When Tomas drew in a long-suffering breath, Nazir just waved a hand. "Oh, relax. He'll be back soon. He never misses dinner."

That, at least, was true, but Tomas was sick of waiting. He didn't like the feeling he was being managed. Of course, it was nothing new and he should be used to it by now. Still, this time the matter was urgent and he didn't relish being treated like a child.

When Parsa did return, however, dinner was long over and he looked strangely troubled. Flustered, which was something Tomas had never thought he'd see.

"What is it?" Nazir asked, sensing the same unusual and worrying atmosphere.

"Too many checkpoints on the streets. They're looking for someone. Cracking down on our people. There were a lot of arrests in the Mire today. A lot of innocent people in jail right now. I had to answer some tricky questions." He glanced at Tomas, a guilty look filling his expression.

Tomas understood right away. "They're looking for me?" he asked.

"They're looking for the Piper. They say he was behind the attack on the Aviary. And they're looking for Ro."

He felt his whole body stiffen in alarm. "Where is she?"

"Safe enough. She's with Ameris, and Devera is keeping a close eye on them. Don't worry. But the Birdsingers and the Windriders are sniffing around and that's not a good thing."

It was not. If he went to her he'd probably just make things worse. He usually did. But he needed to return the hourglass. And more, he needed to talk to her. Somehow, he needed to explain.

But first he needed answers.

"We need to talk about the … item I showed you. I've been waiting for you. You've been elusive all day."

Parsa was always elusive. He liked to say it was part of his charm.

"I'm sorry, Tomas. I was … detained. Not exactly willingly." He dismissed the look of alarm on Nazir's face. "I'm fine. No one important. Just some Windguard functionary with more power than he's used to. There's a lot happening at the moment. I should have come back earlier, but it was an invitation I could not refuse. The Healer had questions. He didn't like the answers either." He shook himself, as if chasing away a bad dream. "Inside. My room. Come along."

By his 'room,' Parsa was talking about his workshop, rather than the quarters he and Nazir shared in the residential area. Material spread everywhere, lengths of bright colours and skeins of wool, coils of thread, everything a Weaver could wish for. There were four tapestries in progress, held tightly on their frames. His students did most of the work, but they were all Parsa's designs and he always made the final intricate touches which made them so sought after. One of the secrets to greatness, he always said, was never to give everything away.

Advice Tomas lived by. Even with those he supposedly trusted.

Never let them know the key component. Never tell anyone everything.

And yet here was Tomas, about to do that very thing.

Parsa threw a large wrap emblazoned with a pattern of red and gold feathers around his shoulders and sat down on the chair beside the workbench. Behind them, Nazir closed the door with a firm finality.

"Well?" Nazir said, as blunt and straightforward as he had ever been. "Where is it?"

Parsa leaned forward, listening intently. They often did this, the switching of power dynamics, to keep people off balance, to keep anyone from guessing who was in charge of what. Even Tomas was never entirely sure. "Show me, Tomas."

Reluctantly, he took out the hourglass. When he had tried to show Parsa last night, the Weaver had taken one look and shied back in horror, refusing to discuss it. Now, however, he eyed it with a dull dread.

"And this is what Ro's brother is so desperate to obtain?"

Tomas had always thought Saran was an ambitious idiot. He left Ro and her family behind him and never looked back. Not even when she needed him most. Matias had trusted him, and look how that ended up. Tomas couldn't prove that Saran betrayed his own brother to further his rise in his new Guild, but he would not put it past him. And Matias, of course, wouldn't hear of it. Perhaps Saran had just thought Matias would give in to the questioning, that he would betray those in the same organisation. But instead, Matias had showed himself to be a hero of the Unity movement. He'd taken the blame, taken the punishment. It might have cost him his life, but thankfully Parsa had managed to pull enough strings to ensure it was just exile.

Just exile. What a joke. Most of the islanders didn't have a clue what lay beyond the ocean, or what awaited them. It was the great unknown. The movement had a few contacts. They had done what they could. Sometimes Matias had been able to slip a message back home through their network. Rarely. And not of late, not since the Birdsingers decided to crack down on trade access entirely.

"Yes, Saran wants it, but Ro was the one who found it," he said, and told Parsa everything. Or at least everything she had told him. He still wasn't sure it was the full story. Parsa listened intently, never moving, while Nazir paced silently back and forth behind him like a shadow.

Eventually, Parsa took the hourglass, his long elegant fingers holding it gingerly, as if it was a firework about to go off.

The moment he touched it, he sucked in a harsh breath and his whole body stiffened. For a moment it looked as if he'd been turned to stone, his eyes wide, his grip on the hourglass so tight Tomas thought he would crush it any second.

"Parsa?"

Tomas started forward, intending to shake him back into reality, but Nazir grabbed him. "Hold on. Don't wake him. It's dangerous when it's this strong."

"What is it?"

"A vision."

"But—" He'd seen Parsa have many visions. He'd had one just the other day in Harbour House. But nothing like this. It looked violent and painful. As if he'd been struck by lightning.

"A strong one." Nazir released Tomas and crept forward warily. "Talk to me, Parsa, my love. What do you see?"

The voice that emerged from Parsa's mouth wavered. "We have to … I can't … the sky is dark. A shadow over Arcadiana. Light the candle … light the— The sky! The sky is falling. The water … rising. Can't breathe. Can't … the earth is shaking, tearing itself apart. There's a lake where the Aviary was. It's gone, Nazir. It's all gone. Swim for the light, Tomas. For the light. Flames on the walls … Everything is falling. A bolt to my heart. It's the end, Nazir. The end of everything."

"Is it the Collapse? Do you see it?"

"We must be ready. We must … Ro must be there. In the chamber, with the hourglass. She must … She's the only one who can do it. Light the candle. Save the world. But she won't be safe. They'll take her. Remake her. Manipulate her. Drain her. Drive her into the arms of the blind. They are coming for her. Do you … do you see the mist? The lights dancing? Do you see? They're coming for her."

Suddenly his head jerked down, and he was looking at Tomas again, directly at him. Looking deep inside him and seeing everything.

The vision broke and now Parsa froze, shellshocked.

"What is it?" Tomas blurted out.

Parsa opened and closed his mouth, as if trying to remember how to speak. When he did, Tomas almost wished he had not. "She's in danger, Tomas. Terrible danger. Right now. The lights, the mist … the hunger …"

And Tomas knew. Just from those few words.

"Shimmerwisps …" he hissed, the name of the fairy tale monsters spilling over his lips.

"They're coming for her. You have to reach her."

"Where is she?"

"In a garden, a knot garden with … with herbs, lavender and a birdbath and …" He frowned as if trying to drag the picture up inside his mind again, to place it. His forehead knotted in frustration. "Surrounded by high walls on three sides, and a low one looking out over the bay, carved with birds in flight. You know it. I know you know it. She isn't alone but she's … they'll surround her. They'll kill her. Tomas, take this to her now. She needs it."

Tomas didn't wait to hear any more. He grabbed the hourglass and threw himself towards the door.

A knot garden, surrounded by high walls, with a low wall looking out over the bay. One he knew.

The Ateliers' garden. She was with Ameris. Parsa had said as much. He'd said she was safe with Devera and her Guild.

And then suddenly she wasn't.

She was all the way across the city.

"Tomas, be careful! There are checkpoints and guards everywhere." He barely heard Parsa's voice trailing after him as he rushed outside.

The Weaver wasn't wrong. He came upon the first checkpoint just in time to duck down an alleyway unseen. Cursing softly to himself, he leaned back against the wall, trying to calm his heaving breath. They were stopping everyone, taking details. He might be able to bluff his way through, but it would take time, time he really didn't have. If Parsa said Ro was in danger he knew better than to argue.

The quickest way was closed to him. The main streets were full of Windguards and checkpoints. There had to be another way. No one knew the city like he did. The narrow lanes and cobbled streets were his home, all of them. The good and the bad.

He glanced up as one of the soaring isles passed overhead. He stared at it, wishing he could get a ride on that. Fire up a grappling hook and let it carry him over the roofs of Arcadiana.

But he didn't have to do that to get higher. He could make his own path.

He found a drainpipe and hauled himself up the side of the building, spilling onto the roof and climbing over the skittering tiles. From there, he ran, leaping from rooftop to rooftop. He slipped across the top of the trade hall, dodging between its fluttering pennants of blue and yellow, sliding down its curved dome, and climbed hand over hand up the side of the watch tower. He hung there for a moment, his hand finding an anchoring point on one of the carved stone eagles which served as water spouts, and studied the city below, the people, the water channels, the clogged streets, the bustling plazas and gardens. Still too many guards and checkpoints. No wonder nothing was moving.

But he was almost there. The Ateliers' Guild came into view at last. Finally, Tomas scaled the wall overlooking the gardens and came to a halt. He sat there, perched, like a bird.

He could see Ro below him, not in danger at all, just sitting there with Saran, beautiful in the setting sun. The light lit her hair to flames, and she was gazing into her brother's face with rapt attention. They were holding hands.

Something inside him thudded against his ribs, a great weight, and his breath came out in a pained gasp. It felt like ice.

"I've studied the archives, and here you are with the final part of the puzzle," Saran was saying. "I need you, not just the hourglass. You. The Birdsingers need you. All of Arcadiana needs you ..."

He wanted her by his side. He wanted her, his sister, to take her place among the Birdsingers, just as Matias had warned so long ago.

Ro would be crazy not to accept. She'd be safe at last, away from the Windriders and that awful bully Hale. And Grayden Mistral too. Saran would look after her. He should have stepped in when their parents died, to shoulder some responsibility.

Tomas just would never have thought it would feel like this.

That sort of access to the Birdsingers' Guild was priceless and rare. Oh, Nazir would love it, wouldn't he? He'd push Tomas even more into Ro's life if she decided to accept Saran's offer. He'd be betraying her with every action, spying on her whether he wanted to or not. If she found out, she'd never forgive him. His heart sank. Would she take the opportunity? At this stage there wasn't much choice left for her.

Suddenly she pulled back and Tomas knew her well enough to see the concern she was trying desperately to hide. She disentangled her hands from Saran's, but he went on, pleading, cajoling and maybe even threatening. What had he said to worry her? What had he done to break the spell he seemed to have cast? His words were too quiet to hear from this distance. Never let it be said Saran would raise his voice in anger. He didn't need to.

Ro, on the other hand, sounded distraught. "I didn't say I don't accept. I just ... I need to think." She stopped, staring at the garden and Tomas felt the hair on the back of his neck lift with instinctive alarm.

Something was wrong. Terribly wrong.

Saran rose to his feet, his robes sweeping against the stone with a hiss, an aura of power rippling around him.

Lights burst into life around them, glimmering lights caught in patches of mist, so uncomfortably bright in the twilight.

Shimmerwisps, just as she had described, just as Parsa had warned.

Tomas was moving before his mind caught up. It didn't matter that she was with Saran, that she called for her brother's help, and that as a Birdsinger he was far better placed to protect her. She didn't even know Tomas was there, but he had to reach her.

He dropped down into the garden.

Ro turned sharply, staring at him in shock, an expression which quickly transformed to fear. Not fear of him, but *for* him. It was written all over her beautiful face. He had just fallen into the utmost peril.

"Tomas? What are you—" But imminent danger made her surprise fall away at once. She'd always been good in a crisis. "Whatever you do, don't let them touch you! Do you understand?"

He didn't, though it hardly mattered because whatever the things were, they weren't paying the slightest bit of attention to him. They rushed towards Ro. Saran spread his arms wide, the long sleeves fluttering like wings. He was already pulling magic from the air and the earth around them, preparing for the attack.

"Ro, get behind me," Saran commanded and Tomas felt the earth between them tremble again. Was Saran doing that?

But whatever magic the Birdsinger controlled, it didn't stop the shimmerwisps. If anything, it seemed to accelerate their attack.

They surged towards Ro and Saran. Saran shouted something, words in a language Tomas didn't recognise, and brought his hands sweeping together in a circle, his robe swirling with his movement.

His fingers made shapes like birds in flight and he reached up. Saran unleashed something from his raised hands as he snarled. Tomas couldn't see what, but he felt it. A spear of air, shot at the shimmer-wisp. The mist parted, the lights scattered and then, to his horror, the terrifying creature reformed.

Bigger, stronger.

It hung there, the others circling it, and then in another mad rush, it headed straight for Ro.

Saran flung his arms out again, his palms flat this time, and the creatures bounced off some kind of shield around the two of them. Whatever this did to the monsters, it enraged them. They threw themselves at the shield, again and again. The frustration on Saran's face began to turn to something else. Fear. He was weakening. One only had to look at the sweat on his skin and his strained expression to see that much.

Tomas was halfway across the garden when the things noticed him. Three of them stopped their assault on Saran and moved back, towards him, floating across the grass like children's balloons. While the others continued their mad attack on the shield, these three spread out. They were slow, but the movement was determined, distinctive. They were fanning out, encircling him.

"Tomas!" Ro yelled, recognising his danger. "Get away."

But they still didn't come at him. He had seen the speed at which they could move. But this was something different. They weren't trying to rush him. They were closing in. Wary of him. Or of what he carried.

Understanding, he reached his hand into the pouch at his belt, his hand closing on the hourglass. It was magic. It contained a glittering, shimmering sand.

The hourglass looked like the shimmerwisps, if you thought about it. They were connected somehow. They had to be.

He pulled it out and held it up high.

"Is this what you're after?" he shouted.

Light burst from the hourglass, so many blinding colours, as if the midday sun had struck a crystal and split into a million shards of light.

Saran let out an agonised cry and collapsed, like a puppet whose strings had been cut. He went down in a heap and four of the creatures swarmed over him in an instant. The remaining shimmerwisps turned back towards Ro, flying towards her. They tangled around her in a clump, a glowing mist which smothered her, swallowed her whole.

He saw her mouth distend in a silent cry of agony. She dropped to her knees, her back arching as the shimmerwisps sucked the magic and the life from her.

The hourglass was a cold weight in his hand. They hadn't come at him because he had it, the very thing Parsa had told him to get back to Ro, to save her.

Tomas shouted her name and hurled the hourglass in her direction.

She snatched it with ease and held it tightly. She took a single breath and then her eyes went wide in some unknown shock.

Light exploded beneath her skin. It rippled out through the air like a wave, sweeping the darkness away.

The majority of the shimmerwisps vanished, swirling back into the darkness and disappearing in an instant. Saran slumped on the ground, unmoving. But the biggest one, the one that had reached Ro first, seemed to hang there, half lodged in her chest, its misty form struggling against her, trying to tear itself free. Ro slowly curled in around it, the hourglass crushed against her chest, inside the mist and lights which formed the shimmerwisp. Tears traced silver lines down her cheeks and her face crumpled up with the sheer effort of whatever she was instinctively trying to do.

She gave a gasp, although whether from pain or relief, he didn't know. Suddenly her arms flew out wide, her head went back and her back arched. Her shout was incoherent and wild. The mist took form, the lights coalesced. A bird burst from her body, the shape of an eagle, but made of smoke and reflections, as if someone had shone a light on a cloud. Its wings spread wide as did her arms as it ripped itself free of her, translucent and insubstantial but all the same real and undeniable, glowing from within. It opened its beak to let out a long, trembling cry of release, like an echo from long ago.

Then it flew, spiralling away from them, up into the clouds so high overhead, heading for the soaring isles. Tomas saw the moon and the stars through its body, saw the clouds light up as it passed through them. It gave that same wavering cry again, and this time he could hear its joy, ringing out over the islands.

Ro pitched forward silently, all her strength wiped out by the effort of whatever she had just done. Tomas only just managed to catch her in time.

"Ro? Talk to me. Are you okay? Please, talk to me."

She blinked, her eyes trying to focus on his face. She looked so pale and worn out. But she smiled.

"Did you feel it?" she whispered just before she passed out, her tone transformed to one of ecstasy. "Did you see? Tomas, I set it free."

CHAPTER 14

The shimmerwisps surged around Ro's body, swamping her, scrabbling against her skin, digging inside her to pull out something vital. It was like acid in her veins, like claws inside her lungs. She gasped for air and that just made it worse. Their light burrowed through her, hungry and determined, a blind sort of need driving them, creatures without thought but only hunger. All they knew was the need for magic, for the life force inside her. And they drank down everything, heedless of her struggles. She wasn't strong enough. She would never be strong enough.

Her brother was down, pinned there as the creatures fed on his magic, helpless and no longer able to help her. He barely moved. She wasn't even sure he was breathing. This couldn't be happening. He was the one who could really perform magic, not her. He was the strong one …

But Tomas—Tomas who shouldn't have been there, who arrived like a miracle in her nightmare—threw the hourglass to her and somehow she found the strength to catch it. Her hand moved of its own volition, the tendons in her arm screaming. But she caught it, its slim and delicate shape like a lifeline in her hand. The light that washed out of it bathed her in liquid gold. It felt hot to the touch, but not uncomfortable. Soothing. Her fingers curled around it, and she pulled it in to her chest.

Most of the shimmerwisps fled, but the largest one was still there, still merging with her, dragging all that was light and hope and strength out of her. She had pins and needles in her limbs and white noise in the back of her mind, but it didn't matter. The light from the hourglass told her it didn't matter. She just had to hold on.

She focused on the shimmerwisp. It struggled against her, trapped now, caught in a snare of its own making. Its own hunger had betrayed it.

And it was terrified. Desperate. She could feel that cold need, blind to everything else, melting away as the light of the hourglass flooded them both. The shimmerwisp had been infecting her but now …

Now she turned everything back on it, all her strength, all her vitality. She hurled herself into the ghostly creature and found something else within it. A shape. The shape of what it had once been. Echoes, Saran had called them. She found the echo of what had been there before …

Wind underneath mighty wings, the strength of its body, the keenness of its eyes, its joy in flight and the pleasure of the hunt … It hung on a stream of air, hovering over the fertile fields beneath. It plunged, folding the wings behind it, claws extended, the thrill of it coursing through her veins. It arched back into the air, triumph and elation driving its movement. It was speed, strength and joy, and a beating heart which knew only the need to fly.

An eagle, she realised, graceful and deadly, able to soar as high as any other bird. It had flown with Golden Aurics. It had seen the shadow of Amare as she flew through the dawn and cried out to her in greeting.

The shimmerwisp had once been an eagle.

She didn't know what kind, or what it had looked like, but she knew its heart, the quintessence of the creature. She didn't know what had happened, other than there had been pain, and terror. She could feel the humiliation and betrayal.

But deep down inside the shimmerwisp, there still beat the heart of an eagle. Desperate, heartbroken, betrayed.

Ro wrapped her mind around it, cradled it in her consciousness and then, with all the strength she possessed, she flung it up, back into the air, willing it to take form again and to fly free. She acted on instinct alone, fuelled by the power in the hourglass. She found enough magic in her own body to insist that it was released, set free from this half-life of fear and hunger, liberated from its prison of mist and dancing lights.

It felt like ripping out a part of her soul, of everything that made her human, but she had to do it. This beautiful creature needed to be released. Her body convulsed and she threw her head back, spreading her arms wide. The eagle, or the thing that had been the eagle, tore itself free of her.

A ghostly winged form took flight, lighting up the night, launching itself out of her chest and spiralling up towards the stars overhead.

She could hear it now, calling out in a sharp cry as it made for the Eyrie, for the Shimmering Tree, the place it was meant to be. She wasn't even sure how she knew that, but the truth of it blazed inside her mind. Lingering behind it was a sense of gratitude, of determination, of knowledge that it would be safe now, that the Tree would take it in and make it part of the eternal magic, that its strength would add to the whole and its magic would live on in their world. It was whole. Free. Safe.

Strong arms enfolded her and she collapsed in Tomas' embrace.

"Ro? Talk to me. Are you okay? Please, talk to me."

He was here. She didn't know how or why, but he was here and that was all that mattered. All those times she had made excuses and told herself that they were just friends, all those times she had wondered, even the recent doubts she had harboured, whether he was the Piper and what that might mean, his involvement in Matias' exile and the Unity movement itself … none of it mattered now. Because Tomas was here in this moment. For her.

"Did you feel it?" She wasn't sure where she found the strength to speak. Her voice sounded like no more than a breath. It grated like sandpaper on the inside of her throat. "I set it free." Darkness surged up around her. His face faded as her strength finally failed her and she passed out.

¤

Ro woke to a different darkness, a cocoon of safety, and found herself cradled in a warm, soft bed. She shifted and tried to sit up, but everything hurt. Her whole body, every muscle protested, her skin too sensitive, and her lungs aching.

"Ro?" Ameris' voice came out of the darkness. "Wait a second."

Ro heard the clicking of her tinderbox, and then light blossomed around the wick of a lamp. She was in Ameris' bed.

"Are you all right? They said to let you sleep, but I didn't want to leave you on your own. That was okay, wasn't it? Can you talk?"

"If I was allowed to get a word in edgeways, possibly?" Ro smiled. Ameris blushed and put the lamp down with a clunk on the bedside table. Ro instantly felt contrite. Her friend had been scared for her, really scared. "I'm fine, Ameris. I'm just … I'm tired. And sore. I feel like I ran for miles."

"I'll get Tomas."

Before Ro could protest, Ameris was already at the door, opening it a crack and hissing Tomas' name. And then he was there as well, appearing out of the darkness.

He looked tired, shadows under his eyes like bruises, but he was there and that was all that mattered.

"Were you sleeping in the corridor?" Ro asked, pushing herself up on her elbows.

He raked his hand through his dishevelled hair. "I didn't want to go too far and I wanted to make sure you were safe. It seemed like the best way."

He'd been guarding the door, sleeping out there so anyone who came for her would have to go through him first. She didn't know how she knew, but she did.

Ro looked from one to the other of her friends. "You both do too much for me. Thank you."

They had stayed with her. And for a moment back there with Saran, she had been tempted to accept, to join him and the Birdsingers, even if it had meant leaving Tomas and Ameris behind. He was family and blood ties were meant to be the strongest.

"Where's Saran?"

Ameris hugged her. "The Birdsingers took him back to the Aviary. He's fine. He recovered much more quickly than you. I think his ego's bruised, but that's all."

He would never have admitted otherwise, Ro thought, but she didn't say it.

"Weaver Craft and the Master Atelier want to talk to you," Ameris said hesitantly.

"About what happened?"

Tomas sat on the bed and held out his hand. She took it gratefully. At least she still had this, and his friendship, to hold on to. "They want you, the Birdsingers. It was all we could do to stop them carting you off along with your brother. We're not sure why, but it has something to do with the hourglass, and something to do with what happened to you at the Eyrie. And, no doubt, concerning what happened with the shimmerwisps. It was magic, Ro. Perhaps more than magic. I can't explain what I saw. No one can. And we were not the only witnesses. Several Ateliers had arrived, alerted by the noise. Saran said you somehow freed that bird, its spirit, that it was the ghost of a bird killed by magic, or killed when the magic was stolen from it. He said that what you did should not be possible. You set it free, that's what you told me before you passed out. Do you remember?"

Remember? Everything was so hazy and confused in her mind. But she remembered the bird. She remembered feeling what it was feeling, the freedom, the joy.

It had taken every last scrap of strength she had to release it, but it had been the right thing to do. The only thing to do.

"How did you know to come?" she asked. "And that I needed the hourglass?"

"Parsa told me."

Ro gave him a careful look. "Your friend Parsa seems to know a lot about all of this."

"He does."

"How?"

The openness in his gaze faltered and he looked both cagey and ashamed. She could tell he didn't want to answer that. She didn't entirely blame him. She could guess why.

"If you'll talk to him, he'll explain. He has a form of magic himself, not as strong as a Birdsinger." *Or you,* his eyes seemed to say, although his mouth didn't follow suit. But the hesitation was there, the doubt. "He has visions, Ro, and he has seen you. He can explain what happened to you."

"He's seen me? What does that mean?"

But Tomas was already gone, out the door in search of his friends who would, apparently, explain everything.

The ghost of a bird killed by magic, or killed when the magic was stolen from it.

That was what she had felt when the shimmerwisp had embraced her. The heart of a bird, its quintessence, the most essential part of its being. How was it possible? She didn't even know that something could be killed in that way, all its magic taken from it.

Ro was aware that magic flowed through every living thing. They were all taught that. It was part of the world in which they lived, part of their nature, what made them living creatures. Magic was the pulse of life, the breath in the lungs or the beat of a heart.

To steal it from another … that was a heinous act.

She'd heard stories. They had all heard stories. Childish tales of horror, to scare the young and the foolish, or so she'd thought.

No one would ever actually contemplate doing it. No one would even know how.

But someone had. The shimmerwisps were evidence of that.

And they were meant to be no more than stories to scare children too.

Ro sat up, bringing her knees up to her chest and wrapping her arms around them. Something was happening, something that should never happen. She didn't know how she knew, but she was certain. If the shimmerwisps were in the cave on the High Eyrie, it had happened there as well. That could just be remnants of the old world, that far away time of fairy tales when anything could happen. But the world had moved on since then. People were better. They had the Guilds and rules to stop such wild abuses of magic. That had been the whole reason for their creation. Yes, the Birdsingers might gather magic from the clouds but that was all. Clouds were not living things.

The shimmerwisps had not come from the clouds. And the one she had encountered here in the gardens of the Ateliers' Guildhouse had not come from the old world. It wasn't exiled to one of the soaring isles. So unless it had followed her down here—which was a frightening enough idea in itself—it had been created here. There had only been a few in the cave. Now there were many more.

Someone had stolen the magic from a bird and created the shimmerwisp, accidentally or intentionally. It really didn't matter which. Someone here, on her island home, had taken the magic and trapped the heart and soul of an eagle …

And she had set it free.

She didn't know how. She'd been working by instinct alone. She didn't know how she had done it or what she had done. Not really.

But she had a strong feeling that she was going to have to do it again. That wasn't the only shimmerwisp. There had been dozens of them. Saran hadn't even been able to drive them off. They were powerful and terrible. They had almost killed him, both of them. If it hadn't been for Tomas …

But deep down inside each and every one of them there was just a lost soul, reaching out blindly, trying to find help.

¤

The Master Atelier's office was a circular room at the top of the Guildhouse. There were four arched windows, three looking over the city and the fourth over the walls to the ocean beyond it. The floor was a beautiful mosaic made of thousands of tiny coloured glass tiles, with the Atelier's hammer in a central position, surrounded by the various instruments they used to create all those clever lifechanging inventions. Ro stared at the gleaming surface and shuffled her feet a little, wishing she had found some time to wash and maybe change her clothes. Although Tomas and Ameris had accompanied her, they stood back now, flanking the door, her only hope of escape. This was the second time in as many sunrises she had stood in the presence of a leader of a Guild and this one, she feared, liked her even less than the last one.

The Windrider, because Ro had rejected her son.

The Atelier, because Ro constantly got her precious daughter in trouble.

Ameris' mother sat behind a desk, resplendent as a queen in a long work apron over her neat and functional clothing. She was a study in muted shades of browns and blacks, her thickly curled hair tied back from her face, her bronzed skin glowing, and her endlessly dark eyes fixed on Ro as keenly as those of the raven that perched on the back of her chair. Unlike the playful and often naughty Zen, Devera's bird, Otto, was every bit as intimidating as she was.

The man standing beside Devera was as different from her as could be. As most Weavers did, he wore flowing robes which fell in layers of colour and seemed to be constantly in movement, even when he was ostensibly standing still. His glossy brown hair was long and loose, greying at the temples. His hawkish eyes watched her from either side of a pronounced nose, and his mouth seemed to be constantly suppressing a smile. She knew him, knew his face. She was sure of it. Was this Tomas' mentor, Parsa? She had no idea he stood this high in his guild to be up there alongside the Master Atelier herself.

Off to the left, standing against the wall in the shadows between the eastern and northern window, was another man, dressed in grey, who had to be Nazir, his husband. Ro had never met the two men who raised Tomas in person, but she'd heard their names and descriptions. Now she realised they had lingered on the edge of her life since childhood.

"In trouble yet again, Ro," said Devera, recapturing Ro's attention instantly. "Why am I not in the slightest bit surprised?"

To Ro's surprise, she almost sounded amused, but Ro didn't have the time or the energy to sort through why that could be right now. She would never underestimate Devera Flint.

"Ma'am," she replied, fixing her eyes on the wall behind her, where a huge tapestry map of Arcadiana and the attendant islands hung. Ro could pick out the great water wheel of the Weaver's Guild, the wide sweep of the harbour and Mount Nest. The detail in it was exquisite. The water was picked out in silver threads which caught the light from the windows and shimmered as if it was moving. All along the walls of the city, gold thread in intricate stitching depicted flaming torches. In the sky over the city flew a host of birds. Every bird imaginable. And above them, the soaring isles …

Ro stared at it, hoping this would be over quickly. Maybe if she just focused on the tapestry … maybe …

She just had to get through this. She was starting to worry that if word got back to the Windriders about what had happened this time, she was going to be heading straight into a Guildless life of exile no matter what she said. Commander Mistral would happily lock her up in the darkest cell available and throw away the key, hourglass or not. Either way, she'd never see Arcadiana again. She tried to use the tapestry to fix the image of it in her mind, so that she'd never forget it. Tears in her eyes made the image blur.

"Perhaps," said Parsa in a more placatory tone, "you might like to tell us your side of what happened. I would start at the beginning of it all, with the Golden Auric."

Ro blinked at him, trying to banish the threatening tears. Had Tomas told him everything? She heard her friend shift uncomfortably behind her, and clear his throat—he did that when he felt guilty. How did he ever manage to get away with all his deceptions? If she could see through him without even looking at him …

"The Golden Auric?" she echoed, without knowing what to say.

"Yes." He smiled at her, a winning smile, a smile that encouraged you to trust the wearer. A smile she instantly found deeply suspicious. If Tomas really was the Piper, she realised, this could be the man he took his orders from. She knew that Unity had a group of leaders rather than just one. They were known by codenames. "The one that took you to the High Eyrie, where you found that marvellous little hourglass that is so chock full of magic it is drawing every shimmerwisp in the city to it."

Every shimmerwisp in the city? She shivered. "How do you know about them?"

Clearly Tomas had told them everything.

"I know about many, many things, my dear young lady," said Parsa. "It is a vital part of what I do."

"You're a Weaver." Why couldn't she shut up?

"Indeed. Weavers gather information. We spin tales. We make sure the right things make it to the right place. Weavers—"

"Ancestors, enough Parsa." Ameris' mother groaned with frustration. "You are not that special. We all have roles to play. This movement is more than just one person. It is time we levelled with Ro and told her everything we can. Trust can only be expected if offered in return." Parsa seemed to consider this and then gave a brief nod. Devera turned her attention back to Ro. "As you have gathered, Ro, Tomas is the Piper. He calls people to help the Unity movement. I am called the Fulcrum, the centre point, the control. I hold things in balance."

She waited for Ro's reaction, but at the same time her gaze drifted back to Ameris.

"You're part of it?" her daughter murmured. Devera pursed her lips in a tight line which said she didn't want to get into this discussion right now. Ro had no doubt the two of them would be having a much longer conversation at a later moment. She didn't envy either of them.

"Yes. For many turnings. You both know that I would never risk you or this Guild, but the islands cannot survive as things are and we have to do something. Only together is there strength enough. The Healer you will meet later. His position is perilous now and he cannot be with us. Parsa here is the Arrow, reaching out to the future, his visions guiding us. Nazir is the Blade." Devera gave no explanation of his title, nor did she need to. Ro could imagine what the role of Blade was for, and looking at the dour face of the man, it fitted. "Now, with that trust in you demonstrated, we need the full story. Not the one your brother told. He has plans within plans and ambitions of his own. I don't know what he's up to, but it begins and ends with you." She lifted her strong, elegant fingers to the bridge of her nose and pinched, as if trying to drive off a headache. When Devera opened her eyes again they were fixed solely on Ro once more. "Where did you get the hourglass? No lies now. Not to me. I have known you for far too long. You are like another daughter to me."

"The troublesome one," Ro murmured before she thought about what she was saying.

Devera's mouth quirked up into a momentary grin, which was quickly smothered.

Trust. It went both ways. Ro glanced over her shoulder at last. Tomas was staring at her, his expression both desperate and filled with longing. He wanted her to trust them, needed it. A lump rose in her throat and she turned back, looking at the leaders of the Unity movement, now she could finally confirm that's who they were.

She began at the very beginning, with the feather.

CHAPTER 15

The calligraphy and illuminated edges of the scroll were beautiful, a work of art in their own right. Tomas had found Ro reading the message, poring over each word as she sat in the garden where she had last seen her brother, where she had performed a miracle. It was an invitation from Saran, to join him at the opening of the Carnival of the Birds, in the Aviary.

"What's wrong?" Tomas asked.

"I was thinking," she told him carefully, never looking up from the invitation.

He sat down beside her. "That's never a good start to one of your sentences."

"Saran knows about the hourglass and about what's happening to the islands. He said as much. He has information, all kinds of information about the old world, and … and he showed us a book, Ameris and me."

"A book." He didn't sound certain about where this was going. She wasn't either. But she knew what she had to do.

"Devera says you need to know what he's planning, for the—for your movement. If we can get into his room, we could find that book. Find out what he isn't telling me. Tomas, if we go to this celebration of theirs, when everyone's distracted—"

He frowned rather than seized on the idea like she'd expected. "That could be dangerous. If they catch us …"

She flashed him her most brilliant smile, even though they both knew it was all for show. "When have they ever been able to catch us?"

The Carnival of the Birds was the moment when the Ateliers' Prize would be announced, and so Ameris' attention had turned entirely back to the second version of the Wing. She worked on it with her every free moment. They even had to fetch her to meals. Ro and Tomas were tasked with helping her, but they were both fairly certain they were just getting in her way. Ro was more and more convinced it was all designed to keep her within the safety of the Ateliers' Guildhouse. More worryingly, no one suggested she should leave. But it also came as a relief. So did having Tomas there.

They still hadn't talked about the Mire, or the Piper. Or even what had happened in the gardens. She just knew he had arrived in the nick of time with the hourglass. He'd thrown himself into danger without a moment's hesitation. For her. But still, they didn't seem able to discuss it. Perhaps part of her didn't want to know. Because that way she could pretend everything was still fine. That her world hadn't changed.

Just after dawn, everyone had been shaken awake by tremors so powerful they sent things flying from shelves and brought a rain of dust from the ceiling. It felt as if someone had grabbed Ro's bed and rattled it, jerking her to consciousness with a panicked cry. Everyone rushed outside to see the sky full of the balloons carrying emergency crews heading east. Ro knew she should have been there too. But she wasn't. She was locked up in the Ateliers' Guild, hiding.

Guilt gnawed at her.

Midway through the morning, the city bells rang. Every bell, all over Arcadiana. Ro ran from the garden to the main courtyard, spotting Tomas and Ameris arriving just ahead of her. They looked as disconcerted as she felt. Everyone did. Everyone except Devera Flint, the rock at the centre of her Guild.

The Master Atelier stood in the middle of her courtyard, already handing out orders, all the while taking scrolls from her assistant, marking them with a quill and passing them back.

"All projects are suspended. Ready the dormitories. I want everyone lending a hand. These people will be traumatised and need our help. Get moving!" She clapped her hands and turned to her assistant who had another scroll ready for her.

"What's happened?" Ameris asked. "What is it?"

"Camri, the little island off the south west, the one with the orchards," her mother said, without glancing at her. "It's gone, torn apart in an earthquake. Few people escaped, and many of the boats carrying survivors were wrecked by the waves which struck the two nearest islands as well, compounding the disaster. We have evacuees coming in. All the Guilds are taking a share. Go and make sure we have supplies."

Ro found herself handing out blankets and food to shocked people with wide staring eyes. She helped children settle in cots while Ameris went through lists of people, trying to trace family members.

There had to be something more she could do. They couldn't go on like this, at the mercy of a world determined to destroy them all, always reacting, never getting ahead of the disasters. Saran was right. His spell, or ritual, whatever it was, could be their only hope.

She just needed to know more about the hourglass, more about the spell. She had to know it was safe. The plan to infiltrate his room and gather information became even more fixed in her mind. She just had to wait for the first night of the Carnival when the festivities would begin and the doors of the Aviary would open. She even had an invitation.

There didn't seem to be much to celebrate, and yet no one suggested cancelling the festival. If anything, Arcadiana just threw itself even harder at the preparations. Maybe the Carnival was only a celebration that they were still here, for the time being. Maybe it was a form of collective defiance. Arcadiana was good at that. They'd shut the whole world out, after all, following an ancient war, an attempted invasion from the outside world to plunder the precious magic which had ultimately doomed them all. The people of Arcadiana had defended their walls to the last. Ro wasn't sure of the details as her lessons on the subject had been long ago and she'd probably been watching the birds through the window when the teacher was droning on about it.

All she knew right now was she had to find out if Saran really had a way to save the islands and what the hourglass had to do with it. And she was certain that secret lay in her brother's book.

¤

The first day of the Carnival came with an explosion of music and celebration all over Arcadiana. The streets were thronged with people. It was supposed to be a time of charity and love, of sharing wonders and riches. People from the remaining outer islands came inside the city walls. The refugees gave thanks for their safety. Even those in the Mire moved freely through the streets. There was music everywhere. Children ran around with little flying models made of paper and string, elaborate kites, windmills and whirligigs. Some were Atelier-crafted but most were handmade, proudly created by the same little hands wielding them now. People wore elaborate costumes, wings and bird masks, headdresses made of feathers of a thousand sizes and colours. They flew kites of all shapes and sizes, each more brightly decorated than the last, and launched balloons of every kind. The air above Arcadiana came alive with them all. The Windriders not on duty leaped from building to building, from height to height like acrobats, engaging in ever increasingly dizzying feats of daring and danger. All the birds joined in, whirling and dancing around them.

The Carnival always included exhibitions of the Ateliers' inventions and the judging of the coveted Ateliers' Prize. The Weavers displayed their magnificent artistry, with music and poetry on every plaza, in every garden and park. The finest food and wine produced by the Labourers were available to all. The whole city was alive with celebration, in every house, on every street. Each Guild opened the doors of their Guildhouses and over the next three days Arcadiana would celebrate the wondrous variety of their islands.

Well, most of them. The Birdsingers kept access to the Aviary by invitation only. So many wanted to visit the Heart of Arcadiana fountain. It had once been central to the Carnival. But over the past three turnings the Birdsingers had become more and more reluctant to allow just anyone entry. Ro remembered as a child going there with her family, running through the dome to greet all the birds until she'd got lost in the dense foliage and her mother had been afraid she'd never see her again. Matias had found her, hefting her up on his shoulders and carrying her back home in triumph, while Saran trailed behind in a mood.

Ro watched the Ateliers setting up their displays for the Prize in front of their Guildhouse, among them new balloons, a number of flying machines, engines which ran on steam, and tiny mechanical birds which sang like real ones. Ameris had set the prototype Wing up in a quiet corner of the main courtyard. As far away from the centre of everything as she could. Anyone could see she was trying to avoid putting herself forward. But at the same time the moment it appeared the invention drew every eye.

The metal glimmered in the sunlight, flecks of gold dancing in the depths of the metal. It was elegant and beautiful, a work of art. Ameris circled it warily, her arms tightly folded, as others began to inspect it. But after a few moments, each one of the experts turned to Ameris with looks of delight and pride. She took a few steps back in surprise. They asked her questions and listened intently to her answers. Respectfully. When Ro approached, Ameris grabbed her arm and pulled her close.

"Did you hear?" she whispered. "Did you hear what Master Gage said?"

Ro shook her head.

"He said it was exemplary, Ro. Exemplary. He never says things like that."

The wave of relief washing through her, the rush of pride in her friend and her talent, made her head spin. She smiled. It felt like the first time she had done so in days. "But you're a genius. We keep telling you."

Ameris hugged her tightly. "It was your idea."

Ameris couldn't even take the credit she was due. But one day she would. Ro just hoped she would be there to see it. "As if I could make that," Ro replied with a nod to the Wing.

"And yet you inspired her to do so." The voice was deep, clever, and filled with pride. They turned to see Ameris' mother approaching. She was magnificent in her robes of office, even when worn over her blacksmith's apron, a paragon of the Ateliers. And she smiled. Ro wasn't sure she'd ever seen her smile in genuine pleasure before. More than pleasure. Pride. "The alloy alone has a dozen uses, many of which we are already implementing. So light, and imbued with the magic of the Auric feather … just perfect." She ran a long slender fingertip along the edge of one of the feathers and sighed. "We have so many plans for it already. And so many volunteers vying to work with it."

"My alloy?" Ameris interrupted, instantly suspicious. "When did you get access to my alloy?"

"I am the Master Atelier, my dear. This is my Guild. No one owns an alloy."

"You've been taking it? I knew the stock was going down. Mother—"

Devera held up an imperious hand. "Enough, Ameris. We do not hoard materials. We do not keep them from our brethren who need them. Calm yourself." It was as close to a reprimand as she would give in public. It was so cold and formal that Ro was sure she saw Ameris shrink in on herself in shame. It wasn't fair. Not now. Not when everyone was heaping praise on her. Ro put her arm around Ameris' shoulders and pulled her into a hug.

Devera saw that as well. "Thank you, Ro. For being her friend," she murmured, more quietly so only the two young women could hear. The tone was entirely different.

Had the coldness been for show? For the benefit of the other Ateliers?

"You never said that before," Ro blurted out before she could stop herself.

Master Atelier Flint smiled, a small knowing smile, but she didn't look angry. For once. "I never had reason before. Shouldn't you two be getting ready for tonight? Parsa has arrived with all manner of fabric and paraphernalia. He's most insistent that you need time to get dressed." She waved her hand dismissively. "And everything associated with that."

It was Ameris who groaned out loud. "Mother …"

Devera embraced her daughter. "I know you won't disgrace me. I am so proud of you, my love. Now, go and indulge the Weaver. I'll see you later when we go to the Aviary. The Prize will be announced there. The Birdsingers requested the honour."

Ro wondered whose idea that had really been, but she didn't dare ask.

¤

"Stand still and stop fidgeting," Parsa said for what felt like the hundredth time. Ro wasn't even aware she had been moving. She clenched her fists at her sides and tried to distract herself by glaring into the wall at the far side of the room but that didn't seem to work. She supposed she should just be happy the Weaver didn't jab her with one of the thousand or so pins he was using to fit the gown.

And what a gown it was. She had never imagined anything like it, especially not on her. It was a deep emerald green, embroidered with gold and amber threads, the colours of a forest in summer. The tiny stitches glittered as she moved—which she was not meant to be doing, of course—and they caught the light like fireflies. Her hair was pulled up on top of her head to keep it out of his way as he worked and her neck looked long and slender. And vulnerable.

Worst of all, she didn't look like a Windrider. She wasn't sure what Guild she looked like. Not anymore. It was the perfect disguise.

The dress fitted Ro like her own skin. As Parsa fussed over it, making final adjustments, Nazir opened a slim case and brought out a mask, which covered her upper face and framed her eyes. There were golden feathers. Not the true gold of Auric feathers, of course. These had been dyed but they glimmered as if they were made of metal and she had to keep touching them to reassure herself they weren't made of gold.

Nazir tied the mask behind her head and rearranged the elaborate arrangement of plaits and curls that another young woman, under Parsa's direction, created out of her wayward hair.

Ro knew she was lucky they were here. Most of the Weavers were employed at the Aviary, decorating it for the Carnival. Parsa had been handing out instructions to people who came and went under his direction. He seemed to be in charge of everything, and he had very particular details on how everything was to look. She'd only caught fragments of conversation, but it sounded like he was creating a wonderland with the precision of a military operation.

Meeting the two men who had raised Tomas and made him the man he was now, his fathers, had been a revelation. She could see much of the two of them in his ways, his nature. The determination, the joy and love, the honour …

"Perfect," Parsa said as he stepped back and admired his work. "No need for further decoration. The Birdsingers will fall over themselves to take you in even if they didn't know about your adventures."

"If I'm in disguise, how will they know it's me?"

Nazir and Parsa both laughed. "Masks like this aren't disguises. They're about giving people the excuse. They'll know who you are the moment you walk in."

She was almost ready with a smart reply when Tomas walked in from an adjoining room and she forgot how to breathe.

Tomas wore a green tailored coat which came down to his thighs, the same shade as her dress. The edges were embroidered in gold and amber. His breeches were a soft material which seemed to be moulded to his legs. She had never seen him in anything other than his work clothes before, but now he looked like a prince from a fairy tale, tall and broad shouldered, sun-kissed skin peeking out beneath the collar of the loose white shirt, dark hair falling over his even darker eyes …

Eyes that widened as his mouth dropped open. He was staring at her the same way she was staring at him.

Parsa cleared his throat to hide a laugh.

"Outside, Tomas," Nazir snapped. "We aren't finished yet."

"But I … Ro …"

"Outside. Here, take a mask."

The mask he handed him was plainer than Ro's, but still beautiful, decorated with much smaller feathers patterned like the body of the wren, brown with speckles that gave a hint of gold as he moved in the light. Less extravagant, less likely to attract attention. It didn't need to. Tomas himself did that, as far as she was concerned. But he held himself differently in that outfit, and when he put the mask on, he seemed to transform into someone else entirely. No one would recognise him.

As he left he flashed her a shy smile which made something flutter in her stomach, something she couldn't define and wasn't sure she should try to.

She had always known that there were things Tomas hid from her. She thought she might be able to guess some of it—his background, his history, and now she suspected his involvement in the Unity movement at quite a high level—but now she feared there was something more. Something that was at the core of his being. Something she couldn't help but be drawn to.

¤

The carriage bearing Ro, Tomas and Ameris lurched through the narrow city streets, navigating through the crowds of celebrants. There were people everywhere, music playing on every corner. In the Great Plaza, people danced amid the huge spreading trees, weaving their way in and out of each other in a complex pattern of steps, laughing and spinning each other around. In previous Carnivals the three of them would have been out there among them, not on their way to the Aviary in all the finery possible. Out there, having fun, where the dance was at its wildest.

As they approached the Aviary, where the streets grew narrower, the cobbles rocked the carriage as it joined a procession of other vehicles. And the crowd grew thicker. They passed the edge of the Mire and Ro couldn't help but shrink back a little, staring into those dark openings. In there it sounded more like a riot was going on. Music blared, all horns and the heady beat of drums, the type of music that promised pleasure and excitement. Voices shouted and sang with full-throated joy, a world away from the tense atmosphere in the carriage. She glanced at Tomas, but he just stared out the other window, at the open plaza where the fountains fed by the underground springs were leaping high into the sky, powered by the new turbines. Even there, people were jumping into the water and whirling around with the sheer thrill of it. She couldn't see his face, but he didn't look at the

Mire at all. No one would think it figured in his life in any way. No one would suspect he was the Piper.

More Windguards walked the streets alongside them, in full uniform, looking more sombre the closer they got to the Aviary gates. They weren't celebrating, Ro realised, but on duty. Perhaps even on high alert. They glared at the revellers, at the people they were meant to be there to protect. But they didn't seem interested in them. They were watching for something else.

"There was trouble last night," Devera said, catching Ro's worried look.

"Where?" asked Tomas.

The Master Atelier fixed him with a stern look. "Down by the harbour. Some arrests for disorderly behaviour, exiles trying to reenter the city without leave, and sedition. That sort of thing. Only to be expected."

"Near Harbour House?" he asked. "And in the Mire?"

She frowned at him. "Yes. I believe so. Why do you ask?"

"I was meant to be there," he replied and looked away, obviously uncomfortable. "The Labourers were celebrating the Carnival's opening. Best party in the world."

Had they been looking for him? Ro wondered. Was that why he had been in the Ateliers' Guild with her? Had Grayden sent Windguards to bring him in?

But Tomas had asked all his questions and wasn't saying anything more. He stared out the window, his expression hidden by the mask, though she could tell he was disturbed by something.

Perhaps Grayden was right to warn her off. Tomas was hiding things and had been all along. He hadn't meant her to find out. She'd known that the moment she saw his face in the Mire, just before that cold mask of indifference had fallen over it.

She had thought she could trust him with anything. Her life. Her heart.

So why didn't he trust her?

CHAPTER 16

The dome of the Aviary was alive with lights. Everywhere they looked, candles burned, and lanterns shone. In between the foliage in the great dome, little specks of illumination made the leaves glow. Ro didn't know if it was natural, Atelier-made, or magical. Perhaps all three. Streamers drifted in the air, lengths of silk and paper of all colours, fluttering as people passed. They stretched up to the top of the dome, rippling over the Heart of Arcadiana and draped out over it like a starburst. Everywhere, she could see delicate porcelain birds, expertly made by master craftspeople. Each one was unique, hand-painted in a vast array of colours. They reminded her of the clay bird she'd made for her father, the one that had been broken, but these ones were created by far more expert a hand and looked ready to take flight at any moment. They hung from wires and every so often they moved, whether through breeze or the vibrations travelling up the streamers. They chimed gently if they touched off each other.

It must have taken days to set this up and she could see the handiwork of the Weavers everywhere. She could sense Parsa's plans. Beauty, elegance, whimsy, and somewhere underneath it a strange sort of interconnectedness which made her wonder.

There was a design here. She just couldn't quite see it.

Music played, soft flutes and harps, and the real birds sang along with them, the chorus marrying with the melody. Ro felt her eyes widen as she saw the people of the upper hierarchies of all the Guilds present. Though they were masked there was no doubting who they were. The servants were discreet and quiet, appearing without fuss, offering a glass of wine or sparkling water, before stepping back and disappearing from view. People laughed and conversed, flirted, all taking in the wonders all around them.

It was so quiet and staid compared to the wild party outside, the whirl of joy and noise that the streets of Arcadiana became during the Carnival. Whereas this … it felt like another world. So strange and different from what she expected of this time of celebration.

She wished she was out there, dancing, singing, laughing. With Tomas and Ameris, just like previous turnings. Not here.

From the moment they entered, Tomas hung back, almost a stranger to her. Part of the pretence, she knew. He seemed to vanish into the crowd before she could say a word, not that she could speak. Wonder had stolen her voice.

The music changed as two Ateliers stepped up to the musicians carrying huge brass horns. The drums struck up a faster beat, and strings joined the delicate pipes in a reel, the sound all amplified by the swirling shell-like contraptions. Suddenly music seemed to be everywhere and the people at the ball laughed with delight.

Up in the vast space of the dome of coloured glass, amid the highest branches of its many trees, with birds on the wing all around them, couples danced faster together on gleaming circles which floated, suspended, in the air. They stepped from one to the other, held aloft, as if by magic.

It wasn't magic, not entirely. The circles vibrated with music, and swirled upwards. The silvery metal of the surface was speckled with flecks of gold, and carried an iridescent sheen. Each one was etched on both sides with an elaborate scene of birds in flight, or stars, or clouds drifting in the wind, and the colours sunken into the metal shimmered. They circled at various heights around the Heart of Arcadiana, the patterns and colours reflected in the crystal clear water underneath. The air was alive with laughter and music now, humming with magic. The fountain ran merrily on, but its song was drowned out, its ancient magic somehow commonplace surrounded by these new wonders.

Behind her, Ameris seemed to have frozen in the middle of the floor, where a stream feeding the pool flowed in a wide loop through the grasses, shrubs and flowers. She was staring upwards at something, her mouth hanging open, her gaze thunderous.

"What is it?" Ro asked.

"That's my alloy." She gestured to the circles in the air. "That's what she's been using it for? To make … *frivolities* for … for this?" She sounded so outraged but as they reached the edge of the pool in centre of the dome it got worse. Much worse.

Not far from the floating fountain, the Wing hung, suspended on wires like one of those ceramic birds, its delicate feathers splayed out on display. A platform stood beneath it, which could be reached by a narrow ladder. It was breathtaking. And it could only mean one thing.

"Ameris," Ro said. "You've won the Ateliers' Prize."

In front of it was another silken streamer which led across to the Heart of Arcadiana fountain, where an unlit candle waited. The only unlit candle in the place as far as Ro could see. An oversight? Or some kind of trick set up for when someone flew the Wing? Because there was no doubt of the intention here. Someone was going to fly the Wing and create a spectacle to celebrate the Carnival of the Birds right at the Heart of Arcadiana.

She gasped, her outrage momentarily forgotten. "I can't have. We haven't even tested the latest modifications. It's purely theoretical. It will have to be demonstrated and it isn't ready. We aren't ready." She glanced back at Ro and the anger was back. "She can't be planning to have someone demonstrate it here."

Ro wasn't going to be able to fly it dressed like this. She felt a shadow of the betrayal Ameris clearly did. But it wasn't unexpected. Why would anyone ask a disgraced Windrider to fly the invention in what should have been the inventor's finest hour? Any kind of association with Ro would always give someone a black mark. In spite of what had been said recently …

Distractions. The word hung in her mind. All of this, everything, distractions.

Ameris swore loudly, using words Ro wasn't even aware that she knew the meaning of. She stormed over towards her mother. Tomas caught her arm at the last minute, stopping her. She glared at him until he released her with an apologetic shrug.

"We aren't here for that. It's probably just another way to keep the Windriders busy. They won't be able to resist the Wing. Not … not that you don't deserve the Prize. It's just … I'm sorry."

"You're sorry? I'll show you sorry." Ameris was almost spitting with rage. Understandably. This was her invention, her treasure. And she felt horribly betrayed. What should have been her greatest honour involved stabbing her best friend in the back. If it even was an honour and not just part of the Unity movement's plan, using Ameris' Wing as a diversion. This wasn't an honour at all.

Who had Devera picked to fly it? Ro had to admit, the thought that nothing had been mentioned to her, as the test pilot of the flawed first Wing, stung.

But she couldn't make this personal. She needed to calm Ameris down if they were to follow through with their plan. "Ameris, we need to—"

"There you are!" Saran appeared from a group of Birdsingers and bore down on Ro in delight. "I have to admit I was worried that you wouldn't make it."

After the encounter with the shimmerwisps, he looked fine, just as Ameris had asserted. More than fine. He was the picture of health. Glowing with it. Clearly the attack had left him none the worse.

"Saran, you weren't hurt?"

He laughed and hugged her. "The healers here are the finest in all the islands. Master Nightingale himself helped me. When the hierarchy heard what you did, they couldn't wait to meet you. You've secured your position already. Come, Ro. Come with me. Everyone is desperate to hear more, to see you, to meet you."

As Saran linked his arm with hers and drew her away from the music and dancing, to quieter area amid the trees, she looked helplessly for Tomas who seemed to have faded away again. A group of Birdsingers lounged in a leafy bower, their flowing featherlike robes and elaborate masks making them look like birds themselves.

How was she supposed to sneak away to search Saran's room? She hadn't expected her brother to actually show an interest in her, not really. He never had before. But after the hourglass, after the garden, the shimmerwisps and his invitation, she should have known better.

This was impossible.

The first Birdsinger she met was old. Not just elderly. Old. He peered at her with cloudy eyes as Saran made his introduction and told all those gathered about what had happened. He explained about her transforming the shimmerwisp in complicated and esoteric terms that Ro would never have thought to use. There were words she had never heard of. But the entire group listened intently.

"Elder Nightingale is the foremost of our healers, Ro," Saran said with a deference which surprised her. "He healed me following the attack."

The old man took her hand in his, ignoring Saran.

"A blessing on you, child." His skin felt tough and knotted as old branches and he trembled slightly. "We have waited on this day. Saran is correct. You worked this wonder."

"Well, I … I just … it seemed the right thing to do." She blushed and stammered out the words. The old man nodded and released her.

"The right thing for all," he agreed. "You saved that creature, you know? None of us could do such a thing. We have tried. It ends … poorly."

For a moment they all fell silent, as if contemplating some terrible fate. Ro shuddered. Having felt the pain involved in the touch of a shimmerwisp, she could imagine. When they had attacked her in the tower, they had killed some of the Birdsingers, injured others. She had never thought to ask any more but now was not the time.

"Elder Nightingale," Saran said, breaking the awkward silence. "Thank you for your blessing. You do us a great honour. I want my sister to meet the Master Birdsinger. She is to join us as an honoured member of the Guild and will study under him directly."

Hushed whispers greeted this announcement, although Elder Nightingale looked sceptical.

"If that is her decision," he said with a knowing glance. "I'm not sure what the Master will be able to teach her though. Birdsinger Starling." He reached out a shaking hand and a young woman with a fall of red hair took his arm like a dutiful carer. "I would like to speak to the Master Atelier. She is here, is she not? Her daughter won the Prize, after all."

"Indeed, Elder Nightingale," said Starling softly. "I'll have someone fetch her." The thought of someone summoning Devera Flint like a child should have made Ro smile, but she didn't have it in her. "Apologies, Windrider. You aren't forgotten." The woman smiled ever so gently. "He just tires easily. He needs to look after himself instead of everyone else."

The old man just shook his head and made a harumphing sound. "I've forgotten more than you know, Bree," he told her. "She is my best student and my greatest hope. Our finest healer."

"Next to you, you mean," Starling laughed. "And your teaching days are not done yet."

He fixed his attention on Ro again. "Choose your own path, young lady," he murmured. "It is the greatest gift we have."

Ro bit her lower lip. Choosing a path for herself seemed to be getting more difficult by the second. She hadn't agreed to join the Birdsingers yet and Saran knew it. He was trying to push her into a path she wasn't sure she wanted. She glanced back over her shoulder and finally saw Tomas watching them from the edge of the stream, overshadowed by the tall trees, the light that was shifting through their leaves casting a dappled pattern of shadows on his face. He looked unaccountably lost and alone. There was no sign of Ameris. Presumably she'd taken off to have it out with her mother.

Their careful plan was falling away into chaos.

All of a sudden a bird called out to her and she turned, recognising the song. A trill, followed by a staccato rap and another trill.

The wren flew to her shoulder and nestled against her neck as it eyed the many people around her. All of them stared at her, and at the little bird.

"A wren?" one of the Birdsingers said haughtily, a tall and stately woman who wore the feathers of a peacock and a gown of iridescent purple. Saran had introduced her as Kira something. Ro hadn't been paying enough attention to catch her family name. Kira glanced at Saran as if for approval, fluttering her long eyelashes behind her elegant mask, before she decided that she could say what she wanted and went on. "Couldn't you get at least a hummingbird to notice you? Or a goldfinch? Anything nearer your own size?"

Someone tittered, one of her friends no doubt. Ro had no idea who, but it really didn't matter. It could have been any of them.

It was going to be the same here as it was with the Windriders, she realised. She'd never fit in. She would always be the upstart, or the threat. Or simply Saran's little sister. Maybe they were just jealous. Part of her wanted to shrink back into her skin, hide behind her beautiful mask. Yet another part wanted to lash out and—

And what? What would she do? She needed to find out the truth, which meant doing what she had come here for, finding Saran's book.

She took a step back from the Birdsingers, mentally and physically. This was not for her. It never would be.

They thought they were above all others.

Not all of them, perhaps. She thought of Elder Nightingale, and his kindness. Of Starling.

"What is it Ro?" Saran murmured. A trace of concern flickered over his face.

"Nothing. I just—I should get back. To my friends."

He grabbed her arm before she could leave. "Nonsense, Ro, you're here to make new friends. Don't make a scene. You want to fit in here."

A scene. No, he couldn't have that. What would people say? What would people think? Well, she'd show him a scene. She was good at that.

With all the force she could muster, she jerked her arm free, drew it back—

And someone else caught it. Not Tomas this time.

"There you are," said Grayden Mistral. He smiled and twirled her into his arms, looking every inch the handsome leader of the Windriders. He wore his best dress uniform and a sword at his side. He was clean shaven, the golden boy. His blue eyes sparkled. No mask for him. "I heard you were here, but I didn't believe it. Shall we dance? For old time's sake? The Ateliers' devices transform the music. It's almost fun. Excuse us, everyone. I can't pass up an opportunity like this. We were engaged to be married once, but she never looked like *this* when we were betrothed."

The woman, Kira, laughed at his joke along with everyone else, but her gaze had sharpened to daggers.

Her brother's expression darkened but what could he say? Grayden was the new commander of the Windriders' Guild and Ro, while the invitation had been extended, was not a Birdsinger yet. So as a Windrider, she was under Grayden's command and she had a feeling he was not above pulling that sort of stunt if the fancy took him.

Grayden swept her away and she was too startled to respond or escape. They entered the flow of the dancers, and the rising music, stepping over the lush grass and across the stepping stones over the river, out of sight of her brother, or so she hoped. Grayden took her hands and danced her to a small hollow surrounded by flowering shrubs on three sides, far from prying eyes. Exactly the sort of spot two old lovers might escape to.

"Were you about to cause a diplomatic incident?" he asked, a strange sort of amusement colouring his voice. "I felt it my duty to intervene just in case. What are you doing here?"

"I was invited," she spluttered indignantly. "By Saran."

But Grayden just gave her his trademark sardonic grin. "You didn't look too happy about it back there."

"I wasn't, but I was going to handle it."

Grayden had perhaps saved her from even more humiliation, but she didn't want to tell him that. Her pride would never handle it. And his would be unbearable.

"I'm sure you were." He smiled, that infuriating smile that drove her up the wall with frustration. "I wish things were different between us, Ro. You lead such an interesting life. It might be good for me to tag along for the ride once in a while."

He had no idea what he was suggesting. The ride she was on right now … it was neither interesting nor good.

She opened her mouth to answer and realised she had no idea how to respond. He had saved her, and probably a few other people and had done it in such a way that had allowed her to save face.

The Grayden she thought she had known would never have done that. He'd have let her fall on her face and laughed about it with his friends. Just like Kira and the other Birdsingers. But not this man.

Maybe she had misjudged him. Or maybe he had changed. Grown up.

They had not been friends, but she was beginning to wonder if in fact they could have been. While she had never loved him in any way, there was a lot to like about him. She would never feel about him the way she felt about Tomas. But there was a lot more to Grayden Mistral than she had thought.

Luckily she didn't have to find an answer to any of these thoughts for at that moment Ameris arrived, striding across the garden as if on a mission. She had spotted them in the hollow and looked possessed of a fury. Her cheeks were flushed and her eyes flashing.

Where was Tomas? Ro couldn't see him anywhere. He wouldn't have gone ahead without them, would he? To begin with, he didn't know where to go.

Ro noticed that Grayden's eyes flicked towards the place where Tomas had last been and she understood immediately. He knew something was up. Not what, perhaps. But he wasn't a fool.

She flashed him an angry glare. Before she could speak, Ameris reached them. She held up her hands to Grayden and smiled in a most un-Ameris-like way, before her eyes lowered. The anger in her seemed to be gone completely. Ro didn't trust that one bit.

"Commander, would you do me the honour of dancing with me?" she murmured, her voice not sounding like her own. "I'm sure Ro can amuse herself. Or at least get into trouble without us." She was wearing her black feathered mask and Ro wasn't entirely sure that Grayden recognised her. She barely recognised her friend herself.

Grayden smiled a very different sort of smile, one that seemed just on the edge of bemused, and took Ameris' hands.

Before Ro knew what was happening, they had gone and she was standing alone by the flowering shrubs.

No, not alone. Tomas appeared beside her. He must have been hiding from Grayden. He even had leaves in his hair. She reached out absentmindedly to pluck them free. He let her.

"We should go. Ameris said she'd keep him busy. She got nowhere with her mother. They're planning to demonstrate the Wing and she's furious. I think Grayden has been talked into doing it. He probably jumped at the chance. When she saw him with you—" He raised his hands helplessly. "We'd better get on with this. Do you remember the way to Saran's room?"

Ro hesitated. The Aviary was vast, and now it was decorated for the ball it looked different than it had the other day. Things had been moved, and the plants now looked different, being decked with lights and other decorations. They'd passed a huge palm, she knew that. And maybe … Tomas followed in silence, his mind clearly not on what they were doing. He kept glancing back behind them and when she met his gaze he looked troubled, distant.

"What's wrong?" she asked.

"Nothing. Let's just find out what Saran is hiding."

"How do you know he's hiding something?" She really didn't like the tone of voice he used when he spoke of her brother. Stopping, she turned back to face him and he came up on her all of a sudden, almost colliding with her. In the narrow pathway, shaded by the trees, there was no way to step around him and neither was prepared to step back.

She stared up at him, trying to figure out what had caused this mood swing. He hadn't been right since they got here. Since they'd left the Ateliers' Guildhouse.

"Tomas?"

"Ro," he said at last, and suddenly he just sounded tired. Exhausted.

"Who are you really?"

"You know who I am. Who I've always been." He was such a bad liar. Or maybe she had just taken him by surprise. He seemed to do pretty well the rest of the time.

"Do I?" She had to know. She had to ask. "Are you Tomas Harper, or are you the Piper? Was Matias exiled for you?"

The guilt was evident on his face. He didn't even need to answer.

"It isn't the time for this, Ro. Let's just—"

But she didn't move. She couldn't. Standing here in the shadows with him so close, all she could hear was her heart beating.

"Perhaps it *is* the time," she said. "What happened, Tomas? Matias told us that the Piper would look after him, that the whole Unity movement would protect him but then …" No one had looked after him, certainly not the mysterious Piper who had faded away as easily as Tomas was able to slip into shadows.

"He made a choice. Not one I agreed with. He was the Piper, long before me. We got him to safety, but it was all we could do."

We.

"You, Parsa, and Nazir, I presume."

"I can't give you names." He didn't need to. They had told her themselves. The Unity movement.

"Not so much can't as won't."

"That's how it works." He swallowed hard and she found her eyes locked on the movement of his Adam's apple. "I promised Matias I'd look after you. And I have. I always will. You know that."

It felt like physical pain. She'd thought they were friends. She'd thought they were more than that. And now—

"Is that all I am to you? A debt to my brother?"

"No. You're not a debt. You're—you're everything." He screwed up his face in frustration and tried to look the other way, but he couldn't. It was as if his gaze was dragged back to her face by an unseen force. "Oh, ancestors, Ro ..." He gave a growl of frustrated dismay.

And before she knew what was happening, he pulled her against him and kissed her.

It wasn't the perfect kiss she'd always imagined. It wasn't even the most expert kiss she'd ever shared, but it was his kiss and that was all that mattered. It didn't help that in the moment she was too shocked to respond. She clung to his chest, trying to make her brain work. But she didn't have a hope of doing that. Not while Tomas was kissing her.

Tomas, who was always so calm and collected, who never lost control; Tomas who always smiled when she tried to flirt and deflected her attention so gently; Tomas who she had loved as long as she had known how to love. Tomas was kissing her, one hand pressed to her back, the other cradling her face, pushing aside the mask so he could caress her skin.

Just as she summoned the wherewithal to kiss him back, he pulled away.

He looked horrified with himself. "I'm sorry. I shouldn't have ..."

"No," she gasped, unwilling to let go of him. She stared at his bewildered face. How was this happening? Now of all moments?

"I just— Don't pick the Birdsingers, Ro. Saran will just use you and he'll never let me near you again. He'll lock you away in that bloody tower forever, no matter what promises he makes now."

The words spilled out of his mouth as if he had no control of them, as if he couldn't stop them. Ro's heart thudded against his chest through her own, trying to get his attention, to make him stop. What was he saying? Didn't he know? Didn't he know anything?

"And as for the Windriders and Grayden …" he went on, heedless of the consequences now. "He'd have you in a heartbeat, I know. I saw how he looked at you tonight, but please, don't pick him. It doesn't have to be me. You don't have to make do with me. There is no debt to Matias, not for either of us. I promised to look after you freely and being with you, being your friend has been the greatest honour. I don't deserve you. I keep too many secrets. Not because I want to but because I *have* to … But please, just don't … Don't leave …"

His voice trailed off and he fell silent, standing down. Still holding her. She could feel his hand tremble against her back, where it pressed lightly against the material of her gown.

That was it, wasn't it? Everyone left Tomas eventually. His family, her brother, and now, he feared, her as well.

"I don't want Grayden," she told him, on a single breath. "I never did. And no one knows Saran like I do. He means well but he's … He's too driven. He wants to save the world, and I don't feature much in his life except as a means to that." The truth hurt, even if she had always known that. But she had to press on. If she didn't get this out now, after his confession, she never would. And she would never forgive herself. "I just want you, Tomas. I only ever wanted you, you idiot. Didn't you know that?"

His mouth opened and closed as if trying to find a reply and coming up empty. But his eyes kindled with an inner fire she had not seen before.

She lifted herself up on her toes and kissed his lips.

For a moment time stood still. She lost all sense of place. There was only him. There was only her. There was only the two of them together.

A sharp trill next to her ear made her jump back. There was the wren, perched on a branch beside her. Tomas laughed unexpectedly and glared at it.

"Well, I've never been chastised by something so small," he told her apologetically. "Except maybe you."

It made her smile. She felt flushed and almost feverish. It was ridiculous. And this was neither the time nor the place. They had a job to do.

"We should get to his room. That's why we're here after all."

He nodded, the magic of the moment gone. But not gone forever. She smiled at him once more and his lips lifted in return immediately. Not gone at all.

The wren fluttered onto the next branch, bobbing up and down until it was sure that they were following. It led them without further pause to the door to the tower. From there they made their way up to Saran's rooms unseen. Ro reached the door first and found it locked.

Of course it was. She rattled the handle again just to make sure and cursed under her breath.

"Let me," Tomas said.

"Don't break it down. Someone will hear." Although given the music and the general noise beneath them, that might be unlikely.

Tomas just shook his head in disbelief that she would suggest such a thing. He slid by her and dropped to his knees. From inside the coat he wore, he pulled out two long, slim tools. She'd never seen the likes of them before. They looked like needles but with bent and serrated ends. Deftly, Tomas slid them both into the lock and moved them slowly, carefully, concentrating on his every move, until something gave a loud click.

The door opened silently.

He got to his feet and the tools vanished back into the pocket inside the coat, as if she had imagined their existence.

"How did you …?"

"Inside, before someone comes."

"We really need to talk about this other life of yours, Tomas."

His grin promised that they would.

The wren went ahead of them, fluttering across the room and up onto the shelves. Ro followed it inside and Tomas shut the door quietly behind them.

CHAPTER 17

Ameris couldn't believe she was doing this. This wasn't like her at all. But something seemed to have broken loose inside her, something that had kept her in check all this time. The Wing—*her* Wing, her invention, all her work—had been brought here without so much as a by your leave, and put on display. They were planning to demonstrate it to everyone and no one had thought to ask her if it was ready. Worst of all they were going to let Grayden Mistral fly it. *Her* Wing.

Her mother had explained all of this to her in curt and clipped tones, with strong implications of 'don't make a scene' and 'we're doing this for your own good.'

She wasn't though. She was doing it for *her* own good, so the world would see what an amazing Guild she ran and how many wonderful inventions that they had yet to give to Arcadiana and the other Guilds. Under her direction, of course. Her mother was nothing if not driven by self-promotion. The consummate politician. She would use anything and anyone to further her own agenda, even her daughter.

And if it helped her Unity movement, so much the better.

Ameris should have known better.

Just today her mother had told her she was proud. Proud! What an idiot she was.

When she spotted Grayden and Ro, something inside her had just snapped. She couldn't help herself.

Those circles that everyone was using as platforms, those floating surfaces which gleamed like oil in sunlight, with their beautiful engravings, they were made of her alloy. It was all her work.

And she had no say in how it was used.

They were using them as amusements. For dancing. All the wonders that could have been made with it—flying machines, safety equipment, structural reinforcement …

No, she was here to be held up as a prize to the other Guilds.

When the handsome fop didn't even recognise her, Ameris found herself holding out her hands to Grayden as if this was the most normal thing in the world. As if she danced with handsome men in uniform at every Carnival. As if everything was perfectly fine.

"Commander, would you do me the honour of dancing with me?" she murmured in a low, flirtatious voice, relishing the deception so she could throw it in his smug face later. "I'm sure Ro can amuse herself. Or at least get into trouble without us."

She smiled meaningfully, and Grayden laughed. Of course he did. The idea of Ro in trouble was as normal to him as breathing.

Hopefully Ro and Tomas would get the hint, take the distraction she was offering and go complete their mission.

Grayden took her hands and they stepped onto the dance floor and, somehow, into that other world. Ameris wasn't sure what happened. She had learned to dance as a child. They all had. It was part of a formal education in any Guild, designed for moments like this. No one wanted to shame their Guild. And even if the majority were not often invited to such events, there was no need to be found lacking in manners and style. Dances at her Guild were altogether less formal. She wished she was back there right now, or out in the streets like every other Carnival. Everyone would be dancing now, spinning each other around in a wild reel, just on the edge of control.

But this was like being swept away on the melody, as if the air itself lifted her and twirled her around. Maybe it was the music, made wilder and more intoxicating by the amplification horns Atelier Silver had invented. It filled the whole dome and left her just a bit bewildered. Grayden was a skilled dancer, leading almost casually, directing her steps with ease. He could make even the most clumsy look elegant, and Ameris was far from clumsy.

The first circular platform they stood on hummed beneath their feet and began to rise as they moved, the vibrations of the music and their footsteps activating it. Part of her wanted to stop and crouch down, to study it and see what had been done to the alloy to make it work this way. But the rest of her overrode that instinct. Besides, she would have to rip herself out of Grayden's arms and then she probably would have toppled over and fallen from the height in front of everyone. Or something similarly catastrophic.

So she danced. She gave herself up to it, to the feeling of his hand against her waist and his other hand in hers, the way he breathed, the way when she looked up into his face, he was gazing down at her with a puzzled expression.

She was grateful for her mask. It mostly hid her identity.

"I haven't seen you attend one of these Birdsinger events." His voice rumbled through her; they stood so close.

She had been to one before though. Once. She'd just hidden on the fringes, watching others, too shy, embarrassed and self-aware to thrust herself out into the limelight like this.

She tried another mysterious smile. "I've never been."

"Never?" he asked. She just shook her head.

"Does it matter?" she asked blithely.

"It does to me. Your Guild must treasure you to hold you so close."

She supposed she should laugh at that, or deflect with a witty comeback, but he said it so seriously her breath caught in her throat for just a moment.

"My Guild doesn't matter tonight," she replied. Truth be told, she meant it in that instant. That surprised her more than she could say. She was so angry with her mother and the other Ateliers, with the Unity movement for getting herself, Ro and Tomas so embroiled in all this, with Grayden for being there to fly her Wing. The Wing which they had announced as winner as yet another distraction.

"Our Guilds always matter."

It almost made her laugh. Except that she was worried she might cry instead.

"Are you really going to fly the Wing?" she asked, swiftly changing the subject. She needed to know. She had to ask him. This was why she was here, now. Not for Ro. Not to distract him so she and Tomas could do what they came here to do. This was why she had approached him in the first place. "The Ateliers' Wing. It's untested. The first prototype fell apart in the air."

"I know. But that won't happen again. I believe a great deal of work has been done."

"It's dangerous. Here, in front of everyone, you don't want to fail. You could be hurt."

His smile broadened and then she watched as it changed, transforming into the smile she knew. Confident, self-possessed, arrogant.

"No one flies like me and I can fly anything. Don't worry. I have every faith in the Atelier that made it."

That made her stumble in shock. "You … you do?"

"Of course I do, Ameris." He released her hand for a moment to press his fingers to the wrist where her bracelet hung, making all the little charms Zen had given her jingle. She jerked back, but his hand snapped around hers and he held her close in a suddenly iron grip. His voice dropped low and rumbled through her where they touched. "Careful. You'll fall."

"Grayden, I mean it, the Wing isn't tested. I haven't had a chance. The first test almost killed Ro."

He spun her around until she was dizzy and dipped her backwards in his arms. She scowled at his smile. "I'm not Ro. You didn't come here to warn me about that, did you?" He pulled her up again, all part of the dance or so it would appear. Ameris didn't know what to think.

"How did you know it was me?"

"I didn't. Not at first. I've never seen you like this. And not just the gown, which is spectacular by the way. Or the mask. You're beautiful."

They had reached the top of the Aviary now, the coloured glass right over their heads. Another circle floated nearby and before she knew what was happening, Grayden jumped onto it, still holding her. It wobbled as they landed and he laughed, holding her even closer when she gave a squeak of fear.

"Ah, that's a bit more like you. When you aren't spitting fire at me. What's got you so angry that you forget yourself? It's something to do with Ro, isn't it? It usually is. Where has she gone anyway?"

No, oh no, this was all going wrong. Ameris squirmed as they continued to dance. She was meant to be diverting him from Ro, not drawing his attention to her.

She did the only thing she could think of, given the circumstances. She threw her arms around his neck and kissed him. Not lightly, not delicately. There was nothing teasing about this. This would cause a scandal. Everyone who was anyone in the hierarchy was looking at the two of them so Ameris kissed him as if she adored him, as if he had just offered to marry her, or had just saved her life. She kissed him as if she really meant it. But she didn't. She really didn't. Even if a secret part of her whispered that she did.

Grayden stumbled back a step in shock. "What are you—?"

The platform came slowly to rest on the floor and they stared at each other.

The music came to an abrupt halt and every alarm bell in the Aviary rang out as if the world was ending.

CHAPTER 18

The dome outside the window of Saran's room was alive with light, casting a multicoloured glow up into the sky, while the music echoed strangely in the darkness beyond. Ro studied the shelves, trying to recall where Saran had put the book. Tomas searched through the papers strewn across the desk.

"He was working here," he said. "Some of the ink is barely dry. What's this? *Five places, one for each Guild, and a focus into which the power will be held.* Instructions? He's added something, a drawing. It looks like the hourglass."

Saran had been obsessed with the artifact from the moment he'd seen it. She knew its magic enthralled him. She'd seen his face when he held it and all he had done ever since that moment was pursue it. And her.

Not just because he wanted his sister back. Or because he wanted to make amends. She feared she was just a means to an end. The end being that hourglass and all the power it contained.

Irritated by the mask against her face, by all the pretence, Ro pulled it off and threw it onto the neatly made bed. The wren started from her shoulder and took off, chiding her as it flew.

"I'm sorry," she said to it. "But if I don't find the book, this has all been for nothing. I have to know what he discovered about the hourglass and it has to be here somewhere."

"Ro," Tomas said, the tone in his voice altering to concern. "Look."

He had picked up a long scroll of paper. There were names and numbers, lots of them.

"What is it?"

"A list of people from various Guilds. I know most of these names. Those from higher in the hierarchy, of course. I guess he couldn't leave them off. And a few lesser beings, as he'd probably call them. Ameris is on here."

"Let me guess, we're not?" She didn't mean it to come out quite so bitterly.

He was quiet for a long time as he read. "I'm not," he said at last. "He's added you near the end."

Typical. Up until now she had been disposable. He was so sure she would accept his offer. It made her stomach twist inside. Why did it feel so wrong? It was just an instinct, little more than a feeling, and yet she had not been able to ignore it.

"What is he planning?"

"It can't be just Saran. There must be more of the Birdsingers involved." He picked up another sheaf of papers, all covered in neat script. "This isn't his handwriting. Someone else put this together."

He paused as he read. “Population density of various islands. Resources. The agricultural outputs of … It’s like they’re justifying the existence of each of the islands and the people on it. And the Guilds. Look at this!”

She didn’t. Every word he said weighed her heart down even further. She reached the final shelf.

“Here!” Ro’s hand closed on the book. It was thick and heavy. She needed both hands to pull it out and carry it to the desk.

She opened the huge tome and flicked through the pages, turning them with care. She shivered as a shadow seemed to pass over her. The air rippled with heat and before her, the world seemed to be overlaid with something shimmering and golden.

That’s when she realised something, something terrifying. The book had been waiting for her.

Saran had told her the right person could just place their hand on the book and see everything, see what needed to be done. He’d told her it was magic.

“Tomas,” she murmured, as loudly as she was able, which was no more than a whisper. The book seemed to steal up her senses and swallow her whole.

Magic, she realised. It was magic. The book was drenched in it. No wonder Saran prized it so. And whatever magic had infested itself in her at the Eyrie responded to it instantly.

It felt like another hand had closed around hers, moving it, as if she were in a dream. She spread her fingers wide, and lay her palm flat on the page, letting herself be guided by someone or something else. She closed her eyes.

The book whispered, the pages rustling beneath her touch though they could no longer turn. They didn’t need to. As she pried her eyes open again, she saw light spilling from her palm, flowing over the table and up the walls. It had the same green-blue luminescence of the lights in the cave and she recognised it instantly.

"Ro?" Tomas' voice sounded far away. "Are you— Are you okay?"

"Yes, but— You're seeing this, aren't you?"

"I am. I'm seeing something anyway." He didn't sound entirely sure what he was seeing. But that was fine. She wasn't sure either. It was nothing she could really define, but she knew enough. It was magic. Ancient magic from the old world, flowing through her into the book, or through the book into her. Or both. Like the ocean and the rain. Feeding each other. Stay too long and she knew she could fall in and be swept away, lost forever in it.

All around them the light climbed the walls and spread across the ceiling, replacing the world around them with something new. Images formed, like a magic lantern show, casting shadows of other worlds, other times. The isles soared overheard. Not just a few, all of them. Ro flew like a bird, her consciousness soaring through the clouds until she saw the shimmering tree on the Eyrie. It was the centre of all of this, the source and the destination of all the magic which arced through the air and rippled in the earth. She plunged into the rock and saw the cave again. Not as it was when she'd last seen it, but alive with light and magic. The same swirling magic surrounding her now was just a faint reflection.

Five figures cast long shadows around the central stone table. Each one stood in place with an object laid at their feet to represent them. A needle and thread for a Weaver, an axe for a Labourer, a hammer for an Atelier, and a sextant for a Windrider … and in the final place, by the Birdsinger's feet, a golden feather. The objects sank into the stone, transforming into the symbols she knew so well, the symbols of the Guilds. The Birdsinger reached out and the candle flickered to life, a tiny dancing flame. The hourglass turned …

Or at least it started to.

There was a great crash and a roar as the Eyrie lurched to one side. Rock crumbled, crashing down, the isles tearing themselves apart, some crashing down into the ocean, others spiralling off into the sky. The world broke apart, the magic shattered, light burst like a new sun rising over the edge of the world, and the people in the chamber, the people of the old world, those workers of magic who had been trying to stop the islands falling, were gone.

Ro gave a gasp and slumped forward, pulling her hand back from the book as if it had burned her.

Tomas caught her in his arms and cradled her against him. He shushed her, trying to calm her and stop her shaking. But nothing could do that. Not now.

"It killed them," she whispered. "Or … or absorbed them. The people. They were trying to save the old world. It went wrong, Tomas. It went terribly wrong. I think they died. All of them."

But they hadn't died. It was worse than that. She thought of the shimmerwisps in the chamber, the ones that had followed her. How many had there been? She couldn't remember now. Were they all that was left of the magicians of the old world?

Shaking, she tried to stand on her own feet again. Tomas seemed reluctant to release her. He just wanted to protect her, but she knew now that this was so much bigger than her. Or the Guilds. Or even the Unity movement.

Saran's papers caught her eye. His lists and plans, schedules and … suddenly she realised. She could see it all mapped out in front of her. His drawing of the hourglass, the symbols of the Guilds. The word in the old world's language—*Adscendo*—the word that had conjured that little swirl of flame from thin air and summoned the shimmerwisps to attack them. Oh, she understood now.

"Saran's going to try it himself. He might have already tried but he didn't get anywhere. Not without the hourglass."

The earthquakes, the rockfalls, the floods …

What had he said? He had a way to save their people, not everyone perhaps but enough. He had a plan. His special project … He had been learning from the past, from the ancestors, from the old world. It was trial and error but in the end …

"Oh, Saran," she whispered, horrified. "What have you done?"

"Only what I've had to do." His voice made them both turn, startled. He'd entered quietly enough and closed the door behind him. He didn't look in any way alarmed to find them here. He sounded perfectly calm. "I should have known you would want to know far more than is good for you. It's a simple enough thing, Ro. We can't save everyone. But we can save some. Don't you understand? The magicians of the old world reached too far and the magic consumed them. But if we just try to save a select few, a small number, we can start again. Up there, among the clouds. Where magic is always within reach. Once we're up there, anything is possible."

She couldn't hide her dismay, both at seeing him and the words he said.

"The others just get left behind to drown? Saran, listen to yourself. This is not our way."

"Isn't it? Have you looked at the hierarchy recently? The leaders of our Guilds? Half of them don't deserve to be saved. They cast out anyone who disagrees with them. Anyone who questions the status quo. And all the time the Collapse continues, the islands sink. And they do nothing. They let people leave. I think they try to promote it. Culling the population. They have no plan for the future. We're barely surviving as it is. But I can save our civilisation and our people. Some of them at least. Enough to start again."

Some of them. The words echoed through like a taunt. *Enough ...*

"And people like me just get left behind?" Tomas asked, a catch in his voice.

Saran sneered. "People like you? What exactly do people like you do for our society, Piper?"

So he knew.

Tomas didn't look shocked or angry. His face was cold with disgust. "How do you live without cooks, or farmers, without fishermen or builders? How do you maintain your lifestyle without—"

Saran waved his hand dismissively. "There will be people to do such things. We will bring them with us."

Tomas stared, his eyes wide now in disbelief. "Just like that?"

But Ro understood Saran too well. She knew how he thought. And it was horrific. "You'll just take people you need whether they want to go or not? That's slavery, Saran. You can't possibly mean that."

"I'll be *saving* them. Give people a choice and there will be mass panic. Rioting. People fleeing and others trying to join us. We could end up with more than we need, the deadweights, the dregs of society, the Guildless. There are ways to get people to cooperate, to make them compliant. Magic can work wonders. It's better this way. Can't you see that?"

Better this way? Abandoning people to their fate in a sinking world, where the islands crumbled and the oceans rose? Taking the opportunity to save yourself and enslaving others, taking away their free will?

No. She could never be a party to that. Never.

But Saran thought he was doing the right thing. He believed that the ends justified everything else, no matter how terrible.

"You can't do this." Tomas spoke before she could find the words. "Using people like that—"

"Like you do?" Saran sneered. "Using my sister. Inveigling yourself into the lives of those who might be of use to you. Those who have power, or whose star is on the rise. Your masters taught you well. The Unity movement hasn't changed much, has it? A funny kind of unity, if you ask me. More like manipulation." He turned to Ro. "He promised our brother he'd take care of you, did you know that? I told Matias he was a fool to trust them. I said he should just turn them in but oh no, not our brother. He made Tomas promise to look after you. He has a funny way of doing that, I must say. But I suppose pretending to be your friend was the easiest way for a member of Unity to get close to you, and keep access to our family and our Guilds."

"That's not how it was," Tomas muttered at last and his face flushed with sudden guilt. "Ro, please—"

"Did he ask you to marry him yet?" Saran went on relentlessly, not giving Tomas a chance to say any more. "Has he professed his undying love for you now that I've asked you to join the Birdsingers? Or has the romancing not progressed quite that quickly yet?"

Tomas had kissed her. He'd begged her … *begged* her, not to leave him.

Saran flexed his hands like a musician approaching his instrument. Ro heard his knuckles crack and saw the gleam of determination in his eyes. She didn't know what to say, how to argue, because he wasn't wrong. Not exactly. She didn't know what to do.

"I'm so sorry, Tomas, but you and your Unity movement have no place in this new world. You cause only dissent and disaffection and we have no need for that. We have an opportunity to make people safe and content. I can't have anyone interfering with our future. Or with Ro. She belongs with us now and with us is where she will stay. Not slumming it with the scum of the Mire like you. It's what our brother would have really wanted, if his head hadn't been turned. That's what got Matias exiled, isn't it? You."

Ro turned to Tomas. Why wasn't he telling Saran to shut up, that he was wrong? He was just staring ahead, not denying anything. Why wasn't he defending himself? It wasn't like that. He'd explained already. It had never been like that.

Matias had been his friend. The accusation was too much for him. Even Ro knew that. She just couldn't stop it happening.

Tomas lunged forward, his hands going straight for Saran's throat. Papers went up in a flutter of chaos and Ro cried out. But it was too late.

The light that burst from Saran's hands sent Tomas reeling back. He crashed into the shelves like a doll. There was a terrible crack, like an oak tree struck by lightning and then he slumped to the ground.

Saran advanced on him, his hands still spread wide. "Let me demonstrate something for you, Ro. Your first lesson, as it were. Magic is held in everything. And if the magic is removed from the thing—"

Tomas' body arched involuntarily, every tendon tightening like a wire, spasming as a mist filled with glimmering lights was dragged through his skin.

"Stop!" Ro yelled, but she couldn't move. She could only watch in horror. "Saran, please. Stop!"

But he didn't stop. He continued to drag the essence of life from Tomas' body, all the magic that was an innate part of him. The mist grew thicker, brighter, swirling through the air and draining all the colour from his skin. His mouth opened in a silent cry of pain and helplessness.

All around her, shimmerwisps appeared, called forth by the use of magic, rising from the floor, leaking out of the walls.

Saran spread his arms wide, not even attempting to drive them back. They surged forward. Ro gave a cry and shied back instinctively, but they were not bothered by her presence. They swarmed around Tomas. There were too many of them. She couldn't deal with them all.

Tomas cried out, a low moan of agony which stretched out, and his back arched like a bent bow until she thought it might break. Saran leaned in over him and made that same strange gesture again and again. Ro watched in horror as Tomas' skin turned grey, slick in a sheen of sweat. His breath slowed, fading. Light rushed out of his body, bleeding through the air. Saran drew in an uneven breath and his whole body became suffused with that light, glowing from within with vitality and strength, with everything he was stealing. It rippled beneath his skin like sunlit water, beautiful and terrible all at once.

Ro grabbed the first thing that came to hand and hurled it at him.

The book slammed into his face. He staggered back, as if dazed, the impact and the magic he had stolen making him reel like a drunk. His control of the spell slipped and two of the shimmerwisps darted out, straight through the closed door, into the tower stairway beyond.

The sound of bells filled the air. The remaining shimmerwisps evaporated like morning mist.

"What have you done?" Saran snarled and then let out a string of curses. "The wards are triggered. The shimmerwisp … Damn it, Ro.

Everyone will come running." He flung open the door and made for the stairs in pursuit of the escaped shimmerwisps.

Tomas slumped down, so still … Too still.

Ro dropped to his side, helpless. Something hollow and empty had torn itself open inside her.

Tomas still didn't move. His eyes were closed and he didn't seem to be breathing. Ro pushed on his chest, trying to shake him into life. But he didn't so much as flinch. He was cold. Far too cold.

No. This couldn't be happening. She wouldn't let it happen. Not to him, not to Tomas.

She shoved him harder, grabbing his shoulders and shaking him, but he wouldn't wake up. His chest didn't move.

"No, please no …" She tried to pull him into her arms, to shake him awake, but she was seized from behind. She hadn't heard anyone arrive, but now Windguards were here and they'd hauled her to her feet, even as she tried to just drop down again. She needed to be with Tomas. Couldn't they see that? She needed to wake him up. She could do it. She just needed a moment. She only had to work out how to do it. She had magic, or so Saran said. It had to be good for something.

"No," she sobbed. "Please … Tomas … please …"

No one was listening to her.

"Secure her," Saran snarled, now back in the room. She no longer recognised him. He wasn't her brother, not anymore. Her brother would never do such a thing. "This must be punished accordingly."

Ro's arms were twisted up behind her back and held there. Something snapped tightly around her wrists. The pain was a shadow of what raged inside her.

And Tomas still didn't move. Perhaps he'd never move again.

She glanced to Saran, desperate for any help, even his.

But he just wiped the blood from his mouth, breathing hard, and glared at her as if this was all her fault. Perhaps it was. She turned to look at Tomas' still, grey face and a sob broke out of her, a wild snarl of anguish. She would have doubled over, fallen to the ground if the guards were not still holding her. She caught a glimpse of Grayden pushing his way through to the room, trying to take control of the situation like a good commander. Maybe Ameris was behind him. A crowd had gathered around the door, too many people, all of them shocked, appalled and far too curious. All come to see what had happened.

But that didn't matter. None of it mattered.

"Lock her up," Saran was saying, his voice twisted with anger and thwarted ambition. This wasn't what he wanted. But he was making the most of the situation. "She brought those cursed things in here to attack us all. It will not go unpunished."

"Wait," Grayden cut in. "She's a Windrider. I'll take her back to our Guild and we'll deal with her. Justice demands it. It's our way."

"Look at her," Saran snarled, but Grayden didn't flinch. He was as self-assured as ever and more than Saran's equal in the hierarchy. "Look at him." Saran flung his arm towards Tomas' still form and Ro flinched, fearing he would use magic again. Even in front of so many people. She would put nothing past him given what she had just seen him do. "There is magic at work here and she has been strange with it since she returned from this so-called adventure of hers. The Birdsingers will get to the bottom of this and no one else. Which reminds me …"

He walked up to her and grabbed the small purse that hung at her waist. She hadn't dared leave it behind. She couldn't risk something happening to it, or it endangering the Ateliers, or the Weavers … or Tomas.

Triumphantly, Saran pulled the hourglass out and hurled the rest of the purse's contents aside, her coins and other belongings meaningless to him.

Meaningless to her now as well. All of it, even the hourglass.

Tomas—*her* Tomas—was gone.

CHAPTER 19

Ameris tried to push her way to Ro's side, but Grayden's hand on her wrist stopped her, his grip like iron. She was too bewildered by all that was happening to resist.

This couldn't be happening. It simply couldn't.

Grayden somehow maintained that casual stance, the perfect Windrider. The perfect soldier.

Tomas didn't move. Ro was dragged away. And Ameris just stood there, in shock, rooted to the spot beside Grayden.

"What do we do?" she whispered.

"Nothing." He didn't sound like himself, his voice so clinical. "There's nothing we can do. Not right now."

They watched as Tomas' limp body was lifted onto a stretcher and a sheet thrown over him. Ameris let out a wild sob and pulled away again. This time Grayden let her go. She turned to run for the stairs but almost slammed straight into Saran who stood in the hallway, watching her with those cold eyes.

How had she ever thought he could be trusted?

"It's a shame," he said, as if he were merely talking about a piece of broken pottery. "But those who meddle in things they should stay away from will come to such an end. He was just a Labourer after all. Aping his betters. He shouldn't even have been here."

Neither should she, Ameris thought. She should be back in her workshop, making things and letting the Ateliers decide what use they should be put to. Her pride had brought her here and look what it had cost. She bit down on the inside of her lip until she tasted blood. She wouldn't show any emotion to him. But she feared Saran was not fooled.

He reached out and pressed his hand to her face. It was all she could do not to flinch from his icy cold touch.

"Your mind really is a wonder, Ameris. You know that, don't you? We would never allow that to be wasted. Our new commander of the Windriders understands, don't you, Grayden?" He looked up past her, his eyes taking on that distant gaze Ro sometimes got when she had to deal with someone she loathed. Ameris alone saw the way his hand rested on the hilt of his sword.

Who wore a sword to a celebration anyway? It was meant to be ceremonial, but she knew it wasn't.

"What are you going to do with Windrider Swift?" Grayden asked.

A chill smile flickered over Saran's lips. "Not a Windrider anymore. She was offered a place here, among the Birdsingers, which I'm pleased to say she accepted. So she is one of ours to deal with as we see fit—"

"She didn't accept," Ameris interrupted. The two men looked at her as if she'd grown another head. Perhaps they'd already forgotten she was there. "She never accepted your offer."

"She came here tonight, didn't she? At my invitation. That's as good as an acceptance. Besides, she even dressed like one of us."

"So did I." She hated every scrap of material she was wearing but that didn't change the fact she was wearing a gown just as Ro was. The bird elements in the mask were a traditional part of the Carnival, but it didn't mean anything.

Saran shook his head as if dealing with a recalcitrant child. "As if your mother would ever let you leave the Ateliers. Your place is assured, Ameris. You just need to keep doing what you've always done and stay out of trouble. Be the pride of your Guild. That is all anyone wants of you."

And just like that she was dismissed.

He turned to leave, but Ameris called after him. She couldn't help herself. "You took the hourglass. It isn't yours."

Saran barely glanced back, but she saw his shoulders stiffen in anger. He had the hourglass. And yet he didn't want anyone else knowing that. Why?

Once again Grayden seemed able to move when Ameris could not. Without saying a word, he hooked her arm with his and swept down the stairs, back into the dome itself. The celebration was well and truly over. Everyone was either being ushered outside, or standing in awkward groups trying to find out what had happened, waiting their turn to be shown out. The place didn't look magical now. The birds were huddled miserably in the trees, flocking together in alarm. There was debris underfoot, abandoned glasses and discarded food. It was a mess. The decorations hung limp and drab overhead.

A few people tried to intercept them—well, to intercept Grayden, Ameris thought bitterly—but he steered her by them with a gracious nod and a few words.

Nothing important. Nothing to worry about. Looking into it. Everything's in hand.

Finally, when they were alone, he let her go and turned away, his arms folding behind him, into the small of his back, all formality and rigid control. He'd never looked more like a Windrider and it set every nerve still able to feel anything on edge.

"I don't know what the three of you were up to or what they were after in there, but you had nothing to do with it. You were with me. Everyone saw us. You had nothing to do with it. Do you understand?"

It wasn't actually a question. It was a command. Ameris knew that much.

"Ro would never have killed Tomas, Grayden. You can't hate her so much as to think—"

"I don't hate her," he snapped. "I never hated her. But she got involved in something dangerous in the extreme, just like her brother. I was trying to help her, but she never listens. And I'm trying to help you now so you don't make the same mistake. The Piper was always trouble. I should have moved on him seasons ago."

"But Tomas—"

"No one can do anything for Tomas now. I'm trying to help you."

"I don't need your help."

"Oh, I think you do." His voice was a growl. "I don't know what you have got yourselves involved in, but it's cost Tomas his life and Ro her freedom. Just shut up and listen to me for once."

Finally her temper snapped. "Or what? You'll turn me in too? You'll lock me up?"

"If I have to. I should have turned in Ro long before my mother and her cronies drove her out of our Guildhouse. I should have known something would happen like this. And that she'd drag you into it. She's always been so—" He broke off with a curse and turned away.

And suddenly Ameris understood. He didn't hate Ro at all. He never had. Just as he said. Grayden didn't lie. He didn't need to.

"What are we going to do?" she said very quietly, too afraid to ask any of the other questions rushing to the front of her mind.

"You are going to go home to your Guild and stay out of trouble. I'll do what I can, which won't be much. Not if the Birdsingers have claimed jurisdiction over Ro. This offer and her blood relationship to Saran … It's his word against hers. As Commander, I may still have a chance if I go above his head and appeal to the Master Birdsinger or the Elders." Abruptly, he softened his voice. "Please, Ameris, let me try. I owe her that at least. I'll come and see you as soon as I … if I can find out anything. But keep your head down. Do you understand?"

There wasn't anything else she could do. Even if she could, he wasn't going to let her and she didn't seem able to convince him otherwise. He thought she was helpless, or hopeless.

"All right," she replied and pulled the mask of dutiful daughter back over her face. They were at a masquerade after all.

But once she was free of Grayden, she was going to do something about this. She didn't know what yet. But something. She had to.

She was not going to stand by anymore.

CHAPTER 20

Deep beneath the Aviary, below the servants' quarters and the cellars, far underground where there was no natural light, the Ancients had hollowed out chambers from the stone itself. In the centre there was a spring, the water bubbling up in a constant stream. It fed the Aviary, its irrigation, its plumbing and by extension most of Arcadiana. By the light of a flickering lamp set beside it, from her alcove off the main chamber, Ro could see the scrape marks of their tools in the rockface, like little bites in the stone. Between her and the water, the metal bars cut off any hope of escape. They might be old, but they were still too strong for her to break. The alcove in which she had been unceremoniously deposited didn't have light, or water, just bars. There was barely room for her to sit down.

Whatever this had been created for, there was no doubting what it was now. A cell. A prison.

Her prison.

She didn't think she was ever getting out of here. She didn't really care.

How could she care about anything anymore?

Something in her was broken, aching. Cold ate into her bones and into what was left of her heart.

Occasionally she heard sounds, the scrap of a boot on stone, a soft skittering, perhaps even a groan. She wasn't even sure whether any of that was real or if she was imagining it. The sound of the water was the only constant.

The air was stale and a chill dampness permeated everything, even the rocks themselves. They were cold and wet to the touch. Ro shivered, wrapped her arms around her knees. She couldn't make herself believe what had happened. Not to Tomas.

But she knew what she had seen, what she had felt. She kept running it over and over in her mind, torturing herself with the knowledge that it had been real. That he was gone.

But she didn't want it to be true.

Her eyes ached. There were no more tears left in her. At least she thought there couldn't be, until she remembered the way he'd smile, or tell her off, or frown and they would start again, until her eyes were red and raw and everything ached. Even breathing felt like knives stabbing into her chest. There was nothing but pain.

Ro didn't know how long she had been there. The lantern light dimmed eventually and she thought they'd just forgotten about her. It would be better that way. Leave her down here, pretend she had never existed. How many other people had been abandoned down here, never to be seen again?

What really happened to people who crossed the Birdsingers?

That was the question. Exile? Who knew for sure? They were never seen again. They were gone. They vanished.

Like this.

Like Tomas.

There had been so many. So many lost and missing people. So many who had been in her life, and now were gone. Like Matias. Like her parents.

At least she knew what had happened to her parents. She'd stood by while they were buried. Alone. Saran wasn't there. And Matias … he'd just vanished.

Where was he? As the Piper, Tomas might have known, but Tomas was gone too.

She closed her eyes again, rested her cheek on her knee. The material was soft and should have been a comfort, but all it did was mock her.

A sweet trill of birdsong brought her head up sharply. It was so out of place.

The wren perched on one of the metal cross bars, so small, so fragile.

"You can't be here," she whispered.

The wren just looked at her and cocked its head to one side. Its eyes, like tiny pieces of jet, glittered. It sang again. She had never heard a sound so beautiful in her life.

"Can you … can you get help? The Golden Aurics or … or Parsa and Nazir … or …" Her voice trailed off.

Yes, Ro thought bitterly, *tell Parsa and Nazir how you got their adopted son killed. That would be quite the moment.*

She didn't even know how it had found her down here. It didn't know what she was saying. It wasn't even one of the noble birds. It was just a wren.

The king of the birds, that was what Saran had said about it, the story he'd used to lure her in. No one believed it. That was a tale for children. But she'd felt a connection to this tiny creature from the first moment she'd seen it. She'd held it in her hand and felt its life return. Or at least that was how it had felt.

She hadn't been able to do the same for Tomas.

"Thank you," she said. "Thank you for being here. But you can't help, can you? It's okay. Really. It doesn't matter. Not anymore. It's too late."

She dropped her head down and the bird began to sing again. Almost like a tune. But wrens didn't sing tunes. Not actual melodies. She closed her eyes, convinced that she was losing her mind.

The wren was singing a melody and it was one she knew, one she had learned as a child. One Tomas used to sing and she'd sang with him, in their unguarded moments, when they were alone.

It was impossible. Grief had addled her mind, that was it. That had to be it.

All the same, she listened and wished with all her heart it was real. The wren sang Tomas' song.

Then, without any warning at all, the little bird took flight again, disappearing up the long tunnel, leaving her all on her own.

She desperately wished it would come back. She had never felt so alone, or so afraid.

She was lost.

The light at the far end of the corridor seemed to grow brighter, the single flickering lantern augmented by another, brighter and more constant.

Saran appeared with three of his comrades, including the woman who had been so snide at the ball, now back in their everyday robes instead of their finery. Kira was even more pinch-faced without her mask, sneering down at Ro.

Perhaps if she ignored them they would go away and leave her to die down here in peace. There was always that last hope.

But even that failed her.

Saran unlocked the cell door.

"Give me a moment with my sister," he told the others, his tone one of unequivocal command, and they backed off to the other side of the chamber. Not far, but far enough. "Ro?" he whispered. He almost sounded like himself again. He crouched down and put his light on the ground between them. "Ro, please, talk to me."

"What is there to say?" She didn't know how she managed to grind out the words.

Saran gave the gentlest of smiles. "I'm trying to help you. Do you know what the Windriders would have done with you? Grayden? He's their commander now. He would have had to make an example of you."

An example. The word turned her stomach. "Like you did of Tomas?"

For a moment he looked as if she'd slapped him in the face. Didn't he realise what he'd done? Didn't he know? For a moment she thought he might deny it, but he didn't.

She watched him school his face to stillness and compassion. "I'm sorry. I didn't mean to hurt him. He attacked me and I didn't think. It was an instinctive reaction. You saw him attack me, didn't you?"

She met his gaze then, her eyes blazing. Each word was a knife to her heart. What did it matter who attacked who? "You killed him."

Saran winced, his expression stricken. "And I can never make amends for that. But I have to try. I meant it about saving our people. I know how, but I need your magic. I need your strength."

He reached out to brush the side of her face with his palm and she jerked back so violently she hit her head against the wall behind her. "I'm not helping you to do anything."

He gave a single, bitter laugh and she sensed the regret. He hadn't lied. Tomas had flung himself at Saran. They had been arguing, sure, but Tomas had attacked first. And for a moment, she wondered … could it have been an accident? Just a terrible accident?

Her brother watched her face closely and then reached out again to touch her cheek. Warmth rippled from his fingertips, like the brush of sunlight in the darkness. "It's what he would have wanted, you know? To save our people. It's all he ever wanted really, though he chose another path. The Unity movement can be difficult for everyone, but I think their hearts are in the right place. I knew Tomas too, remember? He wanted to save everyone, and so do I. But I can't do it alone. Ro, please …"

She closed her eyes, wishing she could just shut out the sound of his voice. Because he wasn't wrong. Tomas wanted to save everyone on Arcadiana and beyond, in all aspects of life. It was all he had worked for, for as long as she had known him. Even when she didn't fully know what he had done, or his involvement with the Unity movement. He would want her to do whatever she could for their people.

Even if it meant working with the man who had killed him.

She knew what Tomas would say. If there was even a chance, even the smallest chance …

"When we were little," Saran went on, "we used to follow the birds outside, do you remember? Up onto the highest crags of Mount Nest, just you and me. And when we were found, I always said it was me, that I'd led you. But that wasn't true, was it?"

She drew in a shuddering breath and fought back tears again. He'd always taken the blame. She had been the one in the lead.

"I know you can do this, Ro. If you lend me your power, I can perform the ritual to raise the Aviary, and up there, where the air is rich with untapped magic, I'll do whatever I can to bring him back."

Her eyes snapped open and she stared at him in surprise. Bring him back? It wasn't possible …

But magic could do anything. And no one knew more about the magic of the old world than her brother. The stories said the people there never got sick, never died. She knew herself that the air had healing and rejuvenating properties. Could he really bring Tomas back?

No, it was a trick. It had to be.

But her treacherous heart ached for it to be true. "Can you?"

He smiled fondly. "There's a spell. There's always a spell. A fragment of his life must still be there; he didn't become a shimmerwisp and we have his body. They worked such wonders up there, our ancestors, and I have the records. But we have to get there first." He held out his hand. "I honestly can't do it without you, Ro. The others will help. They're the strongest amongst us. But they're pale shadows next to you. The five of us, together, though … anything is possible."

She took his hand, only half believing him, but desperately needing him to be telling the truth. In doing so they would be saving other lives, countless lives, saving Arcadiana. If she was as strong as he thought, they could raise the whole island, surely.

And if they did that …

"I have a change of clothes for you," he said. "Something more comfortable."

To be honest, it was a relief to strip out of the heavy green and gold gown which reminded her too keenly of her last hours with Tomas.

While Saran stood with his back to her, she pulled on the loose white dress, which was entirely plain and unadorned. She tugged the various pins from her hair and let it tumble down her back. She combed through the tendrils with her own fingers, a valiant effort, but she knew that, after so long in this cell, she must look a state. She'd lost the mask somewhere, in the tower room, she supposed. She'd taken it off before … before …

She couldn't think about that. The pain that threatened to raise its ugly head again would destroy her. She had to stay calm, pull herself together. Saran's regret seemed genuine. In the heat of the moment, fighting with Tomas, of course he had reached out for the one defence always at his disposal.

The image of his face as he did it flashed up in her mind again and something inside went very cold. No, it couldn't have been an accident. He'd known what he was doing.

The warmth of his touch still lingered on her face and she stood there, confused.

Had he done something to her?

"Ready?" he asked, the gentle tones at odds with what she recalled. He took her hand.

That same warm feeling washed through her. The tingling sensation of magic and belonging comforted her. He was her brother, after all, her blood, her only family. The Birdsingers weren't the enemy. They had to keep a firm control of magic, and here she was running around, causing chaos with it. She belonged with them, she finally realised. They weren't cruel. She thought of Elder Nightingale, his kindness, his blessings.

She could be like that. Saran could be like that. He was like that. Everyone said so. He only wanted what was best. She could help him to be better.

But still, a small voice inside her tried to cry out a warning, that something was wrong. A voice she could barely hear.

"There now," he murmured, as if he was lulling a child to sleep. Light glowed at his fingertips where they touched her arm. The warmth permeated her skin again. That light, that sign of magic at work, ought to warn her. It should make her fight, but she seemed to have lost all ability to argue with him. She needed to help him. That was all that mattered. Together they would save everyone. "There we are. Come on, Ro. We're going to save the Aviary."

No, they were going to save *Arcadiana*. That was the plan. She hesitated, pulling back, but he didn't let her go.

"Are you sure it's working?" Kira asked, peering into Ro's face as if inspecting livestock.

"Yes. She'll cooperate, but the enchantment needs to be maintained. Don't distract her. Take your places." He released Ro, but that same sense of haziness still muffled her body. It was as if she was trapped in a dream. Or a nightmare. "You stand beside me, Ro. Don't worry. It won't take long."

They stood around the spring. It flowed from a perfect round table almost like the one in the Eyrie, Ro realised, with the water still bubbling up in the middle and spilling across the surface and down the sides to pool in the catchment area underneath. One of the men produced a slim white candle in a brass candlestick, which he placed on the stone. Saran took the hourglass out and put it beside the candle. The sand inside it, glimmering with light, still flowed the wrong way.

He lifted his hand over the candle and nodded to the others who dutifully reached out their hands. Ro felt Kira take her right hand while the left hung limply at her side, waiting for Saran.

Something was wrong. She couldn't seem to make her brain figure it out, or force her body to move. Everything was slow and difficult, as if she was moving through treacle. The light from the hourglass danced on the water.

"*Adscendo,*" her brother whispered. The word echoed around the chamber, bouncing off the walls, rippling through the water, and reverberating inside her chest.

Under his outstretched hand, a lick of flame appeared in the air, caressing the wick of the candle. For a moment it seemed as if that would be all, that it would vanish as the one she had inadvertently conjured, but then the wick caught and the candle blossomed to light.

Saran smiled encouragement at the others and took her free hand in his, holding her tightly. The others began to smile as well, but Ro couldn't. Something was wrong. This was terribly wrong. They shouldn't be in the Aviary. They should be up in the High Eyrie. This ritual had no place here. There wasn't enough magic. There would never be enough here. Unless they look it from the lives all around them.

As she thought that, she felt the magic rise. It flooded through her. Kira gave a gasp of surprise. Someone else moaned in pleasure as it rushed through veins and swirled inside their bodies. Rising like the water was rising, burning like the candle was burning, rushing onwards like the sand in the hourglass.

"Ready, Ro?" Saran said. "We need the power in you. We need you to share it with us. Now."

Light swelled between them, golden and bright, sparkling with swirling particles. Ro tried to suck in a breath, but suddenly her lungs were on fire. A thousand tiny hooks dragged along the insides of her veins. Saran and Kira's grip on her hands tightened to bone crushing vices. They weren't sharing; they were taking, plundering.

And then she did scream. She couldn't help it. She couldn't have stopped the noise if she tried. It was wrenched out of her along with her lifeforce, along with all the magic of the Eyrie and the Golden Auric's touch. Her voice echoed off the corridor's stone walls and ceilings, bounced off the floor to come back to her, mocking her as she tried to grab another frantic lungful of air.

It hurt. It was beyond pain. It was agony and abuse, a theft so deep and personal that she knew she would never recover from it. And it didn't stop. The pain went on and on until burning tears carved lines in her skin and she hung between the Birdsingers, limp and pathetic. It seemed to last forever.

Saran released her and stepped back, holding his hands up to his face, marvelling at the golden light suffusing his skin. Shimmering particles that resembled a shimmerwisp danced, but as he closed his fist they were sucked into his flesh. He drew in a shuddering breath. Then he reached out and turned over the hourglass, staring at it with all the intensity of a fanatic.

Nothing happened. There was no change. Nothing.

He muttered a curse and glared at the others, who just stared back uncomprehending. "We need more," he said and grabbed Ro's hand again.

Pain upon pain coursed through her, like barbed wire dragging through her veins, as all the light in her world was drawn out, stolen and ripped away. The misery she felt when Tomas died welled up to swallow her whole again. She was broken and empty, lost. There was nothing left.

When he released her again, she fell to her knees, her eyes still fixed on the hourglass which was steadily flowing in the same direction.

"Now," he snarled at the others. "The doors to the Guild are locked. No one gets in or out. If we don't lift this citadel now, we may not get the chance again."

Not the city. He wasn't even going to try to save the city. Not anymore. Just the Aviary, just his own people …

He'd lied. Lied about his intentions. About Tomas. About everything. She was such a fool, and there was nothing she could do about it now.

The Birdsingers each stepped closer and took a place around the spring, their hands flat on the wet stone.

The ground shook as they used all the remaining magic leeched from her. Saran reached out and turned the hourglass.

This was wrong. Ro knew it. They were doing it wrong. There might be five of them but, apart from her, they were all from the same Guild, and she was hardly a part of this anyway. She was just a vessel full of power to them, to be used and cast aside. The magicians of the old world had come to the ritual with reverence, ready to sacrifice themselves for the sake of all. Saran and his friends had brought nothing except their ambition and their cruelty. It wasn't going to work.

The walls and floor shook again, and this time a noise like thunder joined it. The world lurched to one side and dust fell from the ceiling as a massive crack snaked across it. The water bubbled up in a rush and swept the candle away. The flame was snuffed out.

The only light was from the distant lantern and the swirling, ungrounded magic coursing through them.

Ro didn't know which one of them screamed first. Not Saran. He was in control, drawing on their lives now, just as he had with her, still trying to anchor his spell and work one of the most dangerous rituals of the old world.

Ro could sense the power slipping from his control.

One of the men dropped. He hit the ground, his eyes wide, and then he simply dissolved into specks of light. The shimmerwisp which took his place swirled like a tiny whirlwind for just a moment and then collapsed into the floor.

Beneath them the stone cracked, fissures running like veins through it. The sound was deafening.

Kira went next, her scream higher and stretched out as she broke apart into a sparkling mist which whirled up into the shattered roof.

Saran grabbed the hourglass, cursing. The ritual came to a stuttering halt, but something in the air seemed to stabilise. The earthquake beneath them faded to the odd rumble. The water from the spring continued to flow from the rock.

"What happened?" the remaining man asked. "What … What went wrong? We had the power. I felt it."

"Just shut up and let me think. Lock her up again. Say nothing of this. We can use her again when we're ready."

"If she'll comply."

"She's easily swayed and her reserves of magic quickly restore themselves. The spell works and it's a small effort for such a result."

But his remaining companion didn't move. "What have we done, Saran? The others—"

Ignoring the question, Saran dragged Ro to the cell himself, ignoring her feeble struggles, and heaved her back in, closing the door with a clang. She fell heavily on the ground and lay there, panting for breath.

"They gave themselves up for the greater good," Saran replied, finally getting some kind of mastery over himself and the situation. Taking command. There was no kindness in him now. Only determination.

Ro wanted to scream in frustration at her gullibility, but she didn't have the strength. "They are heroes and we will be too. I'll work it out. I'll get it right. I have to or we are all lost; do you understand?"

They left, still arguing, taking the light with them.

Ro lay on the floor of the cell, water reaching her from the rushing stream. She couldn't even lift her head, let alone the rest of her body. He said her magic would restore itself. That meant he'd try again. And he'd keep doing it until—

A voice drifted down the passageway, almost lost in the sound of water, in the creaks and groans of the stone around her. Someone singing. It almost sounded like Tomas. She was hallucinating. Dreaming perhaps.

Except she would know Tomas' voice anywhere.

No, she wasn't hallucinating; she was dying and he was waiting for her on the other side of the veil. It took all the strength she had left in her to join in, to raise her own fragile, broken voice in something that might once have been harmony. Just for a moment or two, before the darkness took her.

CHAPTER 21

Peace surrounded Tomas. Peace, warmth and faintly diffused light. A distant song, familiar and beloved. Tomas thought at first that the ancestors had actually accepted him into the afterlife and he had stepped through the veil without so much as a challenge. In one way it was a blessed relief. In others, a wild surprise.

He lay as if sleeping. It wasn't a voice, he realised, but bird-song. Just birdsong. Or maybe flutes. It changed, flowing from one sound to the other, human voice, birdsong, musical instruments, and back. And the tune … he knew that tune. He and Ro, sitting in the sunshine, looking over the valley, singing. Humming really. The two of them in harmony.

The tune haunted him now, encircling him and calling him to consciousness, or whatever passed for consciousness here. It sounded like the music that the Birdsingers played on high occasions, their many wooden flutes of different registers complementing each other, so beautiful that the song thrushes and nightingales would join in. It had always sounded magical.

But now, he recalled he had seen real magic. He had felt it torn from his body and his soul. It hadn't been beautiful and wonderful. It had been pain and horror.

What had Saran done?

The tune faded. The soft ruffling of wings surrounded him and something gave a deep sigh, both comforting and relaxing. The urge to just sink down into the peace again, to give up and let himself go was powerful.

Then he thought of Ro, of her face as he fell, the horror and terror before the darkness had taken him. The pain. Dear ancestors, there had been such pain.

He couldn't leave her there alone, at the mercy of the Birdsingers. Of Saran.

You would go back? a voice asked. A voice in the back of his mind. It spoke to him directly, without the need for sound. It was just there, inside him. But not part of him. *For her?*

He was safe here; he knew that instinctively. There would be no more need to struggle, or work, or try to better his world. There would be no more pain or suffering. No more threat. There was only peace.

You're not so sure. Part of you wishes to stay.

"Perhaps a bit, but I have to go back to her." His own voice sounded so very small compared to the other. It was all-encompassing, eternal and everywhere, all at once. But when he thought of Ro in danger, the ferocity of his resolve surprised even him.

Something moved around him, lifted. Feathers, he realised. Huge, beautiful feathers. He could see light filtering through them.

It was like standing in a room made of stained glass. The feathers were every colour imaginable, layer upon layer of hues, and as if they were the sun rising, they gradually took the shape of a great Wing. It had been folded around him, sheltering him. Keeping him safe.

While he could see the Wing clearly, every quill of every feather, he had no sense of his own body. He was just there. He felt so small and insignificant in that moment that he shied back. The head, when it appeared before him, was a bird, huge, beautiful and graceful, her eyes golden, her feathers a rainbow, except where they were metal. Traces of gold and copper, of clockwork, of shining wires ran through her body, a blend of living creature and machine, or a living machine, or a living thing which had taken on aspects of the mechanical. It made no logical sense. But she was not a creature of logic and reality. She transcended that. She was not something that had been made by another. She was a blend of all things, a gleaming abundance of life, joy and invention. Of wonder.

"Amare?" he whispered, hardly daring to name her.

The ripple of laughter shook the air around him, shook its way through him, and made him feel the delight that radiated from her. Love. Pure love. For him, for his world where her children lived, for everything.

I can take you back. I fly between worlds, between realities. And you would weigh nothing at all to me. Though there may be just a glimmer of you left, it is enough. But are you sure, Tomas Harper? You are safe here, at peace. Are you really sure?

For Ro? Of course he was sure.

And not just for Ro. The Birdsingers were planning to raise the Aviary and leave everyone else in Arcadiana to die. The islands would fall beneath the ocean. Countless people would die. He couldn't let that happen. He just couldn't.

There was a plan. Parsa had a plan. He always did and Tomas knew him well enough to trust in that. He knew some of the details but by no means everything. No one knew everything except the Weaver himself.

"I am," he said, his voice suddenly loud and certain. It scraped along the inside of his throat, like old wire, forcing him to move, to live, to breathe once again.

¤

He gasped and sat up sharply, as if jerking out of a falling dream. The wren on his chest took off, hopping into the air, and landed again on his shoulder and then on his leg. Then it came back to his chest and sang.

He knew that tune; it was the one he used to sing with Ro. The song he'd heard with Amare. He stared at the tiny bird, unable to make out what was happening.

Everything hurt. His body, his mind, his spirit. Everything.

He wasn't dead then. That was something of a surprise, even more so than the prospect of a blissful afterlife.

The wren began its melody again. Not its usual song but the tune he knew and loved. The one he and Ro had sung together the day she'd saved the wren. Did it remember? Had it learned their song? No, that was impossible. Wrens didn't do that.

From somewhere far away he thought he heard another voice, an answering voice, singing the same melody. Just for a moment.

"Ro?" he said, his first word since waking. He had to find her. She was in terrible danger.

He struggled upright, pulling off the sheet that was still covering the rest of his body. The room was dark and cold. So cold. The type of place you moved dead bodies to store them before—

Don't think about that, he warned himself. He couldn't deal with that at the moment. He needed to move. He needed to do something.

A great crash sounded from outside and the walls shook. The ground bucked beneath him. That brought him to his feet faster than any encouragement he could give his stiff and sore body. He was still wearing the ridiculous outfit from the ball. He pulled off the jacket and tossed it aside. It would just get in the way. The shirt was loose, at least. It would do. He could move in that.

But where to go? Where would they be keeping Ro?

They had to be keeping her somewhere. Saran wouldn't just let her run off again, not after last night.

At lease he hoped yesterday was still just last night.

The cells wouldn't be that far from a morgue, would they? Deep underground, beneath the Aviary, in the cold and the dark. He ought to be able to find her. He'd scouted the underlayers of the Aviary enough times for Parsa and Nazir as a child. And he wasn't the only one. There would still be people here who would help him. He just had to find them.

He needed to get word to Parsa and Nazir. If they had been told he was dead ... well, it wouldn't do, that was all. They were the only parents he had ever known.

One thing at a time, he told himself. *Find help. Find Ro. Then the rest.*

The ground rocked beneath him again. This couldn't be good. He was used to earthquakes. Everyone was. But this felt bigger and more destructive than anything he'd ever felt before.

The door wasn't locked. Why lock a door for a dead man? He pushed it open to reveal a narrow corridor. The sound of footsteps made him duck back inside. They slowed and Tomas took an uncertain glance around the morgue. There was nowhere to hide. He supposed he could climb back onto the slab and pull the sheet back over himself but the thought of it sent a chill of alarm through him that he didn't really want to contemplate right now.

He flattened himself against the wall behind the door, wreathed in shadows, and held his breath.

The door opened slowly, sending a line of light across the morgue and a small figure entered, staring in horror at the fallen sheet and the empty slab. He turned around to flee, revealing his face. Tomas recognised him at once.

"Erik?"

The boy in Nazir's employ, the one who'd followed Tomas that day to Harbour House and almost made it all the way without being spotted. He took one look at Tomas' face and opened his mouth to scream.

But Tomas slammed the door shut before he could, plunging them both into darkness, making the scream die in the boy's throat. He heard a scuffle of movement, a crash and a curse.

"It's okay. It's just me. I promise. Nothing else. I'm not dead."

"You were dead. Everyone said you were dead. I came to check." He still sounded terrified, but at least he wasn't screaming. "There's a lantern, over there."

Tomas had no idea where he was pointing. The light from outside the room had stolen all his sight now he was back in darkness.

"Where?"

He heard the boy move, saw him like a little shadow crossing the room where the thin gap beneath the door still illuminated the room ever so slightly. The lantern glowed softly at first, then it grew bright and warm.

They stared at each other.

"See?" Tomas said at last. "Just me."

Erik reached out one bony finger and poked him hard in the middle of his chest. "How did you do it?"

"Too long to explain." Not to mention he didn't really know himself. Claiming that Amare had sent him back would never be believed, not even by this child. "What are you doing here?"

"I work here. Nazir said to keep an eye on things. I was doing that when I heard that girl killed you so I—"

"Wait, what girl? Ro?"

"The one who was a Windrider and came to be a Birdsinger."

"Where is she?"

"You can't go down there. We've got to get out of the Aviary. There's a tunnel down in the other cellars, leads to the harbour."

The world around them shook again, almost throwing them off their feet this time.

"What sort of tunnel?" He'd never heard tell of such a thing, but Erik had clearly made it his mission to work out the whole place for Nazir, more so than Tomas ever had. He'd underestimated how much the boy was willing to do for their cause.

"Down at the bottom, right down, under the cells even. I thought I might get people out that way but—"

"Wait, get people out?"

"They've locked us all in, Birdsingers, Windguards, even the servants. Keep saying the Collapse is coming, but they're going to save those of us who stay in the Aviary. But I've got friends out there. And there's people here with family outside."

"Slow down," Tomas told him. "What are they saying? Who's saying this?"

"I told you. The Birdsingers. Not all of them. The Elders don't have a clue. It's that younger group. Birdsinger Swift and his friends.

They keep saying to keep calm and he's going to save us. He just needs to do the ritual again and—"

Ancestors, he'd tried it. Here. He'd tried to raise the Aviary and this earthquake was the result.

"Where's Ro? Show me."

"But she—" They'd all been told she was a killer. His killer.

"They're lying. They're lying about all of it. Saran tried to kill me, not Ro. He's stealing magic from people."

The boy's eyes grew wide. "The volunteers! He asked for volunteers to help him, just now, from the servants."

This was bad. Worse than bad.

"We've got to get word to Nazir," he said. "You need to get out of here and get help. I need to find Ro and stop Saran."

The boy nodded firmly and made for the door, Tomas following him. Together, they moved like ghosts through the corridors as they shook and rained dust down on them. Several times they passed people who were too panicked to notice them, too busy gathering belongings and trying to flee. In spite of Saran's assurances that they would be saved, people were still running. Tomas could only imagine what would greet them when they reached the locked gates and the guards. Windguards had been stationed here for the duration of the Carnival to keep order, and to control entry to the Aviary. He didn't know how many or where their orders came from.

They went up another level and across a courtyard where someone was trying to rally people together and failing miserably. Panic was palpable in the air. An outbuilding down on the east side was little more than a pile of rubble now, a huge boulder in the centre of the devastation.

The next tremor was even stronger and, from outside the gates, they could hear a crowd gathering, people banging against the wood.

But they wouldn't open. Not now. Tomas recognised the locking mechanism which rose the full height of the guards, the Ateliers' finest work, newly installed. No one was getting through that. Saran had planned this well. He might not have got all the people he wanted from the ball, but he had his servants, the ones who would end up being no more than slaves.

There are ways to get people to cooperate, he had said, *to make them compliant. Magic can work wonders.*

Wonders, and horrors. Tomas knew that now.

Rocks rained down from above causing the crowd to scatter. One smashed through the dome, sending glass everywhere.

"Rockfall!" someone shouted the alarm from overhead. "Take cover!"

Too bloody late.

"This way," Erik called and pulled him through another narrow door.

They were at the base of the great tower now, and fractures were cutting through the stones around them. It could come down at any moment, Tomas realised. He'd been around enough quarries and stonemasons to recognise the danger signs. He didn't argue with the boy though, just picked up his pace as they fled down into the dark.

Just when he thought they couldn't go any lower, the boy stopped at a hallway leading off into darkness. Water sloshed around their feet. Somewhere, the foundations were flooding.

"The cells are down there," Erik said, handing him the lantern. "But it's a maze of tunnels. I'll show you."

Tomas shook his head. "Go," he said. Time was of the essence. "If you can make it out, do. But not the harbour tunnel. If there's flooding—"

"I know the way," he called back as he vanished down the hallway. "I hope she ain't dead, Piper."

So did he.

He started down the dark tunnel, the light picking out the way ahead. A sense of dread swept through him, and he stopped again. But he couldn't back out now. Ro was down there.

Back before this all started, when they sat together in the sunshine and sang, he'd never imagined they'd end up in darkness like this. Now he lifted his voice in the same tune, shaky and unsure, trying to find his bravery again. For a moment there was nothing but his own echo.

And then he heard it, very faint, distant and frail. Ro's voice, trying to join in. And then failing.

Tomas broke into a run, letting his instincts lead him onwards. He only paused for a moment to pull open the cell door. They hadn't even bothered to lock it. Ro lay sprawled on the ground, unmoving, her skin as grey and lifeless as the dead. The water was already halfway up her prone body, soaking her. The sight made something unseen lodge in his throat, the panic and the terror. Had she felt this for him, when she'd watched him die? He couldn't shake the memory of the horror on her face, his last memory before …

"Ro?"

Her eyes opened, exhausted, but they slowly filled with such wonder. She pushed herself up. "Tomas? You're … you're alive?"

"Yes." He dropped his lantern, heedless of the water and pulled her into his arms, pressing his face into her shoulder.

She wrapped her arms around him, holding him tight, her whole body shaking. "But how are you alive?"

"It's a long story. We have to get you out of here."

But another voice answered from behind him, cold and vindictive. "Oh, she's not going anywhere. And neither are you." The cell door slammed shut, and he heard the key turn. Saran stood on the other side.

"What have you done?" Tomas surged to his feet.

"I don't know how you managed to recover. You ought to be shimmering dust on the wind right now, but we'll figure that out when I take you apart. Now stay here until I'm ready. You can enjoy your last hour together."

"The water's rising. I don't know what you've done but look around you. You've broken the foundations and the spring is— Look! If you leave us here we'll drown."

Saran snorted derisively. "You've time yet. The Aviary will hold. The spring will be part of it. This room will rise with the rest."

"Saran, you're tearing the whole archipelago apart. The soaring isles are falling. Can't you see?"

But Saran was not listening. He had the gleam of a zealot in his eyes. "I will make it work. It's my destiny. These are my people and it's my responsibility to save them. At any cost."

"No," Ro tried to tell him, but her voice was so weak. "Not at any cost. Saran, think about what you're doing. Saran, please!"

But her brother just walked away through the rising water.

Tomas shoved the door, but it was pointless. The lockpicks were back in the jacket, in the morgue. The one he had blithely abandoned. Idiot.

"Can't you open it?" Ro asked.

"No tools."

Tomas lifted Ro in his arms. She was so weak, so exhausted and broken. He didn't know exactly what Saran had done, but he could guess. He'd done to her the same thing that had killed him. How she had survived it, he couldn't fathom, but he was sure it had something to do with her visit to the Eyrie and the hourglass. Or just her being Ro.

"What about these?" she asked and held out a handful of the metal pins she'd worn in her hair. "Go on," she said. "Try."

Even now, she wasn't giving up hope. Even after all that had happened to her. He swallowed down a lump in his throat.

The lantern was dimming, the water rushing up around it. He would be working in the dark but he'd done that before. He released Ro and set to it.

The rumbling continued, far away and then drawing closer. The Collapse was finally going to take them all and Saran, for all his promises, wasn't going to stop it. If anything he was making it worse.

The lock clicked open and for one brief moment Tomas thought they were going to make it.

The hope was short-lived.

Even as they stumbled out of the cell, the ground tremored again and this time it didn't stop. A great crack wrenched the stone in the ceiling apart. For a moment, Tomas thought it might offer a way of escape, that luck might actually be on their side. The crack tore through stone as if it was paper until it reached the spring, where the water was already flooding and ripped it wide open. Freezing water thundered in, filling the cellar and the corridor beyond it. He had to fight to hang on to Ro as the deluge swallowed them up. He gasped for air, trying to find a way to keep afloat, trying to keep her up with him. He couldn't swim. And even if he could, he wouldn't stand a chance against this. He was out of his depth in seconds, swept off his feet by its fury.

It wasn't fair. It wasn't right. The absurdity of it all made him want to howl. But as the water slammed them against the walls he held on to Ro and she held on to him. His final thought, as he took the last breath he could manage and they were dragged down into the darkness, was at least they were together this time.

But then the water pulled them apart.

CHAPTER 22

The water turned black, dragging them down. Ro clung to Tomas not to save herself but because he had come back and he was all she had left in the world. All she could trust.

He slipped from her grip, the water seizing him. Ro broke the surface and gasped in a mouthful of desperately needed air. Where was he? Tomas didn't swim well.

She flipped around, forcing her exhausted body to obey, to swim down, diving under the churning surface. Tomas was sinking away from her, his arms and legs flailing ineffectually, and she arched through the water to grab his outstretched hand. His warm grip closed on hers and she met his panicked gaze. Without thinking, she pressed her lips to his and forced air into his lungs. Bubbles roared around them, but Tomas held on to her. He was fighting the water; that was the problem. That would serve them not at all. Water was like air. You had to work with it.

Ro shook her head, her hair swirling around her face and pointed upwards. Tomas went still, confused but following her lead. He trusted her, even in this. She just prayed she was right. Dark water moved around them and then, the current seized them, the one she was waiting for, carrying them upwards. She hauled him with her. She would never let him go again.

As they approached the swirling surface she saw light, impossible but undeniable light. It wavered, like an unreliable beacon summoning her. The two of them broke through the water as it crashed against the ceiling, where an air pocket had formed. Precious life giving air which they both inhaled in a dizzying rush. The gap in the stone was bigger, wider, and impossibly, still growing. Ro grabbed hold of a slick rocky outcrop, guiding Tomas' hand to it.

And then, from the widening gash in the ceiling above them, where torchlight came through, she heard a voice.

"Here!" The word was garbled, almost lost in the thunder and roar of water, the screaming of the rocks around them. "They're here! Quickly! Help me."

Strong arms grabbed her, ripping her away from Tomas, and she didn't have the strength to fight them off. Soaked and exhausted, she didn't think there could be any fight left in her until someone dragged her out on to cold stone and she came up fighting. Pointlessly as it turned out.

Strong arms quelled her.

"Hush, girl. It's okay. It's us. Take a breath."

"Nazir?" she heard Tomas say. "How did you get here?"

Dazed, Ro sank back down on the wet stone floor above the cellar.

"Erik found us in the tunnels. Just in time too. The water was on our heels. You hadn't accounted for that, had you, you mad popinjay?" The last bit wasn't directed at Tomas but at the Weaver, still in his bright robes in spite of everything. The sight was a blessed relief. It meant some things had not changed.

Parsa gave a brief laugh. "It was just faster than I thought." Carefully, he pulled off the outer layer of brightly coloured material and wrapped it around Ro's shivering form. "There, is that better? We're going to have to get you dry somehow. You'll both catch your deaths."

It sounded so ridiculous that Ro almost laughed. Death was walking hand in hand with them right now. With all of them, perhaps. And he was worried about her getting a chill?

"What's happening out there?" she asked.

"Outside? Chaos. People are panicking. There's rioting in the lower city from the Guildless, those locked out of their own Guilds, even within the Guilds themselves … The Birdsingers have really done it this time. The soaring isles are falling, and Arcadiana is sinking. The other islands too. We've sent as many people as we can to the high ground and alerted the Windriders. They're attempting to evacuate, but there are only so many balloons and boats. The Aviary is lifting, but it's tearing itself apart just trying to break free. It's part of the island."

They were one floor up from the spring, where a gaping hole in the floor showed the water underneath, the level falling now. No, not falling. The Aviary was rising, exactly as Parsa said.

"No time for explanations," Nazir said hurriedly. He twisted the stick he carried and the top detached from it. Smoothly, with an obvious amount of experience, he drew a sword forth, and Ro saw now why the Unity movement called him the Blade. He handled it like an extension of himself. No regular Weaver, him. But he never had been, she realised. He didn't even dress like them. He was something else. "We need to move or we'll have lost everything. It's time. We've got to do it now."

"Give the signal," said Parsa. "Let's just hope there are enough people down on the island still thinking clearly. You lot, up to the courtyard. We need to get those pieces of the alloy. Nazir, once the signal's up, find the people they've taken, the volunteers. Get them to safety. And *Nazir* ..." He paused and took his husband's hand, just for a moment, squeezing it tightly as he gazed into his eyes. "Stay safe."

"And you." A gruff reply, but one that was heartfelt. He turned away, and began to issue his own instructions to his troops.

"Tomas, Ro, with me," Parsa said, without giving anyone an opportunity to dissent. They climbed the stairs towards the walls, which shook wildly beneath them. As they came out in the open air, looking down on the city below, Ro could see the chaos that he had spoken of and the reason why. A huge chunk of the land beneath the Birdsingers' Guildhouse had ripped itself free from the city surrounding it. It hung tentatively in the air, like a fledgling on its first flight, not high, but high enough. It had drifted to the north so they could see the space where it had been. Beneath it the water rushed in to fill the pit, the groundwater filling a churning lake of brown water. Water in which they had almost drowned.

"Ancestors," Tomas gasped. "It worked?"

"Only up to a point," Parsa replied. "There's nothing to control its direction and it is not holding together. This new floating island will disintegrate long before it reaches the upper clouds. We're all going to die if we don't do something. Look!"

As they watched, another chunk of earth and rock fell from the bottom of the Aviary, part of its foundations going too. They rained down on the water, but Ro was sure similar debris was hitting the city elsewhere. She could hear crashes and screams in the distance. Her city, her Arcadiana … She looked to Tomas in alarm. He looked as helpless as she did.

"But the plan, Parsa," Tomas said. "Your plan. You said—"

The Aviary rose past Mount Nest, the balloons still tethered swarming with Windriders, all on alert, scrambling to make ready, hopelessly unprepared for this in spite of all their preparation and drills. Underneath Ro could make out the square where people had been celebrating, or what remained of it, now strewn with boulders and dirt, littered with smashed gazebos and shreds of banners. The first lights sprang up in the dark tangle of streets that made up the Mire, little flickering flames. Candles, she realised. Ten, twenty, hundreds, spreading out through the city, tiny points of light. All over Arcadiana.

"Yes," Parsa said. "Yes!"

Lines shot from the ground beneath them, grappling hooks at the ends which latched onto the outer walls of the Birdsingers' Guildhouse and anchored themselves. She saw one of the Birdsingers rush towards the nearest, drawing a knife, but that was no use against the metal wires, twisted together and fused. The man gave a shout and had to retreat as more cables shot skywards, anchoring the Guildhouse to the island beneath, holding them together. It shuddered to a halt, almost throwing them all from their feet but Ro clung to the wall.

"How did you do this?" she asked.

"Unity," Parsa told her with a delighted wink. "It's not just a word. When people unite, they can work wonders far greater than magic."

The floating Guildhouse complex wasn't drifting anymore, but it was still pulling upwards. The hooks dug into the walls, but even Ro could see it wasn't going to hold forever. She knew from her aeronautics classes about tension and pressure and the things it could do. The lines were already straining and the walls could still crack and crumble. The forces lifting it had already weakened the structure.

Beneath them the water still poured into the space where the Aviary had been, a huge dark lake. It reached the ornate channels of the irrigation system, the very one that had been recently upgraded, and the sluices opened. Water began to spread out through the city, like a web, the little channels suddenly deep and fast flowing.

It reflected the light from above, glittering in moonlight. A silver web. Ro had seen that before. In the tapestries.

"We have a plan to save the island," Parsa said, his voice determined. "The whole island. Saran was right; we can't save the whole archipelago, but Arcadiana can hold us all until it settles. We've been bringing people in from the other islands, as many as we can, ostensibly for the festival or evacuation. I thought it would be last night, at the Carnival. Saran's an arrogant, vainglorious fool. He couldn't resist the opportunity. I just didn't think you and Ro would get quite so tied up in it. I'd never have sent you in there if I'd known what would happen. The things I heard … I'm sorry, son. Truly." For a moment it seemed as if he might say more, but he plunged on, his plan now foremost in his mind again. "Now, if we can use that metal alloy your Atelier friend invented to stabilise this rock we may still have a chance. But if it shakes itself apart first, well, it'll take all of us with it. And the city below too." He looked up and his face went pale. "Look out!"

Parsa shoved Ro aside as a boulder twice her size slammed into the walkway. The soaring isles were collapsing even as this one was attempting to join them. Tomas hauled her back to her feet and they ran for the steps down into the courtyard below. *The Maiden,* Ro realised. The Maiden was crumbling above them, its beautiful flower studded surface falling away from the rocks beneath it and smashing down on the rising Aviary. It was almost as if it was determined to take out the presumptuous islet that had torn itself free from the ground.

"Why do you need the platforms?" Tomas asked. "Ameris didn't even know her mother had them made. She was furious."

"They weren't for the Birdsingers. We had to get them in here somehow. Devera's a genius. Where do you think Ameris got it from? There's more to do. We have to send the signal to let everyone across the city know it's time to act. To do that we just have to light that candle in the dome. The whole thing is set up. We thought Saran intended to perform his ritual last night, when the Carnival was in full swing and all the people he wanted for his new world were inside the Aviary. But you two derailed that. Everything is ready. There's a candle on the platform by the Wing. I set it all up myself. Lighting it will trigger the signal. But without that our teams in the city below won't know when to act and if they don't act, we're all lost."

They hurried along behind him, down into the courtyard, heading for the broken remains of the dome. Ro pulled the colourful coat further around her body and reached out for Tomas' hand for reassurance.

Parsa's people were already hauling the metal platforms out of the dome when they arrived at the entrance and right away he was handing out orders again. "Get the platforms as far underground as you can safely go. Especially below the tower. The foundations there are the worst. The innate magic in them will reinforce the damaged areas. Quickly now. Be careful."

"How did you know all this?" Tomas asked, clearly as bewildered as Ro.

"I saw it, like I saw everything. It's been coming to me for turnings, just a little at a time. Visions are not the most easy things to plan from, but they don't lie. We have been working on this for a long time, a piece at a time. All the things I had to prepare ... When I held that hourglass it suddenly all came clear. I saw the lake where the Aviary had been and I knew then what would happen. And what to do. But we're not out of the woods yet. We still need to complete that ritual properly. I saw you, Ro, right from the start. When I told your brother what I'd seen all those turnings ago, Matias recognised you. He would have done anything to protect you. Even give up his life here and go into exile, so there would be no family connection to the movement which might endanger you. He even bullied Tomas into taking his place as your guardian. He wanted the poor lad to join the Windriders so that he could be closer to you. But Tomas said no. He took over the network though, became the Piper, and oh, how he watched over you."

Matias. So he'd always known what she could do, of the magic she was capable of, perhaps even that she would retrieve the hourglass, knowing all the danger associated with it. She'd thought her brother had been led astray by the movement, used. Instead, he had manipulated the Unity movement, and by extension poor Tomas, to protect her. Unexpected tears stung in the corners of her eyes. But her love was married with dismay.

"Why didn't he tell me?"

The older man's eyes turned soft with sympathy. "You were so young, sweetheart. You had so much to look forward to and he thought he was keeping you safe. He knew you'd be the one we'd have to turn to. To stop this."

"I can't do it here," she said instantly, pushing the rest aside. She couldn't deal with the enormity of it all at the moment. She had to tell them what she knew. They had to understand. "That's the problem. Saran should never have done the ritual here. It's not for one place alone. It's for all of the islands—not just the Aviary and not just Arcadiana. It can save everyone. But we need to get to the Eyrie first."

Parsa's hands closed on her shoulders and he stared into her eyes solemnly. She could see relief and respect there. "He always said that you knew when things had to be done, even if it's dangerous."

She swallowed hard and nodded, remembering what had happened to Kira and the other man in the cellar, and to the original magicians who tried it. They had been part of the old world, the greatest users of magic who had ever existed. Who was she to even attempt this?

Matias' little sister. Chosen by a Golden Auric. Ro Swift who no one really wanted except for Tomas and Ameris. Not that it mattered now. Wanted or not, she was going to try to save the islands. She had to.

"But I can't do it alone. I need someone from each Guild to help me. It will be dangerous for all of us. Not just me. The spell has already destroyed others who tried."

Parsa hugged her abruptly, the relief that she wasn't arguing with fate clear on his face.

He stepped back, spreading his arms wide in a typically dramatic gesture. "Amare will provide. Now, we need to light the candle. And that's my job." With a flourish, he pulled a small tinderbox from one of his many pockets.

At that moment, a streak of shadow shot by Ro's face, so close she could feel the air as it moved. The crossbow bolt punched its way through Parsa's shoulder, sending him spinning away from her so abruptly she hardly had a chance to react. He collapsed in an unmoving heap some feet away.

Before she or Tomas could run to him, they were surrounded by Windguards, all of whom were bristling with weapons.

"I might have known you'd be here," said Hale, his pinched face the most unwelcome thing Ro had ever seen. He aimed the crossbow directly at her and smiled. "On the ground, both of you."

They would have to comply. They didn't have a chance. Ro glanced at Tomas, who was torn between helping Parsa and defending her. If he did either, if he moved at all other than instructed, she had no doubt Hale would put a bolt in him too.

"No. Wait, please." She didn't know where she'd found her voice, but she had to try. She knew these people, knew each of their faces. She didn't exactly like many of them, but that didn't matter right now. They were all going to die if she didn't do something. "You have to listen to me. We can fix this. We can fix all of this. But you have to help us. If we work together—"

"We don't take orders from you," Hale spat. "You aren't even a Windrider anymore. You made that clear."

"I'm not giving orders." The ground beneath her lurched and rocked. There was a boom, like an explosion, and they all spun around to see the top of the north wall cracking under the strain. The hook fell away amid the debris. She turned back to Hale, looked into his pale and strained face. "We're all going to die if we don't do something."

Hale's hand shook. She saw it in the movement of the primed bolt, the aim wavering. He was as scared as she was.

"Ro," said Parsa, his voice a hoarse croak. Ro thanked the ancestors he was still alive. "You need to take this. Light the candle. Inside, at the Heart of Arcadiana. The signal."

Tomas backed up, his hands still held high, and slowly crouched beside Parsa, trying to assess the harm. Hale let him go, his ire still fixed on Ro.

"We need a healer," Tomas said, his voice strained. The injury was bad then. It had to be. "Please." All eyes turned on him, just for a moment.

Ro moved. She didn't think, she didn't pause. She darted towards Parsa, grabbed the tinderbox where it had fallen from his outstretched hand and sprinted for the dome. She could hear shouting, raised voices, Tomas trying to stop them following her. She wouldn't have time. Any second a crossbow could take her out, but she had to do this. Parsa was lying back there in his own blood and if she didn't light the candle and send the signal, no matter how strange it sounded, everything would fail. Arcadiana would be destroyed. She couldn't let that happen.

Heart thundering at the base of her throat, she sprinted for the dome. Inside, among the foliage she had more cover, but she knew they were close on her tail. She dodged left and right, trying to keep as hidden as possible. She knew the noise she was making from running made her an easy target. It didn't matter. It couldn't matter.

The platform with the Wing was just up ahead, over the place where the pool had been. But the water was gone, drained away, leaving only a muddy hollow. Above it the Heart of Arcadiana still hung in the air like a miniature soaring isle, still beautiful but now strangely silent.

There was no water there either, she realised. The constant stream which had been magically linked to the spring was gone. What else had Saran's spell done? What else had he destroyed?

Don't think, she told herself. *Not now.*

She grabbed the bottom rung of the ladder and began to climb, heaving herself aloft. She didn't know where she found the strength. Each time she thought she could give no more, somewhere inside her another reservoir of inner fortitude opened up. It had to be the magic inside her. It was the only thing left.

A crossbow bolt buried itself in the wood by her head and she swung around, almost losing her grip. Hale wasn't about to give up. Still she pushed herself on, ignoring their shouting, blocking out the danger. She was almost there now.

Arms burning, she dragged herself onto the narrow platform and there, just as Parsa had promised, was a candle. It was tied around with silk ribbons, several heading up into the air above it. Whatever it was meant to do, what grand moment of showmanship he had planned as part of the Carnival ball, she had no idea. She just had to trust him.

They were coming up the ladder after her. The platform shook with their approach. It was now or never.

Ro stuck the tinderbox mechanism and the sparks spluttered into life around the wick of the candle. It didn't catch so she tried again. And again. Cursing, she attempted to steady her hand. One more time.

The flame leaped from her hand itself, not from the tinderbox. The candle caught. Light flared up right in front of her face. She gasped in surprise and then shut her mouth, terrified she might accidentally blow it out. While she lay on the shaking platform, she watched as the candle's flame caught one of the ribbons, then another.

The first was a flimsy paper streamer and it went up like a fuse, a line of light rocketing towards the roof of the dome, burning brightly. It set fire to several others and they spread out in a starburst of fire. The ceramic birds on their strings suddenly shook, chiming softly, and then, all at once, they swung down towards the Heart of Arcadiana.

Ceramic crashed against ceramic, shattering. The noise was incredible. Ro gasped as the tiny marvels all broke against each other. From inside each one, liquid spilled out, pouring down into the depths of the fountain, filling it. The liquid moved, circulating up through the cleverly designed channels until it spilled out of the various spouts to fall to the reservoir again. The Heart of Arcadiana flowed once more.

But the sequence wasn't finished yet. As the ceramic birds dropped, releasing the counterweight, the candle, tied to a second more robust ribbon, suddenly lifted. The flame, still burning bright, rose up and swung around in an arc until it impacted against the fountain.

For a moment there was silence, just the sound of Ro's harsh breath and her racing heart. Somewhere below she could hear exclamations and shouts, but she didn't care about them. All she could do was stare at the fountain as she floated effortlessly in the air, waiting, hoping, desperately needing this, whatever it was, to work.

The liquid burst into flames. All she could see was the way it still circulated, ran though the fountain, as if it was building on itself, feeding fire with fire.

And then the Heart of Arcadiana exploded.

CHAPTER 23

High above the Aviary, light erupted everywhere, raining down, illuminating everything in brightness. Spira Wheeler, who drove her cart back and forth all over the city making deliveries for the Weavers' Guild, had been waiting for this very moment, trusting in the leaders of the Unity movement. It was time.

Faces, lit by the glow of their candles, looked upwards in hope. Scrambling up on top of her delivery cart, the old woman raised her voice.

"Now, Labourers! Time to move. Our strength is our contribution! You know what to do. To your tasks!"

Dozens turned towards her immediately and the others followed.

Labourers worked together, always cooperating, a hidden force in the city, but one to be reckoned with. Spira knew everyone else underestimated her Guild. All through her long turnings, she had grown used to it. But they were many, and they were organised. The city wouldn't function without them. And now, if they didn't act quickly, it wouldn't survive. The signal had been given. The candle was alight at last.

Teams raced to their positions, those of Unity directing those few who were not. They climbed the walls, their locations evident by the flickering of their lanterns, and reached for the hidden levers and cranks that had been fitted for this moment. Great anchors they had sunk into the ground at key points, plunging into the earth of Arcadiana. Dragging the chains from their hidden places, the strongest among the Labourers attached them to huge rings while others turned the wheels to lift the sluice gates and open the culverts in the walls. More controls changed the angle on the irrigation channels, deepening them, increasing the flow.

Water raced from the new lake in the middle of the island, the new Heart of Arcadiana, where the spring filled the space left by the lost Aviary. It thundered along the channels, turning the newly installed turbines, speeding along.

Some of the people started to cheer, although what for Spira wasn't sure. This was just the beginning. Though this had been planned and designed by the cleverest amongst them, though they had trained and prepared, drilled like Windriders to bring this about, there was only a slim chance everything would work. The wires clinging to the Aviary were already straining and they would only work for so long. If they lost the new soaring isle, it could all be over before it began.

She looked to the walls, muttering in her anxiety something like a prayer but not to any god. Her people could do this, the people of Arcadiana, those who were part of the Unity movement and those who were not, but who helped them now. They had to. Because if one part failed, they all failed.

¤

Master Atelier Devera Flint, the Fulcrum of the Unity movement, ran along the top of the wall, yelling out her orders as she passed the torches. Ateliers responded at once, long used to obeying her, and as the water in the irrigation system swelled and hastened on its preset course, she saw the waterwheels and turbines racing to keep up. It would only take a few to fail and she hadn't had time to construct all the fail-safes she would have liked.

"Where's the wave?" she called to Atelier Gage, who just shook his head.

This wasn't good. It had to work. For her people, for her movement, for her own daughter. At least Ameris was safe back at the Guildhouse, but soon even their home would not be safe. Not if the island sank, not if the Aviary disintegrated above them and crushed them all. After all the turnings of planning, of design, after everything she had put into this, with all the Ateliers had done to create this system, it had to work.

They had expected it last night. But the chaos Ro had wrought at the ball had thrown all their plans into disarray. And then, without warning, something had happened and the whole centre of Arcadiana had wrenched itself out of the island, magic so complex and terrible lifting it. No one was ready. They had rushed to their places as word of mouth and sheer blind terror spread the news that the moment had come.

The Weavers were nowhere to be seen. That couldn't be good.

Trust the plan, Parsa had always told her. But what if parts of the plan didn't work? She hated this. Parsa trusted everyone and had faith in the world around him doing as he bid, but she didn't. She was always expecting something to go wrong. All the time, she compensated for oversights and errors. But Parsa, with his endless belief in the movement, in the people, in his own visions, never understood the need.

Amare will provide, he would say.

Well, the Great Bird needed to provide today, and soon.

And Parsa, of course, was nowhere to be seen.

Beyond the walls of the city the ocean was rising, the disruption to the earth beneath whipping it into a frenzy. The ground quaked and she could feel the stones beneath her feet grinding and shaking. There was a roar. It came from everywhere, all at once. Not her people, not the ocean. It came from the city.

Faster and faster, the water came, raging along irrigation channels she'd designed to contain this, to funnel it, to fuel the whole process. At predetermined intervals, hundreds of fountains erupted from the water channels winding their way across the entire city, harnessing the overflow which could have ruined the process. Instead the water shot harmlessly up into the sky and when it rejoined the flow, it increased the speed. Her design was working.

"Gage," she yelled to the older Atelier, "you want to be ready for the ignition. Any moment—"

Water struck the base of the wall beneath her, rushing into the culvert, filling it. Devera felt the impact shudder through the wall and up through her body. All around the city the same thing was happening, at key points around the walls, everywhere. She clung to the fortifications but leaned out so far she risked falling. She had to see.

She counted under her breath.

From beneath her, there came the sound of a vast piece of machinery grinding into life. The water struck blades of metal, turning them, slowly at first and then faster and faster. With a wild surge of hope, Devera straightened, looked up across the city. The groan of the mechanism became a rising song of triumph as the machinery she had hidden in the walls came to life. At the base of each signal tower, flints struck. Gas flowed and flames roared up through the glass tubes, lighting up the night, protected from wind and water, incandescent with heat. Fire powered by the flow of water.

She felt tears of relief on her face.

All along the walls, the signal towers flamed into the night, like torches held aloft. Each one was a symbol of hope.

Gage rested his hand on her trembling shoulder. "Magnificent, Master Atelier," he said in a voice that had to be raised over the noise of the machines.

"It's just one cog in the machine," she replied. "But no one will ever say that the Ateliers, nor indeed the Labourers who lent their strength to us, would have let Arcadiana fall."

"What now?" he asked.

"The Weavers. It's their turn. But they should be here already. Their wagons should have already been in place. The gas we've created is useless without them. And then we have to hope that the other Guilds finally see sense."

He nodded up to the black shape of the Aviary, just as another one of the lines gave way and plummeted down, bringing a shower of stone and dirt with it. His eyes were grim indeed. "The Birdsingers have abandoned us, Devera."

She shook her head and tightened her hands into fists at her side. "Not all of them, old friend. Not all of them."

¤

Parsa had told Erik that when he got back to the Weavers' Guildhouse there was not going to be a lot of time, but the boy had no idea it was going to be like this. The place was in chaos. People scrambled everywhere. The other kids were trying to help where they could but half of them were just getting in the way. The carts were loaded already, waiting for drivers, the Weavers in charge trying desperately to keep everything moving. But they were more artists than anything else. They created things of beauty and wonder. Organisation was not their strong point.

Erik jumped up into the cart and grabbed the reins. "What are we still doing here?" he yelled at the Weaver trying to hold on to the panicking horses.

The man looked bewildered. "Who—who are you?"

"I'm Unity," the boy told him. "And we are out of time. These wagons should have been in place ages ago."

"The Windguards wouldn't let us leave them there last night," the man started to argue.

"Well, they ain't stopping us now. Come on, they're waiting for us. Get a move on."

Whatever happened, they needed to get all the carts to the walls, otherwise it was all lost. Erik didn't understand the half of what Parsa said most of the time, but that much had been clear.

Every piece had to be in place. Each part relied on the last stage. And if anyone was missing …

The Weaver jumped up onto the cart beside him. "You know where you're going?" the man asked.

"Right for the torches."

Through the city, the Weavers raced through the streets, their precious cargo strapped to the careening carts. People threw themselves out of the way and the shouts of warning were lost on Erik. There wasn't time for caution.

He reached the tower on the wall by the harbour, and brought the wagon to a halt as Labourers rushed towards them. The Weaver was already on his feet, undoing the straps and tearing open the huge box on the back. A sprawl of coloured material and wires spilled out.

"Over there, that one!" he yelled, as the Labourers grabbed the huge balloon envelope. "Secure it down there, and the mouth needs to go up. No, right up!" He pointed to the walls, guiding the Ateliers who had got involved. "Anchor first, then—yes, then the gas."

All around them, while they worked, Erik saw people piling into the remaining boats, others already setting out into the harbour, dangerously laden. It was a measure of safety, he supposed; the threat of capsize or sinking was less than the danger of being crushed beneath falling rubble. But he didn't want to leave Arcadiana. This was his home. If he could save it, he would.

With the balloons in position, the Atelier fitted the pipe to the torch and the vast envelope began to fill, slowly lifting like a huge animal stirring into wakefulness. The chains connecting it to the anchor went taut, holding it in place but still the torches filled it with hot air. It rose, lifted, and slowly but surely, it began to lift the city of Arcadiana with it.

"It's too slow," Erik murmured, the horrible realisation crawling over him. "It's not going to give us lift fast enough."

Above them, another cable clinging to the Aviary snapped. The length of metal wires crashed down on nearby buildings, reducing them to rubble and kindling. Someone screamed in panic and then people were running for the boats again, fighting to get on board.

What little order Arcadiana still had began to fracture.

¤

Birdsinger Bree Starling wrenched open the door to the infirmary. "Get these people outside. Now! Before the roof comes down."

Several of the acolytes and other Birdsingers looked around to her, but in each face she saw the same panic she, too, was furiously suppressing. The patients needed her. She was a healer. And any moment now, the cracked and groaning roof of her infirmary could come down. The whole place was disintegrating around her. When she found out what had happened she was going to—well, she didn't know what she was going to do. She didn't agree with violence. But a stern talk wasn't going to do much either.

Elder Nightingale stood by the window, staring out at the darkness, his ancient blue eyes reflecting the lights below them. Starling slipped her arm around his.

"Elder, we have to go. It isn't safe in here." The ground beneath them shook violently again and she could hear the grinding of rock on rock.

"Starling, we have to help them," he murmured.

"We're trying, Elder. I promise, we're trying. We're getting everyone out of the infirmary now. Look—" She waved her free arm back at the long row of beds, where other Birdsingers were helping her patients to get up, or simply lifting them and carrying them outside wrapped in blankets. Some of the Windguards were even helping.

Some of them.

She swallowed down the growl of frustration. The Aviary was complete chaos. No one seemed to know what was going on but the entire place had started shaking and rising from the ground and the air around her screamed with the magic unleashed. Far too much magic, fracturing the structure of her little world.

"It's not going to hold," the old Birdsinger told her. "Not unless we help. You and I. Even if there's no one else here willing to do it. We can."

At least he'd started to move, walking with a purpose now. Any remaining sense of frailty dropped away with his determination.

As they reached the door, Starling's glasslarks surged towards her, pipping out their high little cries of alarm and warning. She tried to wave them back, but they were insistent, terrified.

"It's okay," she told them. "It's going to be okay." But it wasn't. They knew that as well as she did. The Aviary was already tearing itself apart.

"Saran did this," Nightingale told her, pulling her along behind him. She was meant to be helping him, but now the old man was unstoppable. "This foolish ritual of his."

"He said he was going to save us," she protested.

Elder Nightingale turned a bleak stare on her and she felt instantly ashamed. "And you believed his nonsense?"

"No. I mean, sort of. But I didn't think … I never thought it would work. What do we do? Can it be stopped?"

"No. Not now. If we fall, all of Arcadiana falls. There is a plan, child. We've worked for so long to prepare. But they need our help."

They had reached the crumbling upper walls and looking down she could see the city, lit up by the great flaming torches, balloons filling above them, tethered by chains to the anchors sunk in the ground.

"What is that?" she gasped.

"Unity," said Nightingale. "There are a few of us up here who still believe in that concept."

And suddenly she understood. "You're the Healer? You're their leader."

He laughed, not exactly a joyous sound. It came out bitter and cynical and barely sounded as if it came from the old man she knew so well. "No. We have many leaders. We work together. And now we need you, little Starling. You and anyone else we can muster."

"For what?"

"Magic. The gift of the Birdsingers. Will you aid me? Those balloons need more lift if they're going to keep the city from sinking. We must bind it all together." He stretched out his hands and Starling could feel the magic in him awaken. All her life, she had been aware that Elder Nightingale was one of the most powerful of the Birdsingers. Everyone said so. But all she had seen him do was tend his patients and run the infirmary. His magic came in little ways, healing a cut, curing an infection, mending a broken bone, or easing the passing when nothing more could be done. He treated each life as precious, and each loss as tragedy.

The glasslarks came to rest on her shoulders, pipping in concern, and she tried to shush them.

Others had followed them. Not many, but they were Birdsingers too and they knew when their city was under threat. They knew that something had gone terribly wrong and magic was to blame. And in this time of crisis, rather than the Master Birdsinger, or Saran, they turned to the Elder.

The Master's owl flew out of the darkness, soft wings whispering over Starling's head as it came to rest on his shoulder. It hooted softly and she saw Elder Nightingale smile.

"What do we do?" she asked. "How can we help?"

"Call the birds," he told her. No, not just her, she realised. All of them. All the Birdsingers arrayed on the walls of the Aviary. "And concentrate."

All the birds around them took flight, spiralling up into the sky, soon joined by others, every bird in the vicinity. Turning, a vast flock of every size, shape and colour, they soared above the city and then flew down towards the balloons.

Starling forced her mind to focus on the link to her fragile little glasslarks, to try to see the world through their shining eyes. They reached one of the enormous balloons that were even now lifting slowly, and grabbed the guide ropes in their claws. All around them, other birds were doing the same thing.

Their wings beat furiously as they poured every scrap of strength they possessed into their task, and she poured her own magic through them.

The balloons began to rise, pulling Arcadiana with them, out of the raging ocean.

And beneath her feet, Starling felt the walls begin to give way.

¤

"Where's that report?" Grayden snapped at the aide. He didn't know what else to do but be up here, manning the watch tower, trying to manage the rescue efforts and keep control of the escalating situation.

"The Aviary is crumbling, Commander."

He cursed under his breath. Anyone could see that. "Get the rescue balloons up there, now!"

"We don't have enough manpower, sir. Half the fleet are at the outer islands, trying to manage the evacuations there. Three islands are underwater already. There's a near riot down at the harbour."

It was going from bad to worse. The coordinated effort in the city seemed to be doing something. What, he didn't exactly know, and no one among the Windriders seemed capable of telling him. When had they become so self-obsessed and isolationist that not a single one of them knew of this secret plan? He supposed it was when his mother had effectively driven out anyone even faintly connected with the Unity movement. Once, he would have agreed with her. He was rapidly realising what a mistake that had been.

Unity had been right. And now they might be the only thing that would save the city.

One of the watchmen gave a shout and pointed. From the Aviary, birds were pouring down, a vast flock of every kind. They reached the huge balloons rising from the walls, and clung to them, their wings desperately working to give extra lift. Grayden felt the ground lurching and watched in growing horror as the whole island began to tilt.

It wasn't possible. It shouldn't be possible. But the balloons to the east were rising faster than those in the west, and the wind was stronger to the south, as if a storm was rising. The Unity movement might have planned this sequence, with Atelier ingenuity at its core, but they didn't know how to fly.

"Get our best Windriders to the walls," he ordered. "Now! The navigation is off and no one is in control of those things."

The aide looked so bewildered that in any other circumstances it would have been amusing. Right now, the situation was far too dire. "But, sir, you're ordering us to work with the Unity movement?"

His voice, when he spoke, was firm and calm and made it clear he would brook no mutiny at all. "I'm ordering you to do your jobs, to protect and defend this city, these islands. We are Windriders. The air is our home. The wind is our power. Commandeer those balloons and use them as they should be used. If they continue uncontrolled, they could do more harm than good. Even the birds are helping. So should we. Now!"

Everyone scrambled into action around him and Grayden stared up at the Aviary. Only a few of the cables holding it to the island city were left now, between the grappling hooks tearing free, the ground and the walls disintegrating under the pressure. The Aviary was pulling Arcadiana up as much as the balloons, perhaps more so.

If they lost that extra force, they might lose everything and the city would be lost.

Even as he watched, another cable plunged down, crashing onto houses in the vicinity of the Mire. He winced, his knuckles tightening on the rail at the edge of the dock.

His falcon Pel came out of nowhere, flying towards him, shrieking in warning. He circled once, but didn't land. He wanted Grayden to move, to do something. But what?

Then he saw it. A small shape, arcing through the air, flying over the city, dodging falling debris, heading steadily for the Aviary. And he knew who it was, who it had to be.

Grayden cursed and launched himself towards his own balloon.

"Sir!" the aide called, horrified.

He knew what was about to happen. Knew it as surely as he knew how to read the wind or navigate by the stars.

"Man the balloons. All of you. Get up there. Now!"

The last of the cables gave way all at once. On one side of the Aviary the walls came down in a rain of stones. The whole thing lurched to the left and swung wildly from side to side.

And beneath them, Arcadiana began to fall.

¤

The last thing Avon Price would have thought was that he'd still be here at a time like this. Not a Guildless miscreant from the Mire like him. His instincts for survival had always told him clearly enough when it was time to get out of a bad situation. And yet here he was, standing in the tangle of misbegotten streets he called home, with people who had gone from handholding, singing and lighting stupid candles to screaming, panicking and running around as if they'd lost all their senses.

He'd just been trying to have a quiet drink.

The Aviary lurched through the sky overhead, the torches turning the night into an inferno. The balloons loomed overhead like grotesque giants, and now the grappling hooks were dropping onto the city below like anchors.

The ground beneath his feet rocked and tremored, as if an earthquake was tearing the island apart. Too many people, trying too many things, and none of it working. It was the Unity movement and the Guilds, and their constant conflict. It was all 'everyone knew better than the man in the street.' And if they'd asked him he could have told them that for all their plans and all their magic, for all their interfering, Arcadiana was most likely doomed. Without the Aviary pulling them up they were all going under the waves.

If someone didn't do something soon …

He rolled his eyes, slammed his tankard onto a nearby wall.

"Lads," he said to his gang, "we're going to have to do it ourselves."

The others shrugged. They were big, and none too bright at the best of times. He hung around with them for their brawn, not their brains.

He didn't know why he felt the need to step in. But no one else was going to. He might not believe in all that happy-clappy horse manure, but if people didn't work together, especially right now, nothing would ever work. That was the problem with this city. They were too busy dividing things up, saying who was in what box and who couldn't join in at all. Too busy with their Guilds and their hierarchy to see what was right in front of their faces.

The real power of Arcadiana had always been the people who lived here.

He grabbed the men nearest to him. "Get to the roofs, and get those grappling hooks, and any others you can find. And you—" he pointed to the next group standing gawping at him "—we need the firing catapults reset, do you know how to do that?"

The next group he encountered he sent to round up more hooks and cables, another to get the panicking crowds under control. He found a bunch of the kids from the Weavers' orphanage and bullied them into acting as messengers. And amazingly people listened. People wanted to listen. They wanted someone to tell them what to do, to take control.

It happened far more quickly than he would have thought possible. Fear could be destructive. It could also be an excellent motivator. No one knew that like Avon Price.

He climbed up onto the rooftop by the nearest catapult. "Man the firing mechanisms and stand ready."

Moonlight broke through the swirling clouds, illuminating the city. "Now!" he shouted and his arm dropped. The catapults hurled the cables high into the air again and all around the lake, they soared towards the Aviary, arching high into the air and coming down into the base of it, where it held firm. Something at the base of the floating isle vibrated with the impact, a ringing metallic hum which sounded like bells.

Everything shuddered, the island below and the Aviary above, the balloons and the towers of flame powering them, the birds clinging to them and the water racing through the irrigation system to power it all. Slowly, and then all at once, every element slotted into place. And Arcadiana began, once more, to rise from the water.

¤

High up in the sky, the ground jerked backwards as if a giant hand had tried to swat it back down. Glass rained down from the dome, and everything shook. The platform holding Ro jerked wildly around and she slipped off the edge. The Windguards grabbed her before she could fall, pulling her back down the ladder with them. She was passed from one to the other like a sack of potatoes as they fled the collapsing roof and they dumped her unceremoniously at Hales' feet in the courtyard. Off to her left, Tomas knelt by Parsa, another Windguard training a crossbow at the back of his neck. Tomas glanced at her and tried to smile, but the situation was still far too grave.

"Nobody moves," Hale said. "You heard me. No one. Especially not you, Swift."

"Where's Grayden?" she asked, desperately trying another tack. "Where's the commander?"

"I'm in charge here. commander Mistral left me to secure the area. You were arrested for—" His gaze flicked to Tomas and he paled, obviously recognising that the man she was supposed to have killed was very much alive. "I don't know what you did or how you pulled it off, but you did this. All of this. You're part of the Unity movement. Don't bother to deny it. We all saw what you did in there. You destroyed the Heart of Arcadiana."

Hale was crumbling like the Aviary itself with the pressure. Something had gone impossibly wrong and he didn't know what to do except blame her. Some things never changed. She didn't even know why he hated her so much. Perhaps he didn't either.

"Hale …" she murmured, trying to calm him with her voice alone. "Please, listen to me …"

The other guards shifted, worried. They wanted out of here, back to their own Guild and their families and that wasn't likely to happen. They were trapped here, on this island that was falling apart even as it went higher.

The crossbow waved around wildly. "You're just like Matias," said Hale. Then Ro remembered. Hale had idolised him. They all had. "He betrayed us all, joining the Unity movement, slumming it with those scum in the Mire. You're just the same."

"Eno," she tried one last time. "I'm no threat to you. After this, if there even is a Guild anymore, I'm not going to be part of it, am I? But you need to listen to me. Just once. We're all in danger. Not just here and now—the city, the Guilds, all the islands. Everything the Windriders and the Windguards are here to protect."

Hale's finger tightened on the trigger, and she saw a flash of hatred in his eyes. Not just the loathing and lack of respect she was used to. Actual hatred. And she knew in that moment he'd kill her. Just because he could.

"You're a threat to all of Arcadiana, Ro Swift."

Her head swam. It couldn't end like this. It just couldn't. The thunder of her heart at the base of her throat swamped her senses.

It was only when the guards opposite her raised their wondering faces to the sky she realised it wasn't just her heart she was hearing. It was the beating of vast wings.

A shadow in the moonlight passed over her, fluid and graceful, huge blue wings outstretched, illuminated from behind by moonlight and she heard a call like music.

The Golden Aurics had come.

CHAPTER 24

Ameris wasted no time making for her workshop. The original prototype Wing was still there, thank the ancestors. She loaded it into the wagon, hitched up the donkey and made her way as quickly as she could to the gates. If she could get to the slopes of Mount Nest with it, she might have a chance.

That hope was dashed the moment she opened the gates of the Ateliers' Guild and looked outside. Panic had turned the streets into chaos. People swarmed everywhere and the city was jammed. The moment the Aviary rose in the air was the last straw. She grabbed the awkward bundle of the prototype, abandoning the cart and the skittish donkey.

There had to be somewhere with enough height within reach. She had to find somewhere. All the other questions—whether she could actually do this, was it going to kill her, how would she manage if she even got airborne?—well, they would have to wait. She had to do something. She needed to help Ro. They had to get the hourglass back. Two things. It was easy to do just two things, wasn't it?

The Ateliers' tower would have to do, she decided. It was probably tall enough. And if not … well, she wouldn't know about it for very long.

So she climbed.

Zen reeled around her as she clambered out onto the flat roof of the tower, as scared and confused as she was.

To the east, the vast shape that had once been the Birdsingers' Guildhouse rose like a behemoth above the city, blotting out the moon.

What had he done? Dear ancestors, what had Saran done?

"Watch out!" someone yelled from beneath her and a fall of rocks and dirt rained down from overhead. The ground shook, and she lost her footing, coming down hard on the stone floor.

She wasn't sure which was more dangerous right now—up here or down there. As it stood, she was about to find out whether she liked it or not.

The prototype wasn't perfect, she knew that. She'd repaired it in order to make the second one better, to work out what had gone wrong, rather than with a view to actually using it again. And certainly not with a mind to flying it herself. Slowly, carefully, she checked everything one more time and slid her hands into the controls on the wings, stretching them wide.

It felt strange, like another part of herself, as if she could feel it like she felt her fingers or her toes. It shouldn't work like that, but it did. Was it the alloy? The gold from the Auric's feather?

Zen landed on her shoulder and gave a croak as if to say stop trying to figure it out and just do it. She stared at the bird, his dark eyes staring back at her.

"Give me a hand here?" she asked, almost amused at her own whimsy. The crow just bobbed his head. His muscles bunched and he took off, light as a feather. Suddenly she understood. He was showing her the way.

Ameris leapt for the air.

For a moment, all she did was fall. She could feel it in her stomach, in her whirling head and then—then she caught the wind and it lifted her up. The Wing moved with her, and she took to the air. Like Amare. Like the Great Bird after whom she was named. Ameris flew.

Ahead of her, Zen navigated a path of air currents she couldn't even see. The odd, almost desultory flap of his wings told her when to move her arms, but the rest of the time she soared effortlessly as they glided up across the city.

Beneath her, she could see the chaos still unfolding. She saw the cables go up, the people underneath struggling to tie them off on the bollards and street posts, holding the Aviary to the city, trying to stabilise the island. In the harbour, great waves were crashing against the walls and the quays, swamping the boats. The area beyond the wall at the Weavers' gate was already underwater.

The irrigation channels filled with water from the newborn lake in the middle of the city, rushing across the landscape, turning waterwheels and moving sluices, increasing in speed as the water careened towards the edges of the island. Fountains shot up every so often, controlling the overflow, speeding up the water. She swooped low to see the waterwheel there turning so fast it almost detached. Water plunged into the culverts around the city's edge, under the walls and then the torches on the city walls ignited, bright and brilliant, flames leaping for the sky.

This was Parsa's work. His design. It had to be. But she also recognised her mother's hand in it, her meticulous engineering, the elegance of it. This is what they had been plotting.

She swung out around the wall, staring down into the darkness now illuminated by the huge towers of flames. Hot air blasted up, disrupting the currents around her, and at the same time she saw the pipes catching it, redirecting and repurposing it. The torches weren't just decorative, despite their beauty.

A balloon filled, rising over the city walls. It was huge. Far bigger than any she had ever seen. It was tethered to one of those great anchoring points, huge metal rings sunk into the ground, which they had been constructing everywhere. Now she knew why. Now she could see it all working together. She had been so caught up in her own work she hadn't noticed. All along the walls, where the torches blazed, balloons of many colours and patterns began to lift into the sky, anchored to the ground of Arcadiana.

The giant balloons filled with hot air, all around the edges of the island. Water fuelled fire, fire produced gas, and the gas lifted the brightly coloured balloons, which in turn strained to lift the ground itself. Or at least to stop it sinking.

It shouldn't have worked. Everything she knew told her that. But she couldn't deny the evidence of her own eyes. They were holding the Aviary to Arcadiana, stopping its destruction, and at the same time keeping the city from the waves. It wouldn't last forever, it couldn't. But for now, for this moment …

Zen gave an alarmed caw and Ameris adjusted her arms just in time to veer away from more debris plunging down from above. She saw it smash into a shack near the south wall and prayed there was no one in there. The danger had not passed yet. Her people might be working in unison to save themselves, but that would only last so long.

She was high now, so high, and the wind was harder to catch. It shook at the Wing, pulled at her already exhausted arms. Zen circled her, trying to encourage her. Tears streamed from her eyes as she forced herself to keep going. She had to. They climbed the side of the floating Aviary, finding an updraft that lifted her so suddenly it felt like her stomach had been left behind. It wasn't that far above the city. Grappling hooks and metal lines held it secure.

And then they were above it, higher than she had ever been in her life. It was dizzying. But the Wing felt like part of her and, with Zen's guidance, she finally understood the thing she had dedicated herself to for so long in a whole new way. She knew now what to do to make the next one perfect, to make it a thing one controlled as much by instinct as—

The tower of the Aviary lurched at her through the darkness and she almost hit it. Tucking herself into a ball, Ameris managed a messy and undignified landing on one of the upper viewing platforms, the metal of the Wing clattering across the tiled floor.

She was barely back on her feet when she felt the ground of the tower giving, crumbling from the impossible forces pressing on it from every direction. Lurching forwards, she threw herself inside seconds before it came away.

She took a moment, forcing herself to breathe, to get her bearings.

The stairs wound downwards, dark and uninviting. Debris and dust covered the steps, belongings scattered. Even the Birdsingers were fleeing. She knew where Saran had his quarters. If he was keeping the hourglass anywhere it had to be there. It just had to be. Just a few floors down, right above the coloured glass of the dome itself. She removed the Wing, and leaned it against the wall. She couldn't carry it with her.

Doubt made her hesitate though. She needed to find Ro and the hourglass. If they came back this way, if the tower hadn't shaken itself apart, could the two of them use the Wing to escape? In theory it should be possible. Using the height here they could glide down. She just had to hope.

One thing at a time. Her head was already reeling with the exhilaration of having flown her own invention. Zen settled on her shoulder and gave her little crooning noises of praise. She lifted her hand and stroked his silken feathers gently.

"Thank you," she whispered. Where would she be without him? Certainly not flying.

Saran's room was a mess. Whatever semblance of order he had once enjoyed had clearly gone out of the window and he hadn't locked the door. There were clothes everywhere, all those beautiful expensive pieces of fabric balled up and scattered over the furniture and the floor. Papers were similarly strewn across the desk and books had fallen over onto the floor. All the things he normally cared so much about were discarded carelessly. It was like looking at the room of an entirely different person.

Had Saran done this?

Ameris stood there, aghast, not sure where to start. She had been so certain the hourglass would be here, where he kept everything he treasured. How could she hope to find it?

"Looking for something?" a ravaged voice asked. The heap of clothes at the other side of the bed moved and she saw Saran.

She hadn't expected him to be here either. Not up in the tower which was so close to collapse. No wonder the door was unlocked.

But the man she saw now barely looked like Saran at all. His hair was loose and tangled over his face. His eyes were wild, gleaming in the half light. His beautiful robes were torn as if someone had grabbed them in panic or pain. Was that … was that blood?

She dragged her gaze back up to his face as he rose slowly. If his appearance gave the impression of something broken and crazed, his movements didn't. It was like watching some kind of predator closing in on her. Ameris' instincts thrummed with alarm and she backed up towards the door.

Saran reached out a hand and she caught a glimmer of light on the end of his fingertips.

The door slammed shut behind her, making her jump. There was nowhere to go and if she turned her back to flee, to try to open the door again, she knew he would be on her.

Instinct told her to keep her voice very quiet and calm. Confrontation wouldn't help here. "Saran, what have you done?"

"Me?" He snarled the word. "Me? This isn't my fault. It's hers. Ro's. If she'd just done what I wanted, if she had just cooperated—"

Ameris tried to circle around, keeping him in view the whole time. On her shoulder, Zen flapped his wings and cawed, whether trying to warn her or trying in his own way to drive Saran back, she wasn't sure. There was no sign of his magpies.

"Where are your birds?" she whispered.

"I needed the magic," he said, and tears brimmed in his eyes. The horror of it passed over his face. Her throat closed over, her heart hammering beneath it, trying to get out. "To save everyone. I have to save everyone. You understand, don't you, Ameris? You have to understand. I don't want to do this, any of it, but I have no choice."

His hand shook as he reached out to her.

Zen took off, diving straight at him, fierce and angry, his cry raucous. But instead of falling back, or raising his hands to defend himself from the furious onslaught, Saran ripped the crow out of the air.

The world seemed to convulse around them. Zen let out a single, terrible shriek and Saran threw his head back, his eyes closed as light tore itself free of the bird and flowed into him. Light so bright that Ameris had to cover her eyes with her arm and she stumbled back, falling to the ground as she tripped over something unseen. She fell hard, hitting her head against the window ledge.

When she looked again, Zen was gone. Just gone. A few black feathers drifted to the floor, and Saran was wreathed in light.

"What have you done?" she whispered, unable to move.

Saran shook his head. "It won't hurt, Ameris. I promise."

She scrambled back up to her feet, looking around in terror for something, anything, to defend herself with. And that was when she saw it, abandoned on the edge of the shelf.

The hourglass.

It was magic, that was what Ro said. The sand inside it still flowed resolutely on, always in one direction, and it glimmered in the same way as the light around Saran's hands. The same way Zen had in the moments before … before …

Her hands shook so hard she almost dropped the hourglass as she grabbed it, but she managed to hang on, holding it out in front of her as if it were some kind of talisman.

Saran smiled. It wasn't a pleasant expression now. It was desperation, twisted with a kind of madness. She wanted to say it wasn't his smile. But it was. And that was even worse.

"That won't help you, Ameris. I don't think it even works. It doesn't control or moderate magic, or do anything I thought it would. It's just a container. Like all of us. It's just a house for magic, a way to keep it locked up. There's magic in all of us, in everything. In you." He came closer and she tried to retreat, but the back of her legs hit the window ledge. There was nowhere else to go. Saran's smile widened, showing his teeth. "Don't fight, Ameris. I have to finish the ritual, save everyone. You have to understand. It is for the greater good. My destiny is to save our people. Sacrifices must be made." He reached out a hand as if to cup her face, so tender and delicate a gesture. Light glimmered on his fingertips. "I'll make sure it doesn't hurt. You'll welcome it."

Ameris threw herself backwards out of the window and for a brief moment the world fell away from her. Wind rushed by her and she saw Saran fling himself towards the window after her. But he was too late.

Too late to stop her, too late to catch her.

The main roof beam of the dome slammed against her back. Ameris lay there, winded and gasping, stretched out on the broad length of metal that formed the centre of the dome and held up the shattered remains, devoid of glass. In the middle was a gaping hole and marks of fire damage. The whole thing trembled beneath her. It might come down at any second. She lay so still, gasping, aware that if she rolled one way or the other, she'd fall, if she slipped, if she breathed the wrong way …

The sky was huge above her, the clouds so much closer, and the Eyrie drifted overhead, far in the distance, just a dark and distant shape against the moon.

She could see a bird, a falcon, circling over her. It gave a cry, a clear high keening sound. Like it was in mourning.

Zen was gone.

Several yards above her she could still see Saran, almost hanging out of the window, yelling. She slid back, pushing her way along the central beam to get as far away from him as she could. Eventually she'd run out of room, she knew that. But she needed to put distance between herself and Saran.

He'd killed Zen. He'd …

She would have said the balloon that changed course towards her was the last thing she wanted to see under these circumstances, but no. It was the face that appeared, the man who reached out to gather her in his arms and pull her to the tentative safety of the basket.

Grayden.

"What is going on?" he asked as he set her back on her feet. Around him his team of three stared at her.

"He … he's gone mad," she whispered, and a sob shattered her words to pieces. "He tried to kill me. He killed Zen. Grayden … he killed … my crow …" Her words trailed away as she saw how wide his eyes grew, and then filled with anger. He glanced upwards, at Saran and then beyond to where Pel circled overhead. The falcon gave his familiar cry as if in answer to that look alone. "Grayden, he's out of control."

He held her close, just for a moment and leaned in to whisper in her ear. "Trust me."

Trust him? Why should she trust him? Why would she need to?

Before she knew what was happening, he spun her around, pushed her against the side of the basket and secured her arms behind her back.

"I have her, Birdsinger Swift. Never fear," he called up.

"Bring her here. Bring her to me."

She heard Grayden curse softly, but he didn't let Saran hear.

He was too smart to do that. Ameris saw him make eye contact with his team and nod curtly. Whatever command he had just given they didn't give a verbal reply; they just calmly and rapidly moved about, fulfilling their duties. The woman turned to the burner, the main control for the balloon. The man made for the valve releases.

"I can't hear you, Birdsinger," Grayden shouted, his voice cheerful and calm as if he wasn't talking to a madman. "The breeze is wrong. I can't bring the balloon in close enough. Not safely. I'll take her to the halls of justice and we'll sort it out there. She isn't going anywhere."

"Grayden," she whispered. "Please."

His voice dropped low again, every tone a warning. "Just be quiet and let me do my job."

"Your job? This is about more than your job! He's going to kill everyone. He's stealing magic. He's—"

A sudden blast of wind sent the balloon reeling to one side. Pel gave a cry of alarm and dived towards them. Grayden let her go, holding out his arm so the falcon had somewhere to land. A kestrel and a brightly coloured jay appeared moments later, feathers fluffed up in concern, seeking out the other Windriders. The sun was rising over the eastern ocean. The sound of enormous wings filled the turbulent air and they could only stare as two huge birds flew past them in wide spirals, blue as the sky with sunlight striking golden feathers gleaming on their heads and parts of the wings, their long tail feathers trailing behind them like streamers.

It was impossible. Even though Ro had described them to her, Ameris realised she hadn't really believed it, not in her heart of hearts. But here they were, undeniably real. Come with the dawn in the time of Arcadiana's greatest need.

Golden Aurics.

They spiralled down towards the courtyard beneath them, where a small group of people, looking like ants from this height, stood frozen in terror.

CHAPTER 25

Only Ro stood firm as the great Golden Aurics descended, spilling the dawn's light over the shattered courtyard. The Windguards scattered. Even Hale himself took a few steps back, but he didn't run. He didn't seem to be able to move.

"What have you done now?" he growled at Ro.

The Auric landed between them, turned to her and lowered its head. Ro lifted her hand and pressed her palm tentatively to its azure feathers, their silken texture giving her the ability to breathe again. She couldn't believe it. They'd come. They'd actually come. Which meant …

She looked for the wren, but there was no sign of it. Ro pressed her face into the feathers, breathing in the scent of spices and flowers she'd only ever smelled on the Eyrie. It was a comfort, a blessing.

"I thought maybe I'd imagined you," she whispered and the bird gave a curious trill, that odd vibration running through her. "Thank you for coming."

A noise behind them made the Auric twist around, sweeping its wings wide to protect Ro. Hale fell back and sprawled on the ground, dropping the crossbow with a clatter. His face stretched in horror as another bird, his own hawk, flew down to join him. To protect him, probably. Although it seemed more fascinated with the Golden Auric, trying to supplicate itself before it, perhaps trying to apologise for the stupid human it had tethered itself to.

Tomas crouched beside Parsa, trying to staunch the flow of blood from his shoulder while the other Golden Auric stood watching them, its head tilted.

"Tomas?" Ro asked, fearing the worst.

"Parsa's hurt. Badly. I can't … Ro, I can't help him."

More Windriders were coming. She could see the balloons. They must have come up from the city thinking to evacuate the people trapped in the Aviary. She hoped so. Rather than wanting to join them. She had to believe that. The Windriders always responded to those in need. That was their whole purpose. Or it had been, once upon a time.

The same went for the Birdsingers. They weren't all like Saran and his friends. She remembered Elder Nightingale, even those like Finch who worked so closely with the Windriders. They couldn't all be so obsessed as her brother.

"We need a healer," she cried out. "Please."

The group of Birdsingers sheltering near the gates didn't move. Nor did the ones trying to pull people out of the rubble of the dormitories. A girl broke into a run from the ruins of the walls, her featherlike robes stained with the blood of the many injured she'd already attended. Her long red hair was tangled and covered in dust. She barely gave them a glance but dropped down beside Parsa, pushing Tomas aside. Ro remembered her from meeting Elder Nightingale. He'd called her Starling. She'd smiled and teased him, clearly fond of the old man she cared for, his finest student, a healer.

She wasn't smiling now.

Tomas stumbled back, helpless, and found Ro's arms. He was shaking so hard she thought he might collapse, but he hardly looked at her.

"We need to find Nazir," he murmured, his numb lips mangling the words together. "Ro, we need to find him. He should be here."

It was the helplessness in his voice that did it. He'd already given up. He just clung to her, staring at the young healer as she tried to assess the damage. When she looked up, Ro could tell the prognosis was not good.

"Fetch Elder Nightingale," Starling shouted, ignoring the two of them completely. "Tell him it's his friend, the Weaver. Get him here now!" She finally turned to Tomas and Ro, her face very pale but fixed with determination. "He's the best of us. I swear it. If anyone can help—"

Which meant she couldn't.

Parsa stared at the Aurics, but Ro wasn't even sure he could see much anymore.

Elder Nightingale finally appeared from the ruins, helped by several others. When he saw Ro there, with the Aurics, he hesitated and bowed to the birds, for just a moment. The wonder on his face was beautiful to behold. But he had a job to do, a duty. He was above all a healer.

When he reached Parsa, his face fell. He didn't even need to examine him.

"It's too late," he said simply. "I'm so sorry, my friend, my brother in Unity."

"But it can't be," Starling replied vehemently. "There must be something we can—"

Nazir appeared, desperately racing across the courtyard, straight for Parsa. When he reached him he dropped to his knees and howled. The old healer put a hand on his shoulder.

It couldn't end like this. It simply couldn't. Ro looked up to where the thin beam of the rising sun was striking the soaring isles, lighting them up with dawn. The Auric beside her let out a soft trumpeting call.

Suddenly she knew what had to be done. One last hope, one last chance.

"Tomas," she whispered as he shuddered against her like someone waking from a nightmare. "Tomas, listen to me. I need you to get Parsa onto the back of one of the Aurics. Take him to the Eyrie. Now."

The air up around the Eyrie had healed her, it had wound back time and rejuvenated her body. Just cuts and bruises perhaps but … it had to work.

Parsa wasn't dead yet.

"What are you talking about?" A sob broke his voice.

"Trust me. I'll follow on the other one. But you have to go now. There's no time to lose."

What had Parsa said? Amare will provide. Well, her children were right here waiting. They had come because she'd begged the wren for help. And the wren had brought Tomas back to her. It couldn't end like this. Parsa's life was too high a price.

"Nazir?" Tomas asked. That was all he said, but Nazir knew and understood.

"If there's a chance. If there's any sort of chance ..." He looked desperately to Ro, who nodded. The two birds craned their necks towards Parsa, making soft trilling sounds of concern deep in their chests. "Please, save him," Nazir said to them. "I'll mind Ro, keep her safe for you. I swear it."

Tomas lifted Parsa as gently as he could, cradling his slight form as he climbed on the back of the first Golden Auric, settling between the wings and holding on as best he could. He looked terrified but resolute. Ro had never loved him more.

"I'll be right behind you," she told him. "I have to find the hourglass."

"Ro." He hesitated, reluctant to leave her, yet unable to not help the man who was a father to him. "Saran won't give it up lightly. Be careful."

Ro tried to smile. He knew her better than to ask something like that. She couldn't make that sort of promise. "You have to go."

The bird spread its wings and took off, so gently, as if it knew it carried a precious cargo.

Ro watched them getting smaller and smaller. Nazir closed his hand on her shoulder. "You need to go too. He'll need you up there."

The remaining Golden Auric bowed its head and nudged her.

"Not without the hourglass," she said grimly.

And then she heard her brother's voice like a wail of agony and rage. "Stop her! Whatever it takes. Windriders, stop her! That's an order. They're members of the Unity movement. They're criminals. This is all their fault."

Saran came sprinting from the base of the tower, his outstretched hands wreathed in glittering magic. Ro gave a gasp of alarm.

No one else moved, not the Windriders, no one. They all seemed frozen in horror as he flung his arms towards her.

Shimmerwisps appeared from everywhere, all at once. They came from the ground, from the walls, they appeared in the air, glowing clouds which twisted and spun around aimlessly for a moment, as if bewildered by their sudden freedom.

No, not freedom. They were anything but free.

He summoned them. Not the ones in the cave in the Eyrie, but all the others. Perhaps he had been calling them all along. Testing her magic, drawing it out, trying to see what she could do and how quickly she could recover. Setting them loose to gather magic for him.

Now he unleashed them to stop her. If she left with the Auric, she'd leave all the people here to be attacked by them. The shimmerwisps were already spreading out, lunging towards the frightened people, drawn to those with the most innate magic, singling them out. Birdsinger Starling and Elder Nightingale backed up, their hands raising ineffective shields, and Nazir tried to shelter Ro from the approaching wall of light.

"What are they?" he snarled, his sword useless against them.

"Ghosts," she whispered. "Memories, echoes." And with that she stepped away from him. She had to stop them and there was only one way to do that. And she, it seemed, was the only one able to do it. Saran had told her as much. It was fitting in a way. He had made them. She could set them free.

"Ro? What are you doing?" Nazir asked.

Her smile wavered. There were so many of them. "You're going to have to help me, Nazir. Don't let me go, okay?"

With that she spread her arms wide and called them to her. Not with her voice, but with all the magic within. She welcomed them, all of them, life after stolen life. Ignoring any other prey, the shimmerwisps rushed blindly towards her, towards freedom.

It hurt. Dear ancestors, it hurt. It ripped through her, dragging out everything she had only recently rebuilt inside her fragile human body. The magic transformed them, released them, birds, and people. Too many people.

A blackbird sang out a ghostly tune as it flew skywards, into the growing light. The magpies—Saran's magpies, she realised with a jolt of grief—gave a raucous cackle as they burst from her in a wave of brightness. She could smell Kira's expensive perfume and disdain for just a moment. She reached for the shimmerwisps, all of them.

Ancestors, what had he done? How many lives had he stolen? How many people had he killed? And all for this folly, this madness, this blind need to raise the Aviary …

Her brother … her brother had done this …

Ro screamed. She couldn't help herself. It was too much. There was so much magic flowing through her and it would burn her out.

Nazir's hands took hers, both of them, holding her tightly in a strong and secure grip, anchoring her to the world. In doing so he reached through the shimmerwisps. It must have hurt him too. It must have been agony.

"Ro? Come back to us," he told her firmly. "That's enough."

No, there were more shimmerwisps, more lives trapped in this half-life which she needed to free.

From a great distance she heard Starling's voice. "She can't take much more of this. No one can."

"Then we must help," Elder Nightingale replied. "Give her strength."

She felt a flood of fresh energy wash through her, as they shared their magic and life force. But it was barely enough. A mere drop in the ocean that she needed.

Behind her, the Golden Auric pressed against her back and its wings spread wide around her and Nazir, mantling them in protection. She could feel its heart fluttering against her, inside her, its magic joining the magic inside. It gave her hope.

There was just one left, one shimmerwisp, but impossibly it dodged her, refusing to be helped. She frowned, reaching for it as it hovered between her and Nazir. Above it she could see a balloon descending, a face looking over the edge.

Ameris.

The shimmerwisp finally relented, falling into her, and the form of a crow burst free, etched in golden light, flying towards Ameris, calling out to her in an echo of a familiar croak.

It vanished before it reached her, but Ro saw her friend open her eyes wide in wonder and grief. And Ro knew it was Zen.

Ro staggered away from Nazir and the bird, and began to run towards the descending balloon and her grief-stricken friend.

Something lifted her off her feet and tackled her to the cobbles of the courtyard. The last shreds of strength she had were ripped away as Saran intercepted her. His grip tore at what little magic remained in her and he kept delving, looking for more, his teeth bared like an animal.

Nazir's body twisted in a blur, wrenching Ro away from Saran and punching him so hard he reeled back, dazed and bloody.

"Quickly," he said as he dragged her upright. "You have to get out of here. Can you hold on? That's all you have to do. Just hold on."

"But I …" The world was melting away in front of her eyes into vague shapes and colours.

"Ro, focus. Just hold on. You can't stay here. Your brother will kill you. He won't stop. And Tomas needs you. Tomas and

Parsa, remember?" He threw her up onto the back of the waiting Golden Auric.

She grabbed a handful of feathers in both hands and felt its muscles bunch beneath her. It leaped for the sky, its cerulean wings spread wide. Barely conscious, she clung to it, desperately afraid as the wind rushed past.

"No!" she heard Saran scream and then the bird jerked beneath her, struck by a sudden impact. "I can save them all. You have to understand. It's for the greater good." His voice was close, too close. She twisted around to see him clinging to the back of the Auric. He dragged himself up, hand by laborious hand. Feathers fell behind him in a trail, blue and gold falling through the sky as he ripped them out. She felt him unleash his dreadful ability, draining magic.

But not from her this time. Not when there was a far greater source right in his grip.

The Auric began to scream.

CHAPTER 26

The wide blue wings of the Golden Auric bore Tomas and Parsa aloft with ease. In his arms, Parsa shuddered, shivering with pain. His hands closed on Tomas' arm in an iron grip.

"What are you doing?" he managed to say through clenched teeth.

"Just lie still," Tomas told him. "I'm getting you to safety."

"Safety?"

"Ro thinks the Eyrie can heal you. The clouds there." Or something. He wasn't really sure what. He just had to believe she was right.

Because if she wasn't …

Parsa's skin had taken on a waxy quality, dotted with sweat. He chewed on his lower lip and for the first time ever, Tomas realised, Parsa was scared. He'd never seen such a thing, never imagined it was possible. Parsa always knew what was going to happen so he was never afraid. Except this time he couldn't know.

"I only wanted to help," Parsa whispered, the wind almost drowning out the words. Tomas bent close, straining to hear.

"You have helped. It's okay."

"Nazir always said it would end up like this … I told him he was overreacting. He'll … he'll rub my face in this, you know. He's going to *I-told-you-so* for days. It will be unbearable."

Tomas' eyes burned and he closed them tightly, trying to fight off tears. He felt Parsa pat his arm wanly, an attempt, even now, to comfort him.

"We always knew it was a risk. That's why he was always so protective. If they found me out, we always knew exile wouldn't be enough for them. That they'd want me dead." He sucked in a breath and his whole body tensed with a fresh wave of pain.

"Parsa?" Tomas snapped.

It took a moment before he replied, his voice barely audible. "Still … here … How far is this magical place?"

Tomas looked up. The Eyrie passed in front of the rising sun, a silhouette now, the tree on the summit even more brilliant, catching the morning rays. It was still so far away. Too far away.

The Auric gave a long wavering call and banked right, forcing Tomas to jerk forward and cling on even more tightly. His body was bent over Parsa's again, pinning him safely in place.

The movement made him cry out in agony and Tomas winced.

"Just hold on," he muttered. "Please, Parsa. Just hold on. It's not far."

He knew he was lying, but he didn't care. If he could get Parsa to believe it …

But Parsa had gone quiet now. Far too quiet. They were almost there. The High Eyrie was achingly close. But still too far.

"Go faster!" Tomas yelled at the Golden Auric. "Please!"

He didn't know whether the bird heard or even if it understood him. Maybe the lure of home was calling it rather than anything to do with him. But that didn't matter. All he could feel was that the creature was straining to fly faster, the great wings catching the wind and powering farther and farther from the ground.

The Auric finally soared up over the edge of the High Eyrie and landed softly. Tomas tumbled off the Great Bird's back before gently sliding Parsa after him. The bolt still protruded from his shoulder. Parsa himself was unconscious again.

Ancestors, he thought, *please, just be unconscious. Especially for this …*

The bolt had gone right through him. Removing it wasn't going to be pretty, but it could be worse. So much worse. He didn't dwell on it. Time to act. Quickly.

He snapped the head off the bolt as best he could and lay Parsa on the ground. Before he could think better of it, he pulled the shaft of the bolt free too.

Parsa arched up beneath him, screaming. All the birds that had gathered around them took flight, even the Golden Auric, the alien sound panicking them. They swirled aloft, up onto the upper ledges of the isle, or to the safety of the Tree itself.

Tomas flung the arrow aside and watched as fresh blood blossomed on Parsa's beautifully embroidered robes, crimson and bright, drowning out all the colours he so loved.

And then, just as suddenly, it stopped.

"Please," Tomas whispered, over and over again. He didn't know what else to say. "Please, please, please …"

It wasn't a prayer. He didn't even know who a prayer would be sent to. Amare? Their ancestors, perhaps? The people who had once lived here and started all this awful mess? He just needed Parsa to live. Needed the man who had been a father to him to survive, to open his eyes, to be the same smart-mouthed idealist that he had always been.

To live.

Tomas didn't know what the Unity movement would do without him. Nor did he know what he would do if Parsa wasn't there.

Parsa slumped back down, his eyes staring past Tomas' head, fixed on the clouds and the sky above them. Unmoving.

"No," Tomas whispered. "Please." Again, he didn't know who he was talking to. But there had to be someone, something, somewhere listening to him.

Parsa drew in one shuddering breath. It sounded as pained as when he was shot.

Then he swore viciously, like one of the fishermen in Harbour House, and slumped back down again, screwing up his face and trying to grab another breath. It was just as awful.

Tomas held Parsa's hands as he struggled back to life. Finally, after what, seemed an age, the agony lessened and his breath, while still laboured, was at least less tortured.

"Where are we?" he asked, when he could actually form coherent words.

"The Eyrie," Tomas replied, still unwilling to release his hands. He rubbed his palms gently with his thumbs. Parsa gave him a firm glare and then pried one hand free. He pressed it to Tomas' face.

There could be no doubt what he was trying to say—that he was proud, that he was grateful, that he was lucky to be alive and that he owed that to Tomas. But of course, he didn't say any of those things.

"Good man," he whispered at last. Then he disentangled himself and stood on trembling legs. Tomas still supported him though he knew that if Parsa could have stood alone he would have, even at the risk of falling on his face.

"Take it easy," he warned. "You were just—"

Parsa, of course, completely ignored him. "Amazing," he murmured as he looked around. "Just as I saw when I first held the hourglass. Speaking of which, where is the hourglass?"

"Ro went to get it." She should be here by now. Tomas' heart gave an unwelcome stutter. He'd abandoned her down there. True, she had told him to go and he'd needed to save Parsa, but still.

He'd left her.

They weren't far from the edge of the soaring isle. He looked out and the wave of dizziness that swept through him almost took him off his feet.

Clouds passed beneath them. The islands below looked so small and the ocean was vast, morning sunlight glinting on the waves. The sky all around him was huge, stretching from horizon to horizon in an immense dome of blue.

He glanced back at Parsa who was checking his shoulder, rolling it back and forth and then pulling his shirt to one side to reveal a scar but no obvious injury.

"Remarkable," he murmured to himself.

"Does it hurt?"

"No. Not really. It's more like … like it remembers it was hurt but that was long ago." He drew in a breath of the sweetly scented air. A strange peace filled his face and even as Tomas watched, the lines of stress that had always marked his face seemed to ease.

"What do we do now?" Tomas asked, hoping Parsa at least had some semblance of a plan. He usually did. But this time he shook his head.

"I don't know. Perhaps we can coax the bird back. Ro should be here."

She should. She said she was going to follow.

Tomas looked down again, this time prepared for the sensation of teetering on the edge of the world. Far below he could see Arcadiana. He could make out the Aviary straining above it, crumbling with the effort of rising, tearing itself and everything else apart. The island city was etched with lines of light where the sun hit the irrigation channels. Like the silver web Parsa had worked into so many of his designs recently, sending the message out to all who knew how to read it.

The balloons were a hundred different colours and patterns, all around the walls, rising from every tethering point. Tomas even recognised some of them from the designs in Parsa's tapestries. He'd prepared this, all of this. Balloons were bright patches of colour in the sky, flames rose from the torches around the walls to create the gas to fill them, and the water, still flowing onwards, powered the whole contraption designed to save the city.

"Parsa, look what you did."

Parsa had found himself a rock to sit on and was trying to work out if he could salvage the robe, pulling at the torn threads and rubbing at the bloodstain. He looked up. He hadn't even been listening. His dark hair, threaded with grey, fell over his face and in that moment, he almost looked … childish. A gleeful delight sparkled in his eyes.

"What did I do when? I've done lots of things."

"Parsa!" Tomas scolded and threw one hand out to indicate the city below.

"Oh, that." He got up and approached the edge a little more cautiously than Tomas had. He had never liked heights. "It's working?

So far anyway. If they don't keep the balloons fully inflated though …" He grimaced. "The plates underneath the Aviary should have kicked in by now. Of course, if one things fails, it all fails."

"What are you talking about? You planned this."

"Plan is a very big word, Tomas."

"No, it isn't. It's … Parsa, stop talking in riddles."

Parsa gazed down at the city, his city, his dark eyes soft with fondness. With love, Tomas realised. Because he knew that kind of love, the love of all those ridiculous wonderful people, of his home, of a place so tied up in itself and home to so many miracles. The kind of love you'd do anything to maintain.

Tomas had learned to love it from Parsa, after all.

"I couldn't let it sink, Tomas. I saw it, long ago, saw the end. And I knew there had to be a way to stop it. When Matias appeared on the scene, when he told me about Ro … I saw the first glimmerings of how it would work. And I followed those visions."

"You pushed me to look after her, watch over her and—"

"And to love her. *Encouraged,* I would rather say. Not that you needed much encouragement really. Be honest now."

Honest? He'd loved her for as long as he could remember. Ro was exasperating, reckless, any number of things. But she was also very easy to love.

Parsa saw the look on his face and smiled fondly. "When I held the hourglass, I knew. I saw it all and I had to act fast. The irrigation project was already under way so it just took a few tweaks, deepening the channels and changing the course in a few cases. Altering the incline. Once the Aviary lifted, the hollow behind filled with groundwater and the various springs. Water is one of the most perfect driving forces, incredibly hard to stop, did you know that? Water wheels are easy to install and we did, everywhere we could. They turn all kinds of machinery. And once you have that sort of power anything is possible. Your clever little Atelier came up with that wonderful alloy and Devera saw the possible applications instantly. And the balloons were the final touch, a lift for the island. It won't last forever but hopefully long enough."

"Long enough for what?"

"For her. She's what I saw. She's the answer. Look!"

A flash of blue and gold rose from the city, the other Golden Auric, flying hard, desperate to gain height above the ground. It was making for the Eyrie and he could make out a small dark shape clinging to its back.

Ro. It had to be Ro.

But the bird was screaming, its harsh and guttural shriek rising in alarm. It shook the air and, above them, in the shimmering tree other birds echoed the cry. The other Golden Aurics took to the air, swooping down towards their sibling.

"What is it?" Parsa asked. "What's happening? Something's wrong. Tomas?"

There was another figure on the beleaguered bird, clawing his way up its back towards Ro. Every time his hands dug their way through the feathers to the skin and muscle beneath, the bird let out another shriek. Ro was clinging to its neck, her head bent down, as she desperately shouted encouragement to it.

Saran was stealing magic from the Auric, draining it as he had drained Tomas. The memory of what he'd done, of the pain and the helplessness, speared through Tomas' body even now. How the creature was still flying, he couldn't imagine. He hadn't even been able to move. And yet it kept going, trying desperately to reach the Eyrie and the hoped-for safety.

The Auric wasn't going to make it though. The strain on its body was already showing. Its wings were faltering, but still it pushed on.

Tomas locked eyes with Ro, her gaze picking him out even from so far away.

"Ro," he whispered.

He saw her tighten her jaw, her expression filled with some kind of resolve and then, he watched as she pushed her own hands into the Auric's feathers in the same way Saran did.

"No!" he shouted, but it was too late. He knew her, knew what she was doing, giving all the magic in her own body to save the bird. There was nothing he could do to stop her, not from here. Parsa grabbed him, pulling him back from the edge.

He struggled free, pushing Parsa away and in the ensuing struggle he lost sight of what was happening. By the time he had gathered his senses, it was just in time to see the Golden Auric rise over him, a flash of blue and gold, so close he could have reached out and touched it.

The wind of its wings sent him sprawling backwards onto the sandy ground.

It arched overhead and crashed into the rockface high above them, falling like a stone onto the upper ledge, out of his reach and out of his sight.

CHAPTER 27

Grayden set the balloon down in the courtyard. The ground beneath them shook and strained as the city below held back the Aviary's rise. The Auric, Ro, and Saran were a distant speck already and all around them there was utter chaos. Grayden passed through it all as if nothing was happening, barking orders, gathering reports.

Ameris scrambled after him, climbing out of the gondola and running. She didn't care how it looked.

Nazir and his comrades were surrounded by a number of the Windguards and a dishevelled and dusty Hale was screaming orders at the somewhat mutinous rest.

Grayden came to a stop behind him, waiting in ominous silence for Hale to realise he was there. Anyone could go in shouting and yelling. It took real control to stand there and wait for a petty bully like Hale to figure out that his time was up.

The way his voice died was a joy. He turned around slowly, his expression ashen.

"Officer Hale, on whose authority are you holding these people?"

"The … the Birdsingers …"

"The Birdsingers do not command the Windriders."

"Your mother—"

"Neither does my mother anymore. She retired, if you recall. Our Guild is mine."

"Grayden—"

"Commander Mistral," he interrupted in so cold a voice Ameris barely recognised it as his. "That shouldn't be too hard to remember. You are to stand down. Effective immediately. Everyone—" He looked at his assembled Windriders, those who had followed him and those who had already been here under Hale's command. "Everyone take a breath and think for a moment. We are all in dire trouble here. The islands are tearing themselves apart, some sinking and some collapsing. The Unity movement have bought us time, but it won't last. We have to work together now. Nazir, isn't it? Nazir Zephyr? Sometimes known as the Blade?" Nazir gave him a suspicious look. "You don't remember me. I was just a boy when you left. But my father spoke of you often."

"You're Mistral's son. She's one of the reasons I left the Guild."

"She's my mother, yes, but she's no longer in charge. And my father—"

Nazir nodded slowly, examining Grayden more closely now. "Lidayal Sirocco. I remember him well. We trained together."

Grayden gave a curt bow. "I know you were one of the foremost Windriders of your generation before you left us. If you have a plan, now is the time to let the rest of us in on it, not just the Unity movement. If unity is truly what you believe in, we all have a part in it."

For a moment Nazir hesitated, but he couldn't deny it any longer. Besides, Grayden was right. Ameris could have hugged him.

"We still need the help of the Windriders," he said, and held his head high.

Grayden nodded. "I've sent teams to the balloons on the walls. What else do you need?"

Nazir regarded him with something like pride. "I knew not all of you would fail us." He held out his hand and Grayden took it, shaking it firmly.

Grayden turned to his aides on board the balloon. "Get everyone. Every flight needs to suit up. Follow Nazir's orders to the letter. He knows this plan inside out. Send out search and rescue. We'll need to completely evacuate the outer islands. Get them over here and inside the walls. Failing that, get them on the ocean or in the air. Make sure that no one is left behind." His people scrambled to obey.

"Grayden," Ameris said. "This is a stopgap measure. The balloons and the torches below certainly can't actually make us rise like the Aviary."

"The Aviary is pulling us up."

"It's pulling itself apart. You can feel it. The tension is too much. The stone won't hold even if the cables do. We haven't got long and you need to get everyone off it before it's destroyed. The only thing that can save us is up on the Eyrie, and this." She held out the hourglass, the sand now determinedly flowing sideways. "We've got to take this to Ro."

He frowned at the small object. "That's it, is it? The reason for all this trouble?"

Ameris was surprised by the distaste she could see in his expression. Everyone else had looked at the little artifact as if it was made of pure gold. But not Grayden, of all people. Perhaps he saw it for what it was.

"This is it," she confirmed. "And it's the solution as well. We have to take it back where it came from. She knows what to do. There's a spell."

"That was what Parsa said," Nazir told them. "The ritual has to happen up there." He glanced skywards, no doubt thinking of his husband and hoping for his safety.

"And how do we get up there?" asked Grayden. "No balloon can take us that high. Besides, we're going to need them all here to get people to safety."

"I'll take my Wing," Ameris replied.

Grayden frowned. "The Wing? I thought you said it wasn't ready to fly. You were convinced it was going to kill me at the Carnival."

Ameris hadn't even been aware he'd been listening to what she was saying. She'd thought he was busy being Commander. "Not that one. The first one."

"You flew the first one? The one Ro crashed?" He didn't have to look quite so disbelieving.

"I understand how to fly it now. Zen and I ..."

But she didn't have Zen anymore ... Her voice failed, and suddenly she thought she might throw up. It was as if the world had dropped out from beneath her. When Ro had been freeing the shimmerwisps she'd thought she saw him, just for a moment, flying towards her like a mirage and then he was gone. As if she had just blinked and everything had changed.

Suddenly she wasn't sure if she could fly the Wing without him.

"I flew the prototype," she said weakly. "He helped me."

An echo of her pain passed over Grayden's features. "Damn it, Ameris, you're braver than I thought. Where's your prototype?"

She pointed up to the tower, just as it picked its moment to lose the fight with gravity. Everyone in the courtyard scattered as bricks, timber and tiles rained down on the western side.

There was another terrible crack and the ground beneath them split like a dropped melon. For a moment, all was dust. People cried out, backing away from the widening crevice.

As Ameris picked herself up again, Grayden was already barking out orders, organising rescue and evacuation parties and sending others to their own balloons. Even as she watched, dazed and defeated, she saw Nazir's people heading for the cables and using them fearlessly to abseil down to the city below. It wasn't far but it was the fastest escape route for those who knew how to do it. The remaining balloons on the Aviary were taking flight, carrying Nazir, the Birdsingers and the other evacuees.

Tethered above Arcadiana, the whole Aviary was breaking up. It was only a matter of time before Arcadiana did the same. Unless she could get the hourglass up to Ro in the Eyrie. And now she had no way to do that.

Or did she?

The other prototype, the one that had been used as the centrepiece at the Carnival of the Birds … that should still be here. She doubted anyone had even paid it the slightest thought with everything that had happened since. She hadn't.

She tucked the hourglass safely away and ran for the broken remains of the dome.

The second Wing was still mounted on its high pedestal. She climbed the ladder leading to it, hand over hand, as quickly as she could.

"Ameris, stop!" Grayden followed her.

Didn't he have enough to do?

"Let me do this, Grayden."

"Not alone. You did it with Zen but … I'm sorry. That sort of link with a bird helps with flight. Why do you think so many Windriders bond with birds? More than any other Guild but the Birdsingers. It's special. You and Zen were special. But he's gone. I'll take you. Pel and I. We'll fly you up there."

She reached the platform and pulled herself up, staring at her creation with a new sensation of dread. Grayden wasn't wrong. She was afraid of that more than anything else. She didn't have Zen and she needed him to do this. She remembered the sensation, the way the crow had seemed to be in the back of her mind, the way he had led her across updrafts and the way she'd imitated his flight.

Grayden hauled himself up onto the platform beside her and Pel gave a high keening sound as he swooped in to join them.

Instead of Grayden's shoulder, however, he alighted on hers. Ameris stood still in shock as the falcon bent his head and nuzzled her hair. Such a small and simple gesture of comfort, she didn't know what to do. The tears burned her eyes.

"Let us help," said Grayden, in the softest voice.

"I don't know if it can take both of us," she whispered back. She had speculated the Wing could manage it, back when she was redesigning it. But it was untested still.

"Yes, it can. You weigh hardly anything. You'll just have to hang on tight. We'll tie ourselves in together."

Did he even know what he was suggesting?

"Grayden …" She held out the hourglass to him. "You have to go. Take this to Ro. You can do it alone. You don't need me."

He laughed, a bleak and bitter noise that surprised her. "I'm not leaving you here, Ameris. Not when the place is falling apart." He pulled her in against him. "Come on. We're going to fly this invention of yours even if it kills us."

"It might."

He shook his head and his smile made something in her heart glow. "Such belief from its inventor. Fills me with confidence, that does."

CHAPTER 28

Ro forgot how to breathe. When her body remembered for her, sucking in a great gulping breath of air like a block of ice in her windpipe, the hot wires of pain contracted around her chest. She'd hit the rockface so hard she must have broken several ribs, but somehow here she was, still alive.

She tried again, her body refusing to give up in spite of everything and this time it was easier. Just a little perhaps.

Lush greenery surrounded her. The strange plants and flowers of the Eyrie reminded her instantly where she was. She could hear the birds all around, their song so loud in her aching mind. Slowly she pushed herself up on her elbows and felt the magic of the place wash over her. It was in the air, permeating everything.

The Auric!

She scrambled around so quickly she almost fell again and saw the Great Bird lying several yards away, its beautiful body too still, the feathers unmoving. Bald patches marred its back from the tail up to the wings.

As she reached it, it stirred fitfully, so weak and wounded that she couldn't believe it was still alive. Its eye opened as she approached the head, the amber orb fixing on her.

"It's okay," she murmured, as gently as she could. "It's just me. I'm … oh, ancestors … I'm sorry. I'm sorry for everything."

It was dying. She didn't need to be an expert to see that. It couldn't even lift its head and the wings were bent awkwardly, feathers splayed in the wrong directions. The dullness in its eyes, the resignation, would have told her if it was otherwise untouched.

What had they done? She'd tried to pour the magic left in her into it, to give it the strength to get this far. She'd hoped that the air of the Eyrie would be as generous to the Aurics as it was to her. But perhaps because they lived here all the time, it didn't work like that. Perhaps there just wasn't enough magic left. Not for a creature as powerful as this.

The Auric was dying and it was her fault.

She sank to her knees and reached out to stroke its face and head. To offer what small comfort she could. Words seemed empty, meaningless. How could she possibly make amends for this? The Aurics had saved her life. Twice now. This one had given everything to get her here. She'd tried to help it, to make it stronger, but she'd failed. And if it hadn't come to help her, Saran would never have got a taste of the vast reservoir of power that the birds embodied. He would never have been able to rip that magic away from it. Magic which, she realised now, was a vital part of its being. Like blood in the veins, or air in the lungs, the Golden Aurics were creatures of magic.

Willingly or not, she had helped to destroy one.

And for what? To save her islands? Maybe they deserved to drown. Maybe anyone who would do this or allow this to happen deserved to be destroyed. She couldn't blame the world if it decided so. To lose a creature like this, so kind and gentle, so noble, so beautiful … it didn't bear thinking about. It wasn't fair.

She curled in against the Great Bird, trying to help it, to bring it comfort. She felt that same rumbling purr pass through it, as if it was trying to do the same for her. Even now. At the end.

"I'm sorry." She wasn't sure the Auric could hear her let alone understand her. It didn't matter. It knew she was here. She closed her eyes and held it close.

"Ro?"

The sound of his voice brought her head up and ignited rage in her mind. How was he still here? How had he done this thing and not been struck down the moment he set foot on the Eyrie?

Saran staggered into view, holding his arm awkwardly. Just one look told her it was broken.

Good, she thought, and hoped it hurt. Even though she knew it would knit itself back together in no time here, in the rejuvenating air. She hoped it hurt every second of that time though. She hoped it was agony.

"Go away," she told him. "You've done enough. Leave us alone."

Not that he would. When had Saran ever listened to anyone?

Only this time he stopped.

"You were right." His voice wobbled.

She looked up at him again, frowning. This didn't sound like the Saran she knew. He sounded more like he'd been when they were younger, before the madness and lust for power set in. Wonder hung to each word and regret echoed afterwards.

"Did you think I made it up?" she asked.

"I didn't know. I thought … maybe? But this is … Ro …"

He stared at the Auric and his face fell.

"It's dying," she said, just to confirm it for him. He had to know. He had to realise. He had to admit what he had done. This time at least. "You took its magic, plundered it."

His mouth opened but no words came out. He just stood there, stupidly, staring at the Auric.

"I tried to give it mine to get here, the magic that was left in me," she went on. "But it wasn't enough."

Saran took a step towards her but she snarled, ready to attack if he came any closer. She didn't know what she'd do or if she would have the strength to defend the Auric but by the ancestors she would try. She just had to hold on and give it the dignity it needed to die.

But Saran stopped again. Slowly he stretched out the arm that had been broken, wriggling his fingers. *He didn't deserve it,* she thought. *He didn't deserve any of it. He shouldn't even be here.*

And yet, here he was, and the Auric was still dying.

"Why isn't it healing?" he asked. "If we're healing, if the air here heals us …"

Ro's grief welled up around her again. "I don't know. Maybe because it's here all the time. Maybe the magic comes from it. Maybe what you did to it cannot be healed."

The last words struck him as if each one were a physical blow. He jerked back, horrified at the implication.

He came closer, peering at the creature. It couldn't move now, its breath shallow and laboured. It was almost time. Ro hugged it again, wrapped her arms around its neck and cried her tears into its sky-blue plumage. She had no more magic to give it, no more strength. She could only try to ease its pain and let it know it was not alone.

Saran sat down beside her, his beautiful robes spreading out around him. He looked dazed and quite unlike himself.

"I was trying to save our people," he said at last.

"*Some* of our people."

"The Birdsingers."

A bitter smile flickered over her face. "There are more people than just the Birdsingers, Saran. There are more people than just the Guilds. And every one of them counts."

"But I—" He sounded so confused. Lost. He'd been so sure he was right. It must have been a shock to find out that he wasn't.

"You left them to die. Even the ones you were so intent on saving. The islands are coming apart, even the Aviary. It's going to take everything with it."

He nodded thoughtfully and she was struck by the lack of madness consuming him now. He was perfectly calm, almost serene.

"You can stop it though," he said. "You just need the hourglass."

"Do you have it with you?" she asked.

"Not anymore. Ameris took it."

For a moment Ro was completely taken aback. Ameris? Well, why not? Ro always knew there was more to her friend than everyone else thought. She had a spine of steel.

"Good for her," she said and closed her eyes, resting her cheek against the Auric's face, listening to the soft whisper of its last breaths. Her tears matted its feathers, but she couldn't bring herself to leave it.

"Ro?"

Far off she could hear wings, almost as big as those of the Auric. But they didn't sound entirely right. There was something harder about them, as if they cut the air rather than brushed it, as if they vibrated with another rhythm. Metal wings, she thought.

"Ro?" Saran said again, more urgently. "Ro, I'm sorry. Forgive me."

She ignored him. He had no place here. She didn't want him to be here and didn't want to acknowledge him. She just wanted the Auric to stay a little longer.

Saran grabbed her shoulders and pulled her away from the great blue bird.

Ro screamed in outrage, but she was already too late.

Saran held the Auric's head in his hands, pulled it up against his chest and released all of the magic that had been building up inside him. Everything, every last glittering scrap of it, poured out of him and into the body of the Golden Auric. Light like molten honey rippled from him and suffused the bird. She cried out his name and made to pull him away before he was drained dry.

Someone else caught her before she could touch him. Tomas. He held her close, his arms around her too strong to break free. Behind him she caught a glimpse of the Wing descending, piloted by Grayden, with Ameris, who was already struggling to loosen the ties holding her against him to get to Ro. Even Parsa was struggling up the steep path from the lower ledges.

But they were all too late to help.

She dragged her gaze back to Saran and the bird.

He had fallen to his knees, his head bent, his skin horribly grey and the exertion making the tendons in his neck stand out like wires.

"This is all my fault," he said. "I'm sorry beyond words. I will make amends. If this is how I save them, if this is my destiny, so be it."

"Stop," she said, or tried to say. The words wouldn't come out. There wasn't time. Even as she tried, he slumped down to the ground like a bag of old rags.

The Golden Auric shivered, its feathers fluffing up, its wings stretching out. Its blue plumage was suffused with light. The metal feathers scraped against the rocks with a shower of sparks. It shook itself from head to tail and then bowed its head to nudge at Saran's still body. It cocked its head to one side and tried again. But nothing happened. When he didn't move, it took off, flying up towards the shimmering tree, letting out its trumpeting cry.

There was nothing left in him. Ro knew it even as she managed to tear herself away from Tomas' protective embrace and run across the short space. She rolled him over and his eyes stared blindly at the sky.

There was a smile on his lips. The kind of smile she hadn't seen him wear since they were children.

For a moment it lingered, and then he dissolved into a mist of shimmering lights which drifted around her for an instant before taking flight towards the Tree above them.

Saran was gone.

CHAPTER 29

For the longest moment, all Ro could do was kneel there, staring at the place Saran had been. Ameris pressed the hourglass into her numb hands. Ro looked at it for a long time. If she'd never taken it, would Saran have tried to change the fate of the islands and doomed them all? If she'd walked away … or would it all have happened anyway, as Parsa had foreseen? Her brother had already been set on this path before she ever showed him the hourglass.

"Ro," Ameris said in a brittle voice. "Ro, are you okay?"

Beneath them, the city and the islands were disintegrating, the soaring isles crumbling. Only the Eyrie seemed untouched. But she could already feel the trembling beginning deep inside the rocks beneath them.

Everything would fall eventually. It was inevitable.

Unless she could stop it.

No, unless *they* stopped it. She couldn't do it alone. And she couldn't give up now. Not after everything that had happened. She rose to her feet, carefully, as if afraid she might shatter at any moment.

"We need to finish this," she told them all. "Before it's too late."

It didn't take long to find the doorway again. The light inside the walls flickered, weaker now, another sign that the magic was failing.

"Don't let the door close," she said to Grayden who was last to enter, seemingly hesitant to follow. He dragged a large stone into the gap just in case and cast Ro a smile of encouragement which she didn't quite know what to do with.

Besides, she didn't know what was going to happen in the next short while, let alone the future. The wise and experienced Ancients who had tried to do this had failed. Saran and his friends, with all their learning and research had failed.

And here she was, quite literally making it up as she went along, trusting in magical birds and her own desperate hope …

She couldn't stop now. Nor could she allow herself to doubt. It had to work. It simply had to. Because if it didn't …

Well, they were all going to die anyway, weren't they?

Ro led them down the steps, the light within the wall flowing like water, swirling around the corners and curling up over their heads like waves. It glimmered, blue-green, with explosions of white, and pooled into a deep amethyst beneath their feet.

The cave was alive with magic, the tree and the birds, the very air itself concentrating all the remaining magic here.

Ro set the hourglass in its place on the stone table. It glowed softly now, the sand inside it still flowing in the same direction, falling slowly, glittering. Stepping back she found the stone circle with the sextant on it and took her place, directing the others to do the same.

The stub of the candle from so long ago stood in the middle, waiting.

Grayden hung back, guarding their retreat perhaps. Old habits. There were no shimmerwisps this time, she realised. Had she set them all free?

She hoped so. She'd felt their elation when she'd released them and that was enough to know she had done the right thing.

Tomas took his place on the circle marked with the axe, Parsa on the one with the needle and thread, and Ameris stood on the one with the hammer. Without Saran there was no one to represent the Birdsingers but she had to hope that his sacrifice would be enough. That the power lingering in this place would know he had been here and what he had forfeited, and that they'd understand. She hoped.

If the magic consumed her as it had the others who had tried this spell, so be it. She just wished her friends weren't also at risk. And they were. All of them.

Ro reached out her hand towards the candle, holding it flat over the wick as she had seen her brother do. She didn't try to pull the strength from the others. They were giving it willingly. No matter what happened, she promised herself, she would not make that mistake.

"*Adscendo,*" she whispered and turned the hourglass over.

Nothing happened. Nothing at all. She didn't even conjure the little flame. The sand still flowed on, now travelling upwards within the tube. And underneath them the ground began to shake.

"I don't … I don't understand," she shouted to the Eyrie itself. "What do you want? What do I have to do?"

"Ro," said Grayden. He had stepped up behind her, waiting expectantly.

She spun around. "What?"

"You're in the wrong place," Ameris said. "Don't you see?" Her voice was firm but gentle.

"You aren't a Windrider anymore." Parsa pointed at the empty space, at the round carving of a bird with a long split tail like the Golden Auric.

"Maybe you never were," Tomas added. "You always had an affinity with birds, just like Saran. Perhaps even stronger. You just refused to accept it. You can't do that anymore. Look."

She turned around to face the area that should have been occupied by Saran. There, the wren was perched at the edge of the table, waiting.

As she made eye contact, it opened its tiny beak and sang. The melody was unlike any birdsong she had ever heard, but she knew it. She remembered it from sunny childhood mornings, from running through long grass, from sitting with her brothers, their legs dangling over the edge of one of the landing platforms of the Windriders' mountain while the birds whirled and danced beneath her.

You were always meant to be a Birdsinger, Saran had told her. He'd taken the path first, but she had been meant to follow. If Matias had stayed, she might have done so. Everything might have been different.

Grayden spoke. "When my mother threatened to cast you from the Windriders' Guild I never thought for a moment it was meant to be in your favour, but it was. It is. And I don't think Saran was trying to do you any favours either when he offered to take you in. But it was meant to be. You were meant to be here, as a Birdsinger. And you are, Ro. You always were. You were just in the wrong box. It took time to find your way out, to set yourself on the right path. And you have. You just have to take the first step."

"When did you …" The words dried up and she swallowed hard before trying again. "When did you grow so wise?"

Grayden shrugged and gave that disarming smile. "When I started listening to the right people."

"I was always afraid you'd join the Birdsingers and leave me behind." Tomas' voice was so gentle that she couldn't ignore him. "But I understand now. It's where you were always meant to be."

It wasn't far to walk, but it seemed like the longest and most difficult journey she had ever made. Grayden took her place for the Windriders, because of course, she realised, that was where he was born to be. Parsa was right.

Whatever was needed had been provided.

"Ready?" she asked. Of course they were ready. They were better prepared for this than she was.

She stood on the circle, reached out her shaking hand and said the word.

"*Adscendo.*"

The flame beneath her palm blossomed warm and bright. The wick took it and the candlelight danced. She drew in a shaky, desperate breath, and then turned the hourglass.

Light exploded around them.

It coursed through the rocks and through the air. It poured through their bodies like lightning. Ro heard Ameris cry out in alarm as she reached for Grayden's hand.

That was part of it, she realised. It had to be. Alone, they couldn't do it. They couldn't hope to channel that much magical energy through their bodies. But together … it had to be together. They weren't sharing strength or magic. They shared bonds of friendship, love and affection, in all its aspects.

"Tomas," she shouted and stretched out her hand towards him.

He gritted his teeth and quicksilver danced in his dark eyes, but from somewhere he found the strength of will to reach out one hand to her and one to Parsa. On the other side, Ro stretched out to take Grayden's free hand in hers and saw Ameris and Parsa do the same.

The world around them flipped over, or perhaps they moved and everything else stayed still. Perhaps nothing changed at all, just the universe turning.

Ro could see Ameris and the men illuminated from within by an array of colour, light pouring through them, aglow with joy. The entire spectrum of life swirled around the room, and inside each of them. But together, as a group, united in their friendship and love, so many different kinds of love—parent and child, lovers, friends, affection for each other and for all people of their world—the light that might have torn them apart instead swelled inside them and emerged more powerful than ever.

She could feel it all flowing through them now, all life, all the magic, all the power contained in the Eyrie, anchored through the shimmering tree to somewhere else, to *something* else, something so great she couldn't hope to comprehend it.

In front of her eyes, the little wren took flight, circled the table, singing at the top of its voice. The light followed it, spiralling up in a cone and then spilling down again like a fountain. It wasn't just a wren, she knew that now. It was more magical than any of the other birds. Perhaps it was magic itself.

The sands in the hourglass stopped, hanging there for the longest moment, and then finally flowed the other way.

Ro gave a cry of elation. It was working.

The magic pouring through her surged again, thundering through her veins, making her head spin. She couldn't control it. She could only hope it wouldn't sweep her away entirely.

Parsa's face showed the strain first, the light beneath his skin growing too bright. Ro could feel the magic in her pressing too hard, demanding too much. She tried to hold on, struggled to keep it in check. But she couldn't. Beside her, Grayden fell to his knees, still clinging to the others, still trying to keep up with the magic, but he was already losing the fight. She could feel the flow of magic falter, the vibrations changing to something else, something wrong.

It would tear them apart, just as it had the Ancients. Just as it had the Birdsingers who had been so arrogant to try to do this in the cellars. It would leave them as echoes of mist and light, torn apart by the attempt to contain it.

She couldn't let it end like this. She wouldn't. They were her friends, the family she had made rather than the one she had been born with. They were everything to her. Tomas, Ameris and the people they loved …

She had lost everyone in her life, her parents, her brothers …

She couldn't lose them as well. She wouldn't.

One thing she always remembered her father saying was that when you loved someone no sacrifice was too great. Even Saran had understood that at the end.

And she loved them. All of them.

If there had to be a sacrifice to do this, so be it. She would not let it be theirs.

Ro felt the world around her turn, felt the islands lift. She felt the rocks tear themselves free of their roots and the city lurch for the heavens. The light from the candle and the sand from the hourglass rained down on the archipelago and lifted it. More birds flocked to the balloons and clung to the supports, flapping their wings to help the lift, to direct the newly born soaring isles skywards to safety. They sang their joy, their triumph. Beneath them cheers were ringing out, all of Arcadiana celebrating and giving thanks.

The other islands of the archipelago spiralled around Arcadiana, drawn higher in a dance at once dizzying and dangerous. She clung to the order of it. There had to be some kind of order. She didn't know how she was seeing this. Not with her eyes. But that didn't matter right now. She knew. She just knew. She saw it because she was part of it, and it was part of her. And it would take every last iota of strength she possessed.

She gave it willingly.

She could see it all, as if she hung suspended over her world. No … as if she was the sky itself. Spread out, all-encompassing and illuminated with magic, with life itself. The islands rose, swirling around each other in an intricate dance, and the ocean rushed in beneath. Light rained down on the land and the water, the magic of the shimmering tree drenching the islands and enchanting them. One at a time the land tore itself from the ocean and lurched higher and higher, the smaller ones first, faster, those already lost beneath the water reemerging, dripping with seaweed and ruins. The lush farmlands of the inner isles leaped for the air, sliding skywards as gracefully as doves taking wing. And Arcadiana itself, her Arcadiana, her stubborn and beautiful city clinging to the rock beneath it, rose like a flower unfolding in sunlight.

She saw the Weavers cheering, standing in the streets, decked in all their brilliant colours and on the top of one of the carts, a young boy punching his fists into the air. She saw an old woman, a Labourer by her garb, hugging person after person regardless of their status or position, just moving through the celebrating crowds with tears of joy streaming down her face. She saw Devera Flint sitting back on top of the walls, sagging with relief and exhaustion, her task finally complete. In the balloons floating above the remains of the Aviary, she saw the healers, Starling and Nightingale, staring up in wonder at the magic raining down on them. And in the Mire, of all places, she saw Price pick up his tankard again and drain it with relish.

The light flowed on and on through her.

It needed more. She knew it needed more. She wasn't finished yet. She had to make this permanent. She had to be sure it would not fail again. They might all be celebrating as if it was over, but it wasn't.

Ro threw back her head with a cry and surrendered herself to the wild rush of magic, gave herself up to it completely. Willingly. She let it take her.

Tomas called her name, fear in his voice as it bounced off the walls of the cave, but she wasn't in the cave anymore. Her body was but not the rest of her. She was part of everything, part of the magic, part of the Tree, a greater consciousness soaring so high. What had to be, would be. She released herself in the same way as she had released the shimmerwisps and flew.

The light inside her turned incandescent and she felt all that she knew of herself incinerated by it.

CHAPTER 30

"Ro?"

It sounded like Tomas, but she had never heard him sound so scared. She wouldn't have thought it was possible. He always knew what to do.

"Ro, please, talk to me."

Did he think she was ignoring him? She would never do that. Tomas was her friend. No, not only that. Tomas was more than a friend. He was everything.

"For the love of all the ancestors, Ro, *please* wake up."

She tried to move. She tried to open her eyes, tried to reply, but she didn't have the strength. Her body felt like a wrung out dishcloth.

"Here," she heard someone else say, their voice shaking. "Put her down over here."

Ameris. That was Ameris. What on earth had happened? What had upset her so much?

"Ro Swift, if you don't wake up right now …" Tomas growled at her. He didn't finish the threat, whatever he was trying to say. Perhaps he couldn't think of a threat bad enough. Tomas, Ro knew in her heart of hearts, would never hurt her. Not intentionally. Although she feared that of all people he had the most power to do so.

"Give her a moment," said Parsa. "After all she endured in there …"

In there … the cave, the spell, the light of magic burning its way through her. The memory rippled back. It had hurt. She remembered that. She'd screamed. At one point her voice had broken completely and she couldn't even make a sound.

The world had moved. She knew that. Everything had changed.

Sunlight fell on her face. The breeze against her skin was scented with flowers and other aromas at once familiar and exotic. She heard birdsong from every direction. So many birds, all of them singing in harmony. It was a song of joy and wonder, of triumph.

They were singing for her.

No, *with* her. Everything inside her was singing, her blood, her breath, the beating of her heart. She could feel it in tune with the world around her. She was soaring over the ocean, spilling around in a complicated orbit, whirling …

Ro drew in a breath and came back to herself again. She was half lying on the ground outside the cave, her upper body cradled in Tomas' arms. He stared into her face, studying her as she opened her eyes, terror and relief at war in his dark eyes.

"Tomas?" she managed to say, her voice hoarse. "Why is everything dancing?"

He choked on his words, couldn't manage to say anything and pulled her hard against his chest, his hands stroking her back and her hair as if he couldn't bear to let her go.

"You passed out. There was so much magic in you we thought … I thought I'd lost you …"

"I'm still here," she reminded him with a smile she barely had the strength for.

"That you are." He smiled down at her, eyes glistening with relieved tears. "And look what you've done this time."

Tomas lifted her carefully from the ground. Everything hurt and she knew for certain that there was no way she could stand right now. She curled in against him, grateful for his strength.

The others stood around them, on the slopes of the Eyrie, the mouth of the cave still open behind them. She could see the snaking light in the walls. The whole Eyrie was alive with magic, flowing through the veins of the earth that made up its being.

How could she feel that so keenly? She bent her mind to investigate it, feeling as if she was dipping into the surface of an endless ocean, one that would sweep her away if she was not careful. Is that what had happened to her?

She focused on their friends instead. Ameris looked exhausted and was leaning heavily on Grayden's arm, but was focused entirely on the wonders unfurling around them. Parsa was down on his hands and knees, right at the edge of the Eyrie's cliffs, staring down. And Tomas just held her.

"Look, Ro," he said. "You saved it. You saved all of it."

She looked down.

Still below them, but rising fast, all the islands joined in a spiral dance, each with its own path, spinning around each other like a child's mobile in the wind. What remained of the Maiden had repaired itself, its brilliant display of greenery and the multitude of blooming flowers drawing closest. The Fountain, its waterfalls sparkling in the sunlight, followed. Below that she could see Arcadiana, her home, broken and battered but somehow holding together. It soared towards them. The balloons around its edge were no longer the only thing pulling it aloft. All of Parsa's clever plans had sustained it long enough for the spell to take effect. Now the magic had taken over. Strange how, if she concentrated for just a moment, she could see it all, recognise each step of the incredible ballet. And if she let it, if she lost focus, it would swallow her up again. She would lose herself in the wonder of it and find herself flying, suspended weightless over the world, part of everything. Every bird, every tree, every life, every cloud, part of the air itself, part of the magic. It would be so easy to let go.

"Stay with me, Ro," Tomas murmured, his lips against the top of her head, as if he sensed the temptation. "Please. Don't go."

Magic was dangerous. Luckily she had Tomas to pull her back from the vortex of its wonder.

"I'm here," she said. "Put me down, Tomas. You can't keep holding me."

"I could hold you forever, if that is what it will take." But he released her all the same. She wobbled on her feet, yet managed to keep her balance. The weakness was draining away as she felt herself becoming rooted in this world again. Magic was tempting, that was certain. But it wasn't everything. She had so much to stay here for. Not least to watch this wonder unfolding.

The forested isle known as the Copse had already risen until it was level with them. A host of birds of the brightest colours burst from its trees. Music filled the air, birdsong that was somehow so much more than just birdsong, a symphony of sound. Light and colour twirled around them. The reflections of the wings of a flock of glasslarks married with the riotous brightness of parrots from the lower isles.

The Fountain came next, whirling around them and water splashed her face. She laughed, refreshed by its touch and spun around like the soaring isle, delighting in it. Tomas joined in, lifting her off her feet, whirling her around in the rain. Light refracted through the mist, sending out rainbows in all directions.

The Eyrie shuddered beneath them, not in a threatening way this time, but more like standing on the back of a great beast shaking itself awake after a long sleep. Slowly it began to descend, floating down towards the other islands, those which were in the air, those even now rising from the ocean. As they watched, the ground around them unfolded like tendrils of vines, alive with the same glowing light in the cave, reaching out to the Copse and the Fountain. The other islands responded in kind, as rocks and plants entwined with those of the Eyrie as if they had always been together. The magical air of the Eyrie enveloped everything.

The tendrils combined to make bridges between them, graceful arches over endless space, connecting the soaring isles in the way the old manuscripts showed them linked. It moved like a living thing, binding the islands together. After a few moments some of them drifted on and the connections parted slowly, like reluctant lovers. Others entwined more strongly, as if promising to stay together forever.

Ro watched, the joy of it all surging through her like the flow of her own blood. The dance was slowing. She could feel that as well. Normalising, reaching a rhythm at once more natural and more sustainable. It felt like a heartbeat slowing, like her breathing, the adrenaline of the initial magic draining away to something else. Like moving from passion to love. Soon they would take up more permanent orbits and connections.

Beneath them, Arcadiana and the other islands rose like a bubble in syrup. As it came within range, several Windrider balloons approached, finally able to reach them. Grayden called out greetings and a voice came back from the nearest balloon.

"Commander, are you hurt? Do you have wounded?"

Grayden glanced at Ro who just shook her head. No, she wasn't wounded.

Grayden and the Windrider shouted back and forth, the reports given as succinctly as possible. His seconds were mainly delighted to find him alive. People were terrified. Someone had to take charge. Who else, Ro thought dryly, but the golden boy of the Windriders? His mother had anointed him when she stepped down. Without the Birdsingers—who knew how many of them had survived the fall of the Aviary—Grayden was the perfect choice. Perhaps the only choice.

"I should see to the city," Grayden said. "People need reassurance. Parsa, Master Arrow … I could do with your assistance. People will listen to you. They trust you. Perhaps you would be good enough to introduce me to the others. The Healer, I believe, and the Fulcrum?"

Parsa looked at him in obvious surprise and nodded, as if reassessing this new young commander and his knowledge. Grayden was not wrong. If anyone could help restore order, it was Parsa and his Unity movement. And the Windriders. Especially if they worked together.

"That sounds like an excellent idea. I'm sure together we can sort things out. In fact, someone should speak for each Guild. And for the Guildless. We have a lot of work to do."

Another balloon came into range and a voice bellowed from it. A man threw himself out of the gondola before it had even touched down on the Eyrie.

Nazir, it could only be Nazir. He flung himself at Parsa, almost bowling him off his feet.

"I thought I'd lost you, you stupid man."

Parsa threw back his head and howled his reckless laughter. "And yet here I am. A miracle."

"You are more than that," his husband told him and pulled him close.

"Did you threaten that poor aeronaut to bring you up here? Honestly, Nazir, we're just trying to rebuild trust between the Guilds," Parsa said.

Ro left them to it, wandering away before Parsa could rope her, or more likely Tomas, into something else. With their fingers entwined, she walked slowly, pulling him after her. He didn't exactly resist. She looked up at the shimmering tree, alive with life and magic, drawing the city and its satellite islands into its embrace and winding its loving arms around them.

Ro sat down on a rocky outcrop to look out at the new world they had created and waited for Tomas to settle at her side.

His voice sounded hesitant, as if afraid to speak, or afraid of what she might say in response. "I … I kept so much from you. I've done things that … that I regret. And I put you in terrible danger."

She laughed, a brief laugh that was born of regret and pain. "I got you killed, Tomas."

The smile on his lips answered her. "And I came back for you. I will always be there for you."

"You always have been. You promised Matias, remember?"

"It wasn't just because of Matias, or the movement. I should have been honest with you." He wrapped his hand around hers, pressed it to his heart. "But now, I'll tell you anything you want, everything you need to know. I'll make it up to you, even if it takes a lifetime."

"A lifetime," she said, and leaned over to rest her head against his shoulder. "That sounds like a good idea. We should get started on that."

The Golden Aurics flew in wide arcs around the Tree, the blue of the sky touched with the gold of the sun, their long tails flowing like ribbons behind them. Their song sounded like trumpets, a beautiful melody which rang out for all to hear. Every other bird joined them, a swirl of life and colour, a symphony of birdsong.

And right at the heart of them all, so small Ro could barely make it out, even though she knew instinctively that it was there, the little wren sang loudest of all.

CHAPTER 31

One turning later

“Are you ready?” Tomas asked.

Ro determinedly shook her head, but it really didn’t matter. It was going to happen anyway, whether she was ready or not. She pulled the delicate robes painted with a multicoloured array of feathers around her. They were beautiful, falling like stained glass around her, Parsa’s finest work, and expected of a Birdsinger, but sometimes she hardly felt like herself. At the same time, she knew she was more fundamentally herself that she’d ever been in her whole life. She embraced it.

Tomas pressed a kiss on the top of her head and smiled.

"You'll be fine."

That niggle of doubt never quite went away. "What if they laugh?"

"They are not going to laugh. Our people love you. They know what you did for them, what you risked. They know you saved them."

She shook her head, her face flushing with embarrassment. "It wasn't just me. It was all of us."

"You gave the most. And we're all here with you."

"Well, if I was you I'd be running away as far and as fast as possible, but I'm a lot brighter than you are, clearly."

Tomas laughed and hugged her. "Come on, everyone is waiting. And our visitors will be here soon."

Ever since the invitations had been issued and answered, she had been waiting for this day to come. They stepped out onto the veranda of the civic building together. It had been built on the edge of the Aviary lake. Above them, on various levels, all that remained of the Aviary had formed terraced gardens floating in the air. A riot of coloured foliage reflected in the water, and flowers and vines draped down like teasing fingertips. In the middle, floating over the mirrorlike lake, the Heart of Arcadiana had been rebuilt, more beautiful than before, the elaborate fountain in a turretlike enclosure, its walls painted blue and gold, carvings of birds decorating its every surface, their wings spread wide. At the top, an eternal flame burned, illuminating it. Beneath that, the water magically flowed once again, fresh and clear as crystal, forever dancing over the little troughs and spouts. The gates remained as well, the sculpture of the Golden Auric in flight like a bridge over the water, welcoming all to the gardens.

Last night fireworks had lit up the darkness and the Carnival of the Birds had roared into life. Across the floating archipelago, candles had been lit, a galaxy of little stars to commemorate those who had been lost, and to celebrate the salvation of their home.

Light the candle, people would now say to each other, freely and without fear. They had danced in the streets and in the parks, wild and unrestrained in their joy.

Now a hushed expectancy filled the air of Arcadiana. Ro didn't like the word hero. But there were other words like saviour she liked even less, so hero it would have to be.

The islands moved in their lazy spiral, having gradually slowed to a more sedate orbit around each other. The bridges and jetties of the islands moved almost constantly, rearranging themselves according to need, or perhaps an unknowable whim. Ro had people trying to map out a pattern, but so far nothing logical was presenting itself. They were like a living, breathing thing, a mix of vegetation and stone. They glowed, swirling with lines of blue-green light. Bioluminescence, Ameris called it. She and Devera were already trying to come up with a way to incorporate it into their inventions. Light without a fuel, living light, a constant wonder. Like so many things up here. Magic and Atelier ingenuity combined. Ro was sure they had already managed something special, but it was secret still. Ameris was always at work, delighting in it.

Ro had not seen her wren since they had worked the impossible magic in the cavern on the Eyrie. She still felt its presence, and sometimes she still heard it as well. But she had not laid eyes on the tiny bird for even a moment since she had surrendered herself to the ocean of magic she had needed to channel in order to save the islands.

She'd become a Birdsinger, albeit one without a bird of her own.

Not that it mattered. All the birds responded to her, even Grayden's haughty falcon Pel, who had a secret passion for stealing food when no one was looking. And Ro was often deliberately not looking.

"There you are," Ameris said by way of greeting. "Wait until you see what we've done. It's wonderful."

"Another invention?" Ro asked Grayden, who just beamed with pride.

"There is always another invention. They should just hand the Ateliers' Prize over to her permanently. Just wait until you see this one. Believe me, Birdsinger, you won't be able to miss it."

The low rising sun turned the ocean far beneath them into a golden pathway. And along that pathway Ro saw the boat appear. Full sailed, moving like a living creature, it sliced through the waves towards them.

"They're here!" Ro shouted, pointing down to the water far below them. There ought to be balloons ready to greet the visitors and bring them up to the city, but none had appeared yet. She glanced at Grayden, who was just smiling to himself. No use at all.

A hum filled the air, like a soft purring and for a moment Ro was reminded of the Golden Aurics. They were up there somewhere, nesting in the shimmering tree, but they didn't tend to show themselves when there were too many people around.

"What is that noise?" she asked.

Ameris hopped from one foot to the other in delight. "Wait for it."

The hum was coming from beneath them. It didn't just fill the air, she realised. It was the air.

The ship opened up a huge glittering spinnaker and from either side, from bow to stern, panels unfolded like wings, catching the light. They shimmered with flecks of sunlight, the unmistakable sheen of the alloy Ameris had made from the Golden Auric feather and framed slender membranes like the wings of glasslarks. The magic of the air around Arcadiana rippled against them, and, caught by the panels, set them aglow. The whole structure shuddered for a moment, like one of the Aurics preparing its plumage for flight.

The ship leapt from the water, rising into the air as gracefully as the myriad birds which wheeled around it, delighting as it joined them. They sang as it lifted upwards, guiding it effortlessly towards the soaring isles and its destination.

"That's impossible!" Ro gasped and Ameris laughed.

"Nothing is impossible Ro. You of all people know that."

"The hull is covered in the alloy," Grayden told them. "And those wings? They're made of it as well. She found a way to stimulate the magic in the air to capture it. The panels use sunlight and magic to—"

Ameris huffed and elbowed him. "Stop giving away all my secrets, Grayden. It's an airship."

It was beautiful, soaring through the air like a bird, a thing made of wood and metal, and magic. So much magic. "I keep telling her we always refer to a ship as she or her," Grayden added and Ro grinned at him. He was loving this.

Ameris rolled her eyes. "*She's* called *The Devera* for my mother." When Ro smiled, her friend just shrugged. "None of this would be here without my mother and her work. She's an inspiration and this is a tribute. Do *not* tell her I said that."

Grayden leaned in conspiratorially and mock whispered, "We are never going to hear the end of it. But Ameris *really* made her for me."

"No, I didn't." But she threaded her fingers with his and smiled. A wonder was unfolding beneath them, but that didn't matter to Ameris, or to her very proud lover. Wonders were her trade.

The delegation of peace envoys from the mainland arrived on the islands with all honours, born aloft on Ameris' ingenuity. The trill of traditional Arcadiana pipes heralded their arrival in an elaborate fanfare as the airship rose gracefully in the morning light. It was a demonstration of both the art and capabilities of the people of Arcadiana and trust in their visitors. Ro didn't understand all the engineering involved, but she knew what it might mean. *We can do all this,* her people were saying, *and we can share it with you.* No one wanted to miss out on that opportunity.

The airship docked effortlessly against a long jetty, decorated with flowers and ribbons which fluttered in the breeze. The sails were lowered, though the alloy and the magic surrounding it kept it aloft. In no time at all it seemed the gangplank was lowered and all around them the people of Arcadiana cheered with wild abandon.

The delegates who emerged on to the walkway gazed around them in wonder, but they moved, carefully at first, still adjusting to the idea of the flying ship and a floating city, towards the group ready to greet them on the veranda of the civic buildings. Each wore their most formal attire, ambassadors to be treated with every honour. They came from every land, from every culture, to learn the wonders of Arcadiana, to find out how to emulate this and hopefully, one day, to join them. It was an invitation that had been controversial at first. Access to the magic here had caused the wars of long ago, but Ro and Parsa had argued that limiting that access had been the thing to cause the problem, their ancestors greedily hoarding it and using it for their benefit alone. By inviting others to share the wonders around them, they could build connections with their neighbours, just as the islands put out their own bridges and jetties, welcoming anyone in their orbit. They could build new bonds and new relations. And end the threat of warfare that had isolated Arcadiana for so long.

In amongst the finely dressed ambassadors, emissaries and dignitaries from so many other countries Ro couldn't even name them all, there were others. Faces known and never forgotten, unseen allies abroad. Their own friends and family now returned, the exiles.

Ro's eyes instantly picked out a familiar figure.

"Matias!"

Her brother shook his head in disbelief as she pushed her way towards him, and he opened his arms to her. He was broader than she remembered, but he still hugged her the same way he always had, like a bear. As representative of the exiles of Arcadiana and a veteran of the Unity movement, he had been among the first to be invited to return. Many more would follow him. Who could resist a chance to come home at last?

"Ro," Matias said. "What have you done? Tomas, I thought I told you to look after her. Not to get her involved in all … this …" He gestured to everything.

"You never had to try to stop her once she's really fixed her mind on something, did you?" Tomas muttered.

Ro turned and planted a kiss on his lips. Matias almost choked.

Tomas sidled back a little, looking shamefaced and cast a pleading glance at Ro. Oh, yes, they were going to have to explain that as well. And it could be awkward, but she knew Matias would come around, eventually.

After all, he'd forced Tomas into her life in the first place.

"It is so good to have you back home," she told him. "I have so much to tell you. But first … just give me a moment."

A moment. It was going to take a lot longer than that. She closed her eyes, steeled herself, and then addressed the visiting dignitaries.

"Honoured guests." She lifted her voice to address the crowd. "Thank you so much for coming to visit us. We're so excited to share the wonders of Arcadiana with you, this archipelago of soaring islands. And soon we hope more of you will join us in this union. We welcome all here, and hope to live in harmony. Opening the gates of Arcadiana is the least we could do to foster good relations with you, our neighbours, and those who have looked after our exiles for so long."

The flood of questions started as soon as she paused for breath and she raised her hands, laughing softly.

"Of course you have questions. And to be honest we're still trying to discover the answers to many of them ourselves. But our finest minds are working on it. Let me introduce our Master Atelier Flint and Birdsinger Starling, experts in engineering and magic." She gestured towards them, Devera and the redhaired healer taking a step forward. Ameris hung back, not quite ready for the limelight yet. "Many of you already know our Weaver, Parsa Craft, and Commander Mistral of the Windriders. They will be happy to help you. As will many of our returned family and friends."

The Unity movement began to do what it did best, reach out the hand of friendship beyond the walls their people had built around them so long ago. Even as she stepped back to join Tomas on the edge of the crowd, watching her people making connections that would help them all, that would spread the news of what had happened here and invite others to join them, she knew that the future of their lands were in safe hands. Arcadiana would grow and thrive, inviting others to join and to discover ways to lift their own cities and islands into the air as well. If they wanted. The choice was up to them.

Tomas threaded his fingers with hers. "You did this," he whispered softly.

Ro smiled, radiant. "No, we did. All of us. Together."

ACKNOWLEDGEMENTS

Here at Tomorrowland, we're thrilled to share *The Rise of Adscendo* with you, our readers. This book represents an exciting new dimension for us and a first look into our expanding fictional universe, developed together with an international editorial team of diverse experience, talents and backgrounds.

First, we would like to acknowledge the whole Tomorrowland team for its years of wonderful, creative work in developing, creating, and writing down the worlds, stories, and themes of the festivals to create its unique and magical fantasy universe.

We'd like to thank our superb author, Jessica Thorne, who became part of the Tomorrowland team by working together with us in turning our origin story for the Adscendo theme, its epic settings and the worldbuilding into a magical piece of writing. From the captivating characters to the Windriders' techniques for flying, Jessica deftly helped us shape the Realm of Birds, Adscendo, into a home for our story.

Thanks also to the brilliant Emily Yau, the lead editor for this book who, working with renowned literary agent Sallyanne Sweeney, brought not only Jessica into the project, but also her own unique and expert editing skills while providing inspiration to the team.

To Michael Rowley, our resident fantasy fiction encyclopaedia, who is always eager to jump into every creative and editorial stage of the Tomorrowland stories, thank you for helping to shape this book to the gem it has become!

And big thanks to *New York Times* bestselling author Chris Roberson, for his amazing ability to take our stories, themes, and worlds, and bring them to life in our worldbuilding documents, and for generally lending his creative eye to the project.

Huge thanks also to Rebecca Brewer for her excellent copy editing skills and Amanda Rutter for her proofreading. Two wonderful and talented editors with amazing attention to detail.

To Jonathan Baker from Seagull Design, huge thanks for his excellent typesetting and design skills, and for turning our manuscript into an actual book!

And last but not least to our literary agent Paul Lucas, a true Tomorrowland Fiction believer, and Nathaniel Alcaraz-Stapleton from the Janklow & Nesbit Foreign Rights team. We are so excited by the doors you've opened for our Tomorrowland stories.

Thanks to all these wonderful, talented, and experienced people, our creative teamwork has come to life in a book that we're immensely proud of.

ABOUT TOMORROWLAND

Established in 2005 by Manu and Michiel Beers, Tomorrowland is one of the most beautiful music festivals in the world, famous for its fantasy themes and unique feeling of global unity, with visitors from every country in the world. Located in the wonderful town of Boom in Belgium, the summer festival sells out in minutes and welcomes more than 400,000 visitors across two amazing weekends every year.

Tomorrowland's motto is Live Today, Love Tomorrow, Unite Forever. Live Today stands for living life to the fullest; Love Tomorrow is for having respect for oneself, including one's mental and physical health, others, and nature, while Unite Forever celebrates unity, diversity, equality, and freedom for all.

Yet, Tomorrowland is so much more than just the summer festival. With new events landing each season in fabulous locations around the world, from Tomorrowland Winter at the magnificent Alpe d'Huez to the beautiful Itu with Tomorrowland Brazil, it is truly a global phenomenon.

Tomorrowland also connects with the People of Tomorrow all year long via One World Radio and its own record label, Tomorrowland Music, while projects like the Tomorrowland Academy DJ & producer school help mentor the next generation of musical talent. Meanwhile, the Tomorrowland Foundation builds music and art schools around the world, giving vulnerable children the opportunity to express themselves creatively, with schools currently running in India, Nepal and Brazil.

With Tomorrowland Fiction now sharing unique stories full of magic to a global audience, Tomorrowland continues to spread its messages of love and unity around the world.